XENA WARRIOR PRINCESS™
A FAR, FA

Join Xena a
journey for justice
and fight

Don't miss others in the exciting trilogy . . .

Xena Warrior Princess™
Go Quest, Young Man

Xena Warrior Princess™
Questward Ho!

XENA
WARRIOR PRINCESS ™

HOW THE QUEST WAS WON

A novel by RU EMERSON
based on the Universal television series
created by
John Schulian and Rob Tapert

ACE BOOKS, NEW YORK

XENA: WARRIOR PRINCESS™ (BOOK III):
HOW THE QUEST WAS WON
A novel by Ru Emerson.
Based on the Universal Television series
"Xena: Warrior Princess™,"
created by John Schulian and Rob Tapert.

An Ace Book / published by arrangement with
Universal Studios Publishing Rights,
a division of Universal Studios Licensing, Inc.

PRINTING HISTORY
Ace edition / September 2000

The Penguin Putnam Inc. World Wide Web site address is
http://www.penguinputnam.com

Check out the ACE Science Fiction & Fantasy newsletter
and much more on the Internet at Club PPI!

ISBN: 0-441-00674-4

ACE®
Ace Books are published
by The Berkley Publishing Group,
a division of Penguin Putnam Inc.,
375 Hudson Street, New York, New York 10014.
ACE and the "A" design are trademarks
belonging to Penguin Putnam Inc.

PRINTED IN THE UNITED STATES OF AMERICA

10   9   8   7   6   5   4   3   2   1

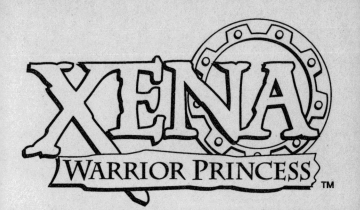

1

Silence.

In a spacious guest chamber in the palace of Knossos, Xena and Gabrielle gazed in astonishment at the small, slender woman framed in the doorway. At her gesture, the room's only other occupants—two serving women—skirted the bed and moved quietly into the bathing chamber separating the two sleeping rooms.

Gabrielle's gaze briefly followed the servants, then came back to shift from Xena to the newcomer, and back again.

She had only been close to the fabled Helen for a short while after the fall of Troy. *I forgot how incredibly beautiful she is,* was her first thought. That amazing cloud of dark hair, those eyes. The second thought followed quickly: *Who would want the burden of all that beauty?* Besides someone like Aphrodite, of course. Or someone like Menelaus, who saw nothing else about Helen.

Xena rose from the bed, red and gold silk guest robe fluttering, and inclined her head, but Helen held up a hand. "Don't," she said, her voice low and pleasant, though her eyes looked worried, Gabrielle thought. "I'm no one of any rank here. Merely Elenya, tutor to the Minos' two children." She shrugged, smiled faintly. "And since I seldom have duties at this hour of the day, I often see to the guests and make certain they're well cared for; the rooms in order and food and drink set out."

Xena glanced toward the bathing chamber; the two women seemed to be busy blotting up water and replacing the drying-cloths, but her voice was lower and softer than usual when she spoke. "Once you're certain the guests aren't from Sparta, I hope?" she asked.

"Yes. The king sends word to me, of course, when guests arrive. Or when unexpected guests give their names." Her eyes were grave, fixed on Xena's. "I am cautious, Xena, yes. Whatever name is given, I still check for myself; the halls leading to this guesting-wing are lined with panels and drapes, and through these are niches and other openings into the passages used by the servants and the children—*and* their tutor. The Minos sent me your name, but I did not come here until I had assured myself that it was you and no enemy. I saw you two women and the—odd man when you came through the Hall of Urns." Brief silence. "I assume he is someone you trust, Xena, or you would not have brought him here."

"He travels with us, and yes, I trust him," the warrior replied evenly and as formally as Helen had spoken. "Within reason. But I came to Knossos for information, Helen. About you. I didn't know that you would be here."

Helen studied the woman's face as she came farther into the room and closed the door behind her. "I believe you. All the same, the man hasn't seen me. I would appreciate it if he never learns that I'm here."

Gabrielle opened her mouth, then closed it without saying anything. Xena laid a hand on her forearm, and when the younger woman glanced that way, the warrior nodded the least bit. *She talks this time—and I guess I listen,* the bard thought, and nearly sat until she remembered that tutor or no, this was still a queen. And the daughter of Zeus. Helen caught both the movement and the hesitation, and smiled. "Go ahead, be comfortable. I am a tutor, remember? One very small step above servant, but not quite good enough for a king's formal dinner, unless by specific invitation. And don't look like that," she added softly. Gabrielle tried to get her face under control. "I never wanted that kind of formality for myself, and now that I have had three years to be an ordinary woman. . . ." She spread her arms in a wide shrug and gracefully moved to the nearest chair. "Well, I find there is very little to miss about being a queen."

Xena used her eyes to sign to Gabrielle to take the other chair, while she herself settled on the edge of the vast bed once more. "What about them?" the warrior asked quietly, indicating the bathing chamber with a motion of her head.

"Myrim is deaf and half mad, and Enosia the only one who can fully understand her sister—and deal with her moods. I know them both well: They come from my father's lands, some of my personal household that Menelaus would not let me bring to Sparta." Her mouth was bitter. "Those like Myrim who weren't pretty enough or properly suited to tend a lady, you know. Or merely odd. Or only useful to me, personally, for their special skills with clay and glazes." She took a deep breath and let it out slowly, briefly closed her eyes. "Never mind. When I came to Knossos a year ago, I found them already here; Father had arranged another position for them with one of his friends here on Crete, when he could no longer maintain a full household. It would seem," she said quietly, "that there is not enough gold in Sparta's coffers these days to support the parents of her once-queen in anything like dignity."

"You should be surprised Menelaus takes care of them at all," Xena replied. Helen merely nodded.

"So—what you're saying is that you trust them, right?"

3

Gabrielle asked. Helen seemed distracted, unable to keep to the line of conversation. Small wonder, though, if she thought she might have been betrayed. Even just being found by Xena probably had shaken her badly. Because if Xena could stumble across her hiding place....

Helen considered Gabrielle's question as though unsure why it had been asked; she finally nodded. "I do trust them. There was never a question of secrecy between Enosia and me, anyway. She knew me at once." The woman was still and quiet for a moment. She leaned back in the chair, folded her arms over her stomach and suddenly demanded. "I find it hard to believe this is an accidental meeting. When I sent for you from Troy, it was well known that Xena hardly ever leaves Greece. So, I wonder why you're here—and how you found me?"

The warrior shook her head. "I told you, we were hoping to find information so we could either get a message to you, or meet with you—if it seemed safe to meet. So, yes, in that sense, it's no accident," Xena replied softly. "But we had no reason to expect to find you in Knossos. And before you ask, yes, we have a very good reason for wanting to get a message to you at the very least."

Silence. The once-queen gestured for her to go on.

"When you sent for me from Troy, you wanted my help with an impossible mission, and even though we had never met, you trusted me then."

Silence.

"Didn't you?"

A faint nod.

"Helen, I haven't changed. I told you then that going back to Menelaus wouldn't end the war, and I warned you that going back to him would not soften his heart."

"I was younger and more naive, then," Helen said flatly. "I would never consider returning to Menelaus now."

"I assumed that," Xena returned, "because you vanished from sight so completely, and you've stayed hidden since the city's fall. That took planning and wit and determination, not blind luck. But I learned a lot about you, back there in Troy. You're stronger than you look, and braver. When we finally decided we needed to find you, I knew it wouldn't be easy—and I knew we'd have to be at least as careful as you had been in hiding."

Nice of her to say "we," Gabrielle thought, mildly amused. So far as she could remember, Xena had been the only one capable of making any real decisions the entire trip down from Thessalonika, and particularly once Gabrielle had been dragged unwillingly out to sea. *Funny,* she thought suddenly. *That stuff—that seasick-goo, when did I last take it?* It must have been early that morning— or had it been the morning before? There had been so much going on as they came in toward the Cretan port: Joxer babbling on about the island and the formations, and then those two ships fighting it out. . . . *Maybe I didn't take any today after all.* Not important, since they were on dry land—*high*, dry land—and would probably remain here for a while, especially since they'd found Helen. *But—yeah. That's funny, I can barely remember anything from being out on the water! It's like my mind wasn't working too good.* Something about badges, something Xena had ripped from Joxer? She couldn't remember! But sea serpents—that was right, there had *been* serpents. Poseidon's pets, Xena'd called them, two of them. And one of the creatures acting as if it was in love with Joxer? She considered this, astonished, then dismissed it. *Naah! In love with Joxer?* All the same, her mind felt full of holes all at once. Better ask Xena a few questions once they were alone again.

Xena and Helen had been talking, and she'd missed something. Helen's end of it, anyway. *You know what Xena's up to—as much as you ever do, at least,* she amended with a faint inner sigh.

Maybe not, though. Xena had leaned forward to brace her elbows on widespread knees, red and gold silk puddling between her legs; she was talking earnestly, her voice still low and noncarrying. Aware of the servants behind her in the bathing chamber, and less trustful of them than Helen. *Not exactly your best Miss Amphipolis posture,* she thought irreverently, *Salmoneous would have something to say about that.* "Once we left the mainland—there were three different ships, and we must have hit every island in the Cyclades *and* the Sporades before we came to Crete. And we only came here by accident when a storm blew us off course on our way to Alexandria. If anyone followed us across all that open water—from one island to the next—without me being aware of them, they're better at tracking than I am." *And no one is better than I am,* was the unspoken—and flatly honest—end of that remark, Gabrielle knew.

"I wasn't trying to insult you," Helen replied evenly; her eyes were dark and narrowed.

"I didn't say you were," Xena shot back. Gabrielle cleared her throat, and both women looked at her in surprise.

"I don't think anyone's trying to insult anyone else here," she said quickly. "Or underestimate anyone, either. Helen, Xena and I both know you've gone through a lot to get away from Menelaus and stay away from him, and that you won't ever go back to him, and Xena, Helen knows that you know that—and that you wouldn't do anything stupid that would let him follow you and find her. So—" She smiled brightly and spread her arms wide, sending sea-foam silk fluttering. "If we're all okay with that, can we go on?"

Helen finally nodded. "It's just that I've had to move so often—any time I thought Menelaus might have sent someone. . . . When I see a man I know, someone who served him—maybe just someone who looks like one of his." Her eyes closed briefly. "So many places, I've nearly lost count. And now—I've been here for nearly a year. I'm—I'm happy in Crete. I like the palace, the Minos is—is not an unkind man, and his children are sweet. I just—"

She met Xena's eyes. "This is the closest I have felt to safe in so long. And happy. I don't want to lose that."

"You won't, then," Xena replied firmly. "I told you, no one could have followed us, and we didn't come here expecting to find you. We were both extremely careful how we asked about you, and we learned nothing except that you had once been on Carpathos. Briefly." Helen's eyes widened at that. Xena shook her head. "And before you ask," she added. "No, Arana didn't give you away." Helen said nothing, but her body was visibly tense as Xena described their stop in Carpathos and the old woman who'd denied recognizing Helen's little, clay man-figure until the two women had followed her home, and asked again. "She told us what she'd been to you, how she'd tended your kilns and had never broken a pot—"

"Not a single cup or vase," Helen said softly; her gaze softened briefly. "I wanted to help her, believe that I did. She's old and alone, and one day she'll die of hunger and cold in that horrid little jumble of boards and stones she calls home, and—and no one will even care. Except for me—and I will never know!" One hand clenched at the other wrist, then relaxed. *She's got amazing self-control,* Gabrielle thought. But any woman who'd lived with Menelaus of Sparta would have learned that very early. Out of self-preservation. "I gave her what coins I had at the time. I tried to send her more, once I had made my place here, and I had a pension. She—sent it back. With a message that it would be suspicious if old Arana suddenly had more than two coppers to rub together, and that my enemies might wonder why. That she had seen such enemies more than once, coming through her market, and she would do nothing to give away one who had done her kindness. No mention of Sparta, my name, anything else." She blinked and blotted one perfect cheek. "Gallant old woman. But she's right; if I would stay hidden, there is nothing I can do for her now." Her mouth was bitter. "Even now, after three years and more, after all the dis-

7

tance I walked and rode from Troy to here, Menelaus *still* controls me! As he will until I die!" She beat her fists on the hard chair arms; Gabrielle leaped from her chair and knelt next to her, gently restraining her wrists.

"Don't," she urged softly. "It won't help Arana, and it won't help you."

Helen drew a deep breath and held it; the anger and frustration were suddenly smoothed from her face. "I remember you now," she said finally. "You came to Troy—with Xena. You're—no, let me think, I remember, he called you Gabrielle." The sudden smile warmed her eyes. "Did he find you, after he left Halicarnassus on the Hittite shore?"

Gabrielle swallowed past a suddenly dry throat. "He? I—"

"Perdicas, of course," Helen said as the bard hesitated. "He went with me from Troy, remember? As a bodyguard, though there wasn't much need for his sword at first. We went south, through the Hittite coastal towns and villages, just—walking, talking, staying the night when there were rooms somewhere. But—but when we got to Halicarnassus, everything went ugly, there was a fleet of ships just offshore, they'd sent word to the king to give over the coast, or prepare to fight for it." Her eyes were distant again, and the breath she drew was shaky. "They—evacuated all the women, children. The old. Sent everyone on the east road to safety in the mountains. Everyone that could, or would, stayed behind to fight. Your—Perdicas was one of them." She swallowed hard. "I felt—responsible for him. He should have been home by then, back in your village, but he'd stayed with me instead. The way we'd traveled took him into danger, and if he hadn't been with me, he wouldn't have felt he had to fight. I—it was only a year ago, in Rhodes, that I learned he'd survived that battle and gone home." She managed a weak smile. "He always said he would go home to Gabrielle. Did—he find you?"

Gabrielle's eyes were too bright, and her throat hurt, the way it always did when she suddenly confronted the whole matter of Perdicas. "He found me," she said finally. "He's—safe now. Happy." Change the subject, she thought. She had to, or she'd start weeping. "You—that little statue—wait. This one." She fumbled in her belt, where she'd tucked the little clay figurine, and held it out. "I found it, in one of the markets, I forget exactly where. You made it to look like him, didn't you?"

Helen's eyes widened as she took the piece; she nodded. "He was—he wasn't like any other man I'd ever met. Not demanding, or bullying. Not hard like they say fathers have to be, or like husbands so often are. He—was a friend, something I'd never had before. He liked me for myself, not for all the rank, the supposed power, things like that. For me. And once he knew I meant for him to treat me like a person, like just ordinary Helen—he did exactly that.

"We talked. All those long days on the road between towns and villages, there wasn't anything else to do. He talked—a lot, once he felt comfortable. About you, Gabrielle. Poteidaia, and all the things you two did as children. The kinds of things I—well, I never knew about, until then."

"What happened after you and Perdicas were separated?" That was Xena—easing her friend out of a difficult conversation, Gabrielle thought, and gave her a grateful smile as she released Helen's hands and went back to her own chair.

Helen shrugged. "I spent a season in the deserts of the Hittites, scarcely knowing the language and without two coppers to rub together, at first. The women helped me: the poorest ones, mostly, because the city matrons and those who'd been wealthy merchants' women were too lost to do more than bewail their fate, too snobbish to accept help from their lessers, too helpless to even try to help themselves.

9

"But the wives of used-goods sellers and reworking-smiths, small tavern holders, and shepherds and I—we understood what we had to do, to keep ourselves alive. Even though we could only communicate by signs at first. When they learned I could turn pottery and that I understood how to load and fire a kiln—well, suddenly, I was one of them." Her smile was rueful.

"Sensible of you," Xena said.

"I hope I was. I tried to be, I still do. At first I made soup pots and water jugs, unglazed plain ware for those who gleaned rice husks and fallen millet from the fields to feed their families. Then practical ware, but incised, for the merchant women who had a soul above the plain." Her smile was briefly ironic. "And once word spread to the higher ranks of what was still only a camp of outcasts, I made the black or whiteware, the patterns I had devised back in Sparta. But there were so many children, so little for them to do, so few things to play with. And I remembered the cloth dolls my nurse used to make for me, and the stick houses for them. And I thought: Why not? Houses of clay, furnishings and people to live within for girl children. There were those who wanted soldiers for their sons, but I could not do it."

"I don't blame you," Gabrielle murmured. "I wouldn't have, either."

She wasn't certain Helen had heard her. "The houses were simple, like the furnishings, but the people. . . . It—was odd. I couldn't make them unless I could see a face. I still can't. A face I know." She smiled at Gabrielle. "And so, Perdicas. My father, my mother. Both my brothers, though only I know how to tell between the figures of Castor and Pollux." She sighed faintly, then turned back to Xena. "You're here. I know how, but you haven't said why. Why look for me at all? Unless—"

"Because Menelaus is looking for you again."

"What?" Helen asked steadily, though she'd paled, and

10

her hands gripped the chair arms. "You think he ever stopped?"

"No. But he's come up with a new campaign. A quest."

"The quest for Helen!" Helen laughed rather wildly, but her eyes were unamused.

Xena nodded. "He sent priests and soldiers out from Sparta not long ago. From what I've seen, they were to locate men who might have some weapons skill, but who weren't—" She paused to find the right word.

"Who weren't worldly," Gabrielle put in. The warrior cast her a grateful smile and gestured for her to go on. "Men who would be proud and honored to be chosen by the king of Sparta for some glorious mission, but not be clever enough to realize they weren't being told the truth—or maybe only a part of it.

"It—didn't make any sense to me for a long time, but it was pretty smart of him, really: Each of these guys thinks he's the only one chosen."

"They did," Xena put in dryly. "Some of them know better by now."

Gabrielle nodded. "Each of them was given a personal meeting with the king, flattered about how perfect he was for it. Then they were told they had to find something—"

"—something he says you took from Sparta when you left with Paris," Xena finished as Gabrielle bogged down.

Helen looked from one to the other, clearly bewildered. "What nonsense is this? I took nothing but what was mine! And very little of that! I left Troy with nothing but the clothes I wore that day; anything still in the city, Menelaus took back with him, surely!"

Gabrielle shook her head. "I told you it was confusing, when you first try to figure it out. He *said* you took something. So—Joxer, you know, the funny-looking guy with us? He's been told to find this necklace. Except it's not really a necklace, it's something that is dangerous to you. Someone else is looking for a special dish. . . ."

The once-queen leaned forward, hands clasped tightly. "But, I don't have any of those things! I don't even know what—!"

"That's not the point," Xena said evenly. "Each of those men thinks you do, because he's seen a vision of you and—and whatever the thing is. And now he has a sacred duty to Apollo to find you and deliver the—whatever it is."

"Apollo." Helen's jaw was set. "Avicus is still with him, isn't he?" Xena nodded. The woman flowed to her feet, began pacing in the small area behind the chair. She stopped abruptly. "I should have expected something like this. Because I know Avicus has tried to find me before now, but he can't on Crete. Neither him *nor* Apollo."

The warrior nodded again. "That explains something I overheard in the palace, some nights ago."

"You mean you're protected?" Gabrielle asked. "Or the island is? How?"

A corner of Helen's mouth twitched. "I don't know exactly how it works, but it's not just me. Oh—I tried. Asked Aphrodite for her help, not long ago. Just—to let me know what Menelaus was up to, if I could stay on here, at least for a little while longer. She—wasn't willing to go against Apollo, just on the least chance he'd find out. No—it's Crete. And particularly the palace.

Her gaze went distant. "The Cretan gods aren't the same as ours. They're older. Different. In some ways weaker, but in others, more powerful. More—apart and unlike humans. They don't like or trust Zeus and his family, any more than the Cretans themselves like or trust Greeks. Particularly Spartan Greeks and especially since Troy. There was one man I knew to be Menelaus, not long after I came here and began teaching the children. He—was seen walking into the Maze, and he never came out."

"You—saw this?" Gabrielle asked. "Or did someone just—"

Helen smiled faintly. "I would think they were being careful with what they told me—keeping me from having nightmares, perhaps, if that were the only incident. Not just Spartans, others who intend the land and its people ill. Many have come and gone without learning anything: one or two Greeks, another man who was Nubian, I think. Menelaus' all three of them, I'm certain, but if they'd been sent as spies for him or for Avicus, they went away without learning anything. The Minos wouldn't give me away anymore than Myrim or Enosia would."

"The king knows who you really are, then," Xena said. Helen nodded. Gabrielle could hear the toneless voice of the deaf woman, Myrim; she couldn't make out the words for the odd accent, on top of everything else. *I hope Helen isn't wrong to trust those two,* she thought suddenly. But if the woman had been here over a year and Menelaus was still resorting to this quest to find her, they hadn't told anyone the secret.

Helen's words caught her attention. "I told King Nossis at once. Nothing else would have been right, or fair. He would have just kept me here, as a guest, but I thought— better if I simply vanished into the household. Safer for me, *and* for him." She drew a hand across her eyes. "And now . . . well, there wasn't ever much chance of it, but I had hoped to stay with the children."

"You don't have to leave," Xena broke in. "That's why we decided to find you, and why we're here—Gabrielle and I—to help keep your secret, to protect you if that's necessary. And to find a way to stop Menelaus and his priest for good."

Helen shook her head, her expression bleak. "You don't know him, Xena. I do. He won't give up unless he's dead. And he's not that old, he's healthy, strong. . . . He'll go on for years!"

"Not if something happens to him," Xena began, but Helen shook her head again.

"King Nossis wouldn't send an assassin to Sparta, even if he had one—even if I chose to let him."

"Why?" Gabrielle wanted to know. Helen blinked; she'd been concentrating so hard on Xena, she'd apparently forgotten about Xena's companion.

"It's not right," she said. "Killing him just to keep me free of him. The qualities that make him a bad husband seem to make him a good king. With no heirs, his death would certainly start a war, and innocent people would die. Let the gods judge him once he's dead." Dark eyes met Xena's. "Do you know what I dream, most often?" she asked softly. "I dream that I return to Sparta with gray hair and lines pulling my mouth down, a sagging throat . . . and Menelaus turns from me in horror." She smiled sadly. "With my mother's choice of father for me, I fear it will be a long time before that happens."

"We'll find a way," Xena said. "There has to be something we can do about him." She rose, walked around the bed, and scooped up a handful of grapes from the low table. "Unfortunately, you're right about Menelaus: Even if he's not a perfect king, he's got things under control in Sparta. If he died now, there'd be open warfare. Not just rioting among the nobles for the throne, either. There is at least one warlord's army I know of within two days of the city. By the next full moon, there wouldn't be two stones left standing together." She absently ate a grape, then turned as footsteps came from the bath chamber: one of the serving women carried the tray, the other a bundle of crumpled drying-cloths. Helen nodded as the two hurried past the bed and out into the hall, pulling the door to behind them. She sighed tiredly.

"Xena, you're only fooling yourself if you think you can change Menelaus. Nothing short of his death or my disfigurement will do that."

"Not necessarily," the warrior countered. "There's always a way—we just haven't found it yet."

Helen turned away, eyes fixed on something beyond

14

the chamber. "You know," she said finally. "I wasn't that unhappy in Sparta. If only I had done the honorable thing when Paris came to me. I could have told him I was a married woman, that he had no right to write poetry to my eyes, and less still to beg me to flee with him." Her lips twisted, her eyes were still distant. "And then, once we'd reached Troy, to learn that I had been nothing but a prize—that Aphrodite had promised me out like a—like a shining solstice toy! If I had told him then that—told him how insulting it was, *made* him believe it, made him send me home. . . ." Silence.

Xena tossed the last grapes back into the bowl and strode across the room, red silk fluttering behind her. "Helen, you *know* better than that! Menelaus would have gone to war if only because Paris had written you poetry, you know that kind of jealousy doesn't forgive anything! But once men find a reason to fight, they don't just—stop."

"You told me that; I remember," Helen whispered. Dark eyes met the warrior's squarely. "But when you've been responsible for as many deaths as I have, maybe you need to try to find a way so that it need not happen."

"I understand that," Gabrielle said gently. "We both do. Even one death—but you weren't responsible, aren't you listening? They both *chose* what they did. Paris chose his path, and when he was offered a married woman as his prize, he didn't do the honorable thing. He took."

"Yes. Because I let him."

"No," Gabrielle said evenly. "Oh, sure you went with him. So what? If you *had* done the right thing and told him to go home alone, do you really think he would have?"

"He'd have had to—"

"Right." Gabrielle's voice was sweet with sarcasm. "So tell me, how many men did Paris bring with him, when he came to visit?"

"I don't—I didn't count—why should it matter?" Helen countered.

15

"Enough to kidnap the woman a shallow, conceited goddess had promised him, if she didn't fall for him?" Xena asked.

Helen was still and quiet for a moment. She finally managed a faint, bleak smile. "I—perhaps. It doesn't matter though; except for Menelaus, it's all done, finished. Past mending." She stood. "I have duties; lessons for the children. Nossis has ordered a banquet for you tonight—both you and your companion. J—?"

"Joxer," Gabrielle reminded her. She gazed at the door, a frown drawing her brows together. "So—where is he, anyway? I mean—I'd just like to be sure he's—okay," she added lamely.

"Staying put," Xena said at the same moment, and the two women exchanged a knowing, tired look.

Helen smiled then, a flash of teeth that warmed her eyes. "Oh—he can't go far. If you want to see him, go right out your door, left at the first passage, and his door will be the one at the end of that passage, on the left. Those are the guest chambers for honored guests the Minos doesn't know well. Those who he either wouldn't want wandering around, or those who might get into danger if they did. You'll be able to go in and out, wherever you like, so long as you wear this." She picked up a pair of small, silver brooches from the table near the door: they were plain, and shaped like the great horns in the courtyard. "With one of these, you can go wherever you choose, though I would avoid the outer courtyards for now, if I were you. But your friend—without one, he won't go far at all." She paused in the doorway. "I will see you at the banquet, but I won't be anywhere near. You don't know me."

"Of course," Xena said, and the door closed behind the woman.

Xena turned to meet Gabrielle's eyes and raised one brow. The bard sighed faintly. "You know, Xena, every

16

time I think things are as confused as they can get, they just keep getting stranger."

"I know."

"What—do you have any idea what she's talking about? I mean, Joxer, and those pins and all of that?" Gabrielle picked up one and turned it over in her fingers. It simply felt like nicely polished silver, a well-made piece of jewelry.

"I've heard things," Xena said after a moment. "Rumors, mostly, and I don't remember a lot about them. Except that the Maze is supposed to be—it's not just all the passages that make it easy to lose your way. Some say the palace is part of that."

Gabrielle set the pin aside to smother a yawn. "Well, you know what? Right now, I don't think I care. We're off that ship, we're away from the water, we found Helen, I'm clean, I've eaten some really good bread and a lot of cherries, and I don't have to listen to Joxer whining. That's enough for me right now. What I need is a nice long nap, and I don't see any reason not to have one."

Xena smiled and wrapped an arm around her shoulders. "Sounds like a plan to me, Gabrielle. I could use one myself. And then some time after that to figure out what all this means."

2

A short distance away, Joxer lay sprawled on a narrow bed, half-buried in soft pillows and bolsters. His hair was clean and freshly slicked, and he wore new clothes: dark trousers of some fine cloth that wouldn't survive a day's fighting and a full-sleeved cream-colored shirt that he privately thought made him look daring and brave. Heroic.

He smiled happily as he raised his head to look around. The chamber wasn't that much bigger than the one he'd had in Sparta, but much nicer. "Now, see," he told himself, "*here* they know how to do these things right. Guests are a sacred responsibility, right?" Especially a guest who was also a mighty warrior *and* bound on a sacred quest. His eyes lit on the small table within easy arm's reach. A dew-beaded ewer of chilled wine, a cup and a footed bowl of bread and fruit there, all of it excellent quality, very fresh. Except the wine, which was nicely aged. Much better than the kind of stuff he drank when he was buying, or when he went someplace like Meg's tavern. "Yeah, this is the kinda stuff you deserve," he told himself happily as he scooped up a couple of dried figs and dropped them into his open mouth. "Wha—uh shooo . . ." He chewed, swallowed. "What you should be drinking, man like yourself. . . ." He contemplated another drink to wash down the figs, but decided not. "Later, maybe. Man's gotta stay alert. Ready. Even in a place like this, anything could happen."

He sat partway up, alert, muscles taut, eyes moving from the narrow window overlooking a vast open courtyard, to the bright yellow door in its red frame, to the small chamber with its pile of soft drying-cloths and that tub of water that still steamed. Sword—over there, against the other side of the bed, out of sight of anyone opening the door. Main dagger, backup daggers, bow, arrows, arrowcase: along the wall, behind the door, in case someone came through that brightly painted piece of wood and the someone wasn't friendly. Javelins, bolos, short spear . . . still in the washing chamber, where he'd stripped out of the grubby, sweaty, salt-encrusted garments he'd worn since before Sparta. Those things were gone, taken away by the king's man for cleaning; he'd made them leave the armor, though. A sensible hero didn't let his armor be taken away.

The boots—he hadn't wanted to let them go, either, but they were about as disreputable and foul-smelling as they could get, and they didn't go well with his current garb. The servant had promised to clean them and bring them back within the hour, and he'd finally relented. "They'd better be back, or I'll—" He frowned, finally shrugged it aside. But there was this banquet later on. No one would want him showing up for that in his bare feet.

He laid back and patted his leg to be certain the new dagger he'd bought one or two ports back was staying where it belonged. Unfortunately, the strap sometimes slipped, leaving him to dig around in his boot for the thing. Once or twice it had simply fallen off. "Nope—right where it should be." His eyes gleamed; he rolled off the bed and onto the floor, ripping the thing from its sheath as he did so. To his surprise, the move worked just the way it should: He finished on one knee, ready to leap to his feet, arms outstretched, dagger in his right hand. "Aha!" he told the empty room triumphantly. Too bad Gabrielle hadn't been here to see *that*.

Fortunately, she wasn't there when he did leap to his feet, caught his toes under the edge of a small carpet, and nearly impaled himself on the blade. He snarled in wordless frustration and fury, rolled onto his back and stared at the ceiling while he caught his breath, glared at the dull little knife as if it had caused the incident, then carefully shoved it back into place and flopped back onto the bed once more.

It was quiet here. Nice after all the noise aboard ship, sailors shouting, the creak of wood, and the snap of sails. Gabrielle yelling at him, the way she always did. Quiet, and warm, he thought sleepily.

He briefly wondered where Gabrielle and Xena had wound up. "Hope they got something as nice as this is." Probably had to share a room, being women and together and all. That king—Nossis, wasn't it? He hadn't seemed to know Xena, the way some of them did. Hadn't looked astonished, the way so many of them did. "Face it," he told himself drowsily. "Xena's a big item back on the mainland, but out here? This is a whole other world, and she's just another woman with a sword." He glanced around warily, as if expecting her to be standing there, listening to him talking to himself, ready to pounce as she so often did. "She shouldn't do things like that," he mumbled. "But forget that. After all, *she* wasn't picked for this quest."

There is no quest. A woman's voice echoed uncomfortably in his head; halfway to sleep as he was, he wasn't sure if it was Xena or Gabrielle. At the moment, he wasn't buying it. "Sure. 'Sss, 's'a fact, gotta be. She's jealous 'cause for once someone else got the 'tention." Because

20

who could make up something like that—whatever it was Helen took that was gonna kill her if she got mad? "Looks like—necklace, 'n' she thinks 's pretty," he mumbled as his eyes sagged shut. "Isn't, though." Was pretty, his mind sorted the thought out. Like Helen. But it wasn't a necklace, it was something dangerous. And Menelaus was only human, still caring about the health of a woman as beautiful as Helen. Of course he wanted someone like Joxer to retrieve the thing before she got hurt or killed. And, of course, he probably really did need it back, like the priest had said.

All those faces; it was as if he was back in Sparta, back in that plain little room, gazing out at the stableyards and what seemed to be twenty or more other men gazing out of nearby rooms. That was another of Xena's arguments against a real quest. *Well, so?* his mind demanded muzzily. So the king had picked more than just Joxer for the quest, so what? It was a big world, even just this part of it. Even Joxer the Mighty couldn't be everywhere. Besides, the king didn't know just what a hero he had, here. "Find her," he muttered, nodded once in satisfaction, and smiled widely at having resolved a long-standing problem, then fell asleep.

He woke over an hour later to find the room still cool, though the beads of dew were gone from his jug of wine. He sampled the cup, set it aside, and suddenly found himself curious about what lay beyond the yellow door. All that open, paved ground out there beyond the window. He crossed to the narrow opening opposite the door, shading his eyes against incoming sunlight, and tried to make out what he was seeing. There seemed to be a colorful pattern to that expanse of floor, but he couldn't be sure of that, let alone see what it was.

The window was grated, but it would have been too narrow for him to go out that way anyhow. He crossed to the door and was relieved to find it not locked. *Why would they lock it?* he asked himself. After all, he was a guest. An honored guest, according to the king. "And no one had said anything like, 'Stay here', did they?" he demanded of the ceiling. "No, because there's no reason. It's a palace, not a fortress." He double-checked the leg-sheath, made sure the dagger was snugged in place, then eased the door open. His boots stood to one side of the opening: cleaner than he could ever remember seeing them, and when he sniffed cautiously, all he could smell was lemon. He went back to the bed with them, considered putting them on, and finally shrugged. *Keep them pretty for the dinner.* The tile felt cool on his bare feet, kind of nice. He resettled the dagger and walked out into the passage.

It was all white out here, except for his door, which was marked with a small green painting of ferns, just at eye level. "Funny," he muttered under his breath. "All those colors in the rooms and out here it's like a snowstorm or something." No tables with jugs and flowers like there had been where they'd first entered the palace. The hallways were narrow, unmarked, broken only by doorways on both sides and an occasional shadow where light came in from above and from both ends of the passage.

Which way? He thought hard for a moment. "Seems I came from—that way?" He looked right, gazed thoughtfully left, shrugged. Couldn't remember. "How lost can you get though?" Inside a palace, there'd eventually be a way out, or a servant to direct him to a way out. He turned right and started down the hall.

One right turn, one left, two long hallways later—he stopped short and stared. "Wait a—huh?" White, unmarked doors, white passages, ceilings, floors . . . and all of a sudden, he was staring at ferns. Green painted ones at eye level on a doorway. "That's weird." He stared at it for some moments, then took a step toward it and tapped at the panel. The door swung open as if unlatched. Joxer's eyes went wide and his jaw dropped: the bed covered in soft pillows and bolsters, a small table with a wine jug, cup, and pedestaled plate of fruit and bread, and the narrow window with its view of an open, deserted courtyard? And there, flopped over next to the bed, were his boots!

"Naah!" he assured himself. "Can't be!" But when he finally edged around the open door to glance behind it, there were the weapons he'd left, just where he'd left them. He stepped back into the passage, pulled the door behind him, and scratched his head. "Okay, that wasn't the way. So—how about left?"

All the way down a long passage without any crossways, then left once, right twice. . . . He almost missed the green marks on the door this time, as fast as he was moving. He froze, then licked his lips nervously. "Look, I'm Master of Geography," he told himself firmly. "Someone like that does *not* get lost in a bunch of indoor halls, okay?" He gazed at the door, willing it to be plain— white, red, purple, anything but painted with ferns! But nothing changed, and when he finally got up the nerve to touch the door, it opened and there was the familiar room and all the rest.

Joxer shoved the door to behind him with a bang and went over to sit on the edge of the bed, one hand tugging at his hair as he tried to think. "This—is just—okay, this is really strange," he finally told himself. "So . . ." His voice faded and his eyes glazed as he tried to recall both routes. "Okay, I did *not* do anything myself to make this happen, so what is it, huh?" he demanded in an aggrieved voice. No answer, of course. "I mean, I don't feel like I ate anything bad, I didn't drink too much—did I?" The ewer was still reassuringly heavy; he'd had about half a cupful of the wine, and it hadn't been that strong to begin with. Not to a man used to drinking the kinds of potent liquors served at a place like Meg's.

Or that tavern just down out of the hills, the second day out of Thessalonika. His mouth twitched, then he smiled widely. "Now *that* place had atmosphere! Not just good food and lots of it, but who could expect so many women who could sing so good?"

He sobered as his thoughts moved beyond the closed door and into that white hallway beyond. "Okay, not drunk, not half asleep—not going the same way twice in a row, even if it all *looks* the same, I'd know, okay?" Silence. "Okay, fine. Think." He mentally retraced his footsteps, shrugged and got to his feet. "One way to figure it. Left, then right, then left, then right. *That* should fix it!"

It did. It took him a lot longer this time—but he eventually wound up in the same place, staring at the same green-marked door that turned out to close off the same rooms.

This time, he dragged the door shut behind him and stayed in the passage, back braced against the wall so he could watch the long, empty corridor that stretched into the distance. Both ways. "Yeah, right," he said sarcastically. "Way I just went, I shoulda been halfway back to the *port* by now!" His eyes narrowed, his gaze flicked from one direction to the other. "So—someone's watching me and moving my stuff, right? From one room behind a fern door to another, right?" He raised his voice sharply. "Well! Thought you'd pull a fast one on me, did you? Well, *no* one fools Joxer the Mighty *that* easily! I'm Master of Geography, and that means I *know* what direction I'm going, and maybe someone else could be faked out by all this, but Joxer knows what's up! Ah-hah!" Silence. Even his words hadn't echoed, he thought nervously, though in a space as long as this, and as high ceilinged, they should have.

Maybe the wine, after all? He held a hand up close to his eyes, wiggled the fingers, and counted carefully. "Thumb, two, three, four, five—no, I know all about too drunk to be sure they're all there." That left two things: "I've lost my mind or Gabrielle and Xena are pulling one on me." He considered this briefly. "Make that three things: I'm gonna wake up and find myself back in Thessalonika with Gabrielle snarling at me while she tries to make a fire with wet wood." He stared at the pale wall opposite and shook his head firmly. "Forget that one. It's bad, it's really bad."

It didn't feel as if he'd lost his mind—of course, mad people were the last to know, he thought gloomily. But that seemed less likely than Gabrielle and Xena pulling a massive joke on him.

And even that didn't seem right, he had to admit, even more gloomily. Both women snarled at him a lot more than was necessary, or even nice. But they didn't pull elaborate hoaxes on him like this.

"Besides," he told himself. "It's not *their* palace. It's the Cretan king's palace. And I never heard anything about a king pulling this kind of joke on his guests."

Uncomfortably, he suddenly remembered Sisyphus—the original jokester, according to the stories Gabrielle told him. A palace that had hidden passages, secret ways, bad magic everywhere. . . . "Yeah, Sisyphus," he growled. He barely remembered anything about that island where Xena had gone to help Ares find his sword. "Well, that's what *they* say she was up to," he reminded himself. After all, both women had assured him it really *was* Xena, but temporarily in Callisto's body. "That's—yeah. Right. As if I don't know Callisto when I see her."

He did recall a little besides: himself and Gabrielle both so angry they were ready to murder each other, and then that monster that turned out to be nothing but a huge, noisemaking machine. . . . And up in a raggedy, dusty palace, a brief glimpse of someone shimmering and fading as Ares snarled curses at him. "Well," he shrugged, "*they* said it was Sisyphus." Maybe so; he had to admit, there hadn't been any way he knew of for Callisto to simply vanish off that beach and Xena to appear in her place.

Weird stuff. He sighed heavily. "You know," he told himself, "I used to remember a *lot* more of what went on in my life before I started being there for Xena and Gabrielle." An image flashed across his mind: himself in a small, darkened chamber, candle in hand, holding the flame to the face of a green-and-orange clad—and very dead—Gabrielle. Ares on his one side, Callisto on the other, and both of them as oddly dressed as he was, as Gabrielle was. The image solidified: Xena in bloodred that clung to her body, her eyes wide in horror. *Because she'd killed Gabrielle . . . ?* He clutched his head, then shook it fiercely. The vision faded.

Don't go there, he told himself silently. "Don't do it." That one *had* been a nightmare. Had to have been. Because hovering right behind that image was the other: a crazed Xena riding into the Amazon camp after the death of her son, brutalizing her friend Ephany and then coming after a grieving Gabrielle—and only himself to stand between the two of them. Somewhere, deep down, he knew he'd never done anything braver or more foolish in all his life. *For both of them.* He knew that, too. If he'd really done it; if it had really happened. He didn't like trying to remember any of that—whether it had happened or just been a nightmare after too much bad wine. A moment later, the thought was gone.

Joxer drew a steadying breath; a smile twitched at the corners of his mouth as his eyes narrowed. "Okay," he murmured. "Someone's playing tricks, and Joxer is gonna figure it out."

He walked back into the hall and turned left. He'd go straight this time. No right turns, no left. He thought briefly, leaned into the room where his things were to check the angle of the sun on the grounds beyond. "East is—that way," he muttered. "Which makes north—that way. So. North you go, every time. Eventually you gotta run out of palace because there's this cliff, right? And the sea beyond, and the port straight down from the cliff, okay?"

Logical, sensible, practical—and utterly wrong. By the time he fetched up against the fern-painted door once again and walked through it, past the bed and over to the window, the sun was at least an hour lower in the sky. Joxer cast his eyes upward, and shrugged widely. "Okay!" he announced loudly. "Whoever's having all this fun, I give up! Done, finished, past it, over with, forget it, not gonna play anymore! Got it?"

No answer, though he'd half expected something. Laughter, if nothing else. "Well, *fine*," he mumbled and crossed the room, closed the door with a ringing slam and threw himself back on the bed. The coverings, pillows, and bolsters were at least comfortable, but now, they seemed to cling to his body and hold him down.

He hadn't intended to sleep, but when he next opened his eyes, the room was much warmer, almost stuffy, and the sun lower. At first, he couldn't remember quite where he was: Not a ship—that was the first thing that occurred to him. *Palace* came into his mind a moment later, but nothing else. Joxer shook his head to clear it—nothing. Finally: "Palace. Knossos. Maze and, yeah, like that." He considered this, his lips twisted. "Yeah, maze all right. Starting on the other side of that door." He staggered to his feet and into the washing, where he splashed reasonably cool water on his face and the back of his neck. A little more alert now, he wandered back into the main room and over to the window.

There definitely was a pattern painted on that floor out beyond this wing of the palace; he could see bright colors and swirled patterns. Beyond that, tantalizingly too flattened by distance to make out, what must be paintings of people or animals.

"Gee," he muttered as he shifted position to catch more of it before the sun left the surface. "They sure do like it *bright* here, don't they?" Yellow door, red frame, all that color outside. Not just the paving, but the walls and the tile roofs, those fat pillars. "Wonder how many people they have just going around and repainting things?" That thought was pushed aside by another, more urgent one as his stomach rumbled. "Wonder if anyone's gonna be able to find me? Since I don't seem to be able to find them?"

He went back to the bed and looked over the contents of the tray next to it: the bread wasn't very soft anymore, and he wasn't interested in fruit at this hour. The wine had definitely gone room temperature. "Fine if it's cheap stuff, or you've already had a few cups. Not for this." He crossed the room, paced back the other way, caught his bare toes on the edge of the nearest small carpet and fell face-first into the bedding.

It took a few moments for him to shovel pillows aside and extricate himself, and he was snarling under his breath as he came up for air. He froze, then. Was that someone in the passage, out there? He managed to wrestle himself around, but instead of regaining his feet, slid down the side of the bed cross-legged onto the floor with a tooth-rattling bump. "Okay, I give up," he mumbled. A tentative-sounding tap at the door and the rattle of the handle silenced him. Somehow, he got upright without pulling anything else to the floor, or tripping over the pillows that were now scattered everywhere, and, cautiously, he slid his feet through them to fetch up against the door.

"Uh—is anybody there?" he asked. Another tap, and the door opened to reveal a sun-bronzed boy of perhaps twelve years—at least by the height and thinness of him. Blond curls clustered above his ears and one hung over his brow, making his face look much younger. *I remember being that age,* Joxer thought with an inward sigh. *Growing taller by the hour, it seemed, and incredibly clumsy because the world, and everything in it, seemed to be the wrong shape and size all at once.* And everybody yelling at him because he was more awkward than normal, even for him. . . .

This youth didn't seem affected by the clumsy part, though, or by the pile of clothing in his arms that he held in place with his chin; he bowed very correctly as he came into the room, eased the door closed behind him with one foot, and gave Joxer a wide-eyed smile. "Sir, I am Newin, come to help you ready for the feast and to escort you to the hall."

Joxer smiled back. *Nice kid. Nice manners.* "Hi," he said. "I'm Joxer the—"

The boy nodded; his eyes fixed on the man's face as if—Joxer couldn't decide as if *what.* The treble voice went up a note. "Oh, yes, sir, I know who *you* are! The men from the ship came with trade goods this afternoon, and it was all they could talk about." He bit his lip. "Sorry, sir, I did not mean to speak out of turn. But it's so—we so seldom get a real hero in Knossos, sir." He bowed again and crossed the room to lay clothing on the bed, then began scooping up fallen cushions.

Joxer squared his shoulders; his mouth twitched. *Hero, huh? Boy, wait until Gabrielle hears that! And Xena, I guess now maybe—* He drew a deep breath, ready to entertain the youth with his exploits, but when the boy turned back and gave him that shining look, somehow, he just couldn't. *Look at the kid; he really means it. Like—like I really was somebody important. Famous. Someone who slays monsters and rescues maidens, and . . . and like it mattered to him.* Newin shook out the shirt he'd just brought; Joxer fumbled with the fastenings of the one he'd worn only since midday, and as he turned to slip it off, Newin neatly dropped the other over his shoulders and snugged the full sleeves to the man's wrists. "They said you tamed a sea serpent, and that you rescued dazed and lost men from Lethe, and that—" He was silent a moment as he concentrated on pleating the sleeves just right, then turned back for fresh trousers: Very dark red, these, and the softest fabric Joxer could ever remember wearing. Silence as he pulled them into place and let Newin help him into a ceremonial dagger belt. "Um—sir, did you *really* encounter one of Poseidon's serpents? And—and tame it?"

If this had been Meg, or any of the women like her, Joxer thought confusedly, it would be no problem: The bigger and wilder the tale, the more of a dash he cut in it, the better. They'd applaud him, buy him rounds of ale or wine, sing with him, and even make up new verses for his anthem. This kid, though, with those wide eyes, holding his breath as he waited for Joxer's reply like he wanted a hero himself to look up to. Or even wanted to become one, maybe. *What do I tell him? I mean*—it just didn't feel right to swagger it, the way he usually would. *So, what would Gabrielle do? Or Xena?* He thought about that for a moment. They wouldn't let the boy down, he finally decided. They would be nice; give the kid a story that was exciting without being too scary. *They wouldn't act like an oaf who belongs in a tavern*, he told himself flatly as he settled the dagger sheath, let the boy make certain the blade was firmly where it belonged, then gave him a friendly smile. "Well—you know? There was this serpent, and it was . . . I mean, it was *big*. Big enough to stand on its tail in the water and be taller than the mast, and boy, could it swim fast!"

"And you tamed it?"

"Wellll. . . . I don't think anyone except Poseidon could actually *tame* a sea serpent. But I saw one—well, two actually, but I only talked to one of them myself, and—you know—it was really weird, because they don't talk out loud like people do. They talk in your head."

The boy's eyes were, if possible, wider. "Really? And they didn't try to crush the ship, like all the tales say?"

Joxer shook his head gravely.

"Well, then, you must have tamed it just like the sailors told me, because everyone knows when Poseidon sends them, they loop around the ship and squeeze until everything breaks apart."

"Well." Joxer thought about that. *There is no way, ever,*

I get into old Fish Breath having this incredible crush on me! It not only made him look foolish, but it sounded completely unbelieveable, even to him. "They didn't crush the ship; I mean, if they had, we wouldn't be here, right? But I don't think it was just because I scared them away." The boy looked as if he didn't quite believe this; he finally shook his head and held out Joxer's boots.

"We had better hurry, sir. The feast usually begins at full dark, and I was—I was a little late, sir."

Sir. *Sir might be a lot of people, but it sure isn't me.* He smiled again, then went back to tugging at his boot. "Um. That's ok. Look, just call me Joxer, all right? Really, it's fine. That's what I'm used to; everybody does." He sat on the edge of the bed to draw on his boots. "And you're Newin, huh?"

The youth nodded enthusiastically. "Eldest son of Nossis, s—I mean, Joxer."

Joxer started to draw on the other boot, then let it fall with a muted *thunk* and blinked at the boy. "Nossis? You—I mean, *that* Nossis? Uh—as in, king of Knossos?" Another nod. "And—*you* came to help me get dressed, instead of a servant?"

"But, s—I mean Joxer, my father says that a king must remember he is a servant. Not like a palace servant, really, but that he takes care of all the people. So, when important guests come, my father tends to them, or I do. Or both, if there are many. It—" He thought a moment. "It keeps him properly humble, he says."

"Oh." Joxer didn't know what else to say to this astonishing notion, but the youth didn't seem to expect any other reply. He scooped up Joxer's discarded garments and carried them into the washing chamber. "Well—ah—thank you," he managed finally. "Ah—not every day someone gets a prince to help him change his shirt, after all."

The boy checked the contents of the tray and set it and the small table over near the door. "My father is really the Minos," he said. "Kings are for other lands, but in Crete we have the Minos. Except, he doesn't like to be called that, because the Minos was his grandfather and his father, he says, not him." Newin stepped back as Joxer got to his feet. "But when *I* am king, I will let them call *me* The Minos." He led the way to the door and stepped into the hall. "Because it is an old and important title, you see," he finished seriously. "And people like old traditions like that." He turned left and started down the passage. "Come on; we'll be late as it is."

But Joxer kept one hand on the door latch. The hallway looked just like it had earlier, except darker, and now there were lanterns and candles at intervals, shining from deep niches. "Ah—you know, I was out here earlier," Joxer said, "and I don't think that's the right direction. Because I wound up right back here, and—" He fell silent as Newin turned back and beckoned; he would have sworn the boy was trying not to laugh.

"It's all right. That's just the palace," he said. "It plays with people who don't know it." He beckoned again. "Come on."

Silence for some moments: intent on Newin's part, wary on Joxer's. Only after they had reached an area he dimly remembered from the morning—and not from his many attempts later on to find his own way out—did he relax. "How did you do that?" he asked.

Newin shrugged. "It's not me, really. Except I was born here, so the palace doesn't try to keep me in one place, or lose me." He glanced back at Joxer, his dark face solemn. "You were fortunate you didn't get *really* lost. People have."

"Lost?" Joxer swallowed. "You mean—like they just—vanish?"

The heir nodded, glanced at Joxer's incredulous face and nodded again. "It's true—well, my tutors say they know of two men who came here and were lost. But they had lied to the Minos about who they were and why they had come here. So, I suppose that's different."

"Yeah," Joxer managed past a dry throat. "Different."

"So, I don't think you should worry, Joxer," Newin finished cheerfully.

"Worry?" The would-be hero managed a confident-sounding laugh. "Why would I be worried?"

3

Gabrielle started awake and lay very still, eyes closed, listening and trying to remember where she was. The last was easy: Clean, soft clothes, soft bed, fresh pillows—palace, obviously. *Knossos*, she suddenly recalled.

The thing that had torn her from sleep wasn't as clear. *Bad dream*, she told herself—whatever it had been. All she could remember was darkness, *heavy* darkness, closing all around her and an absolute certainty that there was no way out. Hard to find air, gasping for it in the dark—her chest still hurt, as if she'd been fighting for breath as she'd slept. "Strange," she murmured. And an odor—though her dreams seldom had scent. *What was it? Animal smell? It was! Wet hair, like a dog in winter. No, worse. Like a sheep left unsheared for a couple of seasons?*

There had been a sheep like that in Poteidaia, when she was a girl. Old widow Grusin had steadfastly refused any help with the shearing in spring, two years running; when she finally died, the poor ewe was a clotted mass of odiferous greenish wool. She'd never forgotten the look of the bloated-seeming creature, or the peculiar reek it gave off. Or what she'd always sworn was the look of gratitude it had after that for the two men who'd finally sheared it.

"What's strange?" asked a low voice close to her ear.

Gabrielle yelped in surprise, then turned her head and sighed faintly as the familiarity of the voice sank in: Xena, of course. *Who did you expect, one of the Hoard asking for water?*

Well, it wasn't one of the Hoard. Nearly as exotic in her own way, though. The face, sure; the hands. But all that brilliant silk in place of the leathers and weaponry— odd. Nice, though. "Don't *do* that," the bard mumbled and sat up, groggily pushing pale hair out of her eyes.

Xena sprawled in the room's only chair, which she'd pulled close to the bed. She still wore red and gold, but this was a different robe, Gabrielle decided. More gold in the weave, maybe, though like the other it was pleated over the shoulders, with wide sleeves that nearly covered her hands. This was maybe just lower cut over her formidable—well, yes. Those. *Wow*, the bard thought. The warrior's legs were crossed at the ankle, her feet bare. A pair of thin-strapped gold sandals lay next to the chair. The dark-brown hair had been recently combed and one long, thin braid ran down past her right temple, caught at the end in a bit of bright red ribbon; next to the plait, half-hidden in thick, dark hair, a blue-gemmed earring gleamed.

As Gabrielle looked her over, Xena raised an eyebrow. "What?"

"Nice."

"Thanks. I had help. That wasn't what I meant, though. What'd I do? After all those days on a ship, all this time on dry land and a good nap to boot, you should be pretty relaxed right now, Gabrielle."

"You startled me. I didn't expect you right there when I woke up."

Xena smiled. "Hey—I was bored with being over there alone, okay? And you're usually not all this jumpy."

Gabrielle smiled back. "Oh, yeah? I guess we're not counting times like when you and Callisto traded bodies? Or when Ares got the Furies to flip you out, and I never knew *what* I was gonna wake up to find?"

A low laugh. "I haven't seen Ares in days. No Furies— no monsters." She grinned widely. "No pointy Bacchae teeth, either."

"No pointy teeth," Gabrielle grinned back. "And, this isn't the fourteenth repeat of the same day in the same stable in the middle of the *same* feuding city where some poor grieving kid got a god to flip the same day back until someone got it right?" Her lips twitched. "Been there, done that."

"I'll rise, but I refuse to shine," Xena replied, and laughed herself. She seemed incredibly relaxed, Gabrielle thought. No bad dreams for Xena; the woman's incredibly blue eyes were warm as she settled more comfortably in the chair's cushions, and she propped her feet on the bed. "This is at least as good as old King Lias ever gave me when I took Princess Diana's place." She considered this. "Better. No yappy little dog."

"And we finally found Helen," Gabrielle said. She sat up and pulled her ankles up under her skirts. "I still don't believe how well you did that: just—riding straight up to the main gates, and there's the king, and then, there *she* is."

"That wasn't me, Gabrielle. That was the storm that blew us off course, remember? If it hadn't been for that, we'd probably be in Alexandria right now and on a very cold trail." She tugged at the braid, then shoved hair behind her ear. "Now, if we can just convince her to let us stay here, figure out a way to help her."

"Help—I don't understand." Gabrielle began separating tangled hair with her fingers. "Didn't she say that Knossos is protected from Avicus? That hardly anyone knows who

36

she is—two servants and the king, see? I remember. But none of them is gonna give her secret away?

"I'm sure they won't. That won't stop Menelaus from looking, though, will it? And if we found her this easily—maybe someone else could. Draco, or Bellerophon, any of the other boys Menelaus sent out to quest. Or—right. Whoever Avicus sends next, when they all fail?"

"Oh." Gabrielle's fingers twisted a strand of unsnarled hair, then shoved it over her shoulder and started working through another tangle. "And, you've got a plan to take care of that, right?"

"Not quite." The warrior shrugged. "For now, we'll be all right if we head off anyone on Menelaus' quest before they reach the palace—or make sure King Nossis is aware of them, so he can. Otherwise . . ." She got to her feet, crossed to the small table and mirror where Gabrielle's personal things had been laid out, and brought her the hairbrush, then went over to the window. "Otherwise, I don't know yet, Gabrielle. It's not as straightforward as dealing with Callisto."

"And that wasn't very," Gabrielle agreed. She eased around to let her legs dangle over the floor and began brushing out her hair. Xena glanced at her, then turned back to study the world outside the guest room.

Callisto. Gabrielle's brush dug into her scalp, and she had to take a deep breath, let the anger out with it. Xena never showed any emotion on that subject. *More than I can say for me.* It was wrong; she knew it was. But there were things she still couldn't completely forgive the crazed warrior for. *A better person would.* But this was not the place to remember. Perdicas so suddenly and appallingly dead the morning after their wedding night, Callisto's sword red with his blood. . . .

The brush was bruising against her scalp; she forced trembling fingers to relax. *Don't. He's safe now, you'll see him again. Don't think about it, not here in Knossos.* It would be too easy to blurt something out. *Helen loved*

Perdicas in her own way, and I don't think she knows he's dead. But even if she does know, she won't ever learn how he died. Not from me. Don't do that to her. Or yourself, she ordered sternly.

The odd, dark dream was gone, she suddenly realized. Along with the feeling of weight on her chest and tightness in her throat. She glanced at Xena as she separated another strand of red-gold hair, but the warrior was apparently intent on the view. Or giving her a moment or two to come properly awake. *Knows me; knows it takes a while.* She smiled at her friend's back.

Interesting, though. That dream: Most of her bad ones involved Callisto. Or Ares. "That's weird," she murmured.

Xena glanced at her again. "What's weird, Gabrielle?"

"Hmmm? Oh, nothing. Just—thinking." Xena merely nodded and went back to whatever she was watching, if anything. She'd sounded distracted, just now. *Like I must've been most of the trip from Sparta.* Because—had she dreamed it, or had Ares really shown up—somewhere, maybe an island? *I remember lots of trees, something about water barrels and Ares' face way too close to mine—like he was going to . . . kiss me?* Now, *that* sounded like a nightmare for certain! Maybe Xena had her own odd memories. If so, she was welcome to them.

She finished her hair, edged off the bed, and brushed at the wrinkled, green silk. *Should have put my top and skirt back on to nap in, or found something else that wasn't as fragile.* She'd meant to, but had suddenly fallen asleep instead.

Ares—she could ask Xena about that particular memory. She'd *have* to ask Xena about a lot of things, eventually. *Sea serpents and a bad storm. And that priestess. Rhodes—yeah, because of the statue, and she was Saroni, I remember that because she was so—yeah, she knew my stories, thanks to some of the guys from the Academy who'd told them in that neat little ampitheater.* Kind of nice to be admired like that; a little embarassing, too.

All the same, she really couldn't remember a lot of things since she'd jumped on that ship on the Spartan shore with the intention of grabbing Joxer and dragging him back onto the pier to wait for Xena—who was, with any luck at all, close behind.

She couldn't remember much else, just—lots of decks, sails, and ships wallowing through water that left her queasy just thinking about it, even now. Funny tasting stuff that Xena dipped out of a pot and slathered on bread for her at sunrise each day.

Another sliver of memory, suddenly: Xena didn't know about Ares. *I did meet up with him, that was true: me panicking because I couldn't remember anything, because I'd met an armed wild-woman, and she was Xena, who couldn't remember anything either.*

Because it was Lethe, that island. She could see it just as she had then, from on deck. Everyone on the ship had gone ashore because there was no water, because that brutal storm had destroyed the water kegs. And once any of them had moved away from the shore, it was like there had never been anything else before that moment. Ares had found Gabrielle after what had seemed a lifetime, and he'd . . . she couldn't remember most of it, just a sense he'd tried to kiss her. *He did douse me with seawater, that's true, so I could rescue the others. For Xena, he'd said. Because even though she isn't his anymore, he'd said. . . .* Something about deserving better, or not wanting to lose a worthy opponent? She wasn't sure. *Lethe—it couldn't have been Lethe, because Lethe is a river.*

I've lost stuff. Lost memory. Scary thought; she put her hairbrush back on the enameled little table and wrinkled her nose at the reflection in the mirror.

What good was a bard who couldn't recall the important things?

Her mouth twitched. *Yeah, like Ares is that important. He wishes.* As for the rest of it, probably when the last of the seasick stuff left her she'd remember.

The closet was behind the dark drape, across from the bathing chamber. At least she remembered that. She smiled, a minor victory, and skirted the bed. As she'd hoped, a change of clothing hung neat, clean, freshly pressed, and ready to put on. From the look of it, this was for the feast: Like Xena's, it was a finer fabric, a little more silver thread in the weave, but otherwise the same sea-foam green.

She carried the garment back over to the bed and glanced up to see Xena watching her, her back against the wall, arms crossed. *Thoughtful, or worried?* "You okay now?" the warrior asked.

Gabrielle nodded. "Sure." She began unlacing the back of the green, then drew her hair aside as Xena came over to deftly unfasten it for her. "Thanks. I like that, Xena. You look good in red." Bright red, the thought crossed her mind. Not dark—bright red, the color of death, and Xena dancing with a red-clad Ares. . . .

But she was done with unpleasant memories for the moment, she decided firmly. She and Xena were guests at a fabled palace, only a fool or an idiot would think about anything just now but comfort, good food, nice clothing, and whatever entertainment was to come.

Between them, she and Xena got her into the pale-green silk, and she spun in place, letting the fabric slither up over her arms and calves, then settle into place. "And, if I didn't say, Xena, you look rested."

The warrior smiled. "Thanks. You look good yourself. And I like red, especially when it's like this: Bright, slithery, and lots of gold to make it interesting. Yeah, I got some sleep. With time left over to think." She moved away, through the separating room and came back with the tray, now holding a very few grapes, a small bowl of cherries, and two ewers with matching cups. She poured herself a dollop of wine and, when Gabrielle nodded, a mug of cider for her. "Not that thinking has helped much so far."

"It will," Gabrielle assured her firmly.

Xena's mouth twitched; her eyes were amused. "Yeah. I wish I had your faith. Because no matter how I go at it, the only way I can see to stop Menelaus from hunting Helen is to kill him. Even just killing Avicus isn't the answer, because Menelaus would find another priest, or another way." She drained the cup and poured another swallow, dropped back into the chair and watched the contents swirl.

Gabrielle set her cup aside. "Xena, hey, listen to me, how many times do we have this conversation? I mean, you can't just kill—" The warrior held up a hand, and she fell silent.

"I know that. And you know I know that." The two women studied each other for a long, still moment. Xena finally broke what felt like an interminible silence. "Gabrielle, if I had thought that that was the right answer, the only way to stop all this, those two would have been dead before I'd left Sparta."

Silence again. Gabrielle swallowed, and finally nodded. Despite her extremely violent past, Xena so often went along with her requests to try resolving things without violence. Now, or back when they'd found the old toy maker, Senticles, during a solstice season in which the local king had refused to allow solstice to be celebrated. *Solstice. Gods, was it two or was it three years ago? It seems like a thousand years ago. Xena and me getting those orphans to help stop the king's soldiers by throwing marbles and other toys, making the guards look silly but not really hurting them, both of us finding a way to make things okay again.*

"Like that town," Xena said, unnervingly echoing her thought. "Remember? The old king who'd lost his wife and we'd thought she was dead? That old toy maker? I try, Gabrielle."

"I know you do," the bard replied warmly. It had probably been the first time since her own childhood—if then—that Xena had 'got' the idea of giving gifts, rather than each of them simply purchasing something she wanted for herself. *And she gave me that carved wooden sheep.* She could still feel the thrill when she'd first seen that toy. So like the one she'd had as a child.

And Gabrielle? *In all the craziness of trying to get that poor old king to let people celebrate solstice—I forgot to buy Xena anything!* She'd felt so awful about it. But the look on Xena's face, then, when she'd smiled so warmly and said, "Gabrielle, you are a gift."

"We'll just both have to keep working at it," she said firmly. "It'll be okay. It has to be. We'll find a way."

Xena didn't agree with that, of course; she'd seen too much in her life go wrong, and though she was more hopeful these days than she'd once been, she still wasn't the most optimistic person around, Gabrielle knew. But Xena merely smiled and nodded, set her cup aside and got to her feet, went back over to the window and gazed out.

Gabrielle's smile faded as she thought about the wonderful toy. That beautifully carved sheep. She had tucked it in the basket with Hope when she'd hurled the baby to what she thought would be safety from a jealous Xena, who'd wanted only to destroy an innocent child. She swallowed again. *My demon child: Poor Hope. But Xena was right; I couldn't save her, any more than I could turn Dahak to Good.* Because the gods knew she had tried and had failed.

Forget it, she ordered herself angrily. It was all behind them now—everything but sudden, painful reminders like this. Solan was dead, Hope had died by Gabrielle's own hands. And the solstice gift from Xena had gone with Hope, part of her pyre—right next to Solan's. *Don't!* she ordered herself fiercely, and blinked to find a concerned Xena coming over to catch hold of her shoulders. She managed a smile, and thought quickly. "Sorry. Must not be awake yet. It really was an—odd dream."

"Great," Xena drew her briefly closed, and smoothed her hair. When she let go of her close companion, her mouth was sardonic. "Don't tell me about it, okay? Your dreams are *all* weird, compared to any of mine."

"Yeah." Gabrielle smiled. "Comes with being a bard. Free stories every time you go to sleep."

"Yeah, sure. Pass." The warrior crossed the room, peered through the bathing chamber, then went back to the window.

"Anything interesting out there?" Gabrielle asked. The warrior shook her head.

"Just—thinking."

Gabrielle watched her settle on the narrow sill, then turned away to pull the bed neat. All the things that had happened to them and between them since the day she'd abandoned her family and village to follow a reformed— make that reforming—woman warlord. It had taken time for Xena to learn to trust Gabrielle, but it had been nearly as much of a struggle for Gabrielle to learn to respect the woman's silences.

Ready for the party—no party yet. If the daylight outside that window was any indication, it might be a while before anyone showed up to escort them to the banquet hall. Gabrielle scooped up a handful of cherries and perched on the edge of the chair to eat them.

"So, you don't think Helen's going to be safe here?"

The warrior didn't turn. "Gabrielle, she's not safe anywhere. Maybe she's safer here than someplace like Rhodes."

Silence. Gabrielle dumped cherry stones back on the tray and contemplated finishing the bowl of fruit. Decided not to. "If only we could—" she shrugged—"I don't know. But he only wants her because of what she is—right?"

"Most beautiful woman in the world," Xena agreed.

"So, maybe, if there was a way to make her look old, or ugly or something?"

Xena glanced at her; smiled briefly. "I thought about that, too. The problem is, in order for it to work, it would have to *be* real. You couldn't fool him with fake warts or something."

Gabrielle grinned. "You mean like the one you wore when you pretended to be a buyer for the gold statue of Pax?"

"Exactly. None of those guys were getting too close to me. Menelaus—you wouldn't be able to keep him from getting close enough to Helen to touch her, and if there's a way to fake old or ugly that close, I don't know what it is."

"Yeah. Me, either." The bard sighed faintly. "Too bad, though. I mean—imagine the look on his face—he shows up here to claim her, and there she is with silver streaks in her hair, bags under her eyes, and missing three teeth, or the last stages of leprosy?"

Xena laughed. "Figure out how to make it work, Gabrielle." She shook her head. "I wish you could," she added soberly. "No, what we have to do is come up with a plan that will make him lose interest without coming to Crete. If that's possible."

"Well—sure."

"That's important. Because Knossos doesn't have an army, the island itself is protected, way it's laid out, and the Minos has treaties with just about everyone close by. And the palace has its own guardians."

"Oh?"

The warrior eyed her briefly. "You heard what Helen said. But an army of Spartan soldiers . . . even if they didn't win, they'd kill innocent people and destroy a way of life."

"And Helen would blame herself for all of it," Gabrielle said. "Every last death. You're right."

Silence, which she broke a moment later.

"You don't make it easy, do you?"

"It's not me, it's life. But there's a way, Gabrielle. There has to be. You can help me find it."

Another silence, but a comfortable one. Gabrielle stirred.

"Did I tell you about that priestess, back in Rhodes? The one I think has something to do with Avicus?"

"The head priestess? Not the one who was all over you?" Xena's mouth quirked.

"Yeah, right," Gabrielle muttered; she could feel her face getting red. Xena was used to that kind of thing, even if she still didn't care for it much. For the bard, this had been a first: Someone goggle-eyed to meet The Bard. Poor Saroni, she thought. The woman must not have much of a life outside that temple. "Saroni—that's the—ah—the woman who likes tales. Anyway, she said something . . . I can't exactly remember what, but it sure sounded to me like it meant that Krista woman was talking to Avicus."

"I don't doubt she is." The warrior shrugged. "Doesn't matter. Helen never went to Rhodes, and she's not there now. Not much the priestess can do to stir up trouble, if that's what she's up to."

"I hope not," Gabrielle began; she was interrupted by a tap on the door. A moment later, a fresh faced, black-haired girl clad in pale blue came through the washing and bobbed a curtsey.

"I am Honoris, here to ready you for the feast."

"Good," Gabrielle said. "Because you know what? I'm *really* hungry!"

"Gabrielle," came the amused reply from the window ledge. "When *aren't* you?"

There are no words, Gabrielle thought irreverently.

A short while later, the two women followe ̶ ̶ ̶oris through long, brightly painted halls. Gabriell ̶ ̶ ̶ ̶ delight at fantastic fields of flowers, and ̶ ̶ ̶ leaping high above a sea with ships on ̶ ̶ ̶ strange creatures below. This shaded ir ̶ ̶ ̶ ruins of an island falling into deep water, the fire and smoky pall of a vast volcano towering above it. "Atlantis!" she exclaimed, and her feet slowed. Xena tugged at her elbow.

"Gabrielle, c'mon! You can look at it later—or tomorrow, when the light's better. If you aren't still hungry, I am."

"Huh?" Gabrielle blinked at her, then at the girl waiting for them at the next joining of hallways. "Oh, right."

Another cross passage, and then another. Gabrielle glanced at their guide, then at Xena, and lowered her voice. "How big *is* this place, anyway?" The warrior shrugged. "I mean—it didn't look this big from the outside. And what is all of it *for*?"

Xena ran a finger along the wall, tracing the line of a bright, green painted vine that opened into an enormous pink and red blossom. "Some of it's for the king's business—scribes and archives; things like that. Some of it's to house the king's nobles and their families."

"Oh." Gabrielle hesitated briefly as the wall to her left became seascape again—sea serpents, one strangling a ship just like they were said to, while two others picked off the sailors who'd been thrown from its deck. *Brrrr*, she thought. *Did we get lucky or what?* "I get it," she said. "It's a city, it's just all under one roof. Right?"

"Something like that."

"And somewhere in all this—" she flung her arms wide, "is Joxer. Except, I thought he was farther back that way than we were."

Xena shrugged.

"Guess we'll find out eventually. I mean, he'll be there tonight, won't he?"

"If we're here that long, I'm sure you'll have plenty of chances to explore," Xena said. Ahead of them, the girl waited at another cross passage, and this time gestured for them to take the left way. "But he's an honored guest, too; he'll be at the feast." She considered this. "Unless

46

he's done something really dumb and wound up at the bottom of the cliff, or in a cell somewhere."

"You know," Joxer's reedy voice came from the right, "I heard that, Xena, and you know what? I resent it! I mean, when is the last time I got thrown in a dungeon?" Gabrielle turned back to look down the hall as Joxer came striding up, a half-grown boy in plain black at his side. The would-be hero smirked. "On account of, I seem to remember, Gabrielle, that *you*—"

"Cut it out," Xena growled. "And start over. This is a palace, and we're guests here."

"Yeah," Gabrielle put in. "It wouldn't hurt to use some manners, would it? Show some class, Joxer." She looked at the boy then; he seemed to be fighting not to laugh, and she smiled at him. "Hi. I'm Gabrielle, and this is Xena. And I guess you know Joxer . . ."

"He knows Joxer," Joxer broke in. "And he's Newin."

Xena nodded and laid a hand on the boy's shoulder. "I thought you might be the heir," she said. "You look like him, and I remember the custom." And, as Gabrielle eyed her curiously, she added, "If Nossis had a queen, she'd have come to help us get ready. He doesn't, but he sent his son to help Joxer."

"Oh." Gabrielle seemed to see Joxer for the first time; she stared. "Wow! Lookin' good, Joxer!" He made her a sweeping bow, and for a wonder, did a neat job of it.

"Yeah," Xena said dryly. "Wonder how long *that'll* stay clean?"

"Manners," Joxer reminded her in a lofty voice. "Which reminds me, you are both radiant, lovely and—gee, I really like the green thing, Gabrielle."

He was trying, he really was. She'd do her best, she decided. "Thank you," she replied simply, and when he bowed the women moved ahead of him and Newin, Gabrielle made sure she and Xena were well ahead of the Prince and the would-be hero before she made a face at Xena. Xena's mouth twitched, and her eyes were wicked.

• • •

It was, Gabrielle decided, some of the best food she'd ever eaten, and probably the most. Course followed course, with toasted, tender, lamb cubes skewered between chunks of apple and other fruits; a bowl of fruit in pale, sweet wine giving way to a fish soup; then some other kind of roasted fish covered in a spicy, crispy layer that crunched agreeably.

The room, fortunately, hadn't been the vast hall she'd expected given the sprawl of the palace as a whole. There was one table fit to hold maybe thirty people closely, instead of a dozen or so tables and herself and Xena widely separated. One side of the chamber was all windows, but with the sun down, she couldn't see much except an occasional torch or lantern somewhere across the palace grounds. The opposite wall was cut into steps, and in the far corner were musical instruments, some benches, and stools.

No music to go with food. She approved of that, especially tonight. She had attended very few royal banquets, and seldom indeed as an honored guest. And there was bardic tradition about such feasts in the halls of the Minos; a person didn't need distractions.

There were twenty-two dining at the long, candlelit table, with the king at one end, his son and heir, Newin, at the other, and various members of his nobility and household between. Joxer had the place at Newin's right hand, then the wife of Nossis' minister of trade—a dark and plainly serious woman of middle years, who seemed much more interested in her plate than the guests. Her husband, Olios, had the next seat, and then Gabrielle and Xena midtable, side by side.

Somewhere between the lamb and the soup, Gabrielle became aware of Helen, a still form near the door clad in dark blue, a sheer scarf of the same color draped over her hair and shadowing most of her face. The two children

48

who had come in with her waited politely until the king saw them, then ran to his side at his gesture. Gabrielle was glad to see the man turn and pull them both close. From the look on his face, he must be very fond of them.

The boy listened as his sister whispered something in the king's ear, then accepted a bit of fruit from his father's plate. Then both ran back to their tutor, who took them out again. Bedtime, the bard assumed, and promptly forgot about them as yet another freshening-course was brought in. Helen returned alone some time later, near the end of the meal, and at a gesture from Nossis, settled on a cushioned sofa on the top step, near the harp.

Now some entertainment would be good, Gabrielle thought. The final item was set before her—a chilled cake filled with dried fruit. She sighed happily and picked around the edges.

Xena nudged her. "Hey, you're not full or anything, are you?"

"Who, me?" Gabrielle took another small bite and washed it down with a sip of very cold and well-watered wine. "I can't remember the last time I was this full. Pinch me so I know I'm not dreaming. Or just remind me I earned this."

Xena glanced beyond her close companion to Joxer, who was quietly talking to Newin. The boy had scarcely touched his last two courses, and gazed at the inept warrior in awe. *Not inept to the prince, at least,* Xena thought. It surprised her how well-behaved Joxer had been throughout the long meal; she'd been sure she'd have to haul him out halfway through the soup. *Not falling in his plate, hasn't spilled anything, and he's not bragging.* Or if he was, she couldn't hear it.

Gabrielle's eyes moved that way, and she pushed her cup away. "Amazing, isn't it? When I first saw those two, I figured we'd be in for at least ten new verses of Joxer the Mighty over dinner."

"I know what you mean. Maybe an innocent kid like that is exactly what he needs," Xena said.

"Well—sure." Gabrielle pinched a little cake between thumb and forefinger and ate it, then reluctantly pushed the rest aside. "It's not like bragging to Meg and her kind, I guess." She turned the other way as King Nossis stood and snapped his fingers. "Do you suppose Helen's gonna play? And do you think that's exactly safe?"

"Gabrielle," the warrior replied softly, "think about it. She's so established as a tutor, what else are these people gonna see except the tutor to the king's babies? It's not uncommon for a tutor to also teach music, you know." She laid a hand on Gabrielle's arm for silence then, as King Nossis began to speak.

"My friends, colleagues, and guests, I welcome you to Knossos, and I trust you have enjoyed the feast so far. To those of you who have not yet met our guests—"

"That would be almost everybody," Gabrielle muttered quietly; Xena nudged her, and she fell silent again.

"I am honored to introduce Xena. I know many of you have heard of Xena the evil warlord, but as we Cretans know, Xena and a companion went to Troy and helped defend her walls to the last. Because of them, many brave Trojans still live." Xena inclined her head as he gestured; she smiled at the polite applause, but her eyes were ironic. *Yeah, right,* Gabrielle thought. *Lookit the two old guys across from us; they're looking at her and thinking 'warlord,' all right.* But the king was speaking again. "Her companion before then, and at Troy, and since: Gabrielle, warrior and bard."

Gee, the warrior/bard thought confusedly, and smiled brightly. The two old men didn't seem to have reservations when they looked at *her*; they were pretty enthusiastic, in fact. *Great. All I need, a couple fellas like that to duck while we're here.*

"And," the king finished grandly, "the warrior Joxer, who has given up his own pursuits to aid Xena in her constant battle against the evil forces in our world." Xena and Gabrielle eyed each other blandly; Joxer waved a hand and smiled, but made no comment whatsoever.

"He's sick, right?" Gabrielle whispered.

Xena shrugged.

"Hey. You got me. *Ssst!* Pay attention, he's not done," she added quietly.

"As you of Knossos all know," Nossis said, "it is custom for the musicians to perform over the final course and wine. But such good fortune as is ours, in the matter of our guests is it possible we could persuade Gabrielle to honor us with some of her tales?"

"What—me?" It came out, fortunately, as a faint, breathy squeak. Xena gripped her friend's elbow, and as Gabrielle glanced wildly her way, nodded firmly. The bard smiled and waved her free hand. "I—sure! I'd be honored. Glad to, in fact." She lowered her voice and leaned close to Xena's near ear. "I did *not* expect this! You didn't, did you?"

"Me? I didn't do anything, it's all his idea. Not that it surprises me, Gabrielle."

"Great! What do I do now?"

"What you're good at. You talk." The warrior smiled. "Just remember, Knossos was friend and ally to Troy, and by and large they don't like a lot of blood and gore."

Gabrielle glanced up and smiled cheerfully, nodding as Nossis gestured, and Helen stood, making her way to the harp. "Okay—so I'd leave Menelaus out of things anyway, and I guess that means nothing about the Hoard—as if I would. I—ah, okay, I can do this." She pushed resolutely to her feet, thinking furiously as she approached the steps, and turned back to face the long table.

Stick with the basics, she told herself, and glanced at Helen who nodded. Ready to follow whatever lead the bard made, she assumed that meant. As it did. "Let me tell you," Gabrielle began, "about the day Xena battled an army and a vengeful giant."

She had to leave a lot out of that tale, as always. What struck her now as wildly funny—her and Xena spatting nonstop the entire day long starting with the argument over a dented frying pan and Xena's 'creative juices.' Poor goofy-looking Howar's drooling crush on the warrior—that was all the kind of thing an audience like this wouldn't get. They enjoyed the rest of it: Xena's creative use of the rampaging giant to destroy the warlord's army, then the even more creative way she'd harnessed lightning to kill the giant.

Xena looked embarassed as Gabrielle's audience broke into applause—but then, no matter what story Gabrielle told here, the warrior would look as if she wanted to be elsewhere.

To Gabrielle's surprise, one tale didn't do it. She went through every story she could think of that wasn't too violent, that wasn't anti-Troy or pro Greek gods. The anti-Troy caution wasn't a problem but the violence thing—it wasn't just enemies like the Hoard, she realized as time after time, she announced a story, only to meet with dead, disapproving silence on the part of some of her audience. The women seemed one and all appalled at the seemingly callous tossing around of the baby that Pandora later adopted when she married King Gregor. Even though the child hadn't been harmed and it was only because of Xena's quick thinking and her own half-quick reactions that the child was still alive. Those sour, matronly faces kept several other stories behind her teeth—things she'd thought reasonably tame, like Ares losing his godhood. *Of course, they don't approve of the Greek gods any more than they like the Greek warlords*, she reminded herself with a faint sigh. That took care of Prometheus, even though she knew she could make a tearful story of Io-laus's near death. And there was no point even starting with Callisto (too violent) or Callisto siding with Ares (Greek gods, odd sex if you could trust Ares on the subject of Xena's body and Callisto's mind in the same form). Never mind Callisto and Xena exchanging bodies (just flat out weirdness, even ignoring the level of violence.

Down at the far end of the table she could see Newin looking slightly annoyed. Because of the way she was choosing her comparatively bland tales? she wondered. Or because none of them . . . She grinned, nodded at Helen and declaimed: "And now, I tell you of Joxer the warrior, who was tricked by the silliest Greek goddess of all into stealing a bride from her beloved, and who by his daring deeds nearly divided two kingdoms." Joxer went red to his hairline. *Hey, deal with it*, she thought happily. The banquet guests adored the story: Aphrodite made to look ridiculous, lovers divided by a whining goddess and then reunited by the very valor of the hero who'd been sucked into pushing them apart. She knew how to make the violence result in zero bloodloss all around, and the swashbuckling hero was rescued at the end by a bard's cleverness in finding a way to ring a bell and tweak Aphrodite's nose at the same time.

It was a story she'd never dared tell before. *Hey, I was never someplace protected from the silly goddess. Raw fish to you, Aphrodite, I could get used to this.*

Unfortunately, the story galvanized her audience. Even Helen looked interested, as opposed to mildly amused the way she had until now. Gabrielle smiled until her jaw ached, her mind turning over story after story: Too violent, too sexy, too just plain odd, too—no, don't go there, *way* too violent, forget about Marcus, Xena wouldn't welcome sharing that. . . .

Inspiration struck just as she was about to bow and plead a sore throat. *Payback*, she thought happily. For Twickenham and the others spreading her stories to Rhodes and wherever else they'd gone. *I wonder where Homer is, and if he's still closing his eyes when he chants*, she thought, and spread her arms wide. "I sing of Spartacus," she declaimed passionately. "Rebel gladiator!"

4

Smoke hung thick and black across a narrow bay near the northeast tip of Crete, making visibility ashore nearly impossible, and breathing anywhere on the bay itself unpleasant. The Gaelic pirate ship *Wode* lay at anchor mid-inlet, tied off to a tree jutting from the steep cliff just beyond her stern, her anchor holding her bow across the center of the deepwater channel, effectively blocking the way in or out. Though at the moment, there were no other ships visible on the open sea. But there was a sleek raider being hauled up onto the sand by a frantic crew. Well, Draco thought with grim amusement, *it isn't going anywhere for a while. Not with a hole that size, and that far below the waterline.*

The smoke faded; the fires were out on the *Wode*, and he couldn't see any flame on the other ship. A light breeze riffled the water and sent most of the sooty cloud east, though the smell clung to everything. The warlord's nose wrinkled. He dropped down off the aft deck and strode forward, leaning over the port rail so he could make out what was happening on shore: Two of the bronze-armored swordsmen were bellowing orders as at least twenty half-naked, soaking wet men hauled on three ropes, dragging at the partly sunken raider ship that lay at a hard angle, sails flapping loose against the port rail.

Those would be the rowers, Draco decided. There hadn't been anyone on deck among the fighters who'd looked raggedy and overly thin like that; slaves, probably, most of them. He didn't know how wet a man'd get, rowing below decks as they did, but more likely they'd gotten drenched when the ship was holed—or getting to shore, of course. They were having a job of it, no surprise, with all the extra water in that bow at the moment. The foremast was half-submerged, and those fighters might as well shut up for all the good they were doing.

Nearby, a clutch of armed and partly armored fighting men eyed the *Wode*. Wondering if they could find a way to attack her, Draco thought. If they should bother. They seemed to think better of it. *Smart ones, aren't they*, he thought dryly. Their catapult was either at the bottom of the bay or underwater, forward, and he'd seen the baskets of shot for the weapon fly off the starboard deck when the bow started taking water so abruptly.

Wode's catapult was lashed down near the port rail, in plain sight, along with the two torches ready to light pitch-coated shot. The warlord's nose wrinkled; he wasn't used to the heavy reek of burning pitch, and he didn't care for it much. *Pine tar laced in the torches to burn out a village—that's a smell a man can appreciate*, he thought.

Another thought briefly flitted across his mind. *You're supposed to be doing good, remember? Yeah. Right.* It suddenly seemed a lifetime ago that he'd made that vow to a very wary looking Gabrielle. In fact, it was difficult to see her face just now, though he'd talked to her only a few days before, the afternoon he'd climbed the back-side of Melos while *Wode*'s crew loaded their water barrels. Funny old small world—him walking right into *her*.

Of course, Xena'd lied to him, back in Menelaus' palace—Gabrielle was *with* her and on the quest for Helen. *Probably that Joxer is with them, too,* he thought gloomily. *I could've made her tell me.* But she'd looked nervous enough, just sitting alone in that high meadow and talking to him. *And "making" someone—that probably isn't doing good, either.*

She'd done a *lot* of laughing that afternoon, he suddenly recalled. That nervous, silly giggle. *You know,* he told himself, *that stupid giggle could get under your skin real bad, after a while.* Maybe, if he had the opportunity, he'd get used to it. But that wasn't important. The *Wode* had lost track of Xena and Gabrielle early on; right now, they could be anywhere, including halfway to fabled India. Besides, there was plenty to do here and now. The fighting just now had been—different enough from a land battle to pique his interest. Similar enough, it felt damned good. *And that part, swinging over to the other ship? Oh, yeah. That* was *good.* He grinned, hitched one leg onto the rail and settled in to keep an eye on shore. And those warriors.

Funny thing about those warriors, though. Habbish's crew might not be typical of the breed, of course. They were from some cold, bleak island well to the north and east, maybe all their kind looked like such a mixed bag: Everything from hardened leather armor to bare chest to cast-off metal plate that had to be lashed in place, and not two swords even remotely alike among the pack of 'em. *Could be he's really lousy at pirating, and this is as good as it gets for these guys.*

He didn't think so, though: The planning and execution of this raid, and the state of that other ship, said Habbish knew his business. *Can't fool another warlord, anyway,* Draco thought. He'd taken to the Gael from the first.

It was something to ask Habbish, though: If those guys on shore were pirates also, how come they were dressed so well? The two prisoners he'd personally taken wore armor that had been smelted for them, and the swords had come from the same smith, he knew the look.

His eyes moved over the lines of the stranded raider ship. It had the look of a fine warhorse: Sleek, smooth, well proportioned. Built for speed. The *Hammer* should have been able to out maneuver *Wode* easily: Habbish's vessel was almost as tubby as a merchantman in comparison.

Draco's admiration for *Wode*'s captain had gone up considerably since Habbish had mentioned the ship following them for so many days, and Draco had said, "Why not stop them and ask them why?" At the time, Draco had thought his comment a rather weak joke and had been surprised when Habbish took the notion seriously.

Draco glanced over his shoulder. Habbish was still up by the wheel, where he maintained the captain should be at such times. Those funny plaid britches and the shock of curly red hair shot with silver. That wild mass of beard. That gut. The man didn't look much like a fighter—not like a fighter at all, the warlord amended. And, in fact, the Gael had done no actual fighting when the ships had finally engaged. But he knew how to plan. *Oh, yeah. Does he ever.* He'd mentioned Crete right away and explained to his guest and passenger why: the island was close, but so were several others. However, Crete was bigger by far than anything else around, long and skinny, with a northwestern tip that was populated only by wild animals and birds, and maybe a herder or so. The current king chose not to waste money patrolling this far end of the island since there was nothing here to protect, no reason for an army to land here and find its way up the cliffs and across hostile highlands simply to sneak up on the towns or the main port. "Or Knossos itself, were a man so foolish as to challenge the power that keeps it safe." *Wonder what he meant by that.* Draco had filed that thought for later, when there was time to talk.

After poring over his charts for some time, Habbish had

picked this particular inlet: for its size and the configuration of the bottom. "There's deep water within, room for two or three ships to maneuver around one another, but t'entry, is narrowed by cliffs. And 'tis known as a good place to stash things and come back for 'em later. And besides," he'd explained to the fascinated warlord, "see this mark? Here—just in from shore? 'Tis a well, good one, too."

Draco'd seen an objection at once, and raised it. "But you said you can land on Crete. That you trade—"

"Sure. But t'captain may not know *Wode* does so. So, would be a normal thing for a ship like this t'put in somewhere away from t'cities, same as we did on Melos. And we've no' made land for water since Melos. Wager they know that, too.

"Now. Way they've followed us so far, like you'll say, 'Habbish, no point to 'em going in there after us; they just wait out of sight until we come out, eh?' Either follow us on as they've done, or ambush us, if that's their long plan. But, say *Wode* sails close along t'island, moving fast and in a straight line, s'if we had some plan and no want to share it?"

Draco had followed this easily enough: "They think we're up to something, you mean? Sneaking around. Picking up treasure, maybe?"

"Or burying our last take."

"Better yet. They want to know what we're up to, and why."

"A man can hope as much." Habbish'd shrugged.

"So, they'll follow?"

The captain had shrugged again. "P'raps. If not this time, then next. There's another place or two t'*Wode* can use t'lure 'em."

The whole conversation had left him impressed with the similarities between land and sea tactics, and the differences, too: Interested enough to want to learn more. *Man could do worse*, he'd thought as he emerged from the captain's cabin to seek his own—the sumptuous little cabin reserved for special passengers. Not as nice as the tent he'd had when he'd commanded his own army, no. Good enough for the time being. *Maybe, until I get a ship of my own?* He'd shrugged the thought aside; too much going on just now, and maybe there wouldn't be enough profit for another ship like *Wode*. Though the waters were vast and there seemed to be no end of merchant-vessels for the taking.

Of course, Habbish might not want to share information like that; might even see the question as a personal threat to his command of this ship. *Wait until you're close enough to shore to swim in, if you have to,* he'd told himself wryly.

Part of him had been surprised, part of him not, when Habbish's plan had succeeded: The old man had done a masterful job of steering his ship on a steady course, sending men to the crow's nest and the aft deck rigging to make a show of seeing the raider for the first time, then sending more men flying into the rigging to pile on more sail and angle the foremast to catch the least breath of wind. The little ship had practically flown over the water until it reached the bay; Habbish had barked out orders and kept the wheel for himself, and Draco'd nearly gone flying as the vessel came around, heeled partway over, then headed straight for the entry of the bay.

They'd vanished into early morning shadow, cast by the high rock walls shielding the rising sun, but not before Habbish had seen the other ship's oars come out. "Taken the bait proper!" he shouted; his men grinned fiercely and went back to their tasks.

Once inside the bay, Habbish had ordered sail drawn in, the foremast tied down flat, and had used what little wind remained to steer *Wode* flawlessly across what even Draco could see was a very uneven depth. *I don't know much of it, and those charts of his might as well be in that Hittite cuneiform instead of straight lettering.* But even a green boy could tell the difference between the deep blue of water a ship could cross, and the paler green that might ground it. *Or the stuff that's so shallow, a man can see the sand and the plants growing in it and clearly make out the shoals of young fishes.*

They were scarcely in place when *Hammer* came into sight, but still well out to open sea. The ship turned sharply in deep water, sails slacking limp as wind was partly blocked by the cliff face. Ranks of oars like a forest of spears cut smoothly into the water and came dripping out, then down again, propelling the slender war machine into calm water.

War machine beyond doubt, once they could see it close up: Archers lined the forerails, and men worked to brace up the catapult while others brought up baskets of shot. Still others stood on the high aft deck, swords out.

Draco could still see the fierce grin on Habbish's face as the other ship moved steadily down the very midst of the inlet and into the bay. The vessel shot by their shadowy hiding place. Draco barely had time to read the name on her bow: *Hammer*.

But once she was inside the relatively pondlike bay, her open-water assets turned into liabilities. Particularly her length. At Habbish's barked order, *Wode* moved out, her own small oar bank moving the ship until the wind could catch the sail; she'd come up behind *Hammer* unnoticed until, with a hellish snapping of wood, her metal-clad prow had sheared off half the port side oars.

Hammer floundered awkwardly until someone bellowed the order for oars up. Dependent now entirely on the wind—what there was of it—the ship came around as awkwardly as an old fishing tub.

Habbish's oarsmen had backed *Wode* away so smoothly, Draco suspected this was a frequent maneuver on their part. The archers on the other ship scrambled for clear shots and catapult workers fought the wallowing ship as they piled shot into the bucket and one of them tried to get his balance long enough to light the pitch. They got off one load: most of that fell harmless into the sea behind the *Wode*, or to starboard. Before the bucket could be filled again and the winch set, *Wode* came at them this time at a sharp angle, the metal-clad prow cutting into the other's port bow. Men went flying as *Hammer* heeled hard to starboard and, moments later, the *Wode* was out of reach.

But only for a moment; this time she went in at the same angle, but Habbish threw the wheel over hard to port at the last moment. Draco and two dozen hardened pirates had been ready; as the ships scraped against each other, men launched themselves from the rails or swung onto the decks of the *Hammer*.

Prisoners, Draco'd reminded himself. It wasn't his usual fighting style, but it hadn't proved that difficult to flatten one man with the hilt of his sword and another with a hard left to the jaw. Two of the men who'd stayed with him dragged the unconscious pair back to the rail, where they were helped aboard *Wode* as she made another pass. Draco stayed behind to make certain the men who'd gone to disable the catapult all made it back; he was the last one across and nearly missed his footing. Fortunately for him, the *Wode* had dropped into a small wave, and he fell onto the deck rather than into the water. Moments later, *Wode* rammed *Hammer* again, this time forward and well below the waterline; the battle was over.

Easy pickings, the warrior thought as he watched the exhausted rowers drop to the sand while other men shoved past them to study the damage to their ship. *Remember to tell the man how impressed you are, when you get the chance.* To this moment, there hadn't been one.

The warlord brought himself back to the moment, and shielded his eyes against midday sun as he gazed up. *Hammer* had actually hit something after all, but the damage seemed to be slight. A few holes in the sail, a sooty streak running up toward the crossbar, and a hole in the floor of the crow's nest. More luck than aim, probably.

Habbish's crew were obviously old hands at all this: Even before the man could bark out an order, and while *Wode* was still menacing *Hammer*, a handful of men had swarmed aloft to put out the fire.

Habbish was still at the wheel, shouting orders in half a dozen directions. Draco stayed where he was—where he'd be out of the way until things were settled.

We coulda settled that ship my way, he thought. He'd said as much to Habbish: "If they're bothering you, get rid of them. Send the ship and every last one of the crew to the bottom."

But Habbish had been firmly against it. "So happen they be Romans, a man'd be foolish to kill 'em all off. They hear of it, and they'll hunt *Wode* until they sink her." *The Romans would never learn what had happened from a drowned ship of dead men,* Draco thought grimly, but the Gael wasn't buying it. "Besides, man'll learn more from a prisoner or two. May be 'tis time for Habbish to move back north and out of these waters entirely."

Well, it's his ship, the warlord reminded himself.

They left the bay a very short time later, the *Hammer* almost as pathetic looking as her rowers, some of the armored men shouting curses and threats. Habbish and his crew ignored them.

There wasn't much wind—just enough to move the ship without the need for oars. Habbish brought *Wode* into deep water, then around toward the northwest before turning the helm over to one of his men; he clattered down from the aft deck and joined Draco at the rail. "A good fight." The captain grinned. "Ye've style, man. And we've three prisoners."

"Three?" Draco raised an eyebrow. "I grabbed two and got out; I didn't see anyone else."

The grin widened. "Two ye took y'self. Third, though: two 'f my men got 'im, fished 'im out of t'water at t'last.

Trying to swim right out of the bay, they thought he was. Funny, don't y'think?"

"A slave trying to escape—?"

"Nae, no oarsman. T'was armored and all; about t'drown when they got hold of 'im, and 'im still tryin' t'get away from 'em." He looked up and shouted, "Just bring that sheet in by half, and drop 't deep anchor! Yon cap'n won't be following *us* anytime soon! We'll bide here a bit!" He turned back to Draco as two men eased out onto the crosspiece and began pulling up loose sail. "Time to ask a question or so, d'ye think?"

"No time like the present," Draco replied cheerfully, and followed the captain across the deck to the starboard rail, hard against the bulkhead of the aft deck where three bound men sat cross-legged, and heavily guarded.

Draco looked them over. The two he'd taken—one with a split lip, the other an impressive, black eye. Both looked back at him sullenly. The third, though: The third man wore hardened leather that looked familiar. So did that shock of pale hair. The smile left his face; his eyes narrowed as he nudged the third fellow with his boot. "You. Look at me."

The man ignored him.

Draco nudged harder.

No reaction.

He drew a long-bladed dagger and squatted on his heels, flipped the blade under the man's chin and with his free hand, grabbed hair, yanking back hard. "I said, look at me. You know how I am about orders." A startled yelp; Draco smiled, but his eyes were hard.

"Brisus," he said quietly. "My old friend Brisus. I sail halfway across the Aegean and who do I find? Only the man I left behind with *my* army!"

"It wasn't your army any more, Draco!" Brisis spat back. "I took it from you because *you*—!" A sudden, convulsive movement of the blade at his throat silenced him.

"Oh, no, Brisus, you got it all wrong. You *cheated* me

out of it. But it's still mine. Now. One more time, and then I start carving: What—did—you—do—with—my—*army*?"

"I didn't—" Terror had tightened the man's throat so that the words came out as a harsh whisper. Draco smiled, shook his head, and slid the blade along Brisus's windpipe and smoothly along the line of his jaw. *Not a drop of blood, either,* he thought with grim amusement. He could see white all the way around the man's eyes. He moved the dagger so Brisus could see all of it, and raised an eyebrow.

The man gasped for breath; his eyelids sagged shut briefly. "It—it was—a coupla days after you left . . ."

"After *you* forced me out," Draco corrected him evenly. "Through the gauntlet, in case you've forgotten that little detail?"

Brisus merely shook his head. He seemed to be fighting for control. After a moment, he went on. "You were gone. Most of the—the men were okay with that, whatever you think," he added spitefully. Draco shifted his grip on the dagger; Brisus sent his gaze down to the deck and kept it there. "We—I was planning a raid, over into Pylos, maybe."

"Yeah, sure you were," Draco said flatly. "Because *I* came up with the idea!"

"Pylos," the man said after a moment. "We—I had everyone in camp, so we—could talk about that. Decide—where the profit was, if it was worth it." He glanced up, away again. "The Spartans came down on the camp from three directions at once. We never had a chance."

Draco stared at him. "You *let* the Spartans take *my* army?"

Brisus's mouth twitched; his eyes were resentful. "I didn't *let* anyone *any*thing! I had guards posted, I—why the Hades do you care, anyway? It wasn't *yours* any more, it was *mine*!"

Silence. Draco was vaguely aware of Habbish just behind him, of men all over the deck listening, and the other two prisoners who now divided their attention between Draco, Habbish, their guards, and Brisus, whom they gazed at with open loathing. "Yeah," the warlord said finally. "I guess you wouldn't get it, would you, Brisus? I put that army together one man at a time. I personally picked every last fighting man, I knew what each one of them was good for, where he'd do best in just about any kind of fight there was." Another long silence. "How many of them were left, when you finished letting the Spartans overrun the camp?"

"We took out a lot of *them*," Brisus began resentfully; the knife moved and he swallowed, hard. "They caught us by surprise, I *told* you. They—"

"You didn't have guards posted on the west entry, did you?"

"It wasn't supposed to have happened like that!" Brisus shouted.

"Yeah. Great excuse. That lets *you* off the hook, doesn't it?" Draco reversed his grip on the knife and threw it; it quivered deep in the aft bulkhead, mere inches from the usurper's ear. Brisus stared at it sidelong, his jaw slack. "So, now tell me how you wound up on *Hammer*."

Brisus licked his lips. "As a slave—"

"Yeah, sure you did. Captain here says they fished you out of the water just like that—armor, weapons. That same nasty knife at the back of your neck, and the other one in your boot, I'll bet. *You* weren't down helping row that boat, you were fighting for her!"

"I didn't—!"

"You stole my army, and then you sold it out, didn't you, Brisus? How much did Menelaus give you to open up the camp for him?"

"No!" The yell echoed across open water. Brisus swallowed again and tried to speak normally. "They—just a couple of us at the end, they gave the choice: Die in the king's torture chamber or volunteer for his ship. I—Hades, Draco, what choice did I have?"

"You had a lot of choices," Draco replied evenly. "Including never coming to me for a job in the first place and never kicking me out."

"Wait," Habbish broke in suddenly. "You mean—yon ship belongs to *Sparta*?" Brisus glanced up as if surprised to find anyone nearby but Draco. He studied the man for some moments, then finally nodded.

"He—his captain, the king's captain, I mean, he said that *Hammer* is supposed to be Roman, or a raider ship manned by Roman deserters. It's his, though. Menelaus'. He keeps a percentage of whatever they take, and—"

"Oh, aye," the Gael snarled, startling Brisus into silence. "T'man duped me!" He bent over to glare at the prisoner. "And what d'ye know of *why* that ship followed my *Wode*, eh?"

"Tell him," Draco suggested softly as he drew another dagger. One of the other prisoners shifted and started to say something, but fell prudently silent as Draco rounded on him. "I'll listen to *you* a little later. Meantime. Brisus—?"

Brisus shook his head. "I—they didn't trust me. I never spoke to the captain, barely even saw him, except when I came—on board."

Draco chuckled quietly; his eyes were all pupil. "Not good enough."

"It's the truth! I swear! But—but, you couldn't help hearing, it's worse than a camp because it's so small and there's nowhere to go away from people. Everyone was talking about it, the last two days. We were supposed to take the *Wode* and strip her; word was, the king didn't trust she was paying full tribute. So—they were gonna teach her a lesson. But there was—something, I don't know, a—a missing badge? The—someone said the king's priest was behind part of it, but no one talks about *him*. They're scared to because he can see things."

Draco laughed again, genuinely amused this time. *Fact*

is, the man really can see things. That water bowl of his. Probably had plenty of ways to see things. After all, he had a powerful god to back him up.

Missing badges—what did that remind him of? He'd worry about that later. Right now, there was this—the amusement was gone—*this scum.* "You bastard," he said quietly. "You shoved me out, took my army, and let it be destroyed. That's assuming I decide to believe your story about the way things happened."

"It's the truth—"

"Shut up. Well, you know what, Brisus? Maybe I'm gonna build a new army. With a new set of rules. Because maybe you heard from some of my men how I pick my fighters? Not just the clever, little men who come in with recommendations about how good they are at building up profit?"

Silence. Brisus had gone a muddy white; he knew, all right.

"I put them ten paces away, give them three arrows, with orders to shoot at me. I catch all three arrows, he's out. The man who can beat my hands is in.

"From now on, same kinda thing to force anyone out. Including me. Wanna see how it's gonna work, Brisus?"

Silence.

"You're gonna stand right there, by the rail. I'm gonna back across the deck, just past the mast. You get three arrows." The warlord got to his feet and began stripping off his armor. He dropped that and dragged the under padding and shirt over his head. "Open target," he added, spreading his arms wide and displaying an impressively muscled chest. He smiled as two of Habbish's men drew Brisus to his feet and untied the ropes. "And if you miss? *When* you miss? Well. Then it's *my* turn."

"I—you can't—!"

"You wanna bet?"

"He can," Habbish said at almost the same moment. He

eyed the wet Brisus with contempt. "He says so, and so do—"

Silence.

"So *you*'re the fine laddie who took m'friend's army, is it?" He clapped Draco on the shoulder. "He's all yours, friend," he said, turned, and went back to the aft deck. "You, aloft!" he yelled as Draco got someone to bring a bow and three arrows. "Keep an eye on that bay, and open water, too! That ship was no Roman, but Spartan! May be another keeping an eye on *it*!" He settled his elbows on the aft rail, watching like most of the rest of his crew, as Draco pressed the bow into Brisus's unwilling hands and propelled him back against the rail, then slowly backed away from the man.

Just as he could begin to see the mast out of the corner of his eye, he stopped. Smiled. It wasn't a nice smile. "I'm giving you better odds than I've given anyone else, Brisus," he said. "Eight paces, not ten. At this range, you don't have to be as good to make the mark—and I have to be a *lot* faster."

Silence. Brisus eyed the warlord sidelong. Draco shrugged widely, then folded his arms across his chest and grinned. Brisus brought the bow up and an arrow to the string in one smooth movement, drew, and fired. Draco caught the first arrow, deflected the second, dodged the third. He was smiling widely as he held out a hand for the bow. "My turn," he said. Brisus took one step toward him. A second. He threw the weapon aside then, turned, and dove into the water. "Stop him!" Habbish yelled. Three of his men were already at the rail, but Draco shoved them aside and held up his hands. Some distance away, Brisus came up for air, arms and feet churning furiously as he swam toward shore.

"Let him go," the warlord said finally and turned away. "If he can make shore with all that extra weight, maybe he deserves to."

"He gets back to *Hammer*," Habbish said flatly, "and like as not, they'll kill him as a spy."

"That's fine with me," Draco said. He scooped up the bow and slipped the string loose. "I didn't kill him."

"And if ever a man deserved it—" Habbish fell silent as Draco clomped across the deck and vanished into his cabin. "Keep those two close-guarded," the captain snapped. "We'll talk to 'em later. A little farther out from shore, p'raps." Neither man showed any emotion whatsoever. Habbish gestured for the three men at the rail to keep watch on them and went back to take the wheel.

Midnight. The nearly full moon slipped from behind clouds to turn the sea a glittering silver and black; Crete was a massive, shadowy bulk. The *Wode* moved slowly north from the island, lifting and settling through gentle waves, her sails barely shifting with the light breeze. One of the boys held watch by the wheel, and another in the bow. Two men sat cross-legged in the crow's nest, talking in low voices as they watched the way they had come.

"Won't be any ship coming t'night," one of them mumbled. "Not after damage we done it."

"Lucky it didn't sink," the other agreed. "Still, 'tis no bad duty, Angus. Air's warm, ship's steady, and—" He drew a jug from inside his shirt; it gurgled. Angus grinned widely. "Mind, now!" the second man urged, and held the jug at arm's length. "Habbish'll have our ears, we don't keep close eye back there!" He uncorked the jug and swallowed a long draught, then handed it over, snatching it back when his companion seemed ready to drain the rest. "And ye'll no watch anything, y'drink it down all 't once."

Angus sighed elaborately and settled his back against the mast. "Bare enough t'wet m'lips, Mobree. And I'm watching, see?" He glanced wistfully at the jug; Mobree's lips twisted and he shoved the cork in, the jug back into his shirt. "Wager Habbish 'n' that warlord're deep in their

69

cups. We got O'Nary on t'wheel, he's got his eyes open like always, and t'prisoners are belowdecks. Nothin' t'fret."

"Like t'be. Was a good job of ship fighting that landsman made of it, and his first on a ship, if the man tells true." He peered into bright moonlight. "Man can't make out a thing of the land back there."

"Nothing to make out," Angus assured him. Mobree considered this for some moments, then broke out the jug again.

Down in the *Wode*'s main cabin, Habbish moved unsteadily from the table to the wooden keg that held his personal supply of ale, empty jug dangling from his fingers. Draco sprawled in a deep chair piled high with cushions, his booted feet crossed and hooked on the edge of the captain's planning table. A pile of hide charts was stacked just beyond his heels, and at his elbow, in a basket lashed to the chair arm, a silver cup still half-full of the captain's ale.

It was only his second cup, but an ale this strong and sour wasn't his idea of a good drunk. It certainly was Habbish's, though. The captain had drained four cups already, and he was on his way to downing a fifth. Halfway through it, he set the thing aside and fixed his companion with bloodshot blue eyes. "Man'll need a new home port, I expect," Habbish said finally. "Menelaus, the tricky bastard. Never a clue that t'*Hammer* was his! What was it made y'let that pale-haired bastard go?" he asked abruptly.

Draco shrugged. "Killing him would've been too easy. Tell me something, though. Letting him go like that—would you call that a *good* act?"

"A—" Habbish stared; he blinked then, and drank deeply, refilling both their cups. "I'd call it daft, is what!"

Draco took a swallow, pushed the cup away. "No, I'm serious. I—there was someone, a while back. I—vowed

70

that I'd try to do things for *good*. Not kill people." He shrugged, retrieved the cup and downed the contents. "I just want to know if that qualifies."

Habbish considered this gravely. "Ye didn't kill 'im, so—I suppose it would count, then."

"Good." *If I ever see her again, I can honestly tell her. I did good.* It might be the one and only time.

Faces suddenly crowded his memory: Men he'd hand chosen to follow him; men he'd known for years, a few of them. Good fighters, good companions all. He snatched the cup and filled it; time to drown memories, drown thought. *Brisus, I hope you died out there. Because I swear to Ares, if you didn't, I'll find you again. And next time.* . . . He smiled, a curving of lips that fell short of hot, black eyes, and drank deeply.

5

Gabrielle woke to full sun streaming into her room. Eyes still closed, she stretched luxuriously and smiled. "This," she announced happily, "is the life."

"Don't you start getting used to it," a familiar voice replied. Gabrielle shielded her eyes and peered across the room. Xena lounged against the doorway, arms folded over her armor. An unfamiliar bit of silver gleamed against her shoulder—the pin Helen had given her, the bard realized after a confused moment.

Gabrielle laughed quietly. "Hey," she told her close companion. "I said I liked it, not that I wanna keep it!" She sat up cross-legged. "So, what's up?"

"Hm? Oh." The warrior brushed a hand across hardened leather and bronze, one finger tapping the edge of the chakram. "All this. King Nossis wanted a meeting, him, me, Helen, one or two of his military advisors that he can trust. You can come if you want to, but—"

But Gabrielle was already shaking her head. "No, that's all right. That kinda stuff isn't really my thing. Just don't forget that I'm here to help, too."

Xena gave her a warm smile. "Gabrielle, would I ever?"

"I know you wouldn't. Tell you what, though; after a day of taking it easy, I'd like to get outside, look around. You know: Explore. Besides," she added as the thought struck her. "Someone's gotta keep Joxer entertained and out of trouble."

"I thought the king's son was doing a pretty good job of that last night," Xena said. "But yeah. Unless Newin knows the secret, it's unlikely Joxer knows Helen is here. And I'm with her, I'd like to keep it that way."

"Even if he does know, I don't think Newin would— well, then again," Gabrielle said thoughtfully. "The way he was looking at Joxer all last night. Like the guy was— really something, you know?"

Xena chuckled softly. "Yeah. Takes all kinds, doesn't it? Joxer the Hero. Bet that kid's tutors were something else."

"Probably told him all the kinds of stories I heard as a kid," Gabrielle agreed. "Except I had a lot better taste when it came time to pick a hero." Xena came over to ruffle her hair.

"You did okay. Even if I wasn't so good with it at the beginning."

"What can I say? I grew on you, right? Anyway, unless Newin's been turned loose to take care of Joxer full-time, he's still pretty young. I'll bet he's got lessons of some kind today, probably lots of them. I'll drag Joxer off with me and make sure he stays unenlightened."

"Good." Xena paused in the doorway to the bathing. "Oh—and Gabrielle?"

"Yeah?"

"Be—careful out there. You'll know the Maze by the big gates that keep people out of it. They'll be locked, and there may be guards."

"They—locked? Why? I mean—think about it, Xena! The place where Theseus found his way in and out be-

73

cause the king's daughter was in love with him and betrayed her people, and he found the Minotaur and killed it and saved all the young Athenians who were supposed to be sacrifices, and—"

Xena's mouth quirked. "Yeah. You and Salmoneous, I bet he'd want to turn it into a tourist attraction, too. It's locked off because it isn't safe."

"But I'd—okay. I understand you wouldn't want to just walk into someplace like that: If it was made for people to get lost in, probably they still could. All the same . . ."

"It's an odd place. Maybe it wouldn't affect you the same way as it did me, the one time I was here."

Gabrielle slid off the bed and reached for her freshly laundered top and short skirt. "And—how was that?"

The warrior shrugged. "I don't know. I was aware of it, I guess. Like it knew I was there—me, personally. And it was trying to draw me in."

"There's a pleasant thought!" Gabrielle's head popped through the short top and she tugged it into place, then snugged the laces down. "Well, I'll tell you what, I'll watch out for anything like that. But it's not like I'm in your class of warrior, am I?"

"Give it time," Xena said gravely, but her eyes were warm. "I'm not sure that was why it was trying to draw me in, though, Gabrielle. Maybe just because I wasn't a native, maybe some other reason. But I gotta go. I'll see you back here—before sundown, anyway. There's another dinner tonight, but it's just for family and us."

"Great." Gabrielle sashed the skirt to her waist and bent down to find her boots—well under the bed, of course. By the time she came back up with them, Xena was gone.

There was food already out: on the table in Xena's room was fresh, white bread, still warm from the ovens, a bright-red sweetened fruit-mash to spread over it; two thin slices of meat and fruit—an entire bowl of cherries, untouched, so far as she could tell—half a dozen figs; and two grapes still clinging to an enormous stem. Gabrielle ate some of the bread and most of the cherries, smiled as she picked up the grape-stem. *That Xena. Left me every single one of the cherries because she knows I'm crazy about 'em. And two grapes, as if to say. . . .* She wasn't sure what it meant to say. Xena being nice, for sure. Thoughtful.

Her throat briefly tightened. "What would I have done without her? If we'd parted, back there. Over Solan and Hope—and just—kept going?" But that was pointless, just now. They *were* together, things just about as good as they had been—before. *Remember that she can tell what you're thinking when your mind goes back to—all that.* Same as she could tell by the look in Xena's eyes. Let it go, she ordered herself.

Time to go play. She cut bread from the loaf and dropped a dollop of the fruit on it, cut a thinner slice and rolled it around the meat. There was an ewer of chilled water and another of pale cider to wash it all down. Gabrielle ate rapidly, drank a mug of the water and poured the rest into her bottle, cut another thick piece of the now-cool bread and shoved it into the small belt pack. "There," she told herself as she patted the pack and went back into her own room for her staff, "now I don't have to come back in at midday if I don't want to."

There were marvelous things throughout Knossos—bardic tradition as well as traveler's stories, and she thought she knew most of them. Unfortunately, the Maze was the most familiar—and intriguing—of those. Still, even if it was off limits—no doubt just like Xena said, locked off *and* guarded—there were other places, plenty of things to see, stuff to do. The theater. *And no priestess of Apollo on Crete to tell me not to declaim,* she thought sourly. The arena where the youths and maidens of Knossos had practiced acrobatics was still standing, and then there was the really exciting thing some traveler had told her about ages ago, when she was still in Poteidaia. "A dancing floor," she murmured, and smiled. It had been a while since she'd had the time, the interest, or a *place* to dance.

That village where dancing had been forbidden—of all the silly things—had probably been the last place. *Who'd've thought Xena could dance that well?* Of course, the warrior was deft-footed, that came with her weapons training. But that kind of grace didn't necessarily go along with swordplay, and the pair of them had been pretty well matched, actually—if you didn't count in all the amazing things Xena could do with her body: all those flips and other moves she used to fight with. *Yeah, but on a dance floor, I could jump just as high as she could. And my feet were every bit as fast.*

Now, if she could find this dance floor, dancing floor. Whatever. Preferably *after* she had found a way to get rid of Joxer, though. Somehow, a combination of a dancing floor and Mr. Two Left Feet didn't sound like a good one to her.

Joxer's room was as easy to find as Helen had suggested; Gabrielle had only just remembered to fasten the pin to her top before she set out to locate him, but either there wasn't any great mystery to the halls, or the thing just did its job. The passageway with his apartment was a little narrower, the rooms smaller and not quite as sumptuous, but he still seemed to be doing just fine. Really poshy for Joxer, anyway. A little to her surprise, he was on his feet, dressed and alone when she tapped at the door—and itching to get outside himself.

"Pretty amazing, isn't it?" He flapped his arms, taking in the narrow room, the tiny bathing chamber that was almost all tub, the view—or maybe all of it together, including the few breadcrumbs and wrinkled fruit stems left on a breakfast tray half again the size of the one she and Xena'd shared. "Newin came by here earlier—the king's heir, remember?" he preened. "But he couldn't stay to guide me anywhere. Duties, you know; I guess all heirs have 'em, *I* wouldn't know. Anyway, he just stayed around long enough to share the breakfast he brought me, and then he had to go off for lessons. And I wasn't dressed, so I didn't leave when he did, but he wasn't gonna have time to get me outside anyway. . . ." He drew a deep breath. "And, you know? I hope *you* know how to get out of this place, Gabrielle, because I sure can't figure it out."

"Joxer," Gabrielle reminded him sweetly as she beckoned, and he followed her into the hall. "You get lost in something the size of one of Aphrodite's temples!"

"Gabrielle, for your information, I have *never* gotten lost in one of Aphrodite's temples, and—and, well," he finished lamely, "I don't get *lost.*"

She turned to flash him a urchin's wicked grin. "Yeah. Right."

"Master of Geography, remember?"

"Rrrr—right."

He tittered. "Face it, Gabrielle; you wouldn't have *found* Sparta if it hadn't been for me leading the way."

"Oh, yeah?" she demanded, suddenly outraged. "Joxer, for *your* information, I would never have *gone* to Sparta!" She turned the next corner and started down an equally plain and long passageway. *What is it with him?* she wondered. *Two minutes back together and we're chewing at each other like he was my kid brother or something. And he's picking on me like. . . .* She wasn't going to go there, though. Uncomfortable memory surfaced briefly: Xena in that town where they'd repeated so many days, *cooing* at her, for the gods' sake, about Joxer having this enormous *crush*—! Or, had it been the other way around, her having one on him? She tugged angrily at a strand of hair and sent the whole half-memory away. Good and likely, she'd never really remember. *And that's just fine with me, because who'd want to?*

"Are you sure we're doing this right?" Joxer broke what had been a reasonably comfortable silence with a reedy demand. "I mean, I *think* I came this way last night, and I wound up back at my own door."

Silence, except for the clomp of his boots.

"Except—I tried the other way, too, and I still. . . ."

"My point exactly, Joxer," Gabrielle said firmly.

"Huh?" he asked blankly; she shook her head and led on. A left turn, a short but wider passage, and there was one of the many porches with its brightly colored, fat-at-the-bottom columns holding up a steep tiled roof. Beyond it, hot sun glared on a brightly painted courtyard. She stopped just short of full sunlight and gazed eagerly over the open ground. "Would you *look* at that?"

"I did, last night—"

She glanced at him sharply.

"I mean, I looked at it through my window, except I—I mean, I am." He was silent for some moments, tribute indeed from Joxer. "Somebody just—did all that, because they could?"

"Well, somebody sure did all that, for whatever reason," Gabrielle told him. Her eyes were searching the near features, all she could make out for the glare and the odd way the ground sloped the least bit away from them. "*Look* at that incredibly complicated swirl of red—and is that a horse or a bull?"

"I can't see anything except something long and squiggly and red, Gabrielle. Why don't we go out there and look?" he replied, and clattered down the broad steps and into the open.

They explored for some time: the painting was a bull, life-sized and enclosed in a lozenge or frame of ornate lines. The animal itself was beautifully done—possibly from a real animal, Gabrielle thought, except the shape of it was elongated and stylized. A mantle of flowers crowned its horns and wreathed the thick neck. "Better someone else than me," Gabrielle said with a shiver.

"Huh?" Joxer blinked at her; his gaze was distant, as if he'd been concentrating on something.

"The bull—all those flowers. I mean, if someone painted it like that because they decorated them—decorate them here, for some festival or something. Because bulls are mean."

"They *look* mean," Joxer said absently. "I wouldn't know from experience, though."

"I don't either," Gabrielle told him firmly. "But there were a couple of bulls back in Poteidaia, and I was smart enough to stay away from them. Just try to put something on a bull's horns like that, and you'll wind up wearing them. Right through you." Joxer wasn't paying attention, she suddenly realized. His gaze was moving slowly along the horizon—mostly ampitheater to the west, that giving way northward to low hills and scrubby, dusty-looking little trees.

"You know," he said finally. "I don't know *why* I'm even here, or why I'm sticking around with you and Xena right now."

Gabrielle moved around to face him and grabbed a double handful of shirt. He eyed her glassily. "Because if you try to go somewhere else, one of us will mangle you? In case you've forgotten, Joxer, that was one of the new rules when I got on that ship with you back in Sparta! You do not go *any*where without us! Okay?"

"Oh—yeah. I guess so." His vaguely puzzled look fixed on her for the least moment, then moved on again. Her hands twisted in his shirt, tightening fabric against his throat; he blinked and seemed to take in what she'd just said. "Oh. Sure. That. But, you know? I have something to do, and just because neither of you believes in this quest, doesn't mean I shouldn't just go off and do what I gotta—"

He broke off as Gabrielle gave him a shake. "Joxer! What is the matter with you? We did this! We did it to death! There is no quest!"

"Look. Gabrielle. All I know is, that's what *you* say," Joxer replied loftily. "If you ask me, you and Xena just want to . . . want to find her first and take all the glory yourselves." He considered this outrageous statement, then grinned at her. "Sorry. Helen, I mean. Well, forget it, because she's *mine*. Okay?"

I'm gonna do it, Gabrielle thought angrily. *This time I really am gonna whack him one.* . . . But somehow she couldn't. He must be sick—there must be something wrong with him, anyway, because his eyes looked— funny. Odd. He was *acting* odd, even for Joxer. She eyed him worriedly. "Joxer, did you eat anything weird last night? Or this morning?"

"Why would I do that?" he asked, bewildered, but his eyes were suddenly concerned. "Gabrielle, maybe we need to get you out of the sun, because I think your brain is frying."

"Joxer, will you cut it out? The problem here is *not* me! Here—hold still a minute, let me. . . ." She laid a hand against his brow, testing for fever; he shoved it away. "Okay, fine." She stepped back and looked him over. "I got it. You—ah, didn't happen to see three wild-looking and barely dressed ladies last night, did you?"

"Huh?" He goggled at her. "Ladies—oh, you mean, like, at dinner?" He thought for a moment. "I'm not ex- actly sure any of them qualified as—"

"Yes, they qualify as ladies but no, *not* like at dinner! The three I'm talking about don't wear anywhere near that much. Ah—half naked?" That got his attention, of course. *That figures,* she thought dryly. But he reluctantly shook his head. "Really wild hair? Great dancers? Lots of bright silk, leather, studs?" No reaction this time, except possibly deepening confusion on his part. *So, I was wrong. Still, if it was the Furies who'd got to him,* she told herself with an inner sigh, *he probably wouldn't have a clue they'd even visited him. And after all, Xena didn't see them until they'd already trapped her and driven her mad. They* didn't have to touch someone to make 'em touched.

Joxer's concerned-sounding voice pulled her out of the thought.

"Gabrielle? You know, you're really starting to worry me. Anyway," he went on briskly, "main thing is, I have something to go do. And don't try to tell me again there isn't a quest, because *I* don't believe you."

Gabrielle tapped her foot, thought furiously. She smiled then. "Know what? We were lying to you, and—know what else? You were right, Joxer! There *was* a quest."

"Huh? I mean—there is?"

"*Was.* Because Xena and I already found Helen. And that thingie—necklace, whatever it is? That's on its way back to Sparta."

Joxer stared at her. A smile tugged at the corners of his mouth, then. "Thought you had me fooled, didn't you?" he asked softly, and took a step toward her, his eyes narrowing in that "Joxer the Clever" look that normally left her wanting to smack him one. At the moment, all she could feel was relief: He was buying into it, just exactly the way she wanted him to. "Okay, Gabrielle. Two can play *that* little game. If you found her, where is she? Tell me that!"

She opened her eyes, very wide. "She's here, in Knossos. Disguised as a servant."

Dead silence. Then Joxer began to laugh. "Gabrielle," he chuckled, "you know, if you're gonna try to lie to *me*, you might at *least* come up with a story that I might even *think* about beginning to *pretend* to believe!" He bit back laughter, but it came spluttering out; Gabrielle leaped back as spittle flew. "Helen of Troy here—oh, yeah, right! Let me guess: she's—washing dishes, maybe? Scrubbing floors?"

Go ahead, dig it in the rest of the way, good and deep, Gabrielle told herself, and slammed the end of her staff on the pavement. It echoed, briefly silencing even Joxer's laughter. "You think you know everything yourself?" she demanded furiously. "She's a laundress, Joxer! Probably

the one who washed your grubby old *shirt* last night!"
She shut up abruptly and clapped a hand over her mouth.
Wasted acting, she decided. Because he was laughing so
hard, tears ran down his face; he flapped a hand at her
helplessly and staggered away from her. He finally got
himself under control, staggered back, now holding his
sides, and grinned at her.

"Well, Gabrielle. You know, I'm glad you told me all
this. And tonight, when she comes around with my trousers, I'll get down on one knee and say, 'Your High-
ness. . . .' " He couldn't go on; laughter exploded out of
him again.

He took the whole bait, Gabrielle thought with relief,
and decided it was time to go ahead and laugh with him.

Some time later, Joxer finally heaved a sigh, and reached
over to ruffle her hair; Gabrielle snarled at him wordlessly
and smoothed it again. "So—what? We're gonna look at
paintings of bulls all afternoon? Or is there anything *else*
on this island that's interesting? Up here, I mean." He
thought about this. "Except you know, I forgot? There's
this maze thingie—"

"I know about the Maze," she told him. "They don't
let people go in there, I guess. Dangerous, or something."

"A maze? Dangerous?"

"If you couldn't find your way out? And no one could
find *you?*"

"Ahh—point taken," he replied hastily. "I don't suppose
you're gonna go off on your own and just let me . . . ?"

"Joxer? Do the words, 'In your dreams' tell you anything?" She smiled sweetly; he sighed.

"And I don't suppose you're interested in getting 'way
out, maybe along the western end of the island, where the
rocks are—no," he concluded as she shook her head. "I
can see that doesn't appeal to you. So, what's left?"

"Well . . ." She sighed faintly. *So you stuck yourself*

82

with him. Serves you right, maybe. "Well, there's this thing called a dancing floor, except I don't know where . . . ?"

"Oh, that?" Joxer shrugged blandly; he looked quite pleased with himself, all at once. "You're standing on it."

It was her turn to stare at him. "I beg your pardon?"

"You're standing on it. This whole big paved thingie? I asked Newin about it this morning, and that's what he said. It's the dancing floor." He nudged the bull painting with his foot. "He said he didn't really know much about it, just the name. Well except that the palace holds solstice fests out here. You know—you ask me—that's a funny thing to call a big old open place like this, isn't it? I mean, you could probably take all the people in Melos and they wouldn't fill this thing up. And you'd need—more musicians than—"

"Joxer!"

"Oh." He watched in silence for some time as Gabrielle turned in place on one heel—not really dancing, he thought, just—trying out the possibility of dancing. "Bet it wouldn't be much fun," he finally ventured, "if you had to dance out here for winter solstice. Cold and windy, OK?"

"Maybe they have another floor inside, painted just like this. Okay?" She turned the other way, lifted gracefully onto one booted toe.

"Funny," Joxer said thoughtfully. "I asked him about that. Newin, I mean. He said that—um." He frowned at the distance. "He said, 'No. That's what the Maze is for.' Like I said, funny, huh? Because, I thought the Minotaur was dead, on account of Theseus killing him?"

"I don't know about funny," Gabrielle said. "Is—not was?" Joxer nodded as she glanced his way. She smiled and turned away from him. "Okay, that's odd enough, I guess. Oh well . . ." She spread her arms wide, staff dangling from her right, and slowly moved off in a series of ever-quickening spins, her face turned toward the sky. She smiled as she executed a number of swift, light-footed steps, twirled again, then laughed in sudden delight. "Oh, yes! This is just great! And you don't have to worry about running into a wall, do you?"

"*You* don't!" Joxer called after her. Gabrielle merely laughed again, hooked the staff against her side, clamped her elbows against her waist and her fists tight on her hips, and brought her feet down in a rhythmic pattern. "I hope you don't expect me to join you," he added in alarm as Gabrielle's rapid footsteps brought her back toward him— sideways.

She laughed happily. Probably the happiest he'd heard her laugh since before Hope. . . . He didn't want to think about Hope, he told himself fiercely. Gabrielle clearly wasn't thinking about Hope—about anything but her feet. "Joxer, if you don't understand how *wonderful* it is to dance, then I am really not gonna try to explain it to you!"

He watched in silence for some moments as she circled him, then spun neatly away to dance off once more. His brows drew together. "There is something—very—*odd* about this," he muttered to himself. "Now. For all I know, Gabrielle's one of the best dancers that ever *was* . . ." A smirk tugged at his lips. "Except for a couple of the girls at Meg's of course." He contemplated this, slapped his own face sharply, forehand/backhand, one cheek and then the other. Hard. Certain images faded, replaced by a golden-haired young woman in a minimal green top and short skirt bouncing deftly across the open ground. "Cut it out! Okay?"

Silence.

"Something's off here. Because—lookit her. I mean, even if she's that good, her eyes are closed and her face is tilted toward the sky anyway—and her feet haven't left that skinny red bit of paint, and it's like all *over* the place."

It was true: Gabrielle wasn't watching where she was going; she couldn't be. And that red paint looked like it had been drawn on the whitewashed pavement by a drunk. There wasn't one single bit of it that went straight: It curved, crossed itself, turned back on itself . . . and it drew away from him.

He blinked. So was Gabrielle. "Going, that is," he told himself in sudden alarm. He glanced all around; no one in sight, except the two of them. "Great," he muttered. "I wonder if she realizes just how much trouble she can be, and how often I gotta haul her sorry. . . . Gabrielle!" he yelled. The sound, unnervingly, did *not* echo. Though her staff had, he remembered, and swallowed. Sudden anger swallowed dread. "All right!" he demanded in a loud, aggrieved voice. "Is this gonna be weird, like the halls outside my guest room? Because I am just gonna *hate* it if it gets weird!" Whatever the reason, Gabrielle wasn't answering him; he wasn't even sure she'd heard him. "Gabrielle!" Louder this time. She flinched, glanced his direction and scowled at him.

"Joxer, will you just—shut up?" Her feet were practically flying, the steps faster and higher. More complex, if he was any judge of such things. "I can't hear the music if you're making all that noise!"

"Music?" he asked blankly. "What music?" He listened intently—but except for the soft patter of her boots on the paving—still tight on that meandering red line, he noticed nervously—it was extremely quiet out here. The distant cry of some kind of hunting bird, then silence again.

"I was right," he muttered. "It's weird, and I am hating this." He drew a deep breath, and started walking across the floor, carefully avoiding the red line. "Because, maybe it's some kinda weird magic and if I step on it, I'm caught, too? You know, what Jett told you all those years ago: Step on a crack, break the harpy's back?" And then she gets pissed off, and *eats* you. He hadn't slept for days after that. . . .

He pinched himself. Yeah, better to stay off the red.

Because he could just picture himself bouncing around out here, sweating and gasping for air, bounding along that red line right behind Gabrielle, and both of them being found by Xena. Worse yet: Newin. "So much for Joxer the hero, huh?"

So—what would a hero do, about now? Joxer set his jaw and lengthened his stride. "He'd—ah, right. He'd grab Gabrielle—nice and tight so she doesn't get cutsey with that little stick of hers and bing me one on the nose—and he'd haul her right off her feet, and—" He wasn't sure what he'd do at that point, if breaking the contact between the red line and her feet didn't slow her down. "Probably he'd have the most bruised shins in all the Aegean," he told himself gloomily, and sighed. "What the—yeah, what the hey, she's worth it."

Forty long strides—somehow, he wasn't catching up with her, he realized. "This—is—not good," he panted. So: pursuit wasn't gonna do the trick, maybe. "How 'bout—an—ahhh! Did I need this? I did not need—how 'bout an ambush?" He leaped wildly across the red line, managed to flail himself back upright before he overbalanced, and took off at a dead run. "Great!" he gasped. "She's—"

Receding, the suddenly alarmed thought finished itself. If anything, there was more distance between them than there had been. And she didn't seem to be making that much movement sideways: most of it was that bouncy up-and-down stuff, mostly from the knees down. His breath whooped, and he bent over to rest his palms against his knees. "Okay, new game plan," he wheezed. "Find where the line curves back *this* way, and cut her off? Except, if it doesn't—?" He shook his head, sending rough-cut brown hair flying. "Bad thought, Joxer. Because this is an island, and a pretty steep-sided one at that, and sooner or later she's gonna run out of level ground and...." He forced himself upright and broke into a run again.

A sudden, shrill cry dropped him flat on his face before

he realized what it was: Xena's war cry, right behind him, and then above him. He rolled partway over, levered up onto one elbow and stared. Xena pulled out of her long, flying tuck, landing right in front of the oblivious Gabrielle; long, hard hands caught the younger woman by the elbows and hauled her off her feet. Xena swung halfway around and virtually threw Gabrielle away from the red line, and somehow still managed to be there to catch her before the dazed bard could fall.

Joxer let his eyes close briefly; he sighed. "Always. Somehow, she's always right there to—yeah. I never get a break."

"It's not like you didn't try, Joxer." He yelped as Xena's low voice came from directly above him. She held out a strong hand and dragged him to his feet. Over her shoulder, he could make out Gabrielle, lying flat and still on the paving, eyes closed. "She's all right, just dazed. I saw what you were trying to do for her." She gripped his shoulders and her blue eyes were very warm. "And I appreciate it. So would Gabrielle, if she knew."

"She—" Joxer's shoulders sagged. "I ran. Tried to cut her off. Everything. I—she just kept getting farther away, and there didn't seem to be a thing I could do."

"Joxer." Fingers tightened, digging into muscle and silencing him. "I know."

Silence.

"It's all right. She'll be fine. Your heart was in the right place." She smiled, her eyes dark. "Like always."

Remembering when she'd tried to kill Gabrielle, tried to drag her to death and then throw the body into the sea, and I had been stupid enough to get between them, and— He swallowed; Xena nodded sharply, then turned away from him.

"I shoulda warned her about this place. Before now, or even just this morning, when I told her to stay away from the Maze. I just didn't think." She gave him a rueful smile. "Everything that's happened lately, sometimes, I forget the details. Like, how much she loves to dance."

"I didn't even know that she did," he said.

"Hey. I didn't even know until recently. Did she tell you about that village where they were trying to ban all dancing?" He gave her a blank look. "Never mind. She found out about this place, though, somehow. That it's called a dancing floor."

Joxer sighed. "Yeah. I'm sorry, Xena. Because I told her—"

Xena cut him off, her fingers tightening on his arm. "And you didn't know any more about it than she did, did you? Just the name?"

He nodded.

"Don't tear at yourself, Joxer. You didn't know."

"Yeah, I guess," he replied doubtfully, then frowned. "Ah—what didn't I know?"

"Dancing floor. Except, it's not that kinda dance. Here, c'mere," she added roughly, and dragged him over to where Gabrielle now sat cross-legged, head cradled in her hands. *"Not,"* Xena repeated as they came up, and the bard cautiously raised her head, "that kinda dance floor, or that kind of dance."

"What other kind is there?" Gabrielle demanded weakly. Xena dropped down beside her and hauled the younger woman halfway around, turned away from her so she could work sword-and-chakram-hardened hands into overly tight neck muscles. Gabrielle made a happy little wordless sound and leaned back.

"Let me know if I get too rough, here," the warrior said quietly, then, including Joxer: "There's a story. Probably only told here in Crete. I just happened to be around my only time through Knossos when I heard it told, the old Minos' bard was a good one, and he made a *real* scary story out of it The kind that I can't imagine would export too well.

"Seems the city had been beseiged—the story doesn't say who they were fighting or when, but the other army

88

won, swept over the port and the other cities, then battled all the way up that road, and up the back of the island, surrounded Knossos and set fire to the palace. The local army wasn't a big one then, any more than it is now— mostly honor guards. Men came out and fought, but they were hopelessly outnumbered and the enemy was deadly. In the end, nearly every Cretan man and boy old enough to hold a spear was dead. The women—" Her fingers dug into Gabrielle's neck, then relaxed as the younger woman tapped urgently at her wrist. "Sorry, Gabrielle. It—gets me. All my years of leading an army, I never did anything like that. Never on purpose. Never anything that— wicked." She shook her head, hard. "The enemy gave the Cretan widows a choice: Come away with them, live out what was left of their lives as slaves—hard labor or the other kind—or—or die, with the young boys and the male babies. Stabbed to death or burned on pyres."

Joxer stared; Gabrielle's eyes were suddenly wide and bleak. "No one would do something that—that horrible," she whispered.

"They would," Xena replied. "The—the women were given two days to choose. They—stayed here."

"They stayed?" Joxer's voice sounded strangled.

"They died," Gabrielle said. Xena nodded, let go her friend's neck and got to her feet.

"They died. That red line supposedly marks the path the women took. One last dance, to honor their men, they said. They begged. The commander of the enemy army looked at them and saw only women made haggard by grief, women who could never defy such a brave army. He gave permission, and he and his men watched the women, the girls, the young boys—they all spread out, arm in arm, a long line of them across the sandy ground facing what was left of the palace, babies on the backs or breasts of whoever could carry them. And they danced: A slow set of steps, the same small pattern over and over again. Drawing steadily away from the palace and the reek of death and smoke and fire.

"Once the captain realized what was happening, it was too late: They tried to reach the line of women, but they couldn't, somehow. The women continued to dance until the last of them fell over the cliff and into the ocean. According to the story, their arms were still locked together when they fell into the sea."

Gabrielle shuddered, and buried her face in her hands. "That's—horrible," she whispered.

"It's terrible," Xena said quietly. "But it's the kind of heroism that—you can believe it would make an impact on the land itself." She smiled deprecatingly and spread her arms wide. "Well! Anyway, it's the story the Minos' bard told that night. Maybe it's true—or maybe, Gabrielle, you just let your feet get carried away with you again."

Gabrielle managed a faint smile in return. "Yeah. That was probably it. Must've been. Like, in Tara's adopted village, you mean?" It was a clear change of subject. "I wonder how she's doing?"

"Dancing up a storm," Xena replied dryly. "C'mon, both of you, it's hot out here." She gave Gabrielle a shake. "No wonder your feet got out of control, the sun fried your brains."

"Yeah, right," Gabrielle said, her voice dark, her eyes moving sidelong toward Joxer, who smirked complacently.

"Well, it's not like I didn't *tell* you so, Gabrielle," he said, and followed them back toward the shaded porch.

6

But as the three started back into the palace, Joxer bumped into Newin, who was on his way out, and at a near-run. Joxer staggered; Gabrielle's hand shot out to steady him and Xena shoved as he fell into her, hard. Joxer overbalanced the other direction, and with a muttered oath, the warrior gripped his shoulders, spun him halfway around, and held him steady until he regained his balance. Belatedly, Newin seemed to catch the drift of a problem, and snatched at Joxer's sleeve.

The two women exchanged looks as Joxer shrugged loose of Xena's grasp with a high air of dignity. Newin released Joxer's sleeve and bobbed a bow at Xena and then Gabrielle, then sketched Joxer a salute; he was grinning hugely and out of breath. "What did I tell you?" the youth demanded enthusiastically. "My master tutor Marboron let me off algebra so I could take you fishing, Joxer! You were absolutely right, too! All I had to do was remind him of the duties owed a hero who is also a guest!"

"Ah—" Joxer couldn't seem to manage anything else, and he looked hideously embarrassed.

"Fishing?"

That, Gabrielle thought with an inner sigh, was of course Xena. Joxer eyed the warrior sidelong.

"Ah—well, fishing or something, right, Newin? But, ah—you know, we wouldn't want to hold you up or anything, Xena. . . ."

To his surprise, Xena merely laughed and waved a hand at him. "Joxer, you and Newin go fish! Hey, most of us could use a break from algebra, right, Newin?" The youth smiled and nodded happily. "I'll get my own chance to fish somewhere around here, before we leave," Xena added. "That is, if I have anything to say about it." She smiled at Newin. "Don't let Joxer fall outta the boat, okay?"

"Oh, no, Xena," Newin replied politely. *He looks like he's not too sure about her*, Gabrielle decided. No surprise there, especially if Joxer'd been filling the boy's ears with tales. Or his tutors had. Anyone in the palace, probably; she'd noticed the night before that half the people at that banquet were giving Xena the same ever-so-polite looks. *Yeah, like you aren't used to that by now.* "Besides," the boy added, "I have a special place along the shore, so we won't need a boat."

"Great," Gabrielle said. "Don't let him fall *in*, then." Joxer gave her a narrow-eyed look; fortunately, before he could find anything snotty to say, Newin merely nodded, then clamped hold of Joxer's wrist and practically dragged him from the porch, and across the wide-open dancing ground.

Gabrielle watched them go, her irritation rising by the moment. "Great. Just—look at them. Does that place grab Joxer? Does the red line clamp onto his boots? No, of course not! Does it even slow the prince down? Certainly not! Why would it? After all, they're off to catch *fish!*

And they're *guys* off to catch fish! Probably come back with a—a—a—a *dolphin*!"

Xena gave her a light shake and smiled as the younger woman blinked at her. "Gabrielle, take it easy! That floor doesn't just—grab everybody who walks across it. If it worked like that, the king woulda covered it up years ago. Or fenced it in."

"Sure." Gabrielle didn't feel convinced of that. "And if the floor didn't *want* to be fenced in or covered up?" Xena studied her, then laid a hand against her forehead. Gabrielle moved it. "Look, I'm all right, it's just that—it spooked me. All the things I can't remember very well from being out on the ship, and then this as soon as I get outside the palace. I'm sorry, it's just very annoying."

"I'd be annoyed, too—wait. You don't remember *what* things from on the ship?"

"That's just it—I don't know if some things actually happened, or I just dreamed them. Sea serpents and a really awful storm—except that should be really clear if it happened, and it's not."

Xena's eyes were grave. "You didn't tell me about that."

Gabrielle shrugged.

"I didn't realize. Why didn't you say something?"

"Because I didn't realize at first, and then I wasn't sure. I'm still not, really. Besides, there hasn't been a lot of time."

Xena drew her close, smoothed her hair. "There's always time, Gabrielle, if you need to talk. Tonight, while we're getting dressed for that dinner. Or after. Both, if you need to. All right?"

The bard nodded.

"I gotta get back inside. We need to decide what to do about Menelaus and Avicus and all these heroes wandering all over the place. That means I gotta learn as much as I can about the palace and all the rest of it."

"They'll tell you?" Gabrielle leaned back to meet

Xena's eyes. "I mean—I thought that was all secret stuff?"

"Not from an ally they trust. And not if keeping it secret means Helen will be in danger. Nossis is determined that's not gonna happen." Xena smiled. "Don't worry about Joxer and Newin bringing back a dolphin, either. Dolphins are sacred here; your friends from the ship are safe."

"Good," Gabrielle muttered. "At least something is."

"Don't worry about Knossos, either. You just have to be cautious. Aware. I *told* you this is a strange place. The Maze tried to draw me in. The old Minos said it does that to a lot of fighters; that's why it's blocked off. I figured it could affect you, as good as you fight these days. That's why I told you to avoid it.

"But I forgot all about this place. About the women, the red line, the dancing." She smiled faintly; her eyes were dark. "I only heard the story once, and it was a long time ago. And, I forgot how much you love to dance."

Gabrielle managed a smile in reply. "I haven't had much time to think about that myself lately." She considered this. "You know—it was so strange," she added thoughtfully, and her gaze swept back across the floor. "Remember, Xena? Back in Tara's village? I mean, the place that adopted her? No dancing allowed, except you found a way around that. You know how much I love to dance. And I'm okay at it."

"Gabrielle, you're *good* at it," the warrior said.

Gabrielle didn't seem to notice. "Out there, though, it was like. . . . Suddenly, I couldn't do anything wrong. I wasn't off balance or tangled up, and even though the ground out there isn't totally smooth or level, I was dancing like it was the best place I ever had for it.

"And—oh, I don't know." She considered this, finally shook her head, and went on. "All right, I'm a good dancer, and I can live with being just good. Because unless you devote yourself to dance, you'll never get to be—*that* kind of dancer. You know? Except, all of a sudden, I was." Dark-pupiled eyes met Xena's briefly, then shifted broodingly back to the dancing floor. "I think it must feel like that sometimes when you fight, Xena. It was all so focused, so simple. I knew *how* to jump, and all the things I normally have to think about just—happened. I could hear each individual step, they were so crisp, and I swear that I actually made a double mid-air spin. And landed like—like a thistle plume."

Silence.

She turned to look out over the dancing floor. "I'm almost sorry you stopped me." Xena took a step forward so she could see her close companion's face, but Gabrielle's eyes were closed, and she was smiling blissfully.

"Gabrielle." Xena gripped her friend's shoulders and gave her a slight shake. To her relief, Gabrielle smiled up at her. "Gabrielle, are you okay?"

"Yeah. I'm okay. And I said 'almost,' remember? I know it wasn't a normal thing. I'm not gonna go back out there and dance my way off the cliff." She shuddered, relaxed into Xena's grasp. "It *was* kinda scary," she said finally. "Because even when it felt so good, I could kinda tell that even if I wanted to stop, I couldn't. Still—it was worth it."

"Even if it almost got you killed?"

"But it didn't, because you were there," Gabrielle replied reasonably. Xena tugged at pale hair.

"Yeah," she growled. "I was there *this* time. Another time, I might not be."

"I know. Thanks." The bard sighed faintly. "I guess I'll have to come back inside with you now, won't I? Unless you know of some place else around here I can explore that's a little safer?"

Xena shrugged.

"Yeah, that's what I thought."

Xena sighed faintly. "Gabrielle, I don't know. Maybe this place and the Maze are the only strange spots; maybe you'd be all right looking around the theater, or the arena.

But even if you wanted to take the chance, I couldn't let you."

"I know." Gabrielle nodded. "I'd feel the same." Her mouth quirked. "I'm not eager to get myself killed, you know. I just want to see as much of Knossos as I can, before we have to move on again. All the stories they tell about this place, and—"

"I know, Gabrielle. And there is a way. Most afternoons, Helen brings the king's two little ones out this way. Lets them play over on the theater steps or out in the open. So, it has to be safe over that way."

"Yeah," Gabrielle replied sarcastically. "For small kids and disguised wives hiding from rotten husbands, anyway. Maybe there's something lurking around the theater, waiting for bards. But, I thought Helen was meeting with you and the king, to figure out what to do—?" She let the question hang, briefly. "Unless you've already worked something out?"

"I wish," Xena said gloomily. "She won't change the routine for the babies, though, Gabrielle. Someone might notice."

"Xena, you're driving me nuts." Gabrielle flung her arms wide. "I thought you said there weren't any Spartan spies here because there couldn't be!"

"That doesn't mean there aren't other spies, does it?" the warrior asked. "But I'm not so concerned about spies. Helen's greatest threat here, as far as I can see, is someone saying the wrong thing to the wrong person. Just some funny little bit of gossip worth repeating, until finally it gets back to Sparta. Or to someone that Avicus can read."

"Avi—oh, yeah." Gabrielle shrugged. "Him, the priest of Apollo." She frowned. "Xena?"

"Yeah?"

"You really think he's that good? Avicus, I mean?"

"Far from it, Gabrielle." Xena's eyes were dark; something she'd just remembered about the priest, the bard thought. "Good and Avicus never did go together."

"I didn't mean it like *that*. Powerful. You know."

"He doesn't have to be: Apollo's powerful enough, and Avicus does whatever the god wants—no matter how low or dirty. *You* heard what Apollo did in Troy, didn't you? Not too long before Helen sent for us? He spread plague through the Greek army. Whatever the commanders had done to wrong the god, those men trusted Apollo, and he betrayed them."

"Xena, I know about Apollo. Not just the Delphi oracle stuff, either. He can be petty and vindictive and—yeah." She laughed. "You'd think he was related to Aphrodite or something!"

That got a chuckle, as she'd hoped. "You got it." The warrior tugged at her own hair, hard. "This stuff is making *me* crazy," she grumbled. "I want something I can *fight*."

"You're telling *me*?" Gabrielle cast one last, wistful glance at the bright courtyard and the incredibly blue sea well away to the south and far below, then wrapped her arm around Xena's waist and went back inside with her.

The small chamber in the Spartan palace that was reserved for the king's priest to commune with his god was very cold and quite dark, even though it was nearly midday. One guttering torch flickered near the door, and only a single candle illuminated the waist-high pillar holding the scrying bowl and the ewer of blessed water to fill it.

At the moment, the sturdy, pale-haired man gripping both sides of the bowl noticed neither chill nor darkness. The total concentration he'd put into the vessel for the past hour had paid off. Avicus gazed through the water for another long moment, then began to laugh. As the bowl went dark, he let his head fall back and roared with laughter.

"Knossos!" By the time he regained control, he was whooping for air. "They're still on Crete! In Knossos!" He spun away from the bowl as it went dark and slammed one fist into the other hand. Absolutely the last thing he'd expected. "But I should have known!" he exulted. He turned away from the bowl and lit two more candles. "I *should* have suspected, anyway," he told himself, his voice once again normal, the mood under control.

It wouldn't do to get too excited, he reminded himself. There were plenty of questions still unanswered, and he'd be a fool to assume the end of the quest was in sight. "And you already made one wrong assumption," he reminded himself. But it was a shift in a so-far immutable pattern: Xena, Gabrielle, and that Joxer had so far not stayed any one place more than a night, and most nights, they'd been aboard one ship or another.

He knew better than to trust patterns like that. But he'd been lulled into carelessness by the meandering route they'd been taking. If Xena *did* know where Helen was, she could be doing that on purpose. But she'd destroyed every one of his patches—except Gabrielle's—and she had no reason to know Gabrielle had one. By now, the warrior should have abandoned the pretense and gone straight to Helen.

If she was actually looking for the woman, they should have simply stopped in Crete long enough to pick up any dockside gossip, then left on *Yeloweh,* or taken a ship going south to Alexandria. "If Saroni was right about where the ship was bound when that storm blew them off course." Maybe they were simply waiting for such a ship.

Maybe anything. *If I had been watching the bowl, I might already know what they're up to. Possibly even why.* It was too bad Menelaus took so much of his attention; he'd been giving the king another of his pointless reports probably just as Xena was being greeted by the Minos. Possibly with Helen at his side.

He'd had just the one brief glimpse of the Cretan harbor, the previous morning, before Menelaus sent for him. By the time he'd finally been able to return here, the patch was sending nothing but black, as if the garment was under a thick cloak or buried in a chest. Didn't matter; she was wearing it again. Maybe the luck would finally turn for him, and Gabrielle's back would be pointing squarely at Helen the next time he accessed the bowl.

"You won't get that lucky," he told himself flatly. For all he knew, Helen could have been out on the palace grounds with Xena and Gabrielle just now, and he'd never have seen *her*. Gabrielle didn't strike him as the sort who would turn her back on a queen. People didn't, ordinarily.

"Don't get too fond of Knossos," he warned himself. The Cretans were pretty good at keeping spies out of the palace, just like their gods kept the Greek ones at bay—but the king didn't reject all Spartan guests. And there were plenty of other Greeks who'd be welcome at the Minos' table—and who knew Menelaus would pay well to learn the location of his errant wife. The warrior princess and her annoying companions were most likely resting after the excitement of the journey from Rhodes. "The Minos would welcome Xena—" He had, clearly. Because the two women seemed to have free run of the palace and grounds; besides, he recognized the silver pin fastened to Xena's armor. The Minos didn't hand those out to just anyone.

And Xena had been on her way south. Could she have somehow learned that Helen was in Egypt? He dismissed that one out of hand. Cleopatra might *think* her household was spy free, but what did she know? The palace in Alexandria was crawling with servants and soldiers both who were in the employ of everyone from Rome to the Hittites and every kingdom between—including Sparta. There was simply no way a woman as striking as Helen could have reached Cleopatra in secret.

So far as he knew, Xena was still as clueless as he. *About Helen.*

Avicus paced the small chamber, thinking furiously. He shrugged finally. The patches and other devices were useful, but they had their drawbacks, too. Unfortunately, he couldn't simply stay fixed to the water, full-time. He might eventually learn something, but so far, the bowl had only shown tantalyzing bits and pieces—and given him a stiff neck. Menelaus would never stand for such a prolongued absence, anyway. The king wanted to talk, make plans—*Vent his spleen and make pointless threats, in case I do not deliver*, Avicus thought sourly. The stubborn fool was inclined to dismiss the bowl, the patches, the rest of it as mostly useless, and he wouldn't be swayed.

"Which means, for now I say nothing to my honored king about Knossos." He might be able to wrangle more time for the bowl, but that would be offset badly by Menelaus' constant demands for more and better information, or worse yet, the king would be at his elbow, demanding to know what was happening *now*. At worst, the man would simply gather a company or two and set sail for Crete. "And Crete is not a—safe—place to attack," he told himself.

Not safe for a walking fury like Menelaus, certainly. "Once *I* find a way, though. . . ." He shoved that thought aside as pointless: the morning might see the women and their inept companion at sea once again. Or he might see nothing for days except the Cretan scenery at Gabrielle's back. Nothing useful in that. He paced some more, muttering quietly to himself, and finally sought the bowl again. A pinch of the blue sand, scattered in a narrow circle across the very middle of the surface. "It might be a bad hour to speak with Saroni," he murmured aloud. But maybe his luck was finally turning.

It might not be turning, but it held. The water steamed, then cleared quickly. He could see the dark little area behind the theater seats and a startled-looking Saroni, her short black hair dripping water onto dark, bare shoulders, staring back at him. The priestess yelped and ducked out of sight. Avicus could make out the rustle of garments; the woman was there again almost immediately, swathed in her everyday robe, the hood sticking damply to her hair. "You startled me!" she gasped, then ducked her head. "Your pardon, Honor," she mumbled contritely, her eyes averted.

Avicus smiled briefly, and his eyes kindled. *Some people know how to treat a man of my talents,* he thought, and cleared his throat, schooling his face to lack of expression as the woman's brown eyes met his across the distance. "I know, Saroni, you did not expect the summons so early. *My* apology, for the surprise." He could afford to be magnanimous with the woman, he thought. And it would make her more willing to do his bidding. "But I will need you, and soon."

"You have found her!" the priestess exclaimed. But Avicus was already shaking his head.

"I know where she may be. By this hour tomorrow, I may be able to tell for certain. But if not—I will need you to go to Knossos, gain entry to the palace, and learn what you can for me."

Silence. The woman's eyes widened and she shoved dripping hair back off her brow. "Knossos? But—what can I do there, if the god cannot—?"

"Saroni, my need is for eyes and a quick wit. Xena is a guest at the palace, she and Gabrielle. I know that by the patch you put on her shoulder. And believe me, Saroni, I will remember that when it is time to reward you. Apollo can do nothing in Knossos, no. But the devices still work—Gabrielle's does anyway. Go—let me think—"

"Ah—Honor?" the priestess broke in warily. "I gave Gabrielle the story I told you; she believes Krista is your ally. If I suddenly appear in Crete and tell her that I fled because the woman learned I had spoken to Gabrielle and not told her at once that the warrior princess was in Rhodes, that I feared for my life and sought the only safe place where I knew Apollo could never find me for her *or* for you . . . ?" Her voice faded. Avicus gravely applauded, and she brightened at once. "Do you think I will find Helen there?"

"You are my best hope of finding out," Avicus replied, his voice as warm and persuasive as he could make it. "Find a way to be near the basin again at this hour, to-morrow."

"Yes, Honor. But—what should I tell Krysta—?"

"The god will give her a vision if he deems it necessary. Do not worry about her, she's not your concern. Gabrielle is. Go and ponder on the best story to convince her." The priest considered this, shook his head sharply. "More importantly: Think how best to convince Xena. She's not as trusting as that silly girl, not by a tenth. And she'll be doubly suspicious of anything touching Apollo."

"I won't fail you, Honor." Avicus merely smiled, the least turning of the corners of his mouth, as he broke the communication.

"She won't," he told himself as he turned toward the door. It must be nearly time for midday food. Impossible to tell in this cave of a room, of course, but all at once he was hungry. He pinched out the candles and left.

Back in Rhodes, Saroni ruffled the water, dried her hands on her thick robe, and used the hood to dry her hair. "There must be a way to warn people—I think he does that on purpose," she grumbled as she stormed into the open courtyard. No one in sight, including Krysta, who was probably muttering her way through the morning ritual. The under priestess turned away from the tiny temple and let the smile spread across her face. "*Yes!*" she whispered fiercely. Out of Rhodes, *away* from the boring rituals! Across the sea and not just to Crete, but high above the sea, into the fabled Knossos of Maze and Minotaur!

If she did the favor for Avicus, actually discovered Helen because she'd tricked the information out of that silly Gabrielle, Avicus would reward her as she'd long before asked. *I think he will*, she revised that thought. She'd never entirely trusted the Spartan priest; he was a little too clever by half, and too careful with his choice of words. *And he started in theater, don't forget.* Started creating illusions to astonish the fools who went to see plays where some benevolent god swung down from the heavens at the last moment to resolve every issue.

Well, some people weren't so foolish as all that. Some people counted on their own resources, just as she herself always had. Deep in a corner of her mind, below the words, where she believed Apollo either couldn't see or didn't bother—especially when the being in question was a very minor under priestess—the notion took form. *Once in Knossos, I can plan how best to present myself as an acolyte to Ares. I can find a way to convince the gorgeous creature that he needs me.*

The open sea northwest of Crete was choppy at midday, with a strong wind blowing the *Wode* toward the top of the mainland. Habbish held the wheel steady for a while, then tacked back and forth, moving his heading toward the passage between Paros and Naxos. Draco casually walked up and down the main deck, pleased with the clean scent of salt air and with the way his legs had adapted to an open deck. The ship wallowed through white-peaked waves and dropped sharply every time the wheel turned the ship straight north, across the waves instead of with them; the solidly built warlord hadn't staggered once.

There were islands visible to the north now: dotting the horizon all the way from well west to far east, and even a couple of black dots astern. *Might be good to set foot ashore for a while,* Draco thought. The Gael's cook went for quantity rather than good food well prepared, which was just as well since Habbish didn't seem to have properly developed taste buds.

"Yeah, but I do," Draco muttered under his breath. He'd always appreciated the services of a decent personal cook—at least, he had since he'd grown to manhood, left home, and learned there was more to food than filling your belly. Back in the days when he and Xena had fought on the same side, he'd made sure the meals they shared were works of art: varied in taste, nicely prepared, only the freshest and finest ingredients (the best that could be 'liberated' from the surrounding countryside, anyway), and presented as nicely as any king could desire. "Xena's forgotten a lot if she thinks I only got hooked on fancy food back when I took Odysseus' island and his wife," he growled. "So I didn't always know what the stuff was called, and I wasn't up on the wines, or the funny things people say when they're tasting them." She'd sure caught him on *that* one; trying to blunder through sampling the various fruits of the absent Ithacan ruler's cellars. The food, though: There'd been a *reason*, and a damned good one, why Lemnos was in charge of the kitchens. *Especially after he learned how to make that fancy before-dinner stuff, like that guy in—where was it we raided that palace?* He couldn't remember.

He shrugged that aside. Raid enough palaces full of enough rich people, you tended to forget which was which. He fetched up against the rail, settled one hip on the wood, and braced the other leg wide to balance himself against the swells—Habbish was heading straight north once again. *That special thing Lemnos did, with shrimp and some kinda hot paste, grape leaves and apple slivers . . . oh, man?* He could almost taste it; he let his eyes close briefly to savor the moment, then shook it off. No point in visualizing epicurean delights—or even fresh cherries at the peak of season—if what you were going to get for midday was another bowl of sticky cooked oats: this one with slivers of overcooked goat, bits of dried fruit, and all of it wildly oversalted.

A startled yell from high above brought his attention back to the moment. The watchers up there were staring astern, pointing at something out there. As usual, excitement or fear pushed their accents to the point that he couldn't make out a word of it. Something up, anyway. Good: A little excitement to break up the afternoon would be welcome. Draco eased off the rail, crossed the deck, and took the aft stairway two steps at a time.

Habbish had already turned the wheel over to his first mate—sure sign of trouble. Draco stared back along their wake and beyond, but all he could see was the black shape of some kind of ship. "What?" he asked.

"My ill fortune is what," the captain snarled. "Never expected t'*Hammer* t'come after us again so fast as all this. Shoulda had more'n t'chance t'get *Wode* into the channels between the Cyclades, maybe even the deep inlets south of Athens, or north in Mycenae, afore we saw 'er again."

Draco shielded his eyes against the glare of sun on water and stared at the distant ship. "That's *Hammer*? he asked. The captain nodded. "You're *sure* of it?"

"Not me—them up above, where they can make out more of t'distance."

Draco shook his head firmly. "Not a chance. I saw that hole in the bow, how'd she ever make repairs this fast? Let alone catch up to us like this? You snapped almost half her oars, damnit!"

"Oars," Habbish scoffed. "Landsman wouldn't know; a sensible captain keeps a full spare set, or more, below decks, down with t'ballast. Same wi' a packet o' treated boards t'mend holes. Ship like *Hammer*'d be set for such a mishap as a mere ramming." He sighed heavily. "Sensible captain like I'm said to be woulda scuttled her right then and been done, but no, I had to show some kind of fair play, in case we meet up again. . . ."

"So you played nice and you got burned," Draco broke in when it appeared the commentary would go on forever. "So a lot of us have done the same thing. That's not important here, Habbish. What do we do now?"

The Gael sighed heavily. "That's t'proper question," he

said evenly. He bellowed orders in his own language; men swarmed up the mast and onto the crossbars and other men came running from the crew's quarters and the mess. "Do? We run."

Draco gaped at him. "What—we just—give up?"

"Was not my meaning. We run for a better place t'fight. Out here, on open water, *Hammer* has all the advantages. And 'tis a long, *long* way to t'bottom from here."

Long way down. Draco fought a shudder and was suddenly furious with himself. What did it matter how deep the water if you were dead once it closed over your face? It *matters,* he told himself grimly. For him, it sure as Hades did. "Fine," he said evenly, and was relieved to show none of the sudden horror of deepwater in his voice. "So tell me what to do."

"For now, y'stay right here behind the wheel, and keep an eye aft. That frees up two men here t'work ropes. Once we're in our own kind of waters—we'll talk again."

"Good," Draco replied grimly. "That suits me just fine."

7

Gabrielle was thoroughly lost by the time Xena led the way into the king's council chamber. She felt as if they'd crossed the plateau twice and said as much.

Xena smiled. "This place really gets to you, doesn't it?"

"I just don't like the feeling of walking forever and winding up in the same place."

Xena squeezed her companion's shoulder. "Well, we aren't in the same place," she drawled, "because look out the window." Gabrielle looked: the stone risers of the theater were close enough that she could make out individual details in the rock, and the design of the pillow someone had left behind.

"Okay," she said, and smiled. "I'm—good with this." She glanced around the room. An oval table, seven chairs around it, and a slightly finer, cushioned chair at the window end, a bench along the wall next to the door—the room seemed barely large enough to contain that much furniture. Maps covered the opposite wall. "This is small, isn't it? And where is everyone?"

"This is just for the king and his inner council," Xena said as she pulled out two chairs facing the door, mid-table. "He's got other rooms—"

"Yeah." Gabrielle laughed. "You're telling *me*." She turned on one heel, studying the chamber.

"And we're early," the warrior went on, she rubbed her shoulders against the chair back and settled low, legs stretched out before her. The two women could hear voices and footsteps in the hall. "Just not by much," she added as the door swung open and a servant came in with a tray holding two pitchers and cups. Just behind him, king Nossis and Helen, who followed the King at a respectful distance. *Servant*, Gabrielle reminded herself. Helen really *was* doing a good job of not calling attention to herself.

The woman was dressed in simple dark blue. A long, sheer scarf in the same shade covered her hair and cast shadow over most of her face; and not until the servant was gone, door closed behind him, did she shift the fabric away from her brow. She smiled at Gabrielle, laid her fingers on the back of the chair across from Xena. "General Kropin's son will be here this afternoon. At least the general said he would."

Gabrielle glanced at Xena, who shrugged and said, "Korinus was supposed to be here this morning, too. The general spent most of our morning apologizing for the implied insult."

Nossis settled in his chair with a faint sigh. "The man was my father's—a good general in his day but he's getting old, and these days he's more concerned with manners and protocol than anything else. It's customary for a ruler to choose his own council but somehow, I never could find a way to replace the old man."

"I can imagine it isn't easy, getting rid of someone who's had a position like that for so many years," Gabrielle said sympathetically. Nossis merely cast up his eyes. "Since you'd be telling him that he's too old to be useful."

"Kropin knows his business, well enough, I suppose. He made Korinus responsible for the guard down at the port," Nossis said. "I would have left the boy in charge of security along the south beaches for another year, but the old man—somehow, he finds a way to persuade me."

"Because you are kindhearted," Helen said quietly.

Nossis smiled briefly. "You make that sound like a good thing. It can get a ruler into trouble, you know. Because, unfortunately, the boy hasn't yet learned how to delegate. That, and he likes the docks and the company of sailors."

"It all looked well managed to me," Gabrielle said.

"He should have been here this morning, telling us what he knows of the southern defenses," Nossis said flatly.

"It's all right," Xena said. *Sounds like she's said that before, and to the same comment,* Gabrielle thought.

The door opened abruptly and two men came in; the king gestured toward the vacant chairs at the opposite end and glanced at Helen, who sat on the edge of the chair across from Xena.

Gabrielle sat next to the warrior as Nossis introduced the general and his son. The conversation seemed to be picking up an argument started earlier in the day; the bard eased back in the chair and studied the newcomers from under her lashes.

The general looked very old and frail; his pace hadn't been that steady when he crossed the room just now. His hair was white and he wore what there was of it close-cropped; his leathers were clearly old but well cared for, and though he wore sword belt and sheaths for a half-dozen daggers, they were all empty. *Manners because of the guests, Cretan custom,* Gabrielle knew. *Unusual.* Xena and she had been in plenty of palaces where they and many of the household kept their blades on. *Usually be-*

cause there's some crisis or another, she reminded herself.

The son looked like he might be the youngest of a large family, or maybe a son born to a man already old: *He* openly wore a fancy-hilted sword, and from the looks the general was giving him, Korinus wasn't supposed to have brought it. She sent her gaze casually around the table as Korinus looked in her direction—past her. He seemed to be scowling at Xena, who was talking to Nossis.

Maybe he was just scowling because he didn't want to be here; it sounded as if his father had practically had to drag him in. Not her worry, she decided. There wasn't anything for her to do at the moment. She didn't know what had already been discussed and dismissed, and she didn't know the island or the palace. And there were those maps on the wall behind her. *You can listen just as well over there, maybe figure out what the lay of the land is, find a way to be useful—besides just telling old stories,* she decided, and slid out of her chair. Xena glanced up at her and she nodded, indicated the maps with her head. The warrior smiled briefly, then went back to her conversation.

The maps were wonderfully detailed, the borders ornate: One showed all of Crete, with colorful ships and monsters scattered across the sea, and next to it, a map showing the sea, with Crete near the southern edge, Greece along the west, and Troy to the northeast. The names of the islands were done in neat lettering, and she spent some time trying to retrace their route. *That would work a lot better if I remembered more,* she thought with an inner sigh, and moved on to the third map, which showed the plateau, the palace, and the grounds.

The last was the palace itself—and the Maze. Gabrielle looked at this one eagerly, but it wasn't much use: None of the rooms and passages were marked, and the Maze itself was merely an open space. As if no one had ever worked out its pattern. *That's odd; after all, if Daedalus made it for the old Minos, wouldn't the Minos have wanted to know what went where?* Surely there must have been times someone needed to get in there and back out again.

Maybe it had been left like that so no one who had no business knowing how the maze worked—but this was the king's map in his own council chamber. She'd have to ask Xena later; the warrior might know.

She went back to the map of the plateau. This was considerably more interesting: Someone had drawn and colored in all of the patterns she'd seen on the dancing floor, and the entire paved area seemed to be covered in patterns and paintings—even the arena and the theater. Most of the pictures, as well as she could make out, were bulls, but there were also snakes and some kind of bird—an eagle, maybe. No red lines aside from the ones she'd followed—but there was a dark, yellow line that cut sharply back and forth across the paving close to the theater. Like the red line, this one also led to the cliffs.

I could probably see that one from here. Well, if there wasn't a planning session going on with the king sitting between the windows. *I wonder how long before Helen goes for the children? And if she'll be okay with me joining them?*

She turned away from the maps and resumed her seat. The general was talking now, something about a trail or an old road up the south face of the island; his son looked impatient, the king politely attentive, Xena bored. Helen had pulled the scarf back over her brow to shield her face, and from under the dark fabric she was steadily watching the king.

The look in her eyes, the bard thought. *Gods, I think she's in love with him!*

Well, why not? Nossis was middle-aged, soft and hardly handsome—but Helen had probably had enough of hard, handsome men. *And he seems like a nice guy. Kind. He's fond of his kids, after all, and not afraid to show it.*

111

Gabrielle's eyes shifted to the king and remained there for a few moments. Nossis, she decided finally, was utterly unaware of Helen's attention.

"Father, I've already said," Korinus broke in, his voice sharp-edged. "No one is going to land on the south shore and come up that—that goat trail! Why should they if the port is wide open? But why would the Spartans go so far out of their way as to sail all the way around Crete, when they could come at us straight on? After all, what can we do, since they outnumber us anyway?"

Xena stirred. "I already told your father and the Minos this morning." *She really was irritated,* Gabrielle thought. Xena wouldn't get correctly formal like that unless she was. "Because Menelaus isn't gonna want to let the other Greek kings know what he's up to."

Korinus sneered. "Oh—yes, I forgot. *Xena* would know what Menelaus is up to, wouldn't she?"

"Son—!" Kropin caught hold of his son's sleeve; the youth shook him off and chopped a hand for silence. When Nossis stirred indignantly, Xena glanced at him and minutely shook her head, then turned to eye Korinus, her expression politely curious.

"I don't suppose you'd mind explaining that?" she asked softly. Steel underlaid the words.

"Explain? You bet I'll explain—no, Father, leave it be, she asked! I serve the king when down on the wharves, so I hear a lot of things the palace doesn't always learn about."

Xena smiled thinly. "You mean, you pick up the gossip. And pass it on."

"It's not gossip if it's true," he retorted. His eyes were hot as they shifted to Helen, then the king. "It's common knowledge out there. Xena was in Troy during the war, on orders from the Spartan king!"

Stunned silence. Helen broke it.

"That's not so, Korinus, I know. I sent for her myself. To help end the war."

"So?" he demanded. "That was the perfect cover for her, wasn't it? *You* sent for her, but she had her own agenda—"

Gabrielle laughed. "That's ridiculous. I was there, with Xena, and believe me, if there'd been a—"

He leveled a finger at her. "You shut up. I've heard about *you*, too, you'd say anything for her. No, you'd just say *any*thing!" Gabrielle's eyes narrowed; Xena laid a hand on her forearm, clear warning to stay put.

"So—Korinus, is it? You know all about it, even though you were a lot too young to be there, right? I was in Troy to grab Helen and take her back to Menelaus, huh?" the warrior drawled. "And since 'everybody' knows this, I'm just stupid enough to come here and offer to help her again, except I'm still doing what Menelaus tells me to—that about it?"

"*They* didn't know until just now," Korinus said, a sweep of his hand indicating the king and Helen. "I told Father, some time ago; he wouldn't believe it."

"Guess we can see who's got the brains in the family," Gabrielle began. Korinus glared at her.

"I said, shut up!"

This time, Gabrielle was halfway to her feet when Xena hauled her back down.

"All right," the warrior snarled. "You've made your point." Tense silence, which she broke. "Gabrielle's right. Only a fool would believe a story like that. I don't fight for kings. Anyone who knows me, or who knows about me, knows that."

"So you say," Korinus growled.

"Yeah, that's right. So I say. But if you're so determined to pick a fight with me, Korinus—fine. You've got one." She smiled grimly as he shoved the chair back, but as he reached for the sword hilt, she shook her head. "Oh, no. Not in here. You may have forgotten the manners due a guest—but I don't destroy other people's council rooms.

113

Particularly not the rooms belonging to a king I respect. We'll do this outside—you choose where."

Gabrielle opened her mouth, closed it again without saying anything. If he chose that dancing floor! Or the Maze. . . .

"Done," he snapped. "The arena. Now!" He stormed out, banging the door behind him. Stunned silence. Then Nossis and Kropin both began talking at the same moment, but Xena shook her head and held up her hands.

"It's all right. No one's responsible for the things he said except him. And I don't make war on foolish children. I'll run him around out there and wear him out. I won't hurt him—and then maybe I can get him to listen to reason."

The general was very red faced. "Warrior—he is my son and still therefore my responsibility," he said heavily. "I thought because he knows the south shore so well, and we could trust his oath to keep quiet about Helen—" He shook his head helplessly and went out after his son. Xena looked at Helen, who managed a wry smile and a shrug, then at Nossis, who had buried his face in his hands.

"King Nossis, it's fine. These things happen."

"They should not happen," the king replied with a faint sigh. "The boy has been a problem ever since his mother died. This is—appalling." He got to his feet. "I will not watch this. . . . I will not by my presence give credence to the foolish lies he has swallowed. If—you will, warrior. If you still see fit to aid us, after the boy's dreadful manners, we'll meet again, after food tonight." Xena nodded; the king left.

Helen watched him go. "I cause him too much trouble," she said helplessly. "He doesn't deserve this."

Gabrielle went to her and laid a hand on her shoulder. "It's not you. Not your fault."

The woman gave her a sad smile. "You and Xena—you both keep saying that. I wish I had reason to believe it.

I'd better go; the children will expect me shortly, anyway."

Gabrielle watched her go. "You know, Xena," she said thoughtfully. "That poor woman—I wonder if she's ever been happy in her life."

"When she was young." Xena came up behind her. "Probably those first days with Paris. When she escaped Troy, probably."

"She deserves more. Better, I mean," Gabrielle said firmly, then turned to eye her companion. "So—what brought all that up?"

Xena shrugged.

"You know, it almost sounded to me as if someone deliberately fed him that story to set him on you?"

"Anything's possible," Xena replied. "C'mon; I haven't got a king to watch me fight, I guess you'll just have to do."

"Oh, yeah?" Gabrielle grinned. "Only if you whack him a good one for me. I don't like it when some snotty kid tells me to shut up like that."

"Two whacks," Xena said. They moved along the passage and out onto a different porch. The theater was twenty paces away, and beyond it, a high curving fence that must be the arena.

"Ah—good." Gabrielle followed the warrior across the pavement and around the bare little stage. "Xena?"

"What?"

"You're not really gonna—" She hesitated.

"What? Mangle him? Gabrielle, I meant what I said in there. He's young and hotheaded. All I'm gonna do is give him a workout."

"Fine. Great. And what if he's good enough with that sword to—?"

"Gabrielle. It would take twenty of him, even if he was that good."

"Great. Xena, getting cocky is not exactly useful here!"

"Who's getting cocky?" The warrior laughed. "I'm

115

good with this, okay? Besides, you know the type as well as I do: All bluster. Besides," she flashed the bard a cheerful grin, "the better he is, the more fun for me. Told you I was spoiling for a fight, didn't I?"

"Great. And he figures out you're playing with him—"

"—and it doesn't matter, either way. Because there's not gonna be anything he can do about it. Anyway, I know that, okay? C'mon." Gabrielle cast up her eyes, and followed.

Korinus was there, sword in hand, going through a frenetically paced series of stretches and bends. General Kropin paced all around him, arms waving, obviously arguing against the duel, but the youth ignored him. When Xena came into the open, the old man threw up his hands in disgust and walked away. Gabrielle gripped Xena's hand and went to join the old man. Korinus bared his teeth in a wolfish grin, laid his sword on the paving, set a dagger next to it, and backed away to make a show of divesting himself of the weapons' belts. He waited; Xena shrugged as if bored, drew her sword and set it down, then removed sword belt, whip, boot dagger, chakram. Daggers, and more daggers, hidden everywhere possible. The youth's eyes moved between her and the growing pile of weapons; his eyes bulged as she fished the ornate little dagger from the midst of her formidable cleavage, and casually tossed it atop the heap.

Gabrielle fought a grin. *Did that on purpose*, she knew. The little blade was hidden well enough he'd never have known it was there. The smile slipped as the old man next to her moaned faintly. "She'll kill him," he whispered.

Gabrielle settled on the sun-warmed stone bench next to him. "She won't—that's not her way. Xena doesn't kill unless there's no way around it, and she doesn't hurt people just because she can."

"The way he—my son isn't really like this," he said. Out on the arena floor, Xena scooped up her sword and waited for Korinus to ready himself. "Just—since his mother died, I haven't known what to do about him. He never used to provoke fights, but his new company, the men he meets from the ships. . . ."

You sound just like every other parent of a spoiled kid, Gabrielle thought sourly. "He'll grow out of it," she said, offering the expected response. The old man gave her a grateful look, then fixed his attention on his son.

Xena held her sword two-handed, at the ready. Korinus began a slow stalk to his left, feinting with his long blade; the warrior merely pivoted in place, her own blade still. The youth suddenly lunged—and stabbed into thin air. With a high, ululating cry that echoed across the plateau, Xena launched herself in a tight tuck and double-flipped over his head, coming down behind him with a loud *thump.* Noise not necessary, Gabrielle knew; the woman could land like a feather, if she chose. But she wanted the boy to know.

He did. Korinus yelped and spun around, sword stabbing wildly; Xena flipped back once, away from him, and as he ran at her, vaulted two high rows of stone benches above Gabrielle and the general.

Korinus swore between his teeth and threw himself headlong up the steep flight of steps, caught one foot and nearly went sprawling; Kropin closed his eyes. Somehow, the youth kept his balance and hurtled on. Xena side-stepped his next half-dozen wild thrusts with the sword; he swore furiously, reversed his grip on the dagger and threw it, but she knocked it aside with the flat of her blade. A moment later, his sword went flying to clatter on the stones far behind him. He paled and began backing away; Xena kept pace with him, but a pace back of her normal reach. He snatched up the sword, let his air out in a gust, and started for her once again, but Xena yelled and threw herself out and down, onto the arena floor again. Korinus went abruptly from pale to red. "You're making fun of me!" he shouted.

"Hey," Xena replied cheerfully, "I'm just down here where the footing's better. You got any objection to that?" For answer, he threw himself back down the stairs and out into the open. For some moments, Xena let him lead the fight, parrying his jabs, lunges, and wild roundhouse swings with equal ease. He was starting to sweat, and the warrior didn't even look properly warmed up. Suddenly, his sword went flying again and a moment later she swept the legs from under him; he landed hard on his back.

That should have taken the fight out of him, Gabrielle thought—but it didn't; he shook his head to clear it, looked around for his sword, and scrambled onto his hands and knees, then lunged awkwardly to his feet and ran toward it. Xena was there first, and the youth once again flat on his back. This time, Xena held her sword steady, the tip hovering just above the base of his throat as she kicked his blade aside.

"Okay," she said evenly. "Let's try this again. I am not working for Menelaus. I am not his ally. Anyone who told you that is passing on a lie, or lying himself. You got that?" Stubborn silence; he glared up at her, lips compressed in a tight line, but his eyes were scared, Gabrielle thought. "Got it?" the warrior demanded, her voice soft and deadly, and now the point pressed against skin. General Kropin let his head fall into his hands.

"It's all right," Gabrielle said quietly. "She isn't gonna hurt him—just maybe scare some sense into him."

"Got it," the youth managed; his voice was almost unrecognizeable, and the words quavered.

"Good. Now—if you've got anything to contribute to this meeting of the king's, I'm okay with you being there. What you said earlier, I never heard. This out here—it didn't happen. That work for you?" He nodded; she stepped back and eyed him measuringly, then turned away and went to squat next to her impressive pile of cast-off weaponry.

Korinus sat up slowly, breathing hard. After a moment,

he staggered to his feet and retrieved his sword, the loose dagger and his belts. Without a backward glance, he walked slowly from the arena. When his father would have followed, Gabrielle caught hold of his sleeve. "Maybe you should just let him go? He probably feels pretty foolish right now. Maybe if he's by himself, he'll think about what he did, and maybe he'll make better sense of it." She considered this. "If you know what I mean."

The old man's eyes warmed. "I think I do, young woman. If I'm not there to heap reproaches on him for what he said and did, he may actually think about what Xena told him."

"My point exactly," the bard agreed. "Better yet, maybe he'll actually believe it." She got up and went over to Xena, who was shoving the small dagger back into her top; the warrior dropped the chakram onto its clip and got to her feet. "So—was that enough to get your creative juices flowing?"

Xena laughed shortly. "What—him, all by himself? Maybe if I'd used the frying pan."

"Yeah. Like I'd let you get your hands on my new pan after what you did to the last one."

"Gabrielle?" The warrior wrapped an arm around her friend's shoulders and started back toward the palace.

"Yeah?"

"I don't care how much you liked it, it was a lousy pan. You've got a new one. Let it go, okay?"

"Got it."

An hour later, Gabrielle was back out in the open, this time with Helen and two very active small children.

"Wanna go see fishes!" the girl shouted gleefully; she might have been six, possibly seven.

"Ideta *always* gets to see the fish," the boy retorted. He was nearer ten. "I want to see where the *fight* was!"

"No fighting, Nebos," Helen said firmly. "Your father

119

would not approve, and I agree with him. You can play in the theater for a while and then I will listen to you recite the verses I gave you to learn." And, to Ideta, "You chose the fishponds yesterday; we can see them tomorrow or the day after, if you can repeat your poem, word perfect. Fair enough?" Two rather subdued nods, then Nebos nudged his sister.

"Race you!" he shouted, and took off.

"That's not fair, 'cos you're older'n me!" the girl screamed, but she was pelting after him. Helen sighed faintly and shook her head.

"They seem like good kids," Gabrielle said.

"They are. A handful, sometimes—but that's normal for children." The women walked slowly, Helen keeping an eye on her charges. "When I first came here, I told Nossis I wouldn't just stay as his guest. He wouldn't accept that, until I convinced him that it was the best way for me to stay hidden. But he didn't want—he couldn't see me in the pottery sheds."

"I can understand that," Gabrielle said. "It's hard, dirty work."

"Yes. But it's—making something out of your own mind." She smiled. "Like you bards do with words. I shape things with my hands, give them form and color and design. It's restful. I like the feel of clay, the way the wheel feels under my feet, the careful movement of a stylus, knowing if you aren't totally calm, you'll probably ruin an entire pot." Another smile, this one ironic. "Of course, I've never had to do the hard work. I've never loaded or unloaded the kilns."

"I don't make my own scrolls, I don't pound reeds or pulp flat and dry it, fasten it to rods," Gabrielle replied easily. "For some of us, the time is better spent creating." They walked around the raised stage and settled in shade where Helen could keep a watchful eye on the children, who were throwing stones at a painted circle on the pavement.

"I suppose." A companionable silence, broken by good-natured squabbling between Nebos and Ideta over whose stone was the one closest to the circle. "Children!" Helen raised her voice only a little; two sidelong glances her direction, and the two began arguing more quietly as they divided up the stones and went back to their mark. "They're really both too young for a tutor, you know. But Nebos is too old for a nurse. And Nossis couldn't find anything else we could agree on for me to do." She shrugged. "I would have washed, changed linens, set the table, it doesn't matter to me."

Gabrielle studied her for a long moment. "I can see that. But I can understand why he wouldn't want that. A guest, and a queen. And I've done my share of laundry; it's hard work, even when it's just for a family."

"I know. I traded my sister off, doing laundry for my family," Helen said. "But Nossis is wrong. I haven't been a queen since I left Sparta for Troy. And I was only queen by title for—it wasn't that long, a year or so. No more than that. In reality, I never was a queen, because Menelaus didn't really want one. Just a—a pretty object to hide away," she finished bitterly.

Gabrielle laid a hand on her shoulder. "It's all right," she said. Helen glanced up to meet her eyes; tears beaded the lashes. "It will be, I swear to you. Xena found a way to help you before, and she'll do it again."

The once-queen searched her face, finally managed a smile. "You really believe in her, don't you?"

"Because I know her," Gabrielle replied passionately. "When she says she'll do something, she means it."

Helen glanced toward the children to make sure they were all right. "I envy you, Gabrielle."

The bard blinked. "You? Envy me?"

"Traveling like you do—freely, not having to hide, not afraid you'll be caught and dragged away. And what you have—your friendship with Xena. I've never had that with anyone." She considered this, then shrugged. "A little, maybe, with my brothers. But I've never known a woman I could be close with like you and Xena are."

Gabrielle smiled and nodded. "I got lucky, really. She just happened to be there when my village was attacked. And then I was stubborn enough to stay after her until she decided I could travel with her."

"I'd like to hear all of that story, sometime," Helen said. She smiled suddenly. "I think I'd like it better than Spartacus, Rebel Gladiator."

"Yeah," Gabrielle smiled back. "At least we don't *die* at the end of that story, like he does."

The woman gazed across the theater pavement and half-stood. "Children! You are not to throw stones at each other!"

Silence.

"Thank you! In fact, you may set the stones aside now and practice your verses. You have a real bard, the honored Gabrielle, to impress this afternoon, and not just Elenya!" She settled back down as the king's youngest obediently set the rocks down and moved apart. Gabrielle could see Nebos' brow furrow, his lips moving soundlessly. At the moment, he very much resembled his father; Helen's eyes were warm as they fixed on the boy.

After a moment, the woman shook herself. "Yes, I'd like to hear that story. But that wasn't what I meant, you know. You and Xena seem so close, and you clearly care very deeply about each other. I've never seen any two people so close except for Castor and Pollux—my brothers," she added in explanation.

"I know who they are," Gabrielle replied. "Bardic tradition, you know," she said apologetically.

Helen considered this. "Of course. I forget about that. The—father aspect of things. That we're part of so many tales, whether we'd like to be or not."

"I understand, really I do. I forget that about Xena, unless something happens to remind me. And she doesn't think about it any more than you do." Gabrielle hesitated,

122

then plunged on. "How long have you been in love with Nossis?"

Helen stared at her. "I—I'm not in—" She swallowed. "I thought I loved Paris, once. I found out I was wrong. I don't love the Minos. He's far above me in rank, but a woman like me has no business loving anyone."

Gabrielle shook her head. "That's no answer. You're the equal to the king of Crete, your father was king of Aetolia, wasn't he? Well, he was. Is, I mean. And so Paris fooled you, was that your fault? He had Aphrodite's help, and trust me, I know how good *she* is at fooling people. And making fools of them."

Helen eyed her in patent disbelief.

"Really. Remind me to tell you about the time she got mad at Xena and got her fixated on fishing, even though there was a warlord loose and trying to do some *serious* damage. Or, better yet, the time she tricked Joxer into almost breaking up a royal marriage and sending two countries to war—just so she wouldn't lose a crummy temple or two." *And let's not get into Gabrielle getting fixated on her own perfectly adorable self,* she told herself firmly. That was one tale no one else was ever going to hear—especially not the woman called the most beautiful in the world. Even at this close range, Gabrielle could see why the title stuck. *And I'm Gabby with her little stick . . . except that's fine with me. At least I don't have a crazed husband chasing me down because of my looks!*

Helen sighed, exasperated. "Gabrielle, don't you see? That's just the kind of thing that's always going to happen! Even if Aphrodite's banned forever from Crete, along with the rest of her family, things are still going to go wrong when I'm around! Because of this—this ridiculous legend! All these stories about me that—for all any of us know—they aren't even true! Even I don't know, how could I? Zeus has never come to me and claimed to be my father! Or to my brother Castor." Her eyes were briefly black with grief, and she bit her lip, turned away.

No, Gabrielle thought, *she wouldn't mention her sister. The one who took a lover while Agamemnon was in Troy. The one who conspired with her lover to kill her husband when he returned.* Killed the husband who had sacrificed his eldest daughter so the Greek fleet could sail for Troy. The woman who died at the hands of her own son, who had then been driven mad by the Furies. She could still see poor crazed Orestes in that madhouse, rocking back and forth; there hadn't been anything anyone could do to save him, and none of it had been his fault.

I'm with Xena on this one; Agamemnon deserved to die, and not as cleanly as they say he did. But poor Helen, having to live with that, on top of everything else. Because, if she hadn't gone with Paris, her niece would still be alive . . . ? And her nephew still sane. She couldn't think about that. The woman needed reassurance and strength, not someone bursting into tears all over her. *Get a grip!* the bard ordered herself fiercely.

"We weren't talking about all that to start with," she said evenly. "We were talking about you, in love with the Minos."

Helen gave her a watery smile. "*We* were? And he hates being called "the Minos," you know. I can understand that—trying to live up to a legend, or even just deal with it on a daily basis."

Silence. Gabrielle held the woman's gaze.

Helen finally looked away and sighed. "All right. Yes, I'm in love with Nossis. That probably seems odd to you."

"No, it doesn't!" Gabrielle protested softly. "Why would I? Remember, I loved Perdicas, and he wasn't exactly Hercules for looks and build, was he?" Her vision blurred and she blinked furiously to clear it. "He was sweet, and kind, and he cared for me—not just that kind of blindly adoring love, but the kind that counts: What I liked, what mattered to me. I think that was why he was able to let go in Troy, at the last. Let me go on with Xena,

124

when I couldn't be certain what I wanted. He understood I'd feel trapped later, if I'd just gone back to Poteidaia with him right then. That—that there was a whole wide world I'd only just discovered with Xena, that I needed to explore that, and myself." She considered this, shrugged. "I'm not making a lot of sense, I guess."

"You're making all the sense in the world," Helen said quietly. "I feel that with Nossis. He's kind and caring. He worries that I'm being kept below my place, that I'm not happy, not getting what I want. He'll probably never re- alize that all that matters to me is caring for his children, and being close to him as often and as much as I can. And before you ask, no, I won't ever tell him."

"Why?"

"Gabrielle, think about it. He's accepted the legend, just like Paris and everyone else. Except, in his case, he can't believe that the 'most beautiful woman in the world,'" sarcasm edged the words, "could ever possibly be in love with a small, ordinary-looking king of an insignificant kingdom. He'll never see that. And if I told him, he'd never believe it."

"You can't know that for sure," Gabrielle protested. Helen cast her a world-weary smile.

"Gabrielle, remember who I am, and where I've been. I do know. I won't do that to him." The smile slipped; her eyes moved to the children, who were now seated side-by-side on the edge of the stage, Ideta listening in- tently while Nebos recited to her. "Just do one thing for me, if you can. You and Xena. Get me extra years here. Give me the chance to stay in Knossos until those two don't need the tutor Elenya any more."

Gabrielle opened her mouth. Closed it. Thought hard. "Helen. I can safely promise you that much, for me and for Xena. We will do everything we can to keep you safe and happy."

The woman must have been distracted by her young

charges, the bard thought, as Helen got to her feet and gestured for Nebos to take the stage. *Otherwise, she'd realize I didn't promise to keep Nossis in the dark.* She considered this, bit back a smile. *As if I would.*

8

The children did a good job, Gabrielle thought, and told them so. Helen sent them off to play for a little longer as a reward. "Thank you for being nice about it, Gabrielle. They aren't used to reciting for anyone but me, and sometimes their father," she said. She glanced at the sun. "I can't keep them out here much longer. Are you coming in with me?"

The bard shrugged. "I meant to ask you before. If it's safe for me to just explore out here, I mean."

"Mostly, it is," Helen replied. "Over there," she pointed west, toward the dancing floor, "I avoid that. And of course, the Maze—but it's locked, anyway."

"Xena told me about the Maze." This wasn't the time to admit she'd already discovered the problem 'over there.' Whether the guest had gotten into trouble from ignorance or foolishness—*or both, in my case*—the host would feel responsible. Nossis was harassed enough, and Helen simply didn't need to know, especially since no one was hurt.

She shoved that aside; the other woman was looking throughtfully around the plateau. Finally, she said, "The theater is safe, so is the arena. Anything east of the arena is all right. There's a grove of young oaks, a small planting of olive trees. A mixed orchard past that. If you go through the orchard and along the south side of the vineyard, you'll find a path leading up. It goes to the top of Mt. Idhi—the tall peak."

Gabrielle shaded her eyes and looked up. And up. "That looks interesting, but I bet you don't get all the way up there and back if you start this time of day."

"You can." Helen smiled. "I've done it, and I am not the walker you must be. There's a shrine, at the very top, a—kind of a dell just below that spire you can see, it's sheltered from the winds."

"Shrine?"

"It's the only place the Greek gods can come to on all of Crete." The smile slipped from her face as she turned to gaze at the peak. "I went up there not long ago. I thought if I could just *talk* to Aphrodite, I could convince her to help me." Her lips twisted briefly. "You can imagine how far that went."

"Right. I've had the pleasure," Gabrielle said.

"Well." The woman drew a deep breath, let it out in a gust, and stood.

Flowed to her feet, more like, Gabrielle decided. *It isn't just the beauty, it's the grace of her.*

"Enjoy the plateau, Gabrielle, and I'll see you at supper. I would stay away from the southern cliffs, if I were you. In places, the ledge juts out beyond the cliff face, and it's a horrible drop."

"Ah—right. Thanks." She watched Helen shepherd her two charges across the open pavement and back toward the palace, then settled on the edge of the stage to bask in the afternoon sun. For some time, she leaned back on her hands, face tipped toward the sky, and enjoyed doing absolutely nothing. "Mmmmm. I could get to like this," she murmured, then stretched and got to her feet.

There wasn't much to the theater, and she'd already decided the acoustics weren't that great. Nothing like Rhodes, and not even in a class with the main theater in Athens. After the previous night's banquet, she was pretty much 'storied out' anyway. She wandered across white-washed stones and into the arena, which she hadn't really noticed earlier. "Too busy watching Xena make a fool of that young idiot, Korinus." Her voice echoed off the high seats. "So, why is it there's at least one idiot like that just about everywhere we go?" She considered this, shook her head. "Yeah. That's like trying to figure out why there's so many stupid thugs around everywhere we go. There's just a lot of them, period." She laughed sourly. "Or Xena pulls 'em in like a lodestone." Sometimes, that was the only explanation that made sense to her.

There were two gates in the inner wall of the arena that divided the floor from the seats. Both bore painted bulls, wreathed and crowned in flowers. She looked behind one, into a very complete darkness, and decided not to explore farther. "I wonder if they really did use to dance with bulls in here?" Bardic tradition said they did. But it said a lot of other things that were exaggeration, and looking around the relatively small arena, Gabrielle shook her head. "There isn't room for that in here. Nowhere near enough for fighting them, either." She'd ask if she got the chance.

She left the arena and sought out the path Helen had suggested. She had no desire to join Xena in thrashing out plans, and the palace itself seemed a little over-whelming at the moment. Stifling. *You did want out, after all.* And she could probably see at lot from partway up that mountain. She tipped her head back to peer upward: In places, it was very steep, and the south side was nearly sheer all the way up. Here on the west face, the slope seemed much more gradual, and she could make out the pale, dusty path winding up between grass and flowers.

For a moment, she considered going back for her staff, then decided not to. "It's handy for climbing, sure, but I can do without it." There surely wouldn't be any need for the staff as weapon anywhere on Crete—until and if the Spartans showed up, anyway—and retrieving it would take time she didn't want to waste. "Just get on up there, look around," she told herself, and set off.

It was cool in the grove, despite the fact that the trees weren't much taller than she was and most of the trunks would have made good staves. They grew closely together though, blocking the view very far in any direction. Most of the way through, a small statue or shrine sat next to the path, half hidden under a woven twig roof. She peered at it uncertainly. *Don't go there unless you know what it's for. Who it's for. And unless you're sure they know you don't mean disrespect.* It definitely was an altar, though: formed like a coiled snake with the head resting atop the coils. Just behind the head was a depression filled with water, and at the base, someone had placed a clay bowl of grapes and a few daisies. She ducked her head respectfully, just in case, and moved on.

The path emerged from the oaks, went straight between two small wheat fields, wound through twenty or so massive olive trees, through the middle of another grain field, and plunged into shade once more. Gabrielle picked up the pace slightly here, and moments later broke free of the orchard.

She turned back to look around. The path had been climbing steadily—not enough for her legs to feel, but all at once she was well above the tops of the oaks and could just look across both orchards. From here, she could make out some parts of the pavement, but not all of it. Eastward, the path wound, climbing steadily, and vanished over the lip of a ledge. "That isn't too far," she decided, and started walking again.

It felt decidedly odd, walking such uneven terrain without her staff as a balance. But, like Helen had said, it wasn't nearly as rough a climb as it looked from below. Still, by the time she clambered onto a near-level grassy depression a while later, she was slightly out of breath.

The sun was definitely lower, but it wasn't that late, and the view was exactly what she'd hoped for. "You really *can* see the whole plateau from up here!" Most of it, anyway. The red line on the dancing floor was visible, and she could even make out where it wound through scrubby brush, but she lost it in bushes and low, wind-blown trees, just short of the cliff. Ocean gleamed on all three sides of the island from here, and she could make out the tiny form of a ship, sailing away from the port. Another coming from the west, heading toward it. South of the island, there was another moving spot that must be a fishing boat or even a large ship, but either way, it was far enough out to sea that she couldn't make out anything about it.

She dismissed ships. *No more ships for a while if I have anything to say about it.*

The palace was the interesting thing from here: a huge sprawl of tiled roofs that ran in all directions. Although she still couldn't see all of it. "That tall part is in the way," she mumbled discontentedly. "And that—whatever it is. Tower, or something."

She tried to remember the map in Nossis's council room, to orient herself. *There*, she finally decided, was where the guest quarters were, and the opposite direction, just behind that porch with the fat red pillars, the main entry. At least, the one where the king had greeted them the day before. This side of it, and angling back to face east, was the way they'd come out to the arena earlier. The council room must be—there, then, she decided. Those windows. "Not too bad," she told herself, pleased.

The Maze itself was fascinating, though there was very little she could actually see. To her surprise, it was not only high-walled—that much had been obvious from below, because the walls were at least three stories high, and the massive gates at least two—but it was completely roofed over as well. "Well," she amended doubtfully, "at least the front part of it is." The rest seemed to slope downhill and away, and from this angle, she couldn't make out even which way the walls went.

The roof was different: Flat, with a low parapet, it was mostly tiled, but in three places that she could make out, there were dark squares. She stared avidly for some time, but could make no sense of them. "Unless—right! Unless they're feeding hatches?" That worked. A fierce, half man, half bull, half crazed, half-divine being. "At least, the stories all say it was pretty crazy. He. So, when there aren't a bunch of young Athenians to feed to him, what does he eat? And who carries it in to him?" More likely, the handlers, or guards, simply climbed onto the roof, opened a hatch and tossed in the meat. She considered this and wrinkled her nose. "Yuch. But, they might not be that, either." Maybe the Minotaur's mother, the old Minos's wife, had loved her unnatural child, and. . . .

Gabrielle sat cross-legged on the grass abruptly and let her face fall into her hands. "Don't do this," she ordered herself harshly. "You can't assume the woman was as—as naive as you were. About—about Hope." She beat her fists on the ground. "Don't do this, let it *go*! There's nothing you can do to change what's past—hers, Hope's, or your own!" She drew a ragged breath and let it out slowly. Managed a shaky laugh. "Hey, for all you know, the woman was as appalled by what she gave birth to as Poseidon had intended for her to be. Maybe it was the Minos who liked to look at the creature." She blotted her eyes carefully. "Maybe you were right the first time, and they're to drop food in. Leave it, okay?"

The shadows were notably longer, she decided. Time to leave.

And now that the sun was lower, she could clearly make out the road up from the docks—a darker line between trees and brush, and then moving straight across the otherwise pale pavement. On the east side of the road, near the northern drop-off, she now noticed stables and what were probably barracks. She wondered how large an army Nossis had. "Xena said not much of one. Huh. Probably should have gone back to that planning session, and then I'd know, right?" She considered this, laughed shortly. "Yeah, right. I woulda fallen asleep. That kind of thing does nothing for *my* creative juices. And, speaking of creative juices—I wonder if there's anyplace I can break out my staff and work it?" It didn't do her reflexes any good to take so much time off from practice; Xena would notice at once if she got sluggish, and would give her a hard time about it. "Yeah," she told herself sourly, "and the last person you fought was *Joxer*. Like that was any kind of workout." She hadn't been herself the last time, anyway. "That was the seasick stuff, getting you pissed off. If you can believe what people tell you. Or gods." She got to her feet and took one last look around, then started back down the hill.

Logically, she knew, there had to be some place the king's men practiced. Newin would know; he was old enough to have a weapons tutor. "There's always the arena," she reminded herself. Nothing strange had happened while Xena was letting Korinus chase her around in there. It was certainly private enough, from what she'd seen so far—but on the other side of the dinar, it was closed off. She'd gotten in the habit of working out where she could see for a fair distance all the way around her. "Yeah. Comes of Xena popping up out of nowhere whenever you start concentrating on your moves and scaring you half silly. So? There is no one around here *except* Xena who's gonna sneak up on you. Unless Korinus decides I'd be a better pincushion than Xena was." She stopped short and shook her head, hard. "Cut it out, Gabrielle, it's not gonna happen." She thought about it again and laughed. "And if it does, hey, he's not that good, okay?" Her eyes narrowed. "Yeah. I can take *him*. Easy."

She gazed out across the plateau as movement caught her eye to the north. Someone was slowly walking up the road, a small pack slung over his shoulder.

Something familiar about the walk, maybe the shape? That pack. . . . "Oh, no," she muttered. "It can't be. Gods, tell me it isn't Briax?"

If it was the young would-be hero, he'd apparently separated from Bellerophon, because he was very much alone out there. "Terrific." Gabrielle sighed. Much as she'd never miss the arrogant young Corinthian, all she needed just now was a sweet but young-for-his-years guy like Briax following her around and making sheep's eyes every time he thought she couldn't catch him doing it.

Or Joxer getting huffy about the competition—whatever *he* thought they were competing for. "It had better be about finding Helen," the bard growled. She groaned, then. "Great. Here he comes, right up to Helen's front door! Did I tell Xena? I told her! I knew this would happen, I just *knew* it would!"

She started down the path once more, picking up the pace as she came to more level ground and went into tree shadows; she could make out the traveler only in brief glimpses here, but when she finally came out onto the pavement, there he was, limping slightly and mumbling to himself, steadily making his way up the road toward the main palace doors. Gabrielle sighed quietly, then brought up a bright smile and started toward him.

He looked up, astonished. "Gabrielle! What are you doing here? I thought you and Xena were on your way to Egypt!"

"We were. It's—a long story."

"Oh?" He winced as he started moving again. "Maybe I can hear about it later, then."

"Ah—sure. But what are you doing here? And where's Bellerophon?"

"Here? Well, I'm here because there's no inn down at the port, and I wasn't sure where I was going after Crete.

And they told me that the Minos gives shelter and bread to anyone who asks it, so I thought, well, that's better than trying to sleep on the dock with an empty stomach, and they assured me it was okay, that everyone takes him up on it. Uh—what else did you just ask me?" He blinked. "I'm sorry, Gabrielle, I'm just really tired."

"Bellerophon."

"Oh. Him." The youth's mouth twisted, and he briefly looked very annoyed indeed, but his eyes were warm when he glanced at her. "He said he couldn't see the point. So many of us looking for Helen, and it was—well, only a woman, after all. I mean—no offense, Gabrielle, but that's what he said. Nothing important, he said, whatever Menelaus *thought* he wanted. Well, I'm sorry, but that offended me, because, after all, *you're* a woman. And—anyway, I didn't really understand the other part he was telling me, something Apollo had told him or showed him, when he was tested? In Sparta. Now, that's just—okay, he made it up. Because I went through the same rite, and every time before, what he told me sounded just like what I saw. Except suddenly he's talking about this personal quest for something the god has lost? And a horse with wings that Apollo promised him?" He laughed sourly.

Gabrielle stared. "Winged horse? You mean—you don't mean Pegasus, do you? Really?"

Briax sighed heavily. "He never said Pega—that. Whatever you said. Just a horse with wings, and something about a statue." Another sigh. "Gabrielle, I think he made it up, just to get out of the quest. Because he was bored, and it was beneath him to be looking for any woman, even Helen of Troy! Or maybe he just wanted to get rid of me because *I* bored him."

He was veering off the road: tired or just not paying attention. Gabrielle eased him back the other way and got his feet moving toward the palace—and the main porch where the king had welcomed her, Xena, and Joxer the day before. "Briax, I don't believe you could have bored him. You're too nice a guy." *And there you go, encouraging him*, she told herself with an inner sigh. But the poor guy looked so woebegone.

"I—look, I need to sit down for a minute." He limped over to a stone bench not far from the arena and dropped down with a sigh of relief. "My feet ache," he mumbled. "And my legs are—"

"I'm hardly surprised, that's a bad road. But why did you walk it?"

"Because I got a good look at the cart they wanted me to get in. Besides, it wasn't going anywhere until the next ship came because there's only the one cart." He shrugged. "I don't think I beat it here by much. But I didn't think it looked like that bad a climb from down on the docks." He dismissed that with a wave of his hand. "Bellerophon," he said determinedly. "You know, he really was so nice, to begin with. I'd never have made it this far if he hadn't known how to find the right ship, how to bargain for passage and food. At least I can do all that now, thanks to him.

"And then he just—he just *quit!*" He sighed faintly again. "Well, after he went away, there I was, stuck on Paros and thinking about going north to dry land. Because we kept running across guys who'd been in Sparta—well, Bellerophon said so, anyway. I didn't recognize any of them. Anyway, I thought, maybe she's still on the land bridge that goes east from Thessalonika, over to the isthmus across from Troy? But then I thought, since I was so far south maybe I ought to try Crete. He told me she would never be here, but I thought it was worth looking. Maybe someone would know something, or saw her someplace else." He dug fingers into a calf muscle, caught his breath in an agonized gasp, and cautiously eased the leg out of his hands. Glanced sidelong at Gabrielle. "I guess I was wrong about Helen, though. Since you're here."

So what do I say, and how to say it? "That's not why we came to Knossos, Briax. Xena was here a long time ago. She knew the old Minos, and thought, since we were already in port because we got blown off course, that maybe we should come up. You know, meet him, even if we didn't stay. Because Xena says he doesn't feel like he's the equal of his father, and so he might feel offended, like she didn't think he was worth visiting."

"Oh." He scratched his neck absently. "And—and Helen?"

Gabrielle shook her head. "Briax, haven't you listened to me? How many times have I told you that there is nothing like that—that whatever you're looking for—"

"The Sacred Ewer of Persephone," Briax broke in with quiet dignity. His face was so solemn, she could have laughed, and besides, she didn't dare. *He'd really be offended—and he doesn't deserve that from me.* Anyway, he took this whole thing so seriously that if she laughed at him, he might get really determined—just to show *her*. Which could get him in a lot of trouble, one way or another.

Gabrielle turned away from him to gaze across open pavement, beyond the theater to the distant sea. "There is no Ewer, Briax," she finally said as gently as she could. "It's a trick. Menelaus is trying to get Helen back to Sparta, and, believe me, if that was what she wanted, she'd have gone with him when Troy fell." Silence. She turned back to search his face. "Doesn't the fact that she fled from Troy tell you something?" Briax's eyes were fixed on a spot just above hers, and he was smiling. Gabrielle waved a hand in front of his face. "Briax—you're not listening to me again, are you?"

"Huh?" He blinked. "Oh. I was just thinking. I'd forgotten how b-beautiful you are. And out here, the way the sun shines on your hair—Gabrielle?" he asked in sudden alarm as she jumped to her feet and held out a hand to aid him up; he took it, winced as his feet took his

137

weight, and hobbled along after her. "Did I say something wrong?"

She managed a smile. "No, Briax. You didn't say anything wrong. Well—not much, anyway. But I—never mind. You're gonna get too stiff to walk if you sit here very long, that's all."

"Oh. Ah—ouch! Thanks. I think," he mumbled under his breath.

"Besides, look," she added. "Here comes the cart and there's a passenger. And—" Sure enough, when she looked back toward the palace and the porch with its bright red columns, there was King Nossis. *I wonder how he does that?* she thought. Surely he didn't come out here every day, just in case there were visitors? "Look, there's the king—the Minos."

"Ah—but I don't—I mean, I shouldn't, he doesn't need to—I mean, just for me, or anything . . . ?"

She interrupted what was becoming a very convoluted babble. "He greets all the people who come here, Briax, it's okay. Come on." She slowed as it became clear he couldn't keep up with her, and moments later the cart rattled past. Gabrielle stared after it, eyes fixed on the small, slight figure who was the only passenger. "You're kidding!" she muttered. "It can't be—Saroni?" The cart was far enough ahead now, she couldn't be sure of anything. She tugged at Briax's wrist and got him moving again.

By the time they reached the deep porch, the cart had drawn up and the single passenger was climbing cautiously out of it. Gabrielle let go of Briax and lengthened her stride. "Saroni?" she asked.

The woman spun around, dark eyes wide. "Gabrielle? You startled me! What are you doing in Crete?"

"Storm," Gabrielle said simply. "But what are *you* doing here?" She glanced up as the king came down from

138

the porch and onto the pavement, touched the woman's arm and gestured with chin and eyes.

The priestess turned, saw the plainly dressed little man and glanced back at the bard, who nodded firmly. The woman went to one knee. "Sir—sire? If you are the Minos? Or his representative? I claim ṣanctuary of Crete!"

Nossis took her arm and helped her up. "I am Nossis, king here. And you are welcome as my guest. Sanctuary, though, that's a serious request. From whom do you ask it, and why?"

The woman plaited her fingers together nervously, and she fixed her eyes on the pavement just before her toes. "I'm—I *was* a novice priestess in Rhodes. To Apollo. There was—" She swallowed. "The head priestess, Krysta, was doing some things that began to worry me—I can't say what, I swear I don't dare tell you about any of it. But, when she found out that I knew, my life was in danger. She—has power, sire, and a long reach. Allies in Rhodes and elsewhere, and other priests who would— track me down, see me returned to Rhodes. And—I'd die there, one way or another. I came here because—I heard that this was one sure place I couldn't be found."

Nossis studied her for several long moments, and Gabrielle suddenly became aware of Xena, hanging back in the shadows, thoughtfully looking the woman over. "We will talk of this at another time, when you have bathed and eaten and rested," Nossis said finally. He held up a hand and two women came from the doorway. "These women will conduct you to a chamber, and bring you food."

"Thank you," Saroni whispered. She glanced at Gabrielle, who smiled at her.

"I'll find you later," she promised. Saroni considered this, then nodded, and went with the servants. Gabrielle followed her as far as the porch, while Nossis greeted Briax, who managed a polite bow and a nicely worded greeting he must have learned from Bellerophon. *His fa-*

ther sure never taught him those kinds of manners, she thought.

Nossis was speaking. "If you can wait here for a moment or so, I will have someone lead you to a room where there will be water for bathing, and fresh clothing. Food. I—wait." A clatter of footsteps brought him around—Newin, followed by Joxer, who caught sight of Briax and stopped short, his mouth twisting in irritation. Gabrielle set her jaw and resolved to say nothing. "Son, you come in good time," Nossis said. "This is Briax, a visitor, and Briax, this is my son and heir, Newin. Son, see to it he has a guesting chamber for the night, bathing water, and food."

"Father." The youth had good tutors, Gabrielle thought; his manners were impecable, as was the smile he gave Briax. "Come with us, sir, and I will see you bestowed." He glanced over his shoulder and grinned at his fishing companion. "Joxer, you're coming with me, aren't you?"

"Me? Oh—yeah," the would-be hero replied with lofty irritation, though when the boy looked at him, puzzled, he managed a real enough smile for him. "Yeah, I'm coming." He gave Gabrielle a sidelong, narrow look as he passed her, and went inside with the king's heir and the new guest. *The competition*, Gabrielle thought with an inward sigh.

Xena hadn't missed any of that, of course; her eyes were sardonic as the king passed her and the warrior beckoned. "C'mon, Gabrielle. I'm betting you could use a bath about now."

"What—you can tell from there?" the bard inquired sharply.

Xena shrugged; Gabrielle sighed and brought up a faint smile. "Gabrielle," the warrior drawled. "If I could smell anything from here *on* you, it would be lost under the reek I just got off Joxer."

"Huh? Oh. He fell in?"

"He smells like salt water, and his boots are squishing."

Xena's mouth quirked. She gazed down the hall after the new guests. "So—that was your priestess from Rhodes."

"Saroni," Gabrielle replied. "Odd—I really never expected to see her again. Not this soon, anyway. I wonder what happened? You gotta figure it's something involving Avicus, though, right?"

Silence.

"Xena?" The warrior came back from wherever her thoughts had taken her, smiled and gestured for her to lead the way.

Well to the north, *Wode* had taken temporary shelter in a deepwater bay along the eastern shore of Paros, where the island cast deep, afternoon shadows over the water. Wind blew stiffly from the southwest, straight through the string of islands known as Cyclades. Draco, who again had watch from the aft deck, leaned across the starboard rail and stared intently south, out to relatively open water. This time of day, Habbish had said, few ships came through this passage because there were half-submerged islets and sharp stacks of stone and the mix of sun and long shadow made it nearly impossible to see them. Only those like *Wode,* whose captain knew the safe routes well, would dare it so near sunset. Or local merchanting ships. *Hammer*, he was hoping, might not be one of these and might fall behind them, or simply turn aside and let them go. *Hah*, Draco privately thought. He was getting a feeling about this captain, whoever he might be. Arrogant and stubborn both. Outraged at losing a battle to a ship like *Wode*, humiliated by the simple trick that had cost so many oars.

Or, it could be as Habbish thought: the man might have orders to capture the Gael's ship. He dismissed the thought; he'd been wakeful the night before with it, and there *was* no way to settle it from here. "I still don't see— wait. There she is." By now, he'd become all too familiar with the particular set of *Hammer*'s sail, and the way her

141

sleek bow looked from straight ahead. Habbish briefly relinquished the wheel to his first, and looked aft. He nodded finally.

"Keep close eye on her, m'friend." He turned and raised his voice—but not much. *Wode* was under as complete a silence as possible, at the moment. "Ye mons make ready now! When I sign ye, hold still or get under cover. *No* giving 'em warning by anything—sound *or* movement! Not until she's in position. Angus, down below quick-like, and warn t'oarsmen. Hold 'em *in* t'water and steady. Remember, this sign," he slashed his right arm through the air in a circle, "means 'go'! We've done this before now, remember how y'did it, or we may be swimming to Paros afore t'day's much older!"

Cautious nods.

Draco glanced toward the deck. What few faces he could see were grave and determined. He turned back aft. "Just clearing that point of rock straight behind us," he announced.

Now they could hear the creak of wood as the warship came on, and the slap of a loose rope against the mast. Two men were clearly visible in the crow's nest, one searching Naxos to the east, the other's intent eyes moving over what he could see of Paros.

It must not have been much; Habbish gave the signal and the *Wode* plunged forward in a series of awkward jerks as the oarsmen fought to get her moving again. Her sail flapped, then caught wind. Draco ran across the deck to the port side, bow strung and an arrow on the string, staggering as Habbish brought the wheel around hard, and the ship heeled to starboard. It rolled back a little, and now men were yelling on *Hammer*, someone bellowing for silence and someone else yelling orders; men ran down the deck with torches to light the pitch.

But *Wode*'s catapult was already loaded, and a line of men stood along the rail, bows up, passing fire from arrow tip to arrow tip. As the ship came in close along the aft port quarter, they fired. Fire bloomed all across *Hammer*'s sail and someone in the crow's nest shrieked as his shirt and hair caught fire. Draco saw the two men dive into the water on the far side, then drew his bow down and steadied himself, seeking a target. *That captain would be a good one, for starters*, he thought, and smiled grimly. But just as he loosed the arrow, the catapult fired, the ship heeled slightly, and the arrow lodged itself deep in the aft bulkhead.

A breath later, Habbish bellowed, "Oars flat!" The cry echoed from below. Draco winced as wood cracked, echoing from the rocks to their west. And then *Wode* was away, taking the open passage south of Naxos and moving as quickly as wind and oars could carry her, northeast toward Icaria.

Draco leaned over the rail and peered down. Then grinned at Habbish, who turned the wheel over to his first again. Behind them, they could still—just—see *Hammer*, floundering as men clambered aloft to pour water on the smoldering sail. "Wonder how much damage you actually did," he asked the Gael. "They're still afloat."

"Aye, and too bad of us, I wager. Still." He grinned. "They'll be a small time mending that rudder."

"Mending—not replacing? You didn't get it all, then?"

Habbish shrugged. "Wasn't much chance of that wi'a captain knows t'ship as well as he does. Sensible man sees a ship heading t'way *Wode* was, and he throws it over full to t'same side. But I saw a good bite of it afloat as we moved off." He measured with his hands—a piece as long as the warlord's forearm. "He won't be following us, though; not until that's mended."

"Well, he can quit following us any time now," Draco said flatly. "I'm getting *bored* with seeing that thing in our wake."

"Huh. Y'think I'm not?" Habbish growled. He crossed to the aft rail and shouted out, "Y'done well, ye mons! Mop up now, and ready t'trade off rowers at sundown!

143

There'll be a spare ration for each of ye tonight!" A cheer met this. The captain waved, then beckoned Draco to follow and went into his cabin. "Time t'plan our next meeting, I'm thinking."

Draco sighed quietly and settled in his usual chair.

9

Gabrielle lay sprawled in the bathing pool, her head cushioned on a small pillow, hair streaming around her shoulders, her eyes closed. The room was very quiet, the air and water delicately scented with something that smelled like a crisp green apple. It was clean, just warm enough. No pond scum anywhere, no fish underfoot, no thugs waiting for her to crawl out. *Just—pure bliss,* she thought happily.

Air swirled nearby, brushing across an exposed shoulder. She eased cooled skin under the surface and opened one eye. Xena, already finished with the bath and wrapped in an enormous, red drying-cloth, dropped down cross-legged next to her head cushion and scooped up a fat sponge. "Dinar for your thoughts," the warrior drawled quietly.

"Funny. I was just thinking how *nice* it is to have a clean, quiet place to bathe. Pure bliss, in fact." She resettled her backside on the underwater ledge, bundled wet hair and drew it forward. Xena pressed her head over and began squeezing spongefuls of water over the back of her neck.

"Nothing *pure* about Bliss," Xena said after a moment.

"Huh?" Gabrielle turned partway around to eye her companion; Xena smiled and turned the head back before applying the sponge to her friend's shoulders. "Oh. *That* Bliss. Yeah. Some rotten little godling's got a *bad* case of indulgent parents. Especially Daddy."

"Needs a good thump," Xena agreed quietly. The sponge moved from one shoulder across to the other, back again, then down between the bard's shoulder blades. "Good muscle, Gabrielle. I'm impressed."

"Hey—I try."

"No, you actually *do* things. That's why it looks so good."

Gabrielle came partway around and smiled warmly. "You know, sometimes, it's scary how good you are at figuring out what I'm thinking—or being right there with it. Because this afternoon, I was thinking about how long it's been since I had a good practice or a good workout."

"I don't think you're gonna lose it all in eight days or so," Xena said. She flipped the sponge into the water and sat back; Gabrielle retrieved it and began washing her arms.

"Well, no, I suppose not. Xena! Is that *really* all the time we've been out here?"

"I lost count myself, somewhere around Lethe," Xena said with a shrug. "Close to that, though. Unless we were on that island over a night or two."

Gabrielle swallowed, remembered dread, and leaned forward to wash her knees. "Ah—no. Because Ares said—"

"Ares?" Xena asked sharply. "What does *Ares* have to do with the island of forgetfulness?"

The bard slewed around to look at her close companion. "I didn't tell you about that part?"

Xena shrugged.

"You know, this is a real bore, wondering just what went on out there, and what I said, what I didn't. . . ."

"Gabrielle, we'll talk, I promise. None of it was that important, though."

"It was, if it's my *mind* we're talking about here!"

"Hey! Hey, relax, okay? Gabrielle, I understand. It's happened to me a few times, and I don't like it, either. At least you have me to tell you if there was anything incredibly strange, or ugly or—whatever." She spread her arms wide, then let them fall to her sides. A faint smile. "Except for Lethe; you're on your own there, because all I remember is walking away from that beach, and then being scared. Really scared. Like all I knew was to be afraid and run from that fear." She laid a hand on Gabrielle's shoulder as the other woman would have spoken. "And you, dragging me out into the sea and feeling like I'd just come awake from a *long* night of bad guys and worse wine."

"That's one you don't have to share," Gabrielle said with a faint smile.

"I didn't intend to." Her eyes were suddenly wicked. "You can always get pissed off at Joxer and chase him around the arena, like I did that young idiot Korinus."

Gabrielle laughed and reluctantly got to her feet. Xena fished a drying-cloth from the stack and held it out for her. "Yeah, right. My creative juices are working just fine, Xena. What I *need* is a workout." She wrapped the cloth around her body, tucked the ends in and caught up a smaller one for her hair.

"Actually, I do have an idea for you," Xena said. "Newin's just about old enough for sword training, but Nossis doesn't want him starting with an edged weapon. He's learned bow and sling, and now he wants to try something new."

Gabrielle considered this. "That's more sensible than you'd expect. Except the king seems like a reasonable guy. So, you think he'd let me teach the kid some staff fighting?"

Xena's lips twitched. "Better than letting *Joxer* teach him anything, don't you think?"

The bard groaned faintly and let her eyes close. "Tell me he isn't teaching Newin that—that song of his?"

"You got me, Gabrielle. And if he is, I don't wanna know. He'll be at dinner tonight, though. Even the little ones will. So—ask about the staff, all right?"

"Sure." Gabrielle shook out her hair and wandered back into her own room, where an ice-blue robe had been laid out for her. She gazed at it and sighed faintly. "It's gorgeous—but why don't they give me red, like they do you?"

"Because I'd look like Princess Diana in that?"

"No." Gabrielle sighed again. "It's the hair." She held out a tress of red-blond, wrinkled her nose at it. "People like me, they *always* dress like Princess Diana. At least it's not pink."

"There's a thought. King Lias' daughter has a fondness for pink. *Fluffy* pink."

"Yeah. I remember."

"This—it's clean, it's classy, and besides, who're you gonna impress here?" Xena demanded with an urchin's grin. "Korinus? Or maybe Joxer?" The smile broadened. "How about Briax?"

"Pass," the younger woman replied firmly. "So—will Helen be there?"

The warrior shrugged. "I guess. Why?"

"I just wondered—you know, with Briax and Saroni—?"

"We're eating with the family, Gabrielle. There's a separate room always set up for regular guests. And since I already told King Nossis that Briax is on Menelaus' quest, he'll be well cared for, but he won't be allowed anywhere near Helen. Saroni—" Her face was impassive as she turned away.

148

Gabrielle eyed her sidelong as she finished drying off. "What?" she asked curiously.

The warrior shrugged.

"Xena, you aren't thinking—just because she's a priestess of Apollo—you're not, are you?"

No reply.

The bard sighed, exasperated. "Xena, there is nothing *wrong* with Saroni! I told you about her, back in Rhodes—I did, didn't I?" Xena nodded, her expression neutral; the bard couldn't tell what her close companion was thinking at the moment. "She was worried about that head priestess, the one who was wearing those wooden shoes—clogs? Krysta, I think?"

"I know. That's what she said out front," Xena replied evenly.

"When she asked for sanctuary, in case you've forgotten."

"I didn't forget that, Gabrielle."

"Well—what, then? Look. Saroni told me she thought Krysta was talking to someone who was not on Rhodes. I must have told you about *that*. Because it sounded to me like the priestess was in league with Avicus—Krysta, I mean." Xena gazed at her; one eyebrow went up. Gabrielle tossed the drying-cloth aside and snatched up the pale blue silk, hauled it roughly over her damp hair; when Xena tried to help, she pulled away. "I can manage, all right?"

"Whatever," Xena said; she sounded slightly surprised, but her expression hadn't changed when Gabrielle finally shoved the last of the filmy material off her face and hair.

"Don't tell me you suspect—what? That Saroni made all that up? For me? Why would she bother? She didn't even know me."

"She knew who you were, once you told her your name. Gabrielle, I didn't say anything—"

"No. You didn't have to, Xena, because I *know* how

149

your mind works. And I saw the way you were looking at Saroni this afternoon, out there."

Silence—a tight one. The warrior broke it with a deep sigh. "Gabrielle, I'm not accusing her of anything. Yeah, I'm naturally suspicious of people when they do unusual things, and for a priestess of Apollo to leave her temple and fetch up in a place like Knossos—that's about as unusual as it gets."

"Sure—and you heard why. Because she was afraid they were gonna kill her!"

"No—that's what she *said* was going to happen, Gabrielle. Now, look—it may be true. And I'm not going to say anything to King Nossis that would cause him to send her away, all right? You know I wouldn't do that without some kind of hard proof, and a funny feeling isn't proof."

"Great. So, you're gonna *look* at her like that because of a funny feeling?"

"You know me better than that. I will watch her, though. If you're right about her, it might not hurt to watch over her anyway. What if the head priestess in Rhodes knows she came here?"

"I guess. Maybe."

"Gabrielle, it's not just the coincidence of her showing up here, right after we did. . . ."

Gabrielle sighed loudly, silencing her. "What she said makes sense, Xena! Where else could a priestess of Apollo *go*, that the god couldn't track her down? Oh—sure, there are probably lots of places, we've *been* in some of those places. If she'd sought sanctuary from Queen Bouddica, she'd be just as gone—but how long would it take her to get there, and how much would it cost in passage? Crete is close, and it's known to be a haven from the Greek gods. All right?"

"*You* didn't know that, Gabrielle. Most people don't."

"No." Gabrielle wrapped a silvery sash around a slender waist, knotted it with a yank, and reached for her brush. "But if I were a priestess, I might know it. If I had

150

been a priestess in a temple where a lot of strange and secretive things were going on, and the other priest types made me worry about whether I was gonna wake up for breakfast and prayers the next morning, you can bet I would have been looking for a refuge. And I'll also bet that on a place like Rhodes, all those ships going in and out, that a lot of people would know about Crete being Apollo-proof."

Xena considered this, finally shrugged. "I'll give you that one. Now—you trade me, will you? I am not saying your new friend is dangerous, or anything of the kind. I'm just saying, all you have at the moment is her word. And because she was maybe nice to you and now she seems to be in trouble, she's appealed to the best in you, Gabrielle.

"All I'm asking is that you don't let that blind you to the possibility that she is not what she seems. That doesn't have to mean she's a danger to Helen."

The fight went out of Gabrielle all at once. "Helen— yeah, I know. She has to be our main concern. I have no right getting angry about Saroni when all you're trying to do is protect Helen. But I wasn't going to say anything—"

Xena closed the small space between them and caught hold of the younger woman's shoulders. "Gabrielle, you don't even have to tell me that." She managed a faint smile; it didn't reach her eyes. "Hey. I'm just being me. You know, suspicious, ready to think the worst of everybody, paranoid?"

Gabrielle's eyes kindled, and she brought up a faint smile. "Yeah, that's you. Know what, though? All things considered, I'm glad."

Xena rubbed hard knuckles over her forehead, standing pale bangs on end. "Yeah, that's you. Silly, giddy, ready to think the best of everyone, including Joxer—fluffy."

The bard snorted, and finger-combed hair back flat. "Fluffy? Xena, for your information, Diana—okay, she

151

was, but *Aphrodite* is fluffy!" Her mouth quirked. "I'm just little, blonde, and cute."

Xena let her go, and rolled her eyes. "Yeah. Cute. Did I tell you what Briax said back in Menelaus' reception hall? Why he was on the quest?"

"Gods," Gabrielle whimpered. "Don't tell me. I got a taste of it again this afternoon. I mean, I thought it was *you*, every time. You know, the hair, the legs, the leather?"

"According to Briax, it's the hair, the smile—the many skills, because you're a warrior *and* a bard, according to what you told him." The bard merely closed her eyes and grimaced. "He didn't mention the little stick, though."

"Now, that could be a point in his favor." She considered this. "Not that it's much of one! Xena, how come I get the ones like Joxer and Briax?"

"Gabrielle, what can I tell you? Remember Howar?"

"Forget it," the bard broke in. "Forget Howar, Minya—forget Joxer, okay? Here I've been looking forward to this dinner, and you're trying to kill it for me."

"Me?" the warrior growled; a smile tugged at her mouth. "Who brought up Aphrodite?"

The meal was much less formal, the food as good, and the only entertainment provided by a pair of musicians who occupied a niche near the door, playing several different instruments each—everything from pipes and drums to harp. Joxer was there, seated near the end of the table between Newin and two of his instructors, and Xena across from them; at the moment, the warrior was deep in some conversation with the youth's tutor in weaponry.

Even in this more private setting, Helen kept the scarf over her hair and sat just beyond Gabrielle, across from the king's two youngest, where she could keep an eye on them.

King Nossis had taken a seat between the children, rather than the usual, formal head of table, and he spent most of the meal talking to either Nebos or Ideta so quietly that no one else could hear. Gabrielle glanced their way often. *Imagine, a king that comfortable with his babies, not afraid to be seen caring about them the way he obviously does.* So many of them left the tending to nurses and then passed them on to tutors.

Or they were like the king that Pandora had married—Gregor? Who had mistrusted all children, because of the prophecy that one of the newly born would eventually be king in his place. *So grasping, he never stopped to think that the child might be his chosen heir.* Of course, if it hadn't been for Xena, Gregor never *would* have realized there was an alternative to killing that baby.

No, she suddenly remembered. It hadn't been that kind of macho swagger that had blinded King Gregor. *Grief, because of losing his wife and baby son.* Well, no blame to her for forgetting: That had been a long time back, and more adventures and calamities ago than she could properly remember. Especially with the smell and flavor of such excellent food before her.

She glanced sidelong at Helen, finished the skewer of chicken, vegetable, and fruit cubes that had just been roasted on a brazier at the far end of the room, then looked over at the king again.

Nossis looked up, as if aware of her regard, and smiled. "I appreciate a healthy appetite in a woman," he said.

She laughed. "Yeah, that's what a lot of people say. I guess that should tell me something about myself."

"Healthy," the king repeated firmly; he was still smiling as his gaze strayed to Helen, came back again. "I've thought over what you asked earlier, and I agree that it would be good for Newin to at least see how you fight with a long stick. And if he likes what he sees, you may feel free to instruct him, once a day for as long as you and Xena remain here. Now tomorrow morning, he and his tutors will meet you in the arena. None of Newin's trainers are familiar with staff, I fear, but there may be someone in my barracks who can use a staff against you—for demonstration purposes, of course. Unless your friend, Joxer—?"

"Huh?" Joxer looked up.

He winced; probably Xena kicking him under the table, Gabrielle decided, and bit back a grin.

"Owwww! I mean, I'm sorry, sire, I didn't hear all of that." Newin clapped a hand over his mouth, but sat up straight and swallowed laughter as his instructors both scowled at him and one of them hissed a low, furious order.

Gabrielle smiled across the table at the inept warrior. "We just wanted to know if you were interested in helping me show Newin how to use a staff. Tomorrow morning."

"Ah—swell." He smiled nervously. "I can do that, Gabrielle. Except—um, if I have a choice—ah, frankly, Gabrielle, I get a *lot*—ah—learning experience! Yeah, more of that out of watching you. And besides, maybe Newin could use my help, you know, someone to fix his stance and like that?" He considered this, closed his mouth, and nodded firmly.

Gabrielle bit the corners of her mouth to keep from laughing: He was *so* transparent! Not to Newin, obviously. The heir leaned close to Joxer's ear and whispered something; he looked wildly excited.

The meal ended shortly after. Joxer and Newin left at once, Newin talking rapidly, Joxer looking slightly bemused. Ideta and Nebos stayed behind with their father; they were telling him about declaiming in the theater earlier when Xena and Gabrielle left. Helen, to Gabrielle's surprise, came with them. Once back in the apartment Gabrielle and Xena shared, Helen closed the door and leaned against it.

"The two people who came here today from the docks—the priestess and the young man who claims to be a warrior, the king says you know them." Wary, dark eyes glanced from Gabrielle to Xena, back again. "I heard from him what they said at the greeting, but it wasn't much. I thought—"

"Good thinking," Xena said, as the woman faltered into silence. "I saw Menelaus and Avicus confirm Briax as one of their chosen heroes. Before you worry about it, I saw Avicus attach his badge things to each of the men who were picked. Joxer's is long gone, and I took the one from Briax when we met at Rhodes. They're at the bottom of the ocean."

"Useless, then." Helen sighed faintly. "Thank you. That was one of my first concerns, even though I doubt if either of them will ever see me."

"If I hadn't already known you," Xena replied, "and if you hadn't come here yesterday, I wouldn't have seen you as Helen myself. You do a good job of hiding in plain sight."

"Thank you. Though I doubt that a good job will be enough if Menelaus—" She shook her head firmly.

"Gabrielle can tell you more about both of the king's new guests; she knows them better than I do."

"That isn't very much, though," Gabrielle said. She was comfortably full and about ready to fall asleep. She explained: Briax's village, his father, the innkeeper, bellowing at him all the time, the youth having maybe half a handful of sword lessons from his father, but wanting adventure and a chance to prove himself to a certain bard he'd just met. "You'll have to admit, it's a lot more interesting than washing cups and slicing boar." Helen smiled faintly. "Saroni—I honestly don't know her, I just met her. In the theater, on Rhodes." Helen began to pace as Gabrielle told about the stopover, the odd atmosphere in the temple area, and—a little pink around the ears—about Saroni's exuberant greeting to one of her favorite bards, once she knew who her guest was.

"She said she'd been—collecting my stories, all of them she could get hold of. It was—well, I'm not used to that. She was—nice about it, really." Gabrielle shook herself. "Anyway," she went on briskly, "I didn't think there was much chance of us going back to Rhodes ever again, and I think if you're a priestess in a temple like that, you usually stay put for life. Unless they make you Oracle and send you to Delphi. So I was surprised to see her here, and at the same time, I wasn't."

Helen glanced at Xena, who raised an eyebrow. Gabrielle explained.

"I see," the once-queen said finally. "My concern wasn't just Apollo, or anyone connected with him. It was Rhodes in particular."

"Why?" Xena asked.

Helen shook her head.

"I don't know. Just something I overheard once, a long time ago. I can't remember when, or where I was. Probably on that ledge above the great reception, I used to go down there a lot, to hear what my husband was up to that I'd never learn any other way."

"I know that ledge," Xena said. "I heard about it the last time I was in Sparta—when you were still living there." Once-queen and once-warlord gazed at each other thoughtfully. "I wish we could have met back then. Even though I'm not sure it would have changed anything. Because I was still building my army, and there wasn't much that could have diverted me at that point."

"Anything is possible," Helen said. Her eyes searched the other woman's face; she finally relaxed a little, and managed a faint smile. "I wish we had met, too. Maybe somehow, I would have—not gone with Paris when I had the chance."

"Helen, you can't second-guess the past, and you can't change it," Xena said evenly. "Let it go and concentrate on saving what you have here and whatever good you can take in the future."

Silence. "All right. I will." Helen turned away and drove long fingered, slender hands through her hair. After a moment, she drew a deep breath and turned back to meet the warrior's eyes. "I'm sorry, I'm wasting time we may not have."

"It isn't wasted if it helps you feel more secure here," Xena told her. "Or if it helps us keep you safe. What about Rhodes?"

The woman considered this blankly, then nodded. "Somewhere, sometime back in Sparta, I overheard Menelaus and that pale-eyed priest of his."

"Apollo's, don't you mean?" Gabrielle broke in. Helen and Xena both glanced at her as if they'd forgotten her presence. "Sorry, didn't mean to—"

"He serves Apollo," Helen interrupted her in turn. "Just like the god gives him powers of sorts, I don't know much about them. But he's Menelaus', the two men might have been born at the same hour of the same mother. Nothing matters to either of them except what he wants, how to get it. How to keep it." Her eyes closed briefly; she shook herself and went on. "I remember hearing them talking. Something about Rhodes. As if—maybe there was something special about the temple there, something that Avicus needed. Or used. My—my once-husband asking something about how it could be used, as if it could benefit them both." She spread her hands. "I'm sorry. It can't have been that long ago, but it seems so."

"A lot has happened since," Gabrielle reminded her softly.

"Too many miles, too many years," Helen agreed, as softly. Her eyes were bleak. "Too many deaths."

"Which were not because of you," Gabrielle told her evenly. The woman merely shook her head.

"Something special about the temple." Xena had ignored that; her attention was fixed on the immediate problem. "A way for Avicus to talk to the priests in that temple on Rhodes?"

Helen lifted a shoulder in a graceful shrug. "But he can do that with any of them—any temple that serves Apollo, at least. It takes that bowl of his, and a similar one at the other place, is all I know. Frankly, Xena, I didn't want to know much about it. Avicus—frightened me. He still does."

"He should make you nervous," Xena said. "He's a very dangerous man; it would be a mistake to underestimate him. Still—Gabrielle, you said that priestess had some kind of water bowl?"

"Saroni told me she did. But they speak with the gods that way, don't they?"

"Hey, don't ask me," the warrior said.

"No—wait." Gabrielle closed her eyes and thought. "She said . . . that they used that, the bowl, I mean. In Rhodes? Because there wasn't a steam vent, like at Delphi. So, it's supposed to be a means to speak with the gods."

"That doesn't mean Avicus doesn't have his own use for it," Xena said.

"Count on it," Helen told her. She sighed faintly. "The woman didn't have anything like that with her, though. The king told me."

"A small pack and nothing else," Xena said. "Large enough to hold a change of clothing, maybe. More like a spare pair of sandals, nothing larger than that. Clean underthings, more like, because it was soft. If there had been a bowl in there, I think I would have been able to tell."

"If you're not sure," Helen replied steadily, "we can wait until tomorrow, when the woman is at her meal, or someone is showing her around, and have her room searched." She glanced at Gabrielle, whose eyes had gone wide. "You look surprised."

The bard shook her head. "Not really. At least, not that you'd do it, or have it done, for any guest you weren't sure about," she replied.

The woman smiled faintly. "It wouldn't be me. No. The king broke the ancient tradition of complete trust of any guest who comes to Knossos, when he learned who I was—and what I was trying to escape." The smile faded.

"I'd better get back to the children, they'll be exhausted and their father has another council meeting tonight." She opened the door, but turned back, softly closing it again. "I nearly forgot—the reason for that meeting; he said to let you know. Did you hear there was a battle between two ships yesterday, out on the eastern tip of the island?"

"We saw it," Xena said. "What there was to see. The captain of Yeloweh kept a lot of ocean between us and them."

"The one ship is from somewhere well north and east— Brittanium, I think they said. It's called *Wode*; it puts in down at the harbor now and again, their captain trades here on occasion. The other, though, the men who went to investigate didn't dare get too close, but they could see the damaged ship drawn onto shore and men working to repair it. It's believed to be a Roman raiding ship that answers to their council or maybe to Caesar himself. But certain of the king's council believe it to use that as a screen. That the ship and its captain answer to Sparta." Dark eyes glanced from Xena to Gabrielle. Back again. "I thought you should know." She was gone before either woman could say anything.

Gabrielle vanished into her own chamber and came back moments later, a slender, dark-blue silk sleep gown dragging the floor behind her. She held a handful of the stuff above her knees in front, and shrugged, her smile ironic. "I think they aren't used to women my size here." She came over and flopped on the edge of Xena's enormous bed as the warrior snugged an emerald green robe over the darker green sleep gown. "That's nice, I like it." Gabrielle's eyes slowly closed. "You know, it's gonna feel almost funny, sleeping in my clothes again."

"First night, maybe," Xena replied; she sat to slip sandals off her feet and tossed them into the corner. "After that, it grows on you."

The bard opened an eye. "Nice. Talk to me, Xena."

159

The warrior smiled. "Why should I bother? You're gonna fall asleep right there."

"Hey," Gabrielle murmured. "I'm not used to sleeping away from you, these days." She considered this, levered up onto her elbows and blinked herself partly awake. "What I mean is, you know: One blanket, one fire, both of us under the stars."

"Safer that way, for one thing, unless one of us is trying to crack the other one across the nose with her staff," Xena replied with a smile.

The staff wielder snorted. "Trying? I got you, fair and square! Anyway, forget about that, you said we could talk tonight."

"Think you can stay awake?" Gabrielle sighed faintly, sat up, and crossed her legs under her. "Yeah, I can. Because I'm tired of dreaming things when I do sleep, and not being sure if they really happened, or if that seasick stuff made me *think* they happened, or if *none* of it happened! Including that goo to put on my bread, and the wafers in case it got rough during the day. You don't have to tell me every single thing that happened since I went on that ship to drag Joxer off, back in the Spartan village—just the important stuff."

"Yeah, well, that won't be so hard," Xena said; she stretched hard, then collapsed onto the bed, rolled onto her back, and folded her arms across her chest. "Most of it was what sea travel always is: repetitive, boring, and you sleep a lot. Unless it's a warship and you're looking for trouble." She glanced up at Gabrielle. "Which we weren't."

"I think I'd remember that." Gabrielle propped her elbows on her legs, and cradled her chin on the backs of her hands.

Xena smiled, turned her eyes back to the ceiling. Thought for some moments, mostly to get things in order, then started talking.

For a while, Gabrielle made comments: Mostly of the,

"Yeah, I remember that" variety, or a stunned, "You're kidding me?" Xena reminded her about the *Wode*—her tossing Draco overboard just offshore, using the canny old Gael's ship to reach her friend and Joxer. The cult in Rhodes, the women and children hiding out in the massive statue of the island's patron god, Briax and Bellerophon showing up while she was in town getting supplies. Poseidon's pet sea serpents, and the one's mind-boggling crush on Joxer. The storm that followed, and the utter calm when the storm spent itself overnight.

"That's when we put in for water, that island you said was Lethe, Gabrielle. And I don't remember anything real about *that* part. I certainly don't remember seeing Ares. So, if you don't mind talking for a while? There's a laugh—"

Silence.

She turned to look at her close companion for the first time in a while. Gabrielle still sat cross-legged, head propped up on braced arms—but her eyes were closed and she was clearly deeply asleep. Xena's eyes warmed; she eased cautiously off the bed and went around it, slowly and carefully getting the bard untangled and down on her side, a pillow under her head and a lightweight cover over her legs; the edge where she could reach it if her upper body got cold later. "Sleep well, Gabrielle," she murmured, and turned to pinch out the nearest candles.

At length there were only two burning: one of them in the deep niche by the door since the room was unfamiliar to her. *Yeah. It's not gonna happen, someone breaking in and trying to break heads here. Then again—* She hadn't reached her current years and skills by blissfully dismissing things that should never happen. The other candle was the last one on a small metal stand near the window sill. She quietly moved across the chamber and touched thumb and forefinger against her tongue, pinched out the flame.

Movement beyond the window caught her eyes. "If the candle'd stayed lit, you wouldn't have seen that," she told herself quietly, and moved to one side of the window to peer intently out across the moonlit pavement.

Nothing moved there just now. She glanced quickly around. If somebody was out there—someone who didn't belong—they wouldn't see her, not where she stood in deep shadow. A quick glance across the room as Gabrielle murmured something, but the woman was still asleep. Xena turned back to study the pavement, concentrating on the deeper shadows around the steep risers of the theater. Nothing for some moments. Then a dark-clad figure scurried from a low, scrubby bush near the closest porch, heading toward the low stage.

"Yeah," Xena told herself softly. "That counts as odd." The person was so draped in cloth, so hunched over, she couldn't tell size, shape, or sex. The head was covered in a deep hood as well. Helen? But why would Helen need to sneak across the plateau at this hour?

The person stopped or slowed frequently, the hood turning sharply this way and that. Nervous, and expecting guards or someone or *thing* else, clearly.

Well, there weren't any guards out in the open—at least, there hadn't been any the night before, and the king had said at this morning's meeting that there seldom were guards since the palace and its grounds were their own protection. *That's something Gabrielle needs to talk to him about. I understand about things that aren't normal and everyday, and I'm okay with it. But she can make better sense of it.*

The hooded figure turned halfway around—something had made noise, possibly an owl or a small animal, maybe nothing but the secretive one's guilty conscience. Xena caught a glimpse of pale skin deep in the hood, dark points that were eyes. Her mouth tightened, and she silently crossed the room to fish the chakram from her piled weapons and leathers. "Someone out there can't sleep, I guess. So maybe I can get them to tell me a story." It made a satisfying picture. She scooped up the silver pin, shoved it between robe and sash, and eased the door open. A quick glance assured her Gabrielle slept deeply—a hand cushioning her cheek, a faint smile turning her lips. Xena eased the door closed behind her, hesitated only long enough to get her bearings, and took off down the hall at a dead run.

10

It took time, going through the maze of corridors instead of simply jumping over a windowsill. There was *one* good reason against the hard, clear glass—even if it did protect those inside from the near-constant winds, Xena thought impatiently as she turned a corner and lengthened her stride. The hallway was empty; she glanced behind her, saw no one, and broke into a loping run. Maybe King Nossis had instructed any guards or servants to leave her to her own devices, no matter how odd they looked. She didn't want to have to waste time explaining to some young night guard why she was armed, clad for sleep, barefoot, and running for the outside. *By the time he got it figured out, whoever's out there would be long gone.*

Somehow, she didn't think it would qualify as guest manners to flatten one of the king's guards who was only doing what he'd been taught to do.

Another turn, this time to the right—she slowed only long enough to make certain the hallway and what she could see of the porch at its end were both deserted, then ran once more, silk whipping around her ankles; she snarled a low curse, bunched green fabric in her free hand.

Just short of the porch, she stopped, set her shoulders against the darker wall and eased up to the open doorway, listening intently. No sound out there—nothing she could see, either. She slipped around the doorframe and into the sooty darkness of the covered porch.

Moonlight was a chancy thing. The moon was nearer full than not, but clouds were thick in places, and one moment the pavement flashed a brilliant blue-white, shaded here and there by walls, plants, and the palace itself. The next moment, the light was gone as if shuttered. Xena crouched so she could make out the pattern of clouds overhead, waited for utter darkness, and ran across the open, fetching up against one of the arena walls just east of the theater.

She listened intently. *Was that water?* It sounded as if someone were pouring a little water onto the stones. A sudden grin tweaked her lips. *Or some young guard who drank too much with dinner and got caught short—?* Except it didn't sound like that, it sounded as if someone had spilled a small amount of water—a bowlful, perhaps? The smile was gone. She held her breath; nothing at first, and then the faint, whispery sound of bare feet crossing stone. *Gotcha!* she thought, and threw herself into the open, chakram glittering as the moon sailed from deep cloud.

The dark-clad figure was nearly upon her, moving slowly; possibly feeling each footstep before moving on. Xena pounced and caught hold of thick cloth, then a shoulder.

A breathy, startled shriek broke the silence; the figure twisted, trying to break free. "Give it up," Xena snarled quietly. "It'd take more muscle than you've got to get away from me." The person went briefly still, but as the moon sailed free of cloud cover, made a sharp duck and twist. Xena held on easily, and as blue-white light illuminated them, used her free hand to shove the hood aside.

Saroni blinked up at her, her face and eyes screwed up against the light. She flung up an arm to shield her eyes. "Who—oh, gods, who are you?" the priestess whispered shakily. "Wait—no, you're—you *have* to be Xena."

"I am Xena. And you're that priestess from Rhodes who showed up today to ask the Minos for sanctuary."

"I am." The woman drew herself up straight, her voice trembled. "Where are we?"

"Funny." The warrior didn't look amused at all, and after one quick glance at her face, Saroni kept her eyes fixed on a spot on the pavement just beyond them. "I was gonna ask you something similar. *Why* are you out here?"

"I—don't know." The woman looked around. "I remember bathing, getting into bed, not long after the sun set." She managed a tremulous smile. "I must have slept at once. That's all I remember."

"That's all you remember," Xena said dryly. "That the best you can do, priestess?"

Saroni glanced up at her, then away at once. "Please. I'm just—Saroni. I'm not a priestess anymore. But—I walk in my sleep sometimes. Krysta—the head priestess—told me that. She used to bar my door from the outside, sometimes. She *said* it was because I walked in my sleep," she finished doubtfully.

It *could* be the truth, Xena thought with an inner sigh. It was no crazier than half the *other* things that had happened lately. It just seemed awfully convenient that this woman was out here. *But how did she get out here at all?* Because without one of those special pins, guests couldn't just wander wherever they wanted. And King Nossis wouldn't simply hand one over to a stranger. So far as she knew, even Joxer didn't have one yet. But Joxer certainly hadn't had one his first night.

Maybe those who walked while they slept had a way around such safeguards as those on the palace hallways.

She shoved the inner debate aside. *Later.* What to do with Saroni? And it would be a good idea to make it quick, before one of the guards came by—or one of the household. The priestess was looking at her now, her stance still wary, but dark eyes searching the warrior's face. "You don't believe me, do you, Xena?" Her shoulders sagged. "I can tell—I used to see that look on Krysta's face—my priestess, I mean. And Avicus looked at me like that—"

"Avicus?" Xena asked softly. "Tell me about Avicus, Saroni."

The woman shook her head. Frowned at her hands. "There isn't much to tell. He was in Rhodes once, not long after Troy fell. Seeking the queen for King Menelaus, he said. He—said she'd been stolen from Troy just before it fell, that she hadn't stayed in Troy willingly, or fled willingly, either. He and the high priestess met in private for most of the day." She swallowed hard. "When—they came out, he accused me of listening. To them. He said he could tell. And that maybe *I* knew where Helen was, and that I was helping her kidnappers." Wide eyes gazed into the warrior's. "I swear I wasn't, I wouldn't have done a thing like that! I'm—not brave like that." Silence.

Xena simply waited. When it became clear the woman had nothing else to say on the subject, she shook her head. "Aiding the kind of men who'd steal a helpless woman doesn't take bravery."

The woman gazed at her, eyes wide and expressionless. "That may be true. I wouldn't know. Avicus—he tested me, somehow. The gods' powers, I'm not sure. He must have realized then that I was telling the truth, but he didn't say. He left, not long after. And from then on, Krysta watched me—as if he'd told her to. It was after that, she told me I was walking in my sleep. She said she was afraid I would fall, hurt myself." She shivered down into her robe. "It's cold. And I don't know where my room is from here."

Xena took hold of both her shoulders, ostensibly to turn

167

the woman toward the porch. Her fingers moved deftly and lightly, feeling the surface of the fabric for any patch or for a pin similar to the one stuffed in her sash. Nothing. But as her hands touched the shoulders under the robe, Saroni started and this time twisted free. "I—I'm sorry. I—don't like being. . . ." Her voice faltered.

"Don't like being *what*?" Xena asked mildly. "Pushed around? I wasn't going to shove you. Handled? Touched?"

The priestess merely shook her head.

Xena eyed her for a long moment, then gestured for the woman to precede her. "The porch is straight ahead of you, where you can see light? That way. I'll direct you from there. I won't touch you," she added as the woman glanced back at her.

Fortunately, the warrior knew which wing and which room had been given to the priestess. King Nossis had shown her the palace diagrams and indicated where each of his current guests were staying. *Better yet, I'm good at maps and I can remember these things,* she told herself as the two of them moved quickly and quietly down the hallway. "Turn right, here," she said after a moment. "Left at the next passage, and left again." The fourth door down this hallway was marked with a dolphin arched high above whitecapped waves.

Saroni opened it cautiously, then let out a held breath and stepped into the room. She even managed a smile as she turned back. "Thank you, Xena."

"Thank me by bolting the door," she replied evenly. "So you don't wind up walking around in your sleep out there again. There are dangerous places even within the palace, and out there, the cliffs are high and overhung in places. One wrong step—" She let the thought hang. Saroni gulped and closed the door. Xena waited until she heard the inside bar slide into place, then turned to head back outside once more.

But once out of the passages that held the smaller guest chambers, she hesitated. Finally shrugged. "Maybe I won't find anything; maybe I won't be able to *see* anything." But she'd heard water spilling. And there were no ponds or fountains out where she'd heard that water. Maybe—just maybe there would be some kind of a gazing bowl. "And then, just *maybe* Saroni and I will have another little talk tonight."

Gabrielle would be upset, of course. *No,* the warrior corrected the thought, *she won't be upset if I can prove there was something up, out there.* Say, that priestess talking to the woman in Rhodes? Or, more likely, Avicus?

Or if she could assure herself that the woman was speaking the truth. "Though how in Tartarus I'm supposed to do *that*!" She shook her head and headed back outside.

A short while later, she returned to the rooms she and Gabrielle shared, cold and frustrated. There was no bowl anywhere near where she'd found Saroni—and the woman couldn't have gone far because she hadn't been aware of Xena when she was feeling her way across that pavement. If there'd been a puddle, or damp paving anywhere nearby, the warrior hadn't been able to locate that. "She wasn't trying to misdirect me—not then, at least." She considered this, corrected the thought. "*Maybe* she wasn't."

It was going to drive her crazy, she thought tiredly as she let herself in and closed the door behind her, then walked over to the window ledge and settled on it, eyes fixed absently on what she could see of the grounds beyond. It wasn't much. The moon was nearly down and filmed over with cloud. "What if her story's true?" It could be. It would explain things, including the woman's showing up here, her being outside just now. . . . "But it just doesn't feel right." A warrior who wanted to live beyond her first battle learned to trust hunches like that.

The old Xena wouldn't have hesitated to put the pinch on the woman and force the truth out of her. *The old Xena would have told her, "Talk, or die; you've got less than a minute of life in you, unless I reverse it, and let the bloodflow back into your brain.*" Nobody ignored a command like that—well, no one who valued life more than they feared retribution for talking, and in all the years she'd used the pinch, there'd been precious few of those. Saroni—the woman had been truly afraid of her, that much Xena could tell; not just the eyes, the stuttered words, but the faint, unmistakable smell of fear. She would have babbled everything she knew.

"*If* she knows anything."

The fact was, Xena realized tiredly, she used the pinch less and less of late—only in the most dire need, and *only* against hardened thugs; men who didn't understand anything less than death staring them in the face before they'd spill secrets that weren't theirs.

Even if she'd normally have clamped off the priestess's neck veins, she didn't have the right: Saroni was the king's guest, just as she was—an unknown, with only what she said of herself to tell the king anything. The guest ethos was ancient, and protected not only those who came openly and spoke truly of who and what they were, it also protected enemies coming openly to the court, or those who carried a burden of secrets. "Yeah, sure. He gave me a free hand to keep Helen safe. But if I attacked one of his guests, and my hunch turned out wrong. . . ." Nossis wouldn't send her away, but there'd be a break in the trust between them. For Helen's sake, if no other reason, she didn't want that.

"Admit it," she told herself. "You don't want to disappoint the old Minos' son. Because he's a nice guy, and he's doing a good job here and that's all probably because he's never run into the kindsa people you trip over all the time." There was a naiveté about Nossis that was—well, it was sweet. Particularly since it didn't seem to weaken him as an able ruler. He seemed to govern fairly, he ran an island that was clearly doing well, and he wasn't ashamed to be seen cuddling with his children. *Helen's father shoulda met Nossis before he held an auction on Greece for his daughter and Sparta.*

Saroni—well, she wouldn't solve the puzzle the woman presented her right now. Not tonight. *Soon, though.* If the woman was honest, fine, the warrior would let her know things were all right between them, and with good luck, Gabrielle would never learn about tonight's little adventure. Tomorrow. "I'll alert Helen and the king. They can work out a way to keep a close eye on that priestess. Gabrielle won't need to know unless we find proof that Saroni's up to no good." She considered this, sighed faintly. "Yeah, I'd rather handle it myself until I'm sure either way, but I can't spend all my time watching her." Nossis had surely dealt with suspicious guests before now; he'd be subtle, or the guards who kept an eye on her would be. The woman would likely never have a clue, whether she was cleared or until she was caught.

The warrior yawned and slipped out of her robe, tossing it over the nearest chair. The single candle burning near the door was enough light for her to see that Gabrielle still slept—in fact, it didn't look as though her close companion had moved at all. Xena smiled and eased down on the other side of the bed, settled her shoulders and closed her eyes.

Draco woke with a start as *Wode* heeled over sharply, turning his narrow bed into a slide; a fast grab at the low rail on the bulkhead side saved him a bruising crash to the deck, but wrenched his shoulder painfully. He rubbed his eyes free of sleep and cautiously sat up, one hand kneading outraged upper arm muscle, listening intently. Footsteps pounded down the deck and he could hear men yelling out there, then Habbish's infuriated roar over all. From here, he couldn't make out what anyone was saying, but he didn't need to, he thought grimly. Because, what else was it going to be? *Hammer* was back. Again. He dragged on his boots, caught up sword, bow, and arrow case, and eased out into the open.

The sky was barely brightened with day. He could make out nothing more than the darker shapes of islands against the horizon, and the thin red line of sun-to-come away to the east. Yelling and men flailing wildly overhead caught his attention briefly, but it was only the night guard coming down from the crow's nest. Habbish left off bellowing orders just long enough to level a finger at the two weaving figures and shout, "Both ye mons t'the mess! Angus, I swear I'll deal hard wi' ye later, do we survive this!" One of the two seemed to want to stay and argue the matter, but the other dragged him away. Neither was the least surefooted, and he could smell the reek of wine from where he stood as they staggered through the mess door.

Drunk, the warlord thought in disgust, and vaulted over the aft-deck rail, down to the main deck. *Hammer* wasn't as close as he'd feared, but it was a lot closer than it should ever have gotten. If those two had been *his* night guards, Draco knew, they'd be marked down for death right now. They would have. He didn't know what Habbish had in mind. *And it's possible you'd find reasons to keep them alive, and ways to make them grateful enough that they'd be two of the best guards you ever had.* He snarled and knelt to deal with the bowstring. Xena had tried to make him soft recently; he was becoming afraid that Gabrielle was going to succeed where her dark-haired companion had failed.

Habbish glanced his way as he strung the bow and draped the arrow case over his shoulder. "Good mon," the Celt snarled. "Same as last time, if ye don't mind—ye're t'best shot we have, and I want more fire on that sail; soon or late, they'll run out of patches for it!" Men swarmed up *Wode*'s mast in near silence, two emerging in the crow's nest, others inching their way out onto the spar where they settled in, awaiting orders. Habbish hissed

172

some order in his own tongue and held up an arm. Draco strode up the deck and took the stairs onto the high, aft deck by threes, then clambered onto the near-flat cabin roof, where half a dozen men awaited him.

From here, *Hammer* was close enough that he could make out the embers in the firepot, next to where the catapult must be, and the faint mast shadow cast by those embers. It was still dark enough that he couldn't make out the machine itself. And from the look of things over there, all the yelling aboard *Wode* just now hadn't alerted *Hammer*'s captain that the ship had been sighted. At least the sleek raider ship plowed on behind them, slowly narrowing the gap and there was no hint that the other ship's men were ready for even an active defense, let alone sudden offense. *This,* Draco thought with a grim smile, *could be amusing.*

The now familiar—and no more pleasant—smell of pitch assaulted his nostrils from two directions. Born on the wind from the enemy ship, and just behind him, where one of the ship's boys knelt in the shadow cast by the aft bulkhead behind the wheel, blowing on the small potful of embers. The boy must already have dropped the bits of sticky pitch into the pot because the smell was strong, growing stronger by the moment, and a pungent smoke was rising—a blue-black cloud that obscured the starboard rail.

Draco met the eyes of the middle-aged scrawny man on his right—an inept-looking fellow whose aim was the best of all the ship's archers—and nodded briefly. Korvin nodded in reply, then leaned toward the man on his right, whispering quietly. Men began to ease forward along the roof, then, one at a time, to light the wadding on their arrows. Draco gestured; Korvin nodded; the arrows smoked and smoldered as *Wode*'s men held them forward, below the edge of the roof, pointed toward the aft deck where *Hammer*'s men could not yet see them.

It was a tricky business, Draco knew from the hard

173

experience of two such fights. Light the things too soon, and the arrow shaft went up in flames and fell to ashes. Wait too long to light the wadding and the opportunity was past. At his low and cautious gesture, the men to his left leaned forward long enough to take fire from the men to his right; a sudden clap of hands somewhere near the mast, that was Habbish, giving the order. Draco scrambled to his knees, turned and drew down on *Hammer*'s sail, yelling out the count as *Wode* sank into a trough, then came smoothly out of it. Men slewed around to join him, and at *three!* a fiery hail of arrows arced from *Wode*; all but one sliced through the wind-filled sail. The last—his own—fell short of that, but exactly where he'd planned for it to go: into the broad-sided pitch pot.

Hammer's sail sprouted gouts of flame in half a dozen places where arrows had pierced it, and men scrambled to beat them out or pour water stored in the crow's nest and carried in pots out along the spar by men who had to fight the weight of such pots, as the sea tossed their ship about, with the wind, and the sudden shift in direction as *Hammer*'s captain gave the order to come about. The pitch pot shot flame nearly as high as the spar, and Draco grinned fiercely as frantic orders were shouted out, and men scrambled to catch hold of the pot's handle with long, hooked poles, and work to wrangle it overboard.

Habbish threw himself onto the cabin roof as the pursuing ship turned sideways, portside and away, wallowed into a trough, and abruptly fell out of the hunt. "Will do, for now," the captain allowed mildly. "It will take 'em a bit to put out t'fires and 'tis no laughing matter, hauling away t'pot when it's aflame." He gripped the warlord's forearm and laughed. "P'raps t'pot'll blow up and sink her, and serve 'em all right!"

"You know, it just might do that," Draco replied cheerfully. All around them, men were cheering wildly as *Wode* surged forward and *Hammer* fell far behind, flames still licking at her sails. Privately, Draco thought, it wasn't going to be anywhere near *that* easy. But a little celebration after beating off a sneak attack like that—yeah. That was almost as good as a final victory. *Until next time,* he reminded himself grimly. And probably, the time after that.

The sun was hours up on Crete: The long shadows were gone, the air warm, and the occasional gust of breeze from the south a welcome thing. The entire plateau echoed with the *clack!* of wood striking wood, the sound bouncing off arena walls, the high stone steps where the audience sat, echoed off the southern palace walls and the hillside.

Gabrielle had started by showing Newin the basic moves, just as Ephiny had once taught them to her, back in that Amazon village where she'd been given the privilege to learn fighting from the elite. Given right of cast. All of that despite Ephiny's grave misgivings about training an outsider—one who was obviously no fighter. *Well, I became one,* the bard thought briefly. She'd become queen of the Amazons, too—but this was no place to dwell on that.

Newin stood on the arena floor with her, Joxer sitting casually on a bench against the wall, next to one of the openings where bulls came from.

She knew they did, because she'd remembered to ask about the dark tunnels—and Newin had told her everything she could possibly ever want to know—and more—about the place.

Newin held himself just out of her normal reach, as she'd told him to. His arms tutors drew him a few paces further back as she explained a half-spinning move that was a feint one way, a sharp flip of the staff, and another change in direction that would fool almost any enemy, then executed it. The boy's eyes were wide and very bright; one end of a freshly cut and peeled and fire-hardened staff rested against the wood chip covered pavement.

The chips were her suggestion; a substitute for the needle-covered forest floor where she'd learned her staff skills. *So, in case I get too cute and dump the kid, at least he won't break his neck.* He might be a week getting all the splinters picked out of his skin, of course. But even that little exercise would make him more aware in the future.

All the same. It made her a little nervous; this was the Minos' heir, after all. His eldest son, except the youth wasn't really all that old. At least two years short of a beard, for sure. Still, one day he'd grow into that beard. Just like he'd grow into his father's throne.

Unfortunately, King Nossis didn't have anyone in his company of guards who'd ever trained with staff. And Xena was off doing something with Helen and the king, so. . . . *Well, so, you did okay with a grouchy and impatient Ephiny teaching you, and you didn't have anyone else to practice on, or watch her practice on. And you didn't break your neck, either. And let's face it, Gabrielle, that staff was your first serious weapon. This boy's had training in a lot of weapons before now.* She could almost envy the boy. His muscles were just possibly that much more aware than hers. *Sure. But he's learned in a cloister; you learned at Xena's side, fighting when the alternative was to get killed.* Well, the boy didn't need to hear that from her. She hoped at some point he'd hear it from his weapons tutors, though. Really clever kings learned when to delegate.

She ran a very basic set of moves, ran them slower, then slower yet, finally nodded. Newin, his eyes very wide, stepped away from his tutors and executed the same set: even slower, of course. A little sloppy in places. Still: "Not bad—in fact, that was really good!" she said enthusiastically. And meant it.

Newin flipped the staff back under his arm, trapping it between ribs and biceps, just as she'd done. He looked less pleased than she'd expected—of course, the king's heir was probably used to cheering from his tutors, whether he'd earned it or not. "Really?" he asked uncertainly.

"Really," Gabrielle assured him. "Now—one thing you need to do right from the start? Bend your knees—like this." He copied the move. "Because your legs are stronger than your arms. You move the staff with your arms, but most of the strength of those moves comes from your legs and how you push off. You get a *lot* of the thump in your hits from leg muscle. Okay?"

He took a moment to think about this before he nodded, and suddenly smiled. "That makes good sense. I will remember."

She watched him copy her through a series of individual maneuvers, then a series of mixed maneuvers, then took him on, carefully and at half-speed, through an actual staff-on-staff practice. He stuck with her, staff smacking against hers just the way it should, again and again. Half again faster, and he managed almost everything as well. He looked disappointed when she finally flipped the staff back under her arm and stepped away from him.

"That's all?" he asked wistfully. Gabrielle smiled.

"Trust me, Newin. You've used muscles today that you don't know you *have*. But you'll know what they are and exactly where by this time tomorrow."

"Oh." He grinned. "Tomorrow? My sword master tells me a new muscle skill needs two days in a row of practice to begin with, because otherwise a man—ah, I mean—" His eyes moved over her slender form, the snug green top and the brown skirt that allowed for easy movement, but didn't cover much of her legs.

"Man is okay," Gabrielle assured him with a grin.

He had the good graces to blush. "Well—a *person* feels crippled by the third day."

"Your sword master got that one right," Gabrielle replied. "Been there, done that. But we won't let you stiffen up like that, Newin. Tomorrow, same hour, right here. We'll try it again, okay?"

To her surprise, he didn't look so embarrassed, all at once, and he actually gave her the kind of deep bow that was usually reserved for nobility—from the commons. *Maybe his sword master or one of his other weapons trainers had taught him that the one who knows all the moves when you're learning—well, that it's the same kind of rank difference. Master to apprentice, or something like that.*

It still felt silly, being on the receiving end of such a bow. She returned the courtesy in full and waited until he was moving out across the pavement, Joxer at his side and the two of them talking enthusiastically, then turned to find the water jug. It was noticeably warmer than it had been when they'd started, and the sun was approaching midday in a clear sky.

The water jug was nearly empty and what was left was warm and stale tasting. "That's okay," Gabrielle told herself. "I'm too warm, and I could use food." And there went Joxer, off with Newin. Figures, she thought and was surprised to find herself somewhat irritated. She laughed. "Yeah, like you want *Joxer* hanging all over you today— or tomorrow! Or—yeah. Like any time soon? Right."

The tutors were making their way across the pavement toward the barracks, and there wasn't anyone else in sight. "Wonder when the next meal is?" Maybe there would be food in the rooms she and Xena shared. Likely, there would be, though it still amazed her how things just— appeared in there. As if the servants knew when she and Xena weren't around, scurried in to clean everything up, deliver fresh clothing, fresh food, a new jug of water, and chilled cider for her, then vanish before either woman returned. No matter how long they were gone—or not.

You'd think they'd have to be somewhere close by, just—just watching to see when we go out. There was a spooky thought to give her nasty dreams. Servants—un-

178

seen ones—lurking and keeping track of her every move. "Yeah, sure. Get a grip." More likely, whoever came by to change linens and set out fresh drying-cloths and food listened at the doorway first, and if they heard voices, they went away. If either woman had been around when food was brought, the person bringing it would simply have tapped on the door and passed in the tray. "Probably Xena took this morning's tray in herself, did you ask her? No. Anyway, that sounds a lot better," the bard decided. "Because the other sounds creepy, a lot like spying, and I can't imagine a sweetie like Nossis doing anything like that."

Somehow, she wasn't surprised when a throaty, dark voice answered her. "Good thinking, Gabrielle. Though it isn't just Nossis or his people. Remember, the palace itself has its own life." Gabrielle sighed quietly and turned to look at where the voice was coming from. Xena stood in shadow at the base of the half circle of theater seats, a chilled jug in one hand, a heavy looking cloth sack in the other. "Hey, you're getting better," the warrior said with a raised eyebrow.

"Something here is *better*?" Gabrielle demanded, but she was smiling.

"Yeah. You didn't jump, you didn't cuss me out, and you didn't turn funny colors. Like you're keeping in mind it might not always be *me* that's sneaking up on you."

"Like you're that sneaky, Xena," the bard began. Xena laughed, settled on the lowest riser, and patted the stone bench. "Remember I got you on the nose with my staff, fair and square—"

"Sure you did. It still hurts. And, yeah, I can be that sneaky; you're just getting better at second-guessing me. Now—there's a scary thought."

"You're telling *me*," Gabrielle replied flatly, but when Xena eyed her blankly, the bard laughed. Xena chuckled.

"Hey. Just so happens I can second-guess you, too. I brought food and something to drink." She held up the jug, which gurgled agreeably. "I thought you could use it about now."

"You thought right," Gabrielle said firmly and went to join her. A gesture of the staff took in the jug. "I sure hope that's water, though . . ."

"Fresh from the cisterns," Xena assured her, and unfolded the cloth to reveal bread, a slightly mashed wooden tray of sliced meats and cold pickle, and two smaller cloths that held mixed bunches of ripe fruit.

The women were quiet for some time as they portioned out the food and ate. Gabrielle finally drained her cup and settled back cross-legged on the riser. "Thanks, I needed that. But, I thought you were gonna be inside all day, helping the king and his council?"

"Yeah," Xena replied gloomily. "I was. And I will be, probably so far past dark that—never mind. I had to get outside because I was falling asleep." She scowled at Gabrielle, who clapped a hand over her mouth to silence spluttering laughter. "What?" she demanded.

"Xena, I thought this was the kinda thing you used to live for. Planning, strategy, tactics? What—it's not fun any more? Doesn't get your creative juices—?"

"Leave my creative juices out of it," Xena growled, though her eyes were amused. "I'm just used to working inside a tent, or out in the open, where the air can get to you. That deep in a stone building, all those windows shutting out the breeze—it might as well be a tomb," she finished sourly. Gabrielle gripped her companion's wrist. "What?"

"Don't say things like that," the bard insisted.

Xena chuckled. "C'mon, Gabrielle. You don't believe those kinds of stories, where people call down bad things on themselves just by thinking they might happen?"

"No," Gabrielle said firmly. "I'm remembering this is Crete, and any place that can have something like that dancing floor could just have other things that will jinx you. Or things like what you've told me about the Maze—

except I don't want to know about that. Just—indulge me, okay?" Her eyes went wary as Xena leaned back on her elbows and smiled at her. "What? What did I say?"

"Nothing much," the warrior drawled. "Except it's funny, because in a way I am indulging you."

"Yeah," Gabrielle replied, her eyes narrowing suspiciously. "Tell me about it, before I start laughing with you."

"You wanted to explore, right? The king needs someone to go to the top of the mountain and look around. Just in case Menelaus does attack Knossos and we need an escape route in that direction."

"And—he doesn't know anything about the top of the mountain? An island this size? You're kidding me, right?"

"Gabrielle," Xena said patiently. "He's a nice guy, and he seems to be a good king—and he doesn't look like he was ever good at a long uphill hike, not even at Newin's age. What do *you* think?"

Gabrielle shrugged. "I think you're right about that, he probably doesn't have one hard muscle in his stomach or his arms. But he's a king, he doesn't need that because he's got all these guards and—"

"His father, the old Minos, knew the top of that mountain as well as I know the scratches on both sides of my chakram, Gabrielle. Even though he wasn't much more of a muscle boy than his son."

Silence, as the bard considered this.

"That doesn't matter. What does is that no one from the royal house has gone to the top of the mountain for a long time—not and paid any close attention to anything but the view. Sure, Newin's been up there, but I talked to him this morning, early; he doesn't even have a clue that the little temple on top of the mountain can be used to call up the Greek gods."

"Temple. It—looks like a temple?" Gabrielle asked quietly.

"It *feels* like one, or so I've heard. You'll do better with that than I ever would, Gabrielle. And you've been with me long enough; you know how to see good places to hide, places to plan an attack."

"Xena—I have a little bit of a feel for battle fields," Gabrielle said urgently, quietly. "I never claimed to be *you*."

"I know. I never claimed to accept the gods most of our people worship. This blinds me to some aspects of their power that you can see, Gabrielle. So, maybe you can figure out something the Cretans haven't yet. Which is just how far down the mountain the Greek gods can come, before the local gods stop them."

"You—actually think I could tell something like that?"

"Gabrielle, I don't know. I just know you'd do a better job than I would. Or than Joxer would." The women exchanged tired glances; the warrior sighed wistfully. "Except Joxer isn't available to help us because he's gone *fishing*! With Newin—or so they tell me."

"Xena," Gabrielle replied warmly. "I promise you that you and I will go fishing at *least* once before we leave Knossos. All right? And I'll find out where all the best places are, before we go. Fair?"

Xena shrugged.

"Especially if I take on this mountain for you and the king this afternoon, and see what I can learn up there?"

For reply, Xena bent down and came up with another cloth-wrapped bundle: bread and a clay jug of fruit spread for it, dried meat strips, dried grapes, a leather jug of water.

Gabrielle sorted through this, carefully retied it, then met her close companion's amused gaze with a narrowed one of her own. "You—Xena, you knew I'd do it!"

The warrior opened her eyes very wide.

"Xena! You know, one of these days, I'm not going to be transparent little Gabrielle anymore, and then *you*—!"

"Gabrielle, you haven't been *that* in a long time. A really long time." Xena jumped to her feet and hauled the bard upright. Her hands were warm on the younger woman's hard biceps. "You've got a couple hours to spare up there for looking around and exploring on your own, if you start now. Keep a special eye out for someplace to hide Helen, if there's need."

Gabrielle froze, then turned to stare at the warrior, who eyed her levelly in reply. "Xena? Let's get something straight, here. If Menelaus comes to Crete with an army and makes it all the way up to Knossos *and* invades the palace? Do you really think a small cave or a ditch covered in dry brush is going to save her, even if it's a long climb up there?"

Xena shook her head; her eyes were grave. "Frankly, Gabrielle, I don't know what to think right now. Except I'm gonna be really envious of you, an hour or so from now." She ruffled the younger woman's bangs, and grinned as Gabrielle sighed gustily and combed them down smooth with her fingers. "Get going, okay? Dinner with the family again tonight."

"Great. I think." Gabrielle hoisted the pack over one shoulder and settled the staff in her right hand. Halfway across the pavement, she turned. Xena was already out of sight. *Great,* the bard thought sourly. She was still muttering under her breath as she strode into the shadows of the small olive grove, on her way up the slopes of Mt. Idhi.

11

Not many moments later, she quit muttering: it took wind she didn't have, because the trail was steep near the base of the mountain, and it was hot and windless. The displeasure lingered. *Why do I have the feeling Xena came up with this little hike so I wouldn't be around this afternoon? Say, in case she wanted to corner Saroni?* She stopped abruptly, smacked the staff end hard against the path. "Okay, think it through," she ordered herself, and reached for the water bottle. A quick swallow; she capped the jug and slipped the strap over her shoulder, turned back to gaze down at the palace, eyes narrowed.

"All right," she told herself finally. "Maybe she has. But Xena doesn't lie to you—okay, she used to, when she thought you couldn't handle the truth, or when she thought what you didn't know would keep you safe. She quit doing that a while back, remember? And the one time, when she killed Ming T'ien and said she hadn't . . ." She swallowed, forcing herself to concentrate on T'ien only—nothing else that had happened at the time. "I found out anyway. Eventually. She doesn't lie to me, and anyway, I don't think she could, and me not know."

Besides, if Xena wanted to interrogate Saroni, she'd simply do it, whether Gabrielle was there or not. Gabrielle sighed heavily and turned back to start toward the summit once more. "And I'd have to let her. Because it's not about Saroni, or me—it's Helen." If Saroni was what she seemed, the woman would surely understand once it was safe to explain things to her. "And if not—well, then it's her problem and not mine. Or Xena's."

She stopped again. "I could go back, get Saroni, bring her with me—no, that wouldn't work either." If Apollo was seeking his missing priestess, he'd find her atop Mt. Idhi. Saroni wouldn't go anyway. If she knew about Crete, surely she knew about the mountain. Gabrielle shook her head wearily and went on. "Yeah. This whole adventure has been so insane! There is no way I am *ever* going to be able to get it onto a scroll!"

Maybe later, when the exasperation level has dropped. "Right. Maybe."

Once she passed the high point she'd reached the day before, the path became much easier to follow. It was narrower, and seemed to be less used, but it was still a clear space flanked by thick grass and wildflowers, or wind-bent brush. Here and there, small stretches of forest shaded the way, and she was grateful for them. The afternoon stayed hot, and the breeze had died away to nearly nothing.

The peak wasn't far above the last copse of trees, most of them wind broken, leaning to the north as if most winds here came from the south. Few of them were much taller than she, though by the size of the trunks, they were fairly old. Lower down, there had been hunting birds, small animals—all the usual calls and rustlings in the undergrowth that she'd expect. Here, it was very quiet. Unnerving, except there wasn't any real cover where anyone—any *thing* could be hiding.

She considered this as she emerged onto scrubby grass, hesitated as she looked around. Then laughed. "Yeah, sure," she jeered herself. "Someone just happens to be waiting all the way up *here*, just in case *you* decide to hike to the top. Right!" She flipped the staff up, out, back under her arm, turned slowly in place, then flipped the weapon forward and dug the end into the ground again and walked on.

The path wasn't as clear-cut, but she could still make out where the springy grass had been trampled down, and once she came over the lip of the high dell near the top, it was outlined in small, pale stones.

Gabrielle glanced at the sky and nodded in satisfaction. It hadn't taken her that long to reach the top. "Helen was right, you could make it up and back in a day, easy." She had plenty of time to explore, take note of the terrain and look everything over. "And, hey," she reminded herself. "You don't have to plan things out yourself, never mind what Xena said about your eye. You look around, you remember what things are like and where they are, and you tell her. Then *she* works out a plan." She frowned. "Too bad I wasn't thinking ahead; should've brought a scroll with me to make a map on."

Well, if the king didn't have some kind of map of the top of his own mountain, she and Newin could probably come up with one since he'd been up here often. Helen could help, too. Gabrielle fished in the pack Xena had put together for her, drew out a stick of dried meat, and, chewing happily, strolled down into the bowl-like circle of grass.

It wasn't actually all the way to the top, she realized some moments later. The path took up on the far side of the dell again, heading up a broad, gradual ravine practically roofed over by windblown bushes. Bright red berries gleamed here and there overhead, where sun touched them. No birds fought for them—she couldn't hear the least sound except, just possibly, the surf far below. "If I

186

were a bird, I bet I wouldn't want to come this high up, either. One good gust, and there goes your nest and all the eggs." If there weren't birds, there wouldn't be the kinds of animals that preyed on nests. Or anything bigger.

The upper end of the ravine climbed at a steeper angle, but at some point the slabbed stones had been worked into steps, and there were handgrips on both sides. She clambered out of this and into another dell—this shallower and oval-shaped: not so wide, north to south, but long, and at the far end from where she stood, backed by a final sharp climb to the summit. "Climb—hah," she told herself. It was one of the least appealing fingers of stone she'd ever seen, and that was without remembering the long drop just to the plateau, never mind down to the sea.

But there shouldn't be any need to go higher: The hut that stood close to the eastern buttress must be the temple Xena had mentioned. It didn't look much like a temple—more like a simple stone hut. Except that there was no chimney, and heavy-looking slabbed shutters covered window-sized spaces along the two walls she could see. A door stood ajar, and that was extremely thick and fixed with heavy mounts for an inner bar.

Save the temple for last, she told herself, and walked all the way around the lip of the grassy depression. North, the ground sloped away gradually, and she thought there might be caves just down from the dell. Something to ask Newin. South—after one look down off the south side, she stayed prudently back from the lip. There was plenty of brush behind the hut—or temple—and, around a jumble of stone, she could just make out a very faint trail, leading down and veering away west. Maybe the way to reach those caves. Another thing to ask Newin. "Maybe it's a way down to someplace on the east side of the island—where it's all wild, if Joxer was right about that."

"Funny," a soft masculine voice said from just behind her, "for once the uncoordinated idiot is right about something."

After the heart-stopping moment of shock, Gabrielle was pleased to note that she'd neither jumped nor yelped. *Xena sneaking up on me all the time is good for something.* She schooled her face to an utter lack of expression, turned on one heel, and looked up into the all-too-familiar face of the Greek god of war.

She smiled then, a thin turn of lips that did nothing to warm chill blue eyes. "You know, Ares," she remarked pleasantly, "if I didn't know any better, I would begin to think that you've give up on Xena and started following me around." As she'd hoped, this caught him off guard— probably he was already confused by her lack of reaction to his sudden appearance. "Now, we both know I'm no Xena when it comes to fighting, and I don't think I'm exactly your type when it comes to other—ah—sports. So! What's your game here?"

His eyes flicked away from her, then back; he ran fingers through the neat little beard. *Gotcha,* she thought. He smiled in turn, and looked just as friendly as she felt. "Game? Hey, Gabrielle, this is where the action is lately— out here in the Aegean, right? And since I can't just show up in Knossos, and since Xena doesn't seem that anxious to come up here and talk to me. . . ."

"I don't make a good messenger, either," Gabrielle inserted neatly as he paused for effect. "You wanna tell her things, you tell *her.*"

"No, I've noticed that," he replied dryly, and now his eyes kindled with amusement. "That you make a lousy messenger, I mean. You been forgetting a lot of things lately, haven't you?"

Gabrielle's smile was gone, her eyes narrow as she took a step forward and glared up at him. "You know, I was asking Xena about that. But now I'm thinking why? When all I have to do is get to the source, right? Because she told me about too much of that seasick goo making people violent and that *you* claimed to be responsible for the stuff." He smiled faintly and shrugged, but seemed to be pleased with himself. "So, what about all the things I've forgotten lately? Was that Lethe? Or you? Because of that stuff I was smearing on my bread each morning?"

"Stuff's got funny effects on some people," Ares allowed.

"Yeah, real funny: A bard forgetting things, I'm laughing, Ares." He grinned. She shifted her grip on the staff, and he raised an eyebrow.

"Hey, put the damned little stick away, you think you're *even* gonna get close to me with that? Sure, so what? The stuff fuzzes up your memory."

"And you never bothered to let anyone know that? Like, the woman who created the stuff for you, back on Melos?"

He laughed cheerfully. "Hey—know what?" He leaned close to her and whispered, "I forgot about that part." Half a breath later, he jumped back, just as Gabrielle's staff slammed into the ground where one booted foot had been. "What? That was a *joke*, okay?"

Silence.

"You really could stand to lighten up," he said earnestly. "A tenth of Xena's talents and all of her attitude does *not* make a good combination, and it's a *real* bad look for you."

"Yeah," Gabrielle spat. "I'm *really* sorry you disapprove."

Another silence.

She turned in place slowly, looking all around the dell, then came back to him. "So, what gives with this place? I mean, if the old gods of Crete could kick all the Greek gods off the island, why let you have this much?"

"Hey," Ares said shortly. "That's Dad's kinda business affairs, I do *not* get involved in Dad's politics, okay? If I ever decide I wanna suicide, maybe I'll start sitting in on council sessions and get *bored* to death. What?" He asked in an aggrieved voice as Gabrielle started laughing.

"Nothing—just funny. You and I have something in common after all."

"More than you might think," he mumbled—or she thought he did. But when she frowned and gestured for him to repeat the comment, he merely shrugged and turned away from her.

He's up to something, Gabrielle thought warily, and hoped it was true the gods couldn't read your thoughts. *Maybe if I can find out what—somehow?* Keep him here a little longer, she decided. Ares was such a peacock, he couldn't resist talking if he thought he had an appreciative audience. Well—he seemed to act like that around *her* a lot, anyway. An unnerving half-memory surfaced. *He didn't really try to kiss me on Lethe, did he?* Well, she was herself up here, and if he tried anything like that, he'd find out just how fast she could swing that staff. *I clonked Xena one on the nose; I can land one on him.* But she'd been quiet too long—at least for what Ares expected of her. His eyes were wary and thoughtful as he looked over one shoulder at her. "So—you're not involved in this whole search for Helen, huh?" she asked finally.

"Gabrielle," Ares said with heavy patience. "If I had cared one way or the other, Menelaus woulda had Helen the day after he landed at Troy."

"Well—okay," she conceded. "Maybe. But since Aphrodite gave her to Paris, and *she* was on the side of the Trojans . . . ?" *Oops,* she thought, and bit back a smile. The skin over the god's cheekbones went red and tight. Ares didn't seem to like being reminded of his giddy sister's role in the whole mess. Or maybe it was just that Troy in general gave him a pain. "Ares, I'm just saying that it's bardic tradition. *You* know. One of Zeus' offspring decides to set some plan in motion, and the others don't get to interfere directly."

"Yeah," he scoffed. "Shows what *you* know, Gabrielle. It's like—rules in a knife fight."

"Huh?" She stared. "*What* rules in a knife fight?"

He gave her an evil smile. "My point. So," he added softly, and closed the very small distance between them, "tell me. What's going on down there, and what's Xena up to?"

"Not a chance," Gabrielle said firmly, then swallowed, hard, as the god of war gripped her jaw. There was a *lot* of muscle behind that grip. "Hey, okay, don't break anything! Joxer's on this stupid quest, we got blown off course after Rhodes—and don't try to tell me you didn't know *that*!—and we stopped here because the ship came out closer to here than Egypt, and everyone knows how well the Cretans treat their guests." He didn't look fully convinced, but his grasp eased. She pulled free and stepped back out of his immediate reach. "Thank you! For your information, there is *nothing* wrong with seven-course dinners, and fresh cherries on a tray in your room, okay? And this way, at least for a couple of days, we're keeping stupid Joxer from bumbling around the Aegean and actually finding Helen because he *tripped* over her!"

The god of war contemplated her for some moments. He smiled again, the closest thing she'd seen to a genuine smile on the god's face. "Nice try, Gabrielle. And you know what? I appreciate loyalty in a fighter and an ally—oh, don't say it, not my ally, Xena's. But I know where Helen is. She's hiding in Knossos. She's been up here several times. And I also know *why* she's been up here. Secret's safe with me, okay?"

"Sure," Gabrielle retorted. "Try again."

"Hey—think about it."

Silence.

He paced a few steps from her, turned back. "I already told you, if I'd been on Sparta's side, Helen woulda been back in Sparta, locked in her apartments, the war wouldn't ever have gone that far. *I* didn't send Paris to Sparta, anymore than I saw to it that Menelaus married her—it's not my kinda scene. And Troy wasn't that good for me.

If no one really minds—including you, Gabrielle—I would like to put the whole mess *far* behind me." She shook her head, confused. He smiled faintly. "Oh, don't get me wrong. War's great, I like it a lot. No surprise there. But I don't appreciate a stupid war, fought badly and for too long, *and* for the wrong kinds of reasons. That's leaving out half my dysfunctional family changing sides every other day! Something like that can get a war god in all the wrong kinds of stories."

This was a surprising side of Ares, Gabrielle thought. Probably trying to manipulate her from another angle. But, if not. . . . *Go with it,* she told herself nervously. "What—you don't want to be cast as the buffoon in someone's epic telling of the Fall of Troy?"

"What do *you* think?" he snarled.

Silence.

His eyes stared past her, seeing something not on this mountaintop, she thought. "Yeah—Troy. Heroes on both sides acting like selfish jerks, and who's in charge? Paris—Prince of Troy and a soft young idiot who couldn't see anything in a woman but how *pretty* she was! Menelaus—yeah, the same take on women, but otherwise, the man was an unimaginative jerk. I did *not* need to be caught in the middle of a war between those two."

Silence.

"If I had been running things, that war woulda been over in ten days, not ten years. It woulda been fought *clean*, too. And not over a woman."

"Ares—we will never agree on this one," Gabrielle replied flatly. "There is no such thing as a 'good' war."

He eyed her; raised an eyebrow in mild surprise. "You got one thing right: We're not gonna agree."

He shrugged.

"You ask me, Menelaus deserves everything that happened to his brother, Agamemnon, after Troy. He won't get it from me, though. Any more than I'll deliver Helen to him. I'm outta this one, all the way. Got me?"

"Whatever," Gabrielle said. It was the most seemingly approachable she'd ever seen him. *Go for it*, she urged herself. "Listen, though. I mean, it's not like you don't owe me—"

"Oh, yeah?"

"Yeah. That seasick goo, for starts."

"We're even on that. You found Xena on Lethe and got her away before she was a permanent addition to the landscape, didn't you?"

"Only because *you* wanted her back!" Gabrielle snapped. "This is—just listen, all right?"

His lips twitched.

"What—you have something important to do right now? Like go harass Sisyphus down in Tartarus, or hang out with Aphrodite?"

Silence. He eyed her sidelong. Finally, when she'd nearly given up. "Go ahead. I'll listen."

"It's—it's this priestess. Saroni. From Rhodes."

"Old business. I know about Saroni, Gabrielle."

"She's not happy serving Apollo. She—well, who can figure some people?" Gabrielle said with a faint, forced laugh. "She's got this—*thing*—for you."

He shrugged. "Yeah? So? So she's got better taste than you *or* Xena. I know about that, too. You done?"

"No! I'm just saying, either your brother's pissed off at her, or Avicus is—that priest of his in Sparta, you know? She needs a break—"

"Fine. Good for her. Not with me, though."

"Ares," Gabrielle overrode him sharply, and he stared, visibly surprised. "Look, all I'm saying is, let her see you, let her pitch her line about serving you, what's the big deal? Ask me, she takes one look at you and passes out cold, and so much for the new head priestess of Ares. But at least she'll know it won't work, and why. And she's okay with looking somewhere else."

Ares looked bored. "Gabrielle, enough. I said I'd listen. Now. *You* listen. There is only one woman I'd ever have to serve me, and that's Xena." His mouth quirked. "Unless *you're* interested, of course."

She suddenly couldn't remember how to breathe; the god of war's very wide eyes were fixed on hers, his lips soft, and entirely too close to hers. . . .

He's doing it on purpose, Gabrielle thought angrily. "Nice," she snarled. "It's a joke, right?"

"Oh yeah—a joke."

"Terrific. I'm *really* laughing."

He laid a hand on her shoulder, snatched it back as she shifted her grip on the staff. "Oh, hey, don't hurt me," he murmured; he seemed to be fighting laughter. "The real joke is *you* trusting that priestess. Saroni, remember? Because of who she serves—"

"Ares," Gabrielle broke in sharply, "yours is hardly a recommendation I'm gonna trust! Besides, she's not Apollo's any more."

"You're sure about that? Gabrielle, maybe you happen to remember bardic tradition about my drunken, twisted brother, Apollo? Saroni's been with him long enough, she's capable of being just as twisted."

Silence.

Ares turned away and slammed one fist into his open palm. "My goldenboy brother who pulls in all these worshippers and all these dinars, and why? Because he came up with the perfect gimmick! And it's so simple, all you need is a smelly steam vent and a seeress—"

"*Seer,*" Gabrielle snapped. "Or do you say *bardess,* too?"

"Daydalus, Deedulus, whatever! You show up with a dinar or so for an offering, ask your question, and this— seer*person*—takes a seat over the steam and gives you the answer. And it's so convoluted, you need another seer-*person* to interpret it. But hey, it all comes out in the end, however it works out, the answer's vague enough, if you wanna believe, you can make it fit."

"Don't tell me you're jealous, Ares."

"Jealous of a used-vision seller? Don't make me laugh, Gabrielle. I'm just reminding you who your new friend serves. Apollo's a drunk and the best manipulator in the whole family—that includes Dad, by the way."

She eyed him in visible disbelief, and he laughed shortly.

"Yeah, well you haven't met either of them, have you? I hope for your sake you never do, Gabrielle."

"I—" She swallowed, managed a smile that seemed to catch him off guard. "Hey. Maybe I'm not too worried about that, because you know what? I've gotten a long ways away from squealing and running—if I ever did anything like that. Maybe I'd just do what your brother's dryad shoulda done. Give him a knee where it counts most."

The god of war raised both eyebrows. "Ouch," he murmured.

Gabrielle sighed heavily and cast her eyes up. "Why are we having this conversation? Look, forget it, Ares. I'm just asking. And just because you think Apollo is a jerk doesn't mean everyone who serves him or believes in him is a jerk!"

Ares gazed at her blankly for a long moment; finally, he leveled a finger at her nose and smiled. "You know what?" he murmured. "You're not as dumb as you look, Gabrielle!"

"Oh yeah?" she snarled. "Well, maybe you're not as—!" She wasn't sure how she meant to finish the sentence; it didn't matter. With a flare of light and a vibrating *twang* that set her teeth on edge, the god of war simply vanished.

"Great—I think." She drew a deep breath, let it out, then spun on one heel and furiously slammed the end of her staff into the ground. "He! Is becoming! *Annoying!*" Another slam. "And I am really, really tired! Of being *annoyed!*" She buried the staff end wrist-deep in damp turf. No response from Ares, of course. She ran the staff through a hard series of maneuvers, shouting wordlessly each time she lunged, repeated the series until her fury began to fade.

"So, I wonder what *he* got out of that?" No information she hadn't wanted him to have—she didn't think. "Ahhhh—forget it."

But realistically, it had to be similar to her other recent encounters with Ares. Between him trying to act seductive and her trying to keep him off balance. "I don't get it! What does Saroni *see* in him?" Ares would have so much fun messing with the woman's mind. "She wouldn't even be a challenge! I mean, he can still get *Xena* going!"

Except Xena gave back as good as she got, most often. Gabrielle sighed and let her eyes sag shut briefly as she ran through the odd conversation. "Okay, you did fine." Better yet. *You hit him in his ego, more than once, and he didn't fry you on the spot.* That made it a victory, in her scrolls.

She let out the last of her fury in a gusty sigh, then blinked and gazed out to the south. The sky was noticeably a deeper blue, and a faint, westerly wind soughed over the so-called temple, whistling through the rocks. "It's late," she murmured in surprise. Somehow, a *lot* of time had gotten away from her since she'd stepped into this high dell. She'd be lucky to get back down to the palace grounds before full dark—if she made it halfway down the mountain. *Remember, Helen's been up here a few times, so she probably can make it down after dark. This is your first trip*, she warned herself firmly. Maybe the only one. Especially if she fell. A broken ankle would be the best possible outcome. More likely, she'd break her neck, or take one long last step leading to a long, *long* drop to the waves below. . . .

"Brrr!" She shook herself. "Let's not go there, all right?" Something like a vision, or a half notion, lodged itself in her thought; she shunted it aside. Better not to *think* of anything up here where Certain Beings could overhear her. *If* they could. Better yet—get herself down

196

and off the mountain, uninjured, and once she'd properly cleaned up and eaten, talk to Xena.

Xena will know what to do. She hadn't thought that in a long time; not with such a sense of relief. But things were getting complicated in all the wrong kinds of ways. Xena would, at the very least, know how to deal with a god of war who was showing all the wrong kinds of interest in her personal bard and close friend. "Go, okay? Think about things later," she ordered herself and started across the narrow dell.

But she stopped short of the lip: women's low voices rose from somewhere nearby—one deep and very familiar. Gabrielle peered down the deep ravine. "Xena?" she called softly; the sound still echoed.

"Gabrielle? You okay up there?"

"Yeah."

"Fine. Helen's with me."

She could see both women, at first only as darker shadows moving in shade, then Xena climbing up the steps, the scarfed Helen just behind her. Gabrielle stepped back and leaned against her staff.

The warrior waited until Helen joined them. After a cautious look around of her own, Helen shoved the deep-red scarf from her hair and indicated the temple, then pressed past Xena and walked rapidly toward it.

The bard eyed Xena, who shrugged. "She and I were talking after King Nossis gave up on his planning session. She wanted to come up here, show me something."

"Okay," Gabrielle said cautiously. "But she's gonna be missed down there, isn't she?"

"Change in plans," Xena replied. "You, I, and Helen are eating in our rooms tonight. That way, the king can invite Saroni and Briax to dinner as guests of the family, and they won't have any reason to suspect he has anything to hide."

Gabrielle shook her head. "Xena, I imagine most guests

don't get invited to dine with the king in that private room. So, why would either of them 'suspect' anything?"

"Because Briax believes in the quest he was given and probably assumes he'd be given full honors—and he'll know about the family dining from Joxer, by now."

"Don't tell me, let me guess; they've met."

Xena nodded.

"And, of course, Joxer was bragging—"

"I don't know that; I'd assume so, knowing Joxer. Anyway, forget that. Saroni. We don't really know anything about her, including how much she knows about Knossos."

"I—yeah. So, Helen is up here—who's taking care of the king's kids?"

"Even royal tutors get an afternoon off here and there; the children will eat with their father, like last night, but their old nurse will be there to keep an eye on them."

"Okay—I guess." The bard looked up suddenly. "Xena, are you saying that *Helen* has an idea for how to—?"

The warrior shrugged, her eyes moving across the plateau. "Gabrielle, I have no idea. She wouldn't say."

"Oh. Figures," Gabrielle muttered. "I hope I bored Ares enough just now that he isn't—"

"Ares?" Xena closed the distance between them, and gripped her friend's shoulder. "What was *Ares* doing here?"

"Sure, like I have a clue," Gabrielle retorted.

Xena rolled her eyes in heavy exasperation.

"Look—I really don't know what he's up to, why would I? This is Ares! You can tell he's lying because his lips are moving!"

"Him and everyone else in his lousy family," Xena muttered. "So. What did he *say*?"

Gabrielle shifted the staff to a place between her ribs and one arm and enumerated on her fingers. "Knows Helen's here on Crete; not interested in Helen, or what Menelaus wants with her; Still wants you for his. . . ."

Gabrielle!"

The bard's lips quirked. "That was a joke, Xena. Anyway, from what he said, and how he said it, he's not too proud of his part in the Trojan War—but hey, his lips *were* moving." She flexed the fingers, bunched them into a fist and glowered at it. "And if you have any suggestions for me on how to get him to keep his distance—like out of *touching* range? I'd really appreciate it, Xena."

To her surprise, the warrior chuckled. "Gabrielle, what? Ares is hitting on *you*?"

"What—that's so far off the mark?" Gabrielle demanded sharply.

Xena shook her head, but she clapped a hand over her mouth to hold in laughter; it spluttered out half a breath later.

"Xena, I realize I don't exactly look like you. But he's getting a little too close and a bit too friendly these days—did I mention Lethe when we talked last night? Forget Lethe. All I care about is getting him to go away without getting into the whole, 'Cut it out, or I'll tell Xena,' thing. All right?"

"Hey." Xena got control over her mirth with a visible effort. "You don't need that—but I know what you mean, Gabrielle. Hey, you can always try the reverse approach, it's worked for me."

"Huh?"

Xena cast her a wicked grin as she drew her friend along the dell, toward the small temple. "Act like you're so crazy for him you're about to start drooling. Then watch him run."

"Ah—okay. I could do this." Gabrielle tugged at Xena's armband. "Um," she asked in a small voice, "what happens if he doesn't run?"

"Then you get to clomp him one across the nose with your staff. You got me with it, didn't you?"

Gabrielle shrugged.

The warrior's smile broadened. "You saw him and me

fight back in that temple when the Furies were after me. He's not that much faster than I am—and you're a *lot* faster than you were back when we took out that giant."

"Hey." Gabrielle slowed as she thought this out; a delighted smile curved her lips until Xena tugged at her hair. Hard.

"We're up here because of Helen. Let's help her find a way to get Menelaus off her track for good, so she can get on with her life."

"Yeah—I know. And we can get on with ours, you're right. Maybe—we can get her the chance to let Nossis see how much she loves him," Gabrielle said finally.

Xena smiled warmly. "Saw that, did you? Last night during dinner, the way she looked at him? Well, Gabrielle, I'll tell you something. He's just every bit as much in love with her. But he won't tell her so."

"But—but that's—!"

"I talked to him earlier today—after Helen left us. But when I asked him why he didn't just say something to her, you know what he told me? He said, 'She is incredibly beautiful—but that's fate, or the gods. She didn't choose such beauty, and I would love her even better without it, being the plain man I am. She's kind and witty. Thoughtful. She not only knows how to make me happy, but she lets me see what will make her happy, and then allows me do such things for her—within the boundaries she set when she first told me she was Helen. She cares for my children—all of them, my heir Newin included. But no mortal man could ever dare bespeak the fabled Helen, never mind a plump little man of middle years and ruler only of a minor kingdom. And she knows nothing of how I feel. One day, my babes will outgrow the need for a tutor, and she'll be gone.'"

"Xena!"

"Yeah, I know, Gabrielle. He hasn't got a clue. I tried

to tell him, but he didn't believe me. And he made me swear I wouldn't say anything to her."

The least emphasis on 'me,' Gabrielle thought. She smiled grimly.

"Well, you know what, Xena? He didn't get that promise out of me! I know this isn't the time, but once we've found a way to defeat Menelaus and his priest—"

Xena smiled faintly and drew her friend on, toward the small temple that was now all in evening-shade. "Gabrielle, it's a good thought. Hang on to it, okay? And speaking of that—there's Helen. Probably wondering what we're up to, out here. Let's go."

Half a sea away, a pale-eyed priest leaned back from his gazing bowl and smiled in satisfaction. "Helen," he whispered. "My Helen. I'll come to you soon. How grateful will you be, I wonder, when I free you from Menelaus' obsessive eyes?" She'd be grateful, he thought. *She had better.* If not, she'd *learn* gratitude.

He turned away from the now dark bowl and gazed across the faintly lit grand reception hall, where he and Menelaus had interviewed so many foolish would-be heroes. Despite the gloom here, it could not yet be sundown. At this hour, Menelaus often retired to his apartments—to study, he said. To plan, to read his maps, to work out strategy against the local bandits. It all meant the man was sleeping, waiting for his dinner hour.

A smile twitched the priest's mouth, falling short of his pale intense eyes. "Waken him."

It would be good for the king, being torn from sleep as he himself so often was, on nothing more than a whim. But Menelaus wouldn't see this as whim: Helen found. At last. And sodden with sleep, the king wouldn't realize there was a good deal that his priest withheld.

"Wake him. Get him to immerse himself in planning an invasion. He won't have a spare moment, or any spare

thought to wonder what else the priest might be up to."
The priest smiled grimly, pinched out the candle that had
backlit his efforts at the bowl for the past hour or so, then
strode across the chamber to seek the main hallway, and
his lord's apartments.

12

Xena gripped Gabrielle's forearm and gestured with her chin, across the bowl where Helen awaited them. "You feel like keeping a queen waiting?"

"No worse than some *other* things I've done lately," Gabrielle muttered, but she started across the springy turf, the warrior beside her. Helen smiled as the women came up, then eased a small sack from her shoulder and held it out so the bard could look. "Apples, a flask and one of your cups, flowers—an offering?"

Helen nodded.

Gabrielle fished out one of the apples. "Nice. Very."

The woman's smile widened slightly. "I was always told that she takes any and all offerings. She claimed recently to not understand why I brought her fish, however, so—" She shrugged, indicated the ruddy fruit. She gestured toward the hut with her head. "We have to go inside, bar the door, or she can't come—or won't."

"Ah—maybe not," Gabrielle began. A slight, disorienting sound just behind her interrupted, and a high female voice overrode hers. "Apples! Oh, and, like, really *ripe* ones, too!"

Gabrielle bit back a sigh, met Xena's glance with a tired one of her own, and both women turned to face the goddess.

Aphrodite eyed Xena for a long, wary moment, then glanced dismissively at her companion. "Oh. You," she said. "Well, whatever. Apples and flowers, Helen?"

The dark woman nodded.

"No fish?" she warned.

Helen shook her head composedly.

"Great!" She beckoned. Helen dropped the loose apple in the sack and handed the whole thing over. Aphrodite gave her a brilliant smile. "Offerings always accepted, you know? Like, I'm sorry, but no way it's going to *get* you anywhere, but feel free to keep trying—" She yelped and jumped as light flared right beside her. Ares stood next to her, his hand on her shoulder.

Correction, Gabrielle thought; he had her in one hard grip. Aphrodite winced, freed herself with an effort. Ares grabbed again, this time snatching a long handful of hair and the strap of her inadequate pink bodice. Aphrodite glared up at him. He smiled back cooly.

"Hey," he said evenly. "Always a pleasure, but you know what? We gotta talk. Me and the lady in pink." Aphrodite tried to pull away from him—in vain. Ares winked at Gabrielle, raised an eyebrow in Xena's direction, and ignored Helen. "We'll get back to you," he said.

"As if!" Aphrodite began furiously. Ares tightened his grip, silencing her.

"Count on it," the god of war said—and they vanished.

Gabrielle dropped her staff, sat cross-legged on the grass, and drove both hands through her hair. "One—*more*—crazy thing!" she growled. "Just one!" She gripped two handsful of hair and tugged hard, closed her eyes, and began counting: ". . . eight minotaurs, nine minotaurs, ten—" She expelled a breath in a gust as Xena cleared her throat to get the younger woman's attention, then held out a hand to help her up. "Terrific. You got an explanation for any of that?" she asked.

"I'm not gonna try to work it out up here," Xena replied evenly. She glanced toward the hut, then the spot where Ares and his sister had just been. "Who knows which one of them is gonna show up next?"

"It's a point," Gabrielle said promptly, and led the way back down to level ground. Once they passed the second dell, she could hear Helen and Xena talking, but they were far enough back, she couldn't make out the words. "Fine with me! Well, for now," she muttered. She entertained herself the rest of the journey down with imagining the destruction if she had actually followed through on that vow to Aphrodite. If she had taken Joxer and that cute little bell on a tour of the goddess's temples. "Ring the bell, he turns into—yeah, some *kind* of fighter." Fast, deft, flashy—impressive all the way. Capable of wrecking everything in sight as a byproduct of thrashing two or three sword-wielding thugs, too. Including every single breakable offering brought to the Goddess of Love by her worshippers and supplicants.

Gabrielle smiled, dug her staff savagely into the dusty path and kept going.

The two women had a leisurely hour for bathing and a change of clothes before servants brought trays of food and drink. Helen arrived alone shortly after.

Dinner was a quiet, pleasant affair, with hardly any conversation. Helen seemed distracted and ate little. But as she stepped into the hall on her way back to the king's children, she turned and said, "I'm sorry about today, Xena. All that way for nothing."

"Don't worry about it," Xena told her. "It may prove useful." The woman merely gave her a sad smile, drew the scarf over her head, and left.

Xena gazed at the door for a long moment—or through it, the bard thought. She blinked then, filled her cup and leaned back. "This has gotta end—here on Crete. And now." She crossed one bare ankle over the other. "Tell me about it, Gabrielle. This afternoon, up there."

Gabrielle sighed deeply, finished her cider, and made a reasonably succinct story of it. Xena nodded thoughtfully when she finished. "Anyway, Xena, if you ask me, Ares is acting pretty darned weird, even for him. Involved, you know? Even if he's pretending he's indifferent to the whole mess."

"Mmmmm." The warrior was gazing into the distance.

"Ah—Xena?" Gabrielle leaned forward and waved a hand just short of Xena's face; the woman wrinkled her nose and lightly swatted the hand aside. "He-*lloooo*? Any-one in there?"

"I'm thinking, Gabrielle. And I just might have a plan—"

"Yeah? What?"

But Xena shook her head, her expression grave. "I need to think about it. Sleep on it, at least. As soon as I have something that makes sense—" She shook her head hard then, and smiled warmly. "As soon as I have an idea you can help me work out, you'll know about it, Gabrielle. You don't need any more loose ends, do you? Really?"

Gabrielle cast up her eyes.

"Thought so. About the king: I just remembered. He's taking me in the Maze tomorrow, early. You, too, if you're interested."

"Are you kidding? Who'd turn down an offer like that? But, Xena! I thought you said it wasn't safe!"

"It's not. Except the Minos goes through a ceremony, and he's okay in there, I told you that, right? And anyone he takes under his protection is ok, too. When they're with him, anyway. Except family's always all right, appar-ently."

Silence. Gabrielle finally shook her head. "Xena?" she asked in a small voice.

"Gabrielle?"

"I didn't get hard cider with dinner, did I? Instead of my usual fresh? Because I feel like my *brain* is spinning."

Xena laughed quietly and drew her friend to her feet. "You need sleep, Gabrielle. You had a long day, a long hike, and you got to play with Ares this afternoon. That all by itself would make *me* tired." She considered this as the bard raised her head and gave her a disbelieving look; Xena looked back, then burst out laughing. "Hey, did I say that? I said *play*! You fought him with words, okay?" She nudged Gabrielle with a gentle elbow; the bard gave her a sidelong, tired look, but a grin tweaked her mouth.

"You're getting pretty good with words yourself, Xena; that was a *low* remark." She smothered a yawn. "Tell you what. I refuse to let Ares ruin any more of my day. And you're right, I am tired." She yawned again. "You using the other side of that bed tonight?"

Xena shook her head. "I sleep better when I know where you are, Gabrielle. Feel free."

Two hours after sunset, at least a full day's sail north of the Cretan main harbor, it was dark, but not as dark as it had been moments earlier. The moon rose from behind Andros, less than full and veiled in thin cloud. It was enough, Draco thought with grim satisfaction, to make out *Wode*, anchored just around the easternmost point of Andros in a broad bay. The ship listed slightly, waves now and again shoving her stern east and bringing her more into a north-south line. Her mainsail hung loose, and he could just make out the shapes of men clinging to the spar, high above the deck, apparently hard at work on the thick canvas. If any of her oars were in the water, they weren't visible—and they would have been, thanks to the sharp angle of the new-risen moon and the long shadows cast by it. *Wode* was a ship visibly in trouble, and even if there were guards and watchmen posted, that ship wasn't going *any*where in the immediate future.

My idea. While he crouched on this high spur of land overhanging the sea, ten of the Gael's men huddled behind him. Habbish hadn't been wild about it, when Draco had asked about places like this bay—when he'd suggested a new strategy for dealing with the relentless *Hammer.*

He couldn't blame the old Celt, though. The ship was his baby, the men all his, and many of them had served him for years. And land fighting wasn't something Habbish knew. *You'd have been even less cooperative, if someone like Habbish had come up with some ship plan for your army.* The army he'd had—Hades, any of his armies. *Forget that.* He had more important things to think about. Because this maneuver was gonna work.

Some thoughts wouldn't go away, though: Such as Habbish's notion that the pursuing ship and her men belonged to Sparta. *It all seemed so damned simple when you went to Sparta, looked in that bowl, and agreed to quest!* Just the way the bards said such things worked. He was willing to bet Gabrielle had never run up against a convoluted quest like this one. One of the men with him touched his forearm.

"Sir," the man murmured. More a boy with a thin, red beard, the warlord thought; and the thought was depressing. "It's there—*Hammer.*" It was. All sails billowing in the rising wind, oars dipping in smooth rhythm. Draco held up a warning hand for silence. They could all hear the creak of wood as the long ship slid through the waves, and oars groaned in their locks. The warlord could just make out the deep, muffled boom of the drum that kept the oarsmen working together. He softly snapped his fingers for the attention of *Wode*'s men, then pantomimed pressing down on something. Men and boys moved crouching around him and took hold of the heavy, metal pry rods that had been worked into place hours earlier, when *Wode* had first dropped them here and moved on to anchor mid-bay, when most of the sailors had gone into the holds to shift the ballast stones just enough to give the ship a visible but nonfatal list.

Draco worked his way among the rocks and out the promontory. As he'd known they must, *Hammer* took the bait. *Either way,* he'd urged Habbish the night before. *Either he thinks you're in danger of sinking and have stopped for repairs, or he doesn't believe that. Either way, he'll know you can't escape because you're anchored out of the wind, at a dead stop.*

The watch crew would see the ship first; they'd be wildly excited, and with luck, that would carry the day. Even if the captain were as experienced as Draco—*Yeah. I'd still attack. Because it usually pays when you let your men's energy drive the attack.*

The one doubtful matter was just how *Hammer* would come after the Gael's ship. But after being fought off so many times, Draco was almost certain the other captain would hold his vessel near shore and out of sight until the last moment.

To his grim pleasure, *Hammer*'s captain seemed to be thinking the same way. The brief outcry from the crow's nest was abruptly silenced, and the drum muffled. The raider ship changed course, easing rapidly to port, two men hanging over the side in the bow and conveying messages by hand-signs, most likely being certain she didn't hit anything.

On deck, men scrambled quietly to fasten the catapult, others bringing the bucket of pitch balls from near the aft deck, still others settling into place along the rails, readying swords and bows. Through all of this, no one seemed concerned with the island itself, or the size of the overhang they were about to pass beneath. *True seaman,* Draco thought sourly, then rose to a half crouch, waited until the bow-sprit and the small foresail had passed beneath him, and signed sharply. Men leaned their weight on the bars and with an echoing, splintering crack, a section of stone broke free and hurtled toward the bottom of the sea.

Unfortunately for *Hammer*, most of her bulk was in the way.

The first fall of rocks shattered the foremast and tore away the bow rail. Draco threw his own weight onto the nearest pry bar and a massive boulder ripped loose to crash through the main deck, mid-ships. A second, echoing crash came hard after the first; a plume of water fountained high. The third fall of rock soared out beyond the *Hammer*'s starboard rail to send water high; pebbles clattered on the aft deck.

But the damage had been done; *Hammer* floundered. Men fought to get clear of the sail that covered most of the foredeck; the ship listed to starboard, and Draco could see and smell smoke. The burning pitch was somewhere under the thick canvas.

A stream of men erupted onto the deck from below; oars hung loose in the water. Sailors threw aside bows and arrows as they dove into the sea; others on deck and four men on the high aft deck shouted orders, but to no effect. Someone fell from what was left of the lines that had secured the mast as *Hammer* lurched over a few more degrees.

Half the men had already abandoned her; those who remained were working frantically to save the ship. *No chance,* Draco thought flatly; he hissed out an order of his own. Most of Habbish's men raced down to the boats they'd earlier pulled onto shore and out of sight, but he and two of Habbish's best fighters edged out onto the overhang, checked that all their weaponry was safely snugged down, then launched themselves onto the high aft deck.

As the warlord had hoped, the deck was largely deserted—more men had jumped overboard when it became clear the ship wasn't maneuverable any longer. His sudden arrival scattered more of them, but not *Hammer*'s captain. The man gave him a tight grin and drew his sword as one of Habbish's men took up a watchful stance near what was left of the mast. His companion sprinted over to the hatch ladder and shouted down, "Any of you who are slaves, and any who served the Greek Draco! He is here, to rescue you! Come above, you'll be given safe conduct!"

Draco smiled unpleasantly and brought up his blade. His opponent lost color abruptly, and began backing away. "Draco?" he whispered. Before the warlord could reply, the man reversed his grip and threw the long blade, turned, and dove overboard.

The warlord slapped the sword aside, looked out across the main deck, which was now occupied only by his two comrades, then glanced around him. Deserted, except for the man who lay sprawled against the aft bulkhead, just behind the wheel. Blood pooled beneath him and a large, jagged rock pinned his legs. Draco felt his throat for pulse—nothing. No answers here.

But it was time to go. The ship wallowed as waves slapped against the hull, then suddenly lurched sharply to starboard. Half a dozen men had come from the hold— ragged-looking, soaking wet men, barely clad, and none too steady on their feet. Some of them wore metal clamps around their ankles or waists that gleamed in the light of the rising moon. Slaves who'd been left chained to drown, down there. "No one else down there!" Habbish's man shouted.

If it turns out Menelaus is behind this—"Yeah," he murmured, and smiled. His eyes were still dark with anger. "Well, then. *He* doesn't get Helen, either. Whatever *she* wants!"

None of the slaves were men he recognized; none of them wanted to go on with *Wode*, either, and Habbish's man finally agreed they'd be put ashore at Naxos, that night.

The seven men who'd gone for the boats did what they

could to pull in prisoners, but most of *Hammer*'s crew evaded them and made shore, vanishing into high grasses and woods. Eventually, the boats returned to *Wode* with five men, including one of the officers. Draco himself made the captain his goal, but the man hadn't been seen by anyone after he dove over and after a long search of the water and the shoreline, he finally gave up and let himself be rowed back to *Wode*, his eyes on *Hammer*. The ship was already very low in the water, and as he watched, it slipped beneath the surface, where it settled, just the shattered tip of the mast showing in the wave-troughs.

Habbish was in good spirits, clapping his men on the back, ordering a round of ale for everyone, closely examining the prisoners and laughing grimly as he peered at the pale fragment of wood, now blue-white as the moon cleared the island and shone on the water where it lay. "Doubt any man'll try to up *that*," he chuckled. "What y'think, Draco, m'friend? Let 'em stew overnight in t'holds, or ask 'em things now?"

"Now," the warlord replied evenly. "And then we'll toss 'em overboard, let 'em find their way with the rest of the crew."

"Good plan," the Gael allowed. "But I'm no' so experienced at t'asking."

"Oh." Draco smiled briefly; his eyes smoldered as he moved over to gaze into five dispirited or downright frightened faces. "That's all right. I'm *good* at it."

It didn't take long—but it didn't help much, either. Captain Inada had kept his own council. Once the five had been dropped back into the sea, and *Wode* was on its way once more, Draco let Habbish lead the way to his cabin and settled gloomily into his regular chair. "If I thought any of them was lying—but they weren't; I can see it in a man's eyes."

"So she could've been Rome's or Egypt's or even been paid by t'Hittites," Habbish grumbled. He poured himself wine, added water, and shoved the ewer over where the warlord could reach it.

"Yeah. Except why would any of those have reason to follow *you* around out here?" Draco asked.

Habbish merely shrugged and drank his ale.

Draco sighed faintly, poured a dollop into his cup and drank. "You know what I'd really like, about now? I'd really like to talk to Xena about all this."

"Xena? After how she treated you back in Phalamys? Why?"

"Treated? Oh, yeah. Tossing me overboard. That's just her sense of humor, I'm okay with that. Because she's got the right kind of mind for a problem like this—all this. And she knows more about Menelaus than I do." He gazed into the empty cup, set it aside, and tugged at an earlobe. "Finding her, though. Yeah. She's probably halfway to Carthage by now. Or—whatever's east of Rhodes."

The old Gael grinned suddenly. "Well, if y'really want Xena, I know where she was, matter of a day or so ago. After we first took on *Hammer*, east end of Crete? Saw a ship at t'main docks as never goes to Crete—usual route is north-south, down to Egypt, up into Ionia. Through Rhodes. Was what took m'eye—*Yeloweh* so far off her normal course. Thing is, I'm most certain I saw Xena out on t'docks."

"Crete? Wait—" Draco shook his head. "If you could make out Xena—"

"She's fair unmistakable, even at distance." Habbish grinned.

"No fooling. Did you see a smaller woman? Little green top, lots of long, golden hair?"

"Too far t'make out color, but sun on hair like that, man couldn't mistake that. And certain, she wasn't wearing much."

"Crete," the warlord said thoughtfully.

"Thing is," Habbish went on, "woman like Xena'd be

welcome at t'king's palace; guests're a sacred business for 'em."

"She might figure on learning something there, anyway. You think she'd still *be* there?"

The Celt shrugged. "If not, we'll be able to find out which ship she took, and when." He poured himself ale and raised his cup in a toast. "And they'll even have a man like me as guest, if not in so fine a style. Man such as y'self'd be welcome, too."

Silence.

"Crete, then?"

Draco smiled, and nodded. "Crete."

Gabrielle woke early—before the sun was up. The room was cool, the palace even more silent than usual, and at her side, Xena slept peacefully, pale silk wrapped around her knees and one hand under her cheek. The bard smiled, then eased onto her back and closed her eyes again. *Something exciting: a dream?* She couldn't remember at the moment, but then she did. The Maze. Today, in just a few hours, she was going to be one of the very few Greeks who had *ever* been inside the fabled Maze and come out alive.

With that to look forward to, she wasn't sure she'd be able to sleep any more. *Think about a plan to get Menelaus off Helen for life,* she told herself. After several frustrating moments, though, she gave that up. *Xena said she has a plan. As long as it doesn't involve lots of killing, like so many of her plans do. . . .* But not this time: Xena knew how terrible Helen would feel if anyone else died.

Wonder if I can get Briax to move on, get him out of here before there's trouble? She fell asleep between one thought and the next and didn't awaken until Xena tugged at her hair.

"Hey, I said, anyone *in* there? Or do you want me to go through the Maze alone?"

Gabrielle sat up and yawned. Sun cast long shadows

outside the window, and she could see several people moving out there. "Thought you said the king has to take you or it's dangerous?"

"She remembers," the warrior said. "King Nossis is gonna take me around a few other places, while the other guests are inside; you've got enough time to get up, get dressed, and eat something, then I'll meet you outside those locked gates." Another tug at her hair. "Wake up now; you don't actually have to shine, Gabrielle." That brought her a sleep-bleary smile. "Wait for me, if I'm not there, okay?"

"You kidding?" Gabrielle asked sleepily.

Xena merely laughed, and left. The bard yawned and stretched and slid off the bed. The floor was cold enough against bare feet to thoroughly wake her up.

An hour later, fed, clean, clad in her own practical skirt and top, staff in one hand and the silver pin fastened to one shoulder, she emerged onto the nearest porch to look around.

Several of the serving women were clustered around a shallow, long pool, laughing and doing the laundry; a few men armed with spears were doing some kind of maneuver—clumsily, she thought—just outside the arena, while a gray-haired man snarled orders at them and shook his head. She *thought* she could make out Newin and one of his tutors in the arena itself; if it was the king's heir, he was doing a pretty good job of sword maneuvers. Someone else, farther out, near the south edge of the pavement . . . two guards, she finally decided, walking slowly along and pausing every few paces to gaze out and down.

A low, woman's voice just off the porch caught her attention: Saroni. *How'd she get out here?* the bard wondered. No one had said anything about the woman getting a pin of her own, and Gabrielle privately doubted the woman would, with Xena suspicious of her. Joxer's reedy voice brought her abruptly out of her thoughts; he sounded sullen, annoyed—Joxer at his worst. *You mean, it's not just me that gets him that way?* She would have said as much, but Saroni's next words sent her back a pace, into deeper shadow, where she could listen and not be seen.

"You know who I am, Joxer—a friend of Gabrielle's, from Rhodes. Not that we had that much time to get to know each other, of course—"

"Well, hey, that's Gabrielle, making friends just like that—I mean, like—" *Trying to snap his fingers and having the usual luck at it,* Gabrielle thought and grinned. "But, look, I've heard a little bit about that place from Newin—the king's heir, you know," he preened, "and besides, Xena told me a warrior like myself should stay outta there."

"Oh, she'd *tell* you that," Saroni said evenly. "But remember, I'm a priestess, and I *know* about places like that."

Oh, yeah?" Joxer said loftily.

"I do. I know you're seeking the fabled Helen, Joxer, and I know why."

"I am?—I mean, you do?"

"Aphrodite told me you were. She favors you, you know, Joxer."

"Well—sure she does." He sounded pleased.

"Two things you can gain from this, if you do what I've told you, Joxer. You can learn where the woman is, because I believe you'll be open to a vision. And it's said that the Maze was created—"

"I *know* about that part," he broke in. "Because of the bull—well, the half-bull, half-man, they had to put it somewhere big and safe, on account of, it *ate* people, and that's a bad habit in king's sons, you know?"

"I gather," the woman replied darkly. "But have *you* ever seen anything like that, Joxer? Half-man, half-bull? It sounds more like a bard's story, doesn't it?"

"Well—yeah. Except, you know, I've seen a *lot* of really weird stuff, going around with Xena and all. And some pretty strange stuff right here, too."

"Then you can understand what I'm telling you," Saroni urged quietly. "Why do you think the place is kept locked? If there ever *was* a minotaur, he's dead, isn't he? Killed by Theseus, or so they say?"

"Well—okay. I guess," Joxer replied doubtfully. Gabrielle crouched and edged forward. She'd only known it was Saroni by the timbre of her voice and the faint accent: She sounded like an entirely different person! *Scary*. All she could see, though, was Joxer's face—puzzled, no surprise there—and the top of Saroni's dark head. "So, it's like, a temple or something? Like, whatsit—Delphi?"

"Like that. A place where men favored by certain gods can receive visions, answers to things that deeply concern them. Also," she added casually, as if it had just occurred to her, "it was built as a training hall for master swordsmen, to help them hone their skills."

"Huh?" Joxer gaped; his eyes narrowed then, and he took a step back. "So, *that's* why Xena wanted me to stay away from the Maze. Typical, huh?" he went on bitterly. "Well, we'll just *see* about that!" He turned and took off at a dead run.

Gabrielle scrambled to her feet, hurled herself down the steps, and yelled after him. "Joxer! Don't you *dare*!"

He half turned, shook his head angrily, and kept going. Gabrielle tightened her grip on the staff and started after him; something hard came down across her shins and she fell; Saroni landed on top of her, driving the wind out of her. "I wouldn't," the woman murmured. She seemed amused.

Gabrielle shifted one way, back the other, but the woman shifted with her; she slammed back with her left elbow, and, more by good luck than aim, caught Saroni just under the ribs. Her back fist wasn't anything compared to Xena's, but it was good enough for what she was fighting: The priestess flailed for balance and rolled aside.

Before she could more than clutch at Gabrielle's hem, Gabrielle was on her feet and out of reach. Her eyes were hard as they met the other woman's amused ones. "You and I will talk!" she snapped. "*Real* soon. Right after I grab Joxer!" She took off at a dead run. "And don't think about going anywhere!" she shouted over her shoulder. "Because *that* will make me mad!"

The great doors leading into the Maze were thrown wide; Gabrielle passed the startled-looking launderers just as Joxer stumbled. Somehow, he righted himself and kept going, but the near fall gave her a good chance of catching him before he got inside.

There wasn't anyone else in sight: not so much as a guard. *I thought Xena was gonna meet me?* Surely Saroni hadn't managed to do anything to Xena! "Xena!" she yelled. The cry echoed, but she got no other response. And now she was too winded to even think about yelling any more.

The Maze loomed ahead. It wasn't just dark in there, she thought, it was as if even the outside daylight couldn't penetrate beyond the doors. And she could *feel* something now—something like that uncanny alertness she'd felt back when Ares had lost his sword and his power. . . . *Don't get any closer,* she warned herself. That's a bad kinda feeling, and you know it.

But Joxer—he didn't even hesitate. One moment he was there, almost within reach, and the next, he was simply gone. "Let—him—go," she panted, and slowed. It was hard, fighting the urge to haul him out of danger the way she always did, fighting the lure and the pull that was surely the Maze. But she *could*. She stopped a bare three strides from the entry. "Let—Xena—go in after—him," she gasped. Something hard slammed into her back: hands. She staggered forward and everything went dark.

But behind her she could hear a low, satisfied chuckle.

• • •

Xena let King Nossis lead the way around the south outer wall of the Maze. "That small door isn't any more use than the roof hatches Gabrielle told me she saw, is it?"

"You can't see anything through the hatches. As for the door—I used it once," he said with a shrug. "When I was first initiated. "There are stairs to a ledge, where my mother could watch for—for him. My—half brother. But the ledge doesn't go anywhere else. Daedalus built it especially for her. He rounded the south wall and the open gate, came out onto pavement, and stopped short. "Where are the guards, and how did you—?"

Xena was already around him, moving fast. She had just seen the least flash of green and brown, pale hair before Gabrielle vanished abruptly. Saroni gasped as the warrior gripped her shoulders and hauled her away from the entry. Suspicious blue eyes bored into wide, brown ones. "How'd you get out here? Sleepwalking again, priestess?"

"No. Gabrielle came—" She glanced toward the opening behind her. "She saw someone over here and just started running—! I tried to stop her, but I wasn't fast enough."

"Funny," Xena drawled, her gaze was hard. "That isn't what I saw. Try again, priestess."

The woman's face changed. Hardened. A corner of her mouth twitched into a sly smile. "All right. She's in there. She went in after Joxer."

"Joxer—I shoulda known," Xena snarled. She glanced back at the king, but he was partway across the pavement, shouting angrily at two armed men who were nearly at the southernmost edge of the drop-off. She turned the suspicious glare back to her captive. "And I wonder why *he* went in there. Maybe because someone talked him into it?" She loosed her right hand, bunched it into a fist.

"You want them back?" Saroni said flatly. "Because I know a *lot* about that place. I know how you can get them out—unharmed."

"I don't need you for that, the king can—"

"—thinks he's attuned to the Maze. I know better. But Gabrielle and Joxer aren't; he'll never find them."

Silence.

Saroni smiled; it wasn't a nice smile. "Give me Helen. I'll give you back your precious Gabrielle."

"Helen?" Xena bared her teeth. "I was right about you. You're Avicus', aren't you?" She loomed over the priestess. *"What do you know about Helen?"* she hissed.

"I know she's here, on Crete. I know she's hiding. Make this easy on these people, Xena, Menelaus' army will kill every last person on this island and burn the palace to the ground. Let me—"

"Let you what?"

"Let me talk to her. Helen. All I have to do is tell her what the Spartans are planning; she'll go with me willingly."

"No!" That was Nossis, who'd come up unnoticed by either woman. Xena glanced at him, and Saroni tore free of her grasp, leaving a handful of poorly stitched fabric in the warrior's hands. She staggered back, half turning as she caught her balance. Xena snatched at her again, but the priestess gave her a triumphant smile, drew a broad-bladed dagger from one sleeve, and fled into darkness.

13

Nossis caught hold of Xena's arm as she freed the chakram; she tore loose with no effort at all, but he snatched at her arm again, two-handed this time. "Warrior—Xena! Not like this! Don't go in there—!"

She rounded on him. "Talk fast, then!"

He nodded; he'd gone pale in the last moments. "You can't enter the Maze angry and with a drawn killing weapon. That priestess—she's doomed herself."

"Look, I don't *care* about Saroni, except that she's gone in there after Gabrielle! I'm not going to risk Gabrielle's safety—"

"You don't have to. Put your round blade away, let the rage go." He waited, visibly anxious; Xena sighed faintly, reclipped the chakram, closed her eyes. Two deep breaths later, she opened them and gave him a level look. He studied her face. "Stay close to me. I will be the one thing in there—the *only* thing—that doesn't change."

"Go," the warrior ordered tersely, and followed him into darkness.

• • •

It was very dark, Gabrielle decided; as bad as a clouded over night in deep woods. Oddly, now and again, she could see things—dark shapes that didn't make any sense to her eyes, mostly—but so far, no sign of Joxer. *Funny. He wasn't that many steps ahead of me.* She'd tried calling right at the first, but something about the way her voice sounded—she hadn't spoken aloud since.

She'd lost all sense of direction once the darkness had closed around her, even though she'd immediately turned back, or what she believed to be the direction she'd just come from. The darkness simply *was*: it stretched in all directions, vast, stifling, without limit. Stop that! *You're letting it get to you!* By the time she'd turned in place what she assumed was full circle, she could no longer even guess which way was out.

She stopped again, forced her fingers to loose their death grip on the staff just a little, then held her breath to listen. The lack of sound was so complete, she could hear her heart thudding—but, no, there it was again: a distant, whispery clatter that might be pebbles falling onto a dust-covered floor—or possibly a clumsy oaf tripping over his own boots. It was the only guide she had, and she was more afraid to stay in one place than to move on. When she stood still, the dark shapes she saw *moved*.

Time passed. She couldn't decide then or after how much of it. But a wordless, reedy exclamation stopped her cold. She sagged onto the staff as Joxer's voice came from her left.

"Owwww!"

She wasn't alone in here—and she'd found him.

"Joxer!" Gabrielle hissed urgently. No response. Farther from her than she'd thought, maybe. She swallowed dread, spoke normally with no result, then used a bard's carrying pitch: "Joxer!"

Silence.

Then: "Ga—brielle? What are *you* doing in here?"

"Well, I didn't get tricked by a sneaky priestess." *No, just shoved by one.*

"Oh, fine. Riddles on top of everything else!"

Just keep talking to me, she thought grimly, then nearly laughed. Just try to *keep* Joxer from talking, especially when he was annoyed. "Xena was right about this place, in case you haven't figured that out, Joxer."

"Gee, Gabrielle—you know, I think I just might have figured that *out*? Like, almost as soon as I passed those doors and all the *light* went away? Yikes!" That as Gabrielle's hand flailed across his shoulder and clamped down on his arm. "Don't *do* things like that!" he snarled. "You trying to scare me to death?"

"Don't tempt me!" she snarled back. "And I've got you now, so you can just shut up any time now, okay?"

"Fine," he sniffed, and was momentarily quiet.

Like that'll last long, she thought sourly; it didn't.

"I don't suppose you know how to get *out* of here, do you?"

"Joxer, the way I got it from Xena, only the king knows—"

"Oh, great. So, how long do we wait in here until someone realizes what's happened and sends for him to look for us? I mean, if he'd be even bothered." His voice brightened. "Hey, wait, though, that priestess, Saroni? She knows I came in here."

Gabrielle turned her head; something moving—not quite seen, just a sense of air moving. She shifted her grasp on the staff. "Joxer, you listen to me." She lowered her voice. "Saroni deliberately *shoved* me in here after I caught her telling you all that—stuff to get *you* in here. But the doors were open because King Nossis wants to show Xena what it's like. I was on my way to join her when I overheard Saroni—" Her voice faded; something nearby was panting. Gabrielle swallowed dread and let go Joxer's sleeve.

"Gabrielle?" he whispered. "Where'd you go?

"I'm here," she whispered back. "Something's out there."

"A lot of somethings. I've heard them." A faint screech as he drew his sword.

Gods, all we need is Joxer flailing around with that lousy blade of his; all he'll hit is himself—or me. "Joxer—"

"Something's coming closer. Stand back, Gabrielle; I can't see you, and I don't want to hurt you."

"Oh, no you don't, Joxer." She swung her arm until it connected with his back, then got a firm grip on his sleeve once more. "You're gonna stand back to back with me, where I can *feel* you, okay? That way *you* don't get lost again, and neither one of us hurts the other one!"

He didn't like it; she could tell by the grumbling. *Too bad*, she thought flatly. *Deal with it.*

The panting was nearer—close enough she should have been able to see what was there. For the moment, she actually welcomed Joxer's presence; pressure from his shoulder was the one real thing in the whole Maze, just now.

He squawked and shifted his weight forward, she flailed to catch her balance, planted the staff hard, repositioned herself against Joxer. "Sweet suffering sirens, Gabrielle, what is *that?*"

"Can't tell you," Gabrielle replied tersely. She wasn't about to turn and look; whatever Joxer saw was his business. His responsibility. Because either the chamber was lighter all at once, or her eyes had adjusted somehow. However it worked, she could make out the bulky creature shambling toward her: It walked on hairy man's legs, and brutish arms were outstretched to grab her. But the head was a thing of nightmare: Black, shaggy hair, deep, red eyes, and great, pointed, shining horns.

It hesitated as she brought up the staff, the tip of a thick, pink tongue protruding from the slack mouth as it panted. Behind it—*above* it, skeletal shapes floated, whispy rags

224

of clothing and skin clinging here and there, or hair floating around bony shoulders. And somewhere beyond them, nearly lost in gloom, another skeleton moved. A sense of *face* overlay pale bone here, drawing her eyes, her attention; with a wrench, she hauled both back to the improbable creature standing before her.

It hadn't moved; it—*he*—eyed her thoughtfully.

"Gabrielle!" Joxer suddenly yelled; her heart thudded. Despite the pressure against her left arm, she'd nearly forgotten him. "Gabrielle, *run*! It's the bull, the minotaur, he's coming right at me! A stick's not gonna stop something that big!" He caught his breath in a gasp. "I'm telling you, get out of here!"

"Joxer, that can't be—I'm looking right . . . at . . ." It could be, though, if what they both saw wasn't real. *The minotaur is dead, Theseus killed it, remember?* "It's an illusion!" she shouted.

"Oh, yeah?" he snapped back. "So how come I can *smell* it?"

She tested the air, nose twitching. He was right. The creature reeked. The odor intensified as it let out a low grunt and stalked slowly toward her.

"This place is very odd," Xena said; it was the first thing either of them had said since entering the Maze. As Nossis had suggested, she kept a corner of his short cloak in her left hand. Fortunately for her peace of mind, the man moved faster than his soft bulk would have led her to believe. It still couldn't be fast enough for her. If anything happened to Gabrielle . . .

"I know, warrior. I have only been in here when necessary, once a year ever since the ceremony that attuned me to the place."

Silence. Even their feet seemed to make no noise.

"You may see strange things; they won't try to hurt you, so long as you're with me."

"How—strange?"

"The ghosts of those killed in here—over the years. By my half-brother."

Another small silence. "I'd forgotten. About the relationship."

"I don't think of it much," he replied simply. "One of my priest tutors, when I was younger, told me that Mother haunts the Maze. But I don't believe that."

Brief silence; Xena tried to hear anything that might be Gabrielle, but there was nothing, and she couldn't see far in any direction. "You can't bring a torch in here?" she asked.

"They don't stay lit," he said. "Because the Bull likes it dark. Or, so they tell me."

The Bull—not a bull, or his half-brother the Minotaur, Xena realized. One of the strange, elusive Cretan gods, he must mean.

"You're *certain* nothing in here will harm Gabrielle—or Joxer?"

"There's nothing certain in the Maze," he replied. "But it's unlikely." He was quiet for some moments. "No, I don't think so."

"You don't *think* so?" She had to force herself to breathe normally, to fight cold fury at what the priestess had done. "I should have questioned that woman when I found her sneaking around outside the palace last night," she told herself quietly.

"That opportunity is past," Nossis told her mildly. "She set her own course, and—" He stopped short; Xena practically ran him down. "Listen," he urged softly.

She did. Nothing at first; then what might be a fire-hardened staff slamming into something hard.

"She's in trouble," the warrior said unhappily.

"She fights well; you'll reach her in good time. I—" He fell abruptly silent as the warrior pivoted on one heel and laid fingers on her chakram. The least, faint light seemed to come from the walls, or the very air, all at once.

Or maybe from the thing approaching rapidly from their right.

"Can I use my sword now," Xena asked, eyes fixed on the approaching spindly, flying creature, "or do I have to kill that with my bare hands?"

"You're inside; weapons are acceptable. But that isn't real, things in here are illusion—" Nossis began. Xena edged sideways to put herself between the thing and the Minos.

"Illusion," she spat. "That's a harpy! And I *know* harpies." Nossis started to say something, but she was already gone, racing toward the harpy, sword out and up.

It smelled like pitch, fire and death. Yellow eyes sought hers and it bared a mouthful of pointed teeth. Long claws curved, ready to snatch at her. Xena feinted with the sword once, twice, lunged at it—it fluttered back and up, just out of her reach. Finally, with a snarled oath, she unclipped the chakram and threw it, hard and edge-on. The deadly ring sliced through the harpy's neck, sending the head flying one way while the body crumpled to the dusty, pebble littered floor.

She could see fairly well now: well enough to make out the floor and one nearby wall, its surface painted with some kind of fantastic design and riddled with doorways, stairs, passages and more passages. And the body huddled near her feet. She stared as King Nossis came up behind her. "I—tried to tell you," he said apologetically. "I could see it wasn't one of the shades that haunts this place. That it was her."

Xena stared down at what had been a priestess. Blood ran across the floor, pooling in a shallow cleft; Saroni still gripped her dagger. Nearby, dark eyes stared toward the ceiling. The warrior retrieved her chakram, gazed down at the dead woman for a long moment. She turned the same expressionless gaze on the king, then. "Maybe she didn't deserve to die like that. But she deliberately lured Gabrielle in here in order to get to Helen. She was Avicus's spy." Her eyes flicked toward the dead woman. "You ask me, she got off easy."

Nossis gestured with both hands—a supplication, blessing, possibly averting danger or retribution, the warrior thought. The light faded but didn't leave them entirely. "Let us go," he said quietly. Xena caught hold of the tail of his cloak again and went with him.

Light came and went. Gabrielle peered uncertainly at the creature slowly stalking toward her. At her back, Joxer was mumbling unhappily and she heard and felt him draw another blade. The bull-man flexed his shoulders and began moving sidelong, to her right, approaching slowly but making progress. "Great," Gabrielle muttered.

"Huh?" Joxer, of course. "Gabrielle, it's trying to sneak around me to get to you, would you please just—"

"So's mine," she broke in. "Just—great!" Fortunately, her feet were planted this time; Joxer lunged away from her with a loud, wordless cry of challenge. "Joxer!" she shouted. "You get lost again and you can *stay* lost, you got me?"

No reply. She shifted her grip on the staff, and leaped forward, bringing the weapon up, around and down in a blur. It cracked into the broad face, staggering the brute, but nothing more.

Her fingers went briefly numb. "Oh, you're *real* all right," she said quietly. She let the staff recoil into the stone floor, used the momentum to power it around and down across the hollow between shoulder and throat. The bull-man stumbled, regained his balance, and began stalking the other direction; ruddy eyes never left her face. Gabrielle slammed one end into the floor and launched herself at the brute's throat; she managed two hard kicks before he had time to snatch at her boots. Thick hands came together on thin air.

Behind her, she could hear Joxer's ongoing, one-sided dialog with whatever *he* fought, and metal clanging against metal; she didn't dare look, though. "Gabrielle!" he yelled.

"Joxer, don't distract me—!"

"Just listen to me, will you? Bull head, man body? He's top-heavy, Gabrielle!"

Top-heavy. *Get him off balance and over he goes?* It sounded much too simple. Worth a try, though; his audience or his following was getting closer, and though they didn't look particularly dangerous, she didn't really want any of *those* touching her. She threw herself to one side suddenly, watching closely as he came around. He *was* awkward when it came to sharp moves. "Got it!" she yelled back, planted the staff and launched herself over it in a tight flip, landing just behind the creature. Muscular, hairy arms flailed for balance; when he was halfway around, she swept the legs from under him and he went down with a crash. The follow-up slam to his temple didn't knock him out, but he looked dazed.

Gabrielle risked a glance in Joxer's direction. All she could see was a hairy back and a grubby bit of cloth covering backside and upper legs, a long, skinny tail with a black tuft at the end. Movement near her feet brought her eyes right back to her own opponent, and another hard knock to the head left the monster still once more.

A familiar voice came from some distance then. "Gabrielle! Is that you?"

"Xena?" she yelled back. "Where are you?"

"Coming for you—! I'm with King Nossis, are you all right?"

"I will be when you get here, hurry up!"

Joxer was still dancing around nearby, a blade in each hand, muttering insults at the brute he fought, trying to draw it on so he could trip it, maybe. Gabrielle resisted the urge to take over and flatten the thing for him. He didn't seem to be in any actual danger, and she didn't have the right to do that to him, anyway.

She peered around uncertainly. Xena's voice might

have come from anywhere. But there was a sense of light back beyond the floating skeletons, and one by one, they faded, until only one remained.

Behind her, Joxer suddenly yelled indignantly, "Hey! Where'd you go? Come back here and fight like a—!" A glance his way assured her the bull-man had vanished; when she spun halfway around to make sure of her own, he was gone, too. Gabrielle stared doubtfully at the floor where he'd been: There was a smear of sweat and a small tuft of black, coarse hair, and she could still smell him. "I don't get it," she said.

"Gabrielle!" Xena came running toward her and the bard forgot vanishing monsters, ghosts, soaring skeletons and Joxer. She dropped the staff with a clatter and wrapped her arms around her close companion.

"*You'd* better be real," she murmured. Xena's hands were reassuringly hard on her back; the warrior's cheek rubbed against her hair.

"I'm real, Gabrielle, it's all right." She held the younger woman away from her, gazed searchingly into her eyes. "Are you okay?"

"Yeah—fine. Okay."

"Joxer—?" Gabrielle half turned as Xena got no reply. Joxer was walking around a spot on the floor, staring at it and muttering to himself. "*Joxer!*" Xena shouted; he started and stared at her.

"Oh—hi," he said lamely. "Look, just what is going *on* in here? Because that priestess, that friend of Gabrielle's, you know? Well, anyway, she told me—"

"I can just imagine," Xena broke in. "Spare me."

He turned away from her, one boot scuffing at the floor; dust rose in clouds. "I just wanna know where that—those *things* went."

Nossis came up in time to hear this last; he sounded breathless. "Illusion," he said. "My half-brother was in this place for so many years, it still holds part of him."

Gabrielle managed a weak smile. "Ahh—okay. So, the

skeletons I saw really were what I thought? His—"

"His victims," Nossis supplied when she hesitated. "I'm not offended, bard. What he was—that wasn't anything I could have changed. He had no choice than to be what he was."

She's still there, though, Gabrielle thought, eyes wide as movement beyond and above Xena's dark head caught her eye. Xena half turned to see what was behind her, and Nossis moved aside to look for himself. "Then—why is that one different?" Gabrielle asked. "Because you can almost see who she is, and she hasn't faded. . . ." Her voice faded as the king caught his breath in a faint gasp.

"Mother?" he whispered. The vision or ghost shimmered, then vanished, leaving them in the dark. Gabrielle clung to Xena, who patted her shoulder reassuringly. Nossis cleared his throat, and when he spoke, his voice was a little higher and tighter than it had been. "I think you might all—like to leave this place for now?"

"You've got it," Gabrielle said firmly. Somewhere behind her—or maybe behind Xena, she could hear Joxer's stumbling footsteps and the rattle of stone.

"Hey!" he demanded indignantly. "Where'd everyone go?"

"Joxer?" Xena said flatly. She kept one hand firmly wrapped around Gabrielle's wrist as she leaned away.

"Uh—yeah? Owwww! Don't scare a guy like that!"

"That's *me*, Joxer. I've got you, ok?"

"Fine. Great. I think I bit my *tongue* in half when you did that."

"Joxer?" Gabrielle put in.

"Yeah?"

"Shut up."

It was nearly midday by the time Gabrielle climbed wearily from the tub and wrapped herself in in a thick drying-cloth. Xena sat at the table, absently eating grapes; her eyes were fixed on the window or the view beyond it. "Xena? You okay?"

"Hmmm? Oh—sure. I'm fine. What about you?"

"Well, I feel clean again, and I can actually feel my fingers. I can't believe how hard I hit that monster and then for him to just—vanish. . . ." She picked up a slice of bread, eyed it, set it back down. "And I still can't believe what Saroni did."

"Believe it, Gabrielle."

"I mean, I should've known there'd be a good reason if *you* didn't trust her. It just seemed—well, *too* obvious to me. I mean, just because she served Apollo. And then, everything she said back on Rhodes, and that Krysta really did look kinda spooky. . . ." She sighed, tore a corner from the bread and ate it. "But getting Joxer into the Maze— just to trade you for Helen? I mean, he coulda been killed, and she didn't even care!"

"*You* could've been killed, Gabrielle," the warrior reminded her darkly. "She got off easy." She brooded on this for some moments, glanced at Gabrielle. Away again.

"Xena, I know you wouldn't have just—killed her like that. You didn't have a choice, okay?"

"I didn't know it was her, either. That's what bothers me."

"Either way," the bard insisted. "Look, what are we gonna do? You said you maybe had a plan . . . ? Except, if it involves that place, are you *sure* you want to send Helen into the Maze? Even with Nossis? Because, frankly—"

Xena held up a hand, cutting off the flow of words. "Wait a minute, Gabrielle. I'm thinking. . . ." Her voice faded; she closed her eyes. "Something about that priestess, I—that's it!" Xena leaped from her chair and ran through the bathing room, returning with Gabrielle's dusty green top. "She hugged you, back on Rhodes, right?"

"Ah—yeah. Caught me by surprise. I mean, she was really excited about—she *said* she was really excited to

232

meet me, favorite bard and all that," Gabrielle finished bitterly.

"So, how were you to know?" Xena felt her way across the front, the shoulders, flipped the bit of cloth over and ran her nails down the back. "Gotcha," she said with grim pleasure and began tugging at the fabric. Gabrielle stared as the warrior held up a small bit of something that was more like parchment or hide than cloth. It wasn't green for certain. When she would have spoken, Xena held a finger against her lips, crossed the room and held the little thing in the candle flame until it flared; she dropped it then, watching as the thin line of smoke faded, then savagely crushed the ashes with her thumb.

Gabrielle stood just behind her, watching. She swallowed as Xena met her eyes. "That—was one of them, wasn't it?" the bard asked finally. "One of those patches, like Avicus put on all the guys he sent out on his phony quest?"

The warrior nodded.

"That was—that's been on *me* ever since Rhodes?"

Another nod.

"Xena!" Gabrielle turned away, stumbled to the table, sank into one of the chairs, and buried her head in her hands. "She put that on me. She didn't come here for sanctuary, she *knew* we were here, and she followed us! And she knew Helen was here, and—"

"Gabrielle?" Xena dropped down next to her and wrapped a strong arm around her shoulders, pulling her back up. "Look at me, okay? Listen to me," she went on softly. "What happened is not *your* fault. You couldn't have known. And I'm beginning to think that it's right the whole thing should end here, on Crete. So I don't think it will matter in the end that Saroni marked you for Avicus."

"Yeah, sure," the bard replied bitterly. "Xena, you don't have to say that just to make me feel better—"

"Gabrielle, I'm not." Xena gave her a gentle shake.

"C'mon, think about it. Menelaus is fixated. He's not gonna give up until he finds her. Whatever it takes, okay?"

Silence. Gabrielle reluctantly nodded.

"So we choose the time and the place."

"Fine—except there's no real army here. Menelaus could—" She sought words, finally shook her head.

"I don't think he can just have things his way. Not here. Apollo can't help him, which means there isn't much his priest can do."

"Great. You and me and a bunch of king's guards against an army."

"What—we have to split one measly army between us?" Xena smiled. Gabrielle gave her a rueful grin. "Besides, wouldn't you like to get this over and done with so we can go home?"

Gabrielle sighed faintly. "Yeah. You must be missing Argo something awful. I miss having dry land all around me for days in any direction." A smile tugged at the corners of her mouth. "And I still get to thump Joxer, when we're all done with this."

"And Helen deserves to get on with her life," Xena added gravely.

"Yeah. That most of all." A comfortable silence held; Xena ate a few more grapes, and Gabrielle finished her bread.

"So," the warrior said finally. "You ready to go back into the Maze?"

"No way," the bard replied firmly.

"Why don't you get changed and come with me anyway?" Xena said. "Just to fetch Joxer, then only as far as the family apartments."

"Ah—sure. Why?"

"Because I think it's time Joxer met Helen."

Eventually, Xena went into the children's rooms to speak to Helen while Gabrielle waited in the hall with Briax and

Joxer. "After all," she had insisted, "if Joxer can help us, then so can Briax. Maybe he's not much of a fighter, but neither's Joxer—and he's got a good heart." Xena had reluctantly agreed, and now she leaned into the hall, beckoning.

The children were nowhere in sight, though Gabrielle saw a slate with half-erased figures on it, and an open scroll on the low table. Helen stood mid-room, dark eyes moving curiously from one man to the other. Briax flushed a deep red, then, and looked at the floor. Joxer managed a smile, swallowed hard, and ducked his head. "L-lady, I mean, your majesty—"

"Helen," she told him gravely.

"There was—I mean, the king, Menelaus, I mean—" He winced as Gabrielle kicked him in the ankle, then drew himself up straight. "I was told that you had taken a thing from the Spartan palace, a thing that looks like a necklace?" He fell silent as the woman shook her head.

"I took nothing when I left Sparta, except some of my clothing, and jewels given to me by my father," she told him. "My—once husband wants me to return to his house. I don't want to go back to him."

"Ahhh—well, then!" Joxer smiled. "Then I guess you won't be going anywhere, because we'll just all see to it that you don't. Go anywhere, I mean."

Helen looked extremely doubtful of this, Gabrielle thought. And none too happy. But it was Xena the woman looked at now. *Whatever Xena told her just now—yeah, I'm sure the last thing she wants is any fighting over her here. Too bad she doesn't have any choice.* Except running again. Gabrielle was of Xena's opinion. *She's right. Helen can't go on like this forever, and Menelaus isn't gonna give up.* The woman's next stop might take her right into the man's clutches.

Besides, there was Nossis.

Gabrielle brought herself back to the moment. Briax was doing his best to sound as if he addressed beautiful women every day, and mostly managing, but he was still very red faced. "Then—the thing I was sent to retrieve, the plate with three golden pomegranate seeds? That doesn't exist, either?"

Helen shook her head.

"Then—he *used* us, to get to you?"

The woman nodded.

Briax turned to Gabrielle; his eyes were stormy. "You know, that really makes me very angry," he said. "I should have trusted you, I should have listened. And now, if I've done anything to put her in danger . . ."

"No," Helen said firmly. "I was already in danger. I have been since the day Menelaus first came to my parent's house and looked at me. Think of yourself as my warrior—you, and you, Joxer. Why ever you started your quest, you'll end it by helping me free myself of Menelaus for good." Before either stunned man could find words to respond to this, Helen turned and walked from the room.

Two days of intense meetings and hard planning later, Gabrielle decided she had never been quite so tired—or so busy and so bored at the same time. She'd climbed Mt. Idhi again, looked at more maps of the island than she wanted to believe could exist. She'd gone back into the Maze with Xena and King Nossis and found that this time there was a difference. The king's presence apparently did disarm whatever was strange about the place. At least, she saw no ghosts, monsters or sad-faced floating phantoms. Aside from the painted walls, though, there really wasn't much to see, and the seeming vastness and confusion of the place merely depressed her. The second afternoon, she followed Newin and Joxer down a goat trail cut in the south face of the island to the sea. *Well, it looked and felt like a goat trail to me,* she thought gloomily. The way down had been precipitous, the return journey exhausting. She'd led, afraid to allow the clumsy Joxer any chance to trip and fall on her. The trail itself was wide enough in places for two to walk—or scramble—abreast, but mostly it was barely good for one and the final climb to the pavement required both hands.

Why everyone seemed to think Menelaus would use this. . . . Gabrielle fought a yawn and finally asked.

Xena shrugged. "It's not certain, just likely. He knows the path is there, and that bay it leads to is the only place ships can put in along this end of the south shore. It's well known the Minos doesn't post guard on the plateau, and you wouldn't see anyone coming up that trail until they reached the top."

"The front road's bad enough, but it's gotta be an easier way," Gabrielle argued.

"But there are guards on the docks—the ones you see, plus one or two who look like ordinary dockmen and work the mirrors to send word to the palace when there are visitors coming."

"Oh." Nossis stirred; he looked as exhausted as she felt. "Actually, whenever a ship heads into port, we're warned of that, and then the messenger post sends word either way: that someone is coming, or that no one is. So—" He shrugged.

"So if a ship sails in and suddenly there's *no* message, that means something bad's happened, right? Okay. But Menelaus has an army. If he brings his army up the main road, it won't matter if we're forewarned, will it?"

"But," the king put in, "I do have spies on the mainland. "Friends, actually; old Nestor keeps a watchful eye on the Spartan ports, and there's no way to hide an army massing for transport oversea. He'd have time to warn me."

"Or stop Menelaus," Xena said flatly. "Remember, Gabrielle, there are members of the old Greek alliance against Troy who still resent what Sparta got them into."

"I guess," Gabrielle said.

"Remember, Helen doesn't want any fighting—at least no killing, if it can be helped."

Good luck, Gabrielle thought. She looked up, blinking, as one of the servants came into the stuffy little meeting chamber. Nossis listened, then nodded.

"I'm told there's a ship, just put in to port unexpectedly—the northern vessel *Wode*. According to the messages, the ship is ready to go back to sea after filling its water barrels, but one man remains behind." He glanced inquiringly at Gabrielle, who groaned faintly. "He's on his way up: A dark man, a warrior named—"

"Draco," Gabrielle broke in drearily.

Nossis eyed her in mild surprise, then nodded.

"That was the name. Warrior, he told my men, but I seem to recall hearing of a warlord named Draco. You know him?"

"I know him," Xena said evenly. "I'm not sure I like his coming here."

"You're telling *me*," Gabrielle put in feelingly.

"But maybe it's all right," the warrior went on slowly. "Because if we can get him on our side—"

Gabrielle jumped to her feet. "Xena, I really hope you aren't planning to get *me* to talk him into—!"

"Won't be necessary, Gabrielle," Xena assured her. "I'll explain things. He'll listen—and he'll help."

"Sure. Like it's gonna be *that* easy," Gabrielle mumbled to herself. Xena merely laughed and patted her on the back, then followed Nossis out into the hall. Gabrielle started after them, but at the door, she turned back and settled firmly in her chair. "Me, go out there and wait for Draco to show up? Yeah, right." She tugged at her hair and sighed deeply. "Great. So, what's next? Salmoneus shows up to convince the Minos to turn the Maze into a traveler's site?"

14

The warlord must have taken the steep road at a near run, Gabrielle thought. The king had barely time to take his usual place when the man appeared, striding easily across the paving, past the barracks and around the fish pools. She turned as Nossis caught his breath in surprise; her eyes went wide. Helen came across the shaded porch to stand at the king's side.

"You must go back in," Nossis said urgently. The woman shook her head; her mouth was set in a stubborn line. "This isn't safe! We do not know this man!"

"No. The time for hiding is past. Xena told me about this man—a little. And if our other guests who were named as questors have been given the option of taking my side, then this warlord should also have the right." She managed a shaky smile. "It is all right, my kind and loyal friend. Even if he chose to believe Menelaus, I have Xena here."

"You think he fears her, Helen?"

"Not that," Xena drawled. "He just knows better than

to fight me after a climb like that. But he wouldn't win, anyway. And he's smart enough to know that, too." Her gaze shifted to the man coming rapidly toward them.

He'd seen Xena *and* her companion, Gabrielle thought; that sudden check in his stride, the way he swung his head in visible frustration before he came on again. He was smiling as he neared those waiting for him, but the smile didn't reach his eyes. He hadn't even broken a sweat, warm as the afternoon was, and at whatever pace, he'd taken that ghastly road. His voice was low and even to her suspicious ears, sounded nothing but dutiful. "Sire— if you are King Nossis—I come to pay my respects." The king nodded. Draco's eyes moved, warmed briefly as they touched Gabrielle, slid to the leather-clad woman next to her; a wry smile twisted his mouth. "Xena. Seems to me, I owe you a dunking."

"Draco," she purred. "Any time you wanna try."

"Sure," he agreed. "*Try* whenever you want." His gaze moved past her; his eyes went wide. Helen smiled at him. "And you," he managed, "must be Helen. Lady," he added, and sketched her a neat bow.

"Helen only," the woman replied gravely. "And you are Draco, the warlord who devastated much of western Sparta years ago. Why do you come here—and why alone?"

"Fair question," he allowed. "I am no warlord now— that requires an army, and I no longer have one. I had reasons of my own for responding to the call for a man who could find Helen. If you're concerned, or even just curious, I can tell you what they are. Sometime."

Silence. Helen broke it. "And—what will you do, now that you have found her?"

"Do? What I promised a—a friend." He glanced at Xena. "You don't look like a woman being held prisoner, so I'm guessing you could leave here if you wanted, and no harm would come to you from these people."

She nodded.

"And—if what this friend told me is true, you had plenty of chances to leave Troy and go back to King Menelaus. Free choice on your part?"

Another nod.

"So—if that's true, then I have to suppose that you're here because you don't want to be *there*. So, at this point, there's no reason for me to ask you if you'd like me to escort you back to Sparta, is there? Any more than I should bother asking if you took some fancy dish thing when you left Sparta? Something the king might urgently want returned to him?" His eyes were dark, narrowed as Helen shook her head. "Uh-huh." He spun partway around to glare at Xena. "All right, you win, Xena. I was played for a sucker, and *nobody* gets away with that."

"Nobody?" she drawled. He chopped a hand for silence. She raised an eyebrow and said nothing else.

"So, *now* I gotta ask—what are you up to here, Xena? And how do I help?" He considered this, spread his arms in a wide shrug. "Provided you *want* my help, that is."

Xena smiled briefly. "What is this, Draco, a trick question? For all we know, half the Spartan army may show up here any day now. We'll take all the help we can get. But you know I'd never turn you down. Especially never for something like this."

"You're most welcome," Nossis added. "As my guest, of course."

The warlord inclined his head. "Thanks—but I earn my keep. We need to talk, though. I've seen some things the past few days you might want to know about."

"We can talk that over later today," Nossis said. "For now, my men here will show you to a room; you will find a bath, food, and wine."

The warlord smiled and bowed again, but he looked like the arrangement wasn't so pleasing: *Impatient—either what he has to tell us is urgent, or he's just frustrated*, Gabrielle thought.

Xena seemed to think the same thing. She smiled and

wrapped an arm around Draco's impressive shoulders. When he shook that off, she grabbed him again, her fingers sinking deep into well-defined biceps. "I'll go with him, King Nossis. We'll talk—right, Draco?"

Draco scowled and tore free of her grasp, sketched the king another bow and followed the servants, letting the warrior bring up the rear. Helen watched them go, then walked off across the pavement toward the family apartments; the king went with her.

"Boy, I thought *Joxer* was a pain," Gabrielle mumbled. "Draco—" She sighed faintly and turned to go in.

Someone there, she realized with a start: Newin, Joxer and Briax stood in the shade of the near porch, Joxer gazing suspiciously after Draco. As she came up the steps, the would-be warrior transferred the scowl. "Fine, Gabrielle—so what's *he* doing here?"

Gabrielle rolled her eyes. "Joxer, for your information, I do *not* answer to you! And if you were standing there, you know as much as I do. He's on the quest, too, except—"

Joxer snorted rudely. "Except there's no quest. That doesn't tell me why *he* had to show up." Narrowed eyes glanced her way. "He doesn't still have that *thing* for you, does he?" She gaped at him. He gave her a bitter look. "Don't try to fool me, Gabrielle, I happen to remember that he went crazy for you. The Hestian virgins, remember?"

"Oh, that. Whatever." Her attempt at Xena's best bored and uninterested look didn't seem to distract him, unfortunately. At least Draco hadn't seen Joxer. *Yet.* "It's not an issue for me, Joxer."

"Well, maybe it's an issue for Draco, huh?"

Her eyes narrowed. "Joxer, guess what! I don't care if it's an issue for Draco, or even an issue for you, I don't care! Because—because I just do not care! Got it?"

"Got it," he snapped back, turned and stomped off the porch. Newin followed him, his young brow puckered

242

with concern. Gabrielle stormed into the palace, aware of Briax's wistful gaze following her all the way down the passage. It did nothing to improve her mood.

Nor did finding the rooms she shared with Xena to be empty. She contemplated taking a nap, or another bath, but neither appealed. A walk or a workout. But now that Joxer and Briax had free rein of the palace grounds, her luck would take her right into one of them.

Or Draco. Except he'd be wherever the king had put him, lounging in a steaming, scented tub, getting his back scrubbed by. . . .

"Hey," she ordered herself sharply. "Don't go there!" She paced over to the window, stared out across the pavement. "Besides, what do *you* care? Anyway, Xena'd learn more from him that way." Her eyes brooded on the ampitheater. "It's not like I have some reason to be *jealous* or anything. It's just—yeah. Draco. He's almost as bad as *Ares*." She paced the room one way, back again; caught up an apple and took a savage bite from it. "And I am *tired* of being hassled by both of them!" She glared at the apple, finished it in half a dozen snapping bites. Her fingers drummed on the wall. "Great! So, where *is* Xena?"

The warrior stayed gone for over an hour, and when she finally let herself into the room, she looked tired and irritated. Gabrielle pounced as the door closed. "So? Why's he here?"

"Gabrielle—gimme a minute, okay?" The warrior poured herself water, drank slowly, then flopped on the bed. "He's in a bad mood."

"I gathered that! What did he *say?*"

Xena shrugged. "Wanted to tell me how bad the last few days had been for him. I told him we could trade later, got the details out of him, and came away." Her mouth twitched. "Okay, so I scrubbed his back. It's the best way I know of to get him talking." She made a short, neat tale of Draco's story; Gabrielle listened intently.

"Anyway, *Hammer*'s sunk for good, and nobody they caught knew anything useful. Habbish is sure the ship was Spartan, made up to look like a raider."

"Okay. Why, though?"

"When did Menelaus do anything straight?"

"How'd I know? Wait. You think that ship was out to help him find Helen?"

"Maybe. A ship like that could be useful to Sparta, but if it was supposed to locate Helen, it failed, Gabrielle. I think that's why the quest. Hand me a grape or two, okay?" Gabrielle fished a mostly stripped stem from the bowl and held it out. Xena wrinkled her nose. "What— you're not gonna skin 'em for me?"

"Deal with it," Gabrielle said flatly. "Tell me things."

"Hey—you can always try, right? There isn't much else to tell. Draco got picked just like Joxer did, and he doesn't really know any more. And he's a lot more frustrated."

"Great."

"I know. Except he's on our side—"

Gabrielle shifted uneasily. "Xena—no offense, but are you sure about that?"

The warrior eyed her thoughtfully. "You mean, was he faking it out there when he talked to Helen? No. I know him, Gabrielle; he can't fool me. He may build himself another army after this is resolved, I can't swear he's really gonna turn to good—or stay there. But he's trying to do the right thing." She smiled wickedly. "Just like he did back in Sparta—in the palace, remember? You'd'a been proud of him. Helping me flatten the king's finest and didn't spill a drop of blood." Gabrielle closed her eyes. Xena laid a hand on her arm. "Gabrielle. He's not gonna push you, as much because you don't want it as because I'll mangle him for it. And he's gonna fight for Helen, *and* try not to kill anyone."

The younger woman whimpered faintly and closed her eyes. "Great. But I'd hoped he'd given up on me."

"Not yet. *Wode*'s gone back out to sea; Habbish is

gonna keep an eye out for any Spartan ships heading this way, and he'll get warning to us. If he can. I don't have much confidence in that tubby old boat of his."

"It let you catch up to the one I was on with Joxer," Gabrielle pointed out.

"Yeah, so it can outrun a merchanter. There isn't much that *can't* outrun a merchanter." She poured out the last of the water, drank it down. "But that's okay, at least he's trying to help. And who knows, maybe this is where our luck finally changes."

Gabrielle sighed quietly. "You know what, Xena? I'd like that. I'd like it a lot." She drove a hand through her hair, tugged at the end of a long strand. "But what I'd like a lot more right now is for Joxer, Briax, and Draco *all* to find something or someone else to be—ah—interested in?"

To her surprise—and mild annoyance—Xena burst out laughing. It was some time before the woman got her mirth under control. "Gabrielle," she managed finally. "I'm not laughing *at* you! It's just—Hades, it's the hair, the legs, the funky little green top, the little stick. . . ." She started laughing again, waved her hands helplessly. Gabrielle cast up her eyes. Xena's laugh was normally highly catching. And it did make a funny picture: One Poteidaian bard of indifferent size, personal assets, and nonlethal weaponry being trailed by a pack of wide-eyed males. *It would be funny, if it was someone else,* she thought sourly.

She reluctantly joined Xena for the late planning session and was relieved when Draco more or less ignored her. The warlord told the king and his general what he'd earlier passed on to Xena, pointed out the location on the larger Aegean map where they'd sunk *Hammer* and where her crew had perforce stayed.

"It may not matter," Nossis said finally. "But I should send a message to Kyrkrias, who rules Paros. He should know such stranded and possibly desperate men are on his under-populated back lands—and his people may learn something you were not able to, Draco."

The warlord might have been a little angry at that, Gabrielle thought as she watched his eyes, but he controlled the irritation and even managed a brief smile.

"I was only able to question a few of those men, and only one officer." He was very interested in what had been planned and spent some time pouring over a highly detailed map of the entire island. "Okay," he said finally. "Most of this makes good sense to me; you don't have a real army, and the lady doesn't want all-out battle anyway. Having met the lady, I can see why she'd feel that way, and why you'd respect her wishes. But this south-trail that comes up from the beach; if it's the same one I saw a few days ago from below, it's steep, narrow, downright ugly, and a *damned* long climb. Why's a general as smart as Menelaus is said to be gonna send his men up *that*? And don't give me 'element of surprise,' because if he figures you've got Helen here, he'll also figure you'll have guards posted anywhere that might lead up to the palace, including a trail like that one. Because guarding all possible ways in is just what he'd do, if he was the Minos."

"Good point," Xena replied softly. "Except he also thinks every other king around is soft, weak, or an idiot. Way below his own level. I say he's gonna at least check it out. Maybe send a small company first, half a dozen men dressed so they'll blend into the hillside."

"Maybe—all right," Draco said. "So, a few men to watch . . ."

"Already provided for," Nossis informed him.

So—say everything works out the way you plan. I don't see how you're gonna stop him."

"I'm working on that part," Xena replied. "Actually, Gabrielle is."

"Nothing yet," the bard mumbled as the warlord turned wide, dark, warm eyes on her. "Um—you'll know as soon as I do." Draco looked as if he didn't believe he was hearing everything—which he certainly wasn't—but he finally shrugged and let it pass. Gabrielle was very relieved when Nossis finally broke the meeting so everyone could clean up for dinner, and he could spend a quiet hour with his children.

She was aware of Draco's lingering gaze as she slipped from the room just behind Nossis and ahead of General Kropin. Back in the small chamber, she heard Xena asking Draco something, the warlord's distracted-sounding reply. But when she reached the bend in the passage and looked back, there was no sign of either. *Good. Keep him outta my hair, Xena.*

Not that the warlord—ex-warlord—was being overwhelming. He *could* be. So far, he was polite—though his gaze sought hers too frequently for her comfort.

"He's just not even remotely my type," she said firmly as she walked out onto the porch closest to the arena. A few minutes at one of the fish ponds, she thought. There was something to clear her mind, and improve her mood.

Briax's voice broke the moment. "Who—who's not your type, G-Gabrielle?" Somehow, she managed not to jump through the porch ceiling, and even managed a smile as she turned back toward the palace. The youth stood framed in the door, leaning would-be casually against the sill. "Briax! What a surprise!"

His face fell. "I'm sorry. You don't look happy to see me, Gabrielle. I didn't mean—I mean, I'll go away, I . . ."

She forced a smile. *How does Xena deal with these guys?* "Hey, did I say anything? Briax, it's okay, honestly. It's been—" Images tumbled over one another and she forced them away. "It's been a long day, and I'm tired and I'm frustrated, and none of that has anything to do with you."

"Oh. Oh! It—hasn't?" he asked, so openly hopeful that she almost laughed.

"No, it hasn't. Look, though. I really, truly need a little time to just—go sit and think. Alone."

"Okay," he allowed cautiously. "I can understand that. I feel that way myself. Often."

Face it, Gabrielle, she told herself gloomily, *his type is gonna look for hidden meanings no matter what you say, or how nicely you say it.* "Tell you what," she said finally, "After dinner tonight—the two of us? We can talk then, if you like."

"I—sure. That's—that'll be great," he managed. She bounced down the stairs before he could think of anything else to say and strode across the open. Not the nearest fish pool, she decided firmly. The one closer to the barracks. After all, she hadn't visited that one yet. *And from there, you can't see that poor boy devouring you with his eyes.* "So you just told him—no, suggested to him that you *two* could talk? I thought you were the one who was *good* with words!"

The sun was nearly down behind the mountains west of Sparta, and a strong wind blew across the city. It was a later hour than Avicus would have chosen to begin the trek down to Phalamys and the waiting ships, and he tried to suggest as much, but there was no holding Menelaus back. *Be honest with yourself,* the priest ordered himself. *The man's been uncommonly patient—for Menelaus, anyway.*

No surprise that the king had called the rising wind an 'omen.' Just about anything the past four days had been named an omen—with exuberance or a lot of snarling. Ordinarily the priest would find it annoying, but for now, he was content to let the man rave away. It meant Menelaus was too busy with his plans to recapture lost Helen, or plans for their triumphant return to Sparta to be aware of anything else. *One day very soon, he'll look up from his special niche in Tartarus and know who put him there, and who beds his woman. And there will be nothing he can do about it.*

The thought warmed him; little else did, though, because he had too many loose ends trailing across the Aegean, and no answers for too many questions. Most important of all: Where had Saroni gone? And why? He'd watched with grim satisfaction as the priestess teased Joxer into taking on the Maze, just as he'd suggested to her. He'd laughed aloud as he watched the woman shove that nattering Gabrielle inside, then turn to deliver his ultimatum to Xena.

Xena. He'd underestimated her—concern, call it, for the annoying young woman who followed her everywhere. But there'd been no mistaking the fury in Xena's eyes. Suddenly nothing at all. "But if Saroni went into the Maze, I would have been aware of her." Most likely, Xena had accidentally found Saroni's patch and destroyed it, then killed the woman for endangering her . . . 'friend.'

At least, thanks to Saroni, they knew where Helen was. And he could be fairly certain that no one on Crete was aware he had learned this. With Gabrielle's patch still dark, he couldn't trust to that, of course. Unfortunately, he'd been called away from the bowl not long after he'd seen Xena glaring at Saroni. When he'd returned, over an hour later, there was simply nothing from Crete. Either Gabrielle's skimpy little green top was back in the laundry, buried in a clothes' press, or the patch was gone.

Hammer—Menelaus was furious over the loss of his ship, and Avicus was all too keenly aware the suggestion to send it after *Wode* had been his. Still, there would come a day, very soon, when the king of Sparta had no use for ships. *Sensible king would lock himself and his in the land and leave the sea to others.*

Such as Habbish. Thanks to the devices the priest had

managed to get aboard *Wode* over the past year or so, he knew enough for his purposes. Enough to be fairly sure that Draco was nowhere on that ship.

"He could be anywhere—on land, unless I'm wrong about the man." What he'd seen and heard of Draco, the warlord found ship life boring and deepwater unnerved him. The priest shook his head. Something he'd seen or heard—perhaps a fragment of dream Apollo had sent him—told him the ex-warlord was on his way to Crete. "Without the patch Xena tore from his armor, I have no way to know, though." *Xena.* His eyes narrowed, and an unpleasant smile turned the corners of his mouth. "Xena, compared to you, Menelaus is a mere gadfly. Well. You've done your best to thwart me, but it's not good enough. Crete is the one place I can destroy you. And I will."

Early morning, two days later, Gabrielle strode up a much-too-familiar path and over the lip of the long dell, stopping just short of the squatty, plain little temple. "Third time had *better* be the charm," she grumbled. The last two mornings, and now today, she'd scrambled up here, shielding her eyes against the hot, level rays of an early sun to find—nothing. No sense of godly power lingering anywhere atop the mountain. No Ares; no Aphrodite. And nothing—no song, no tale she could devise, none of the tasteless jokes she could remember about pale-haired, boneheaded females—produced either god. *Maybe they're still arguing. Maybe she flounced at him once too often and he strangled her—nah.* Amusing thought, at the moment, with the sweat drying on the back of her neck, and her eyes fried by the sun. *She's a goddess; they don't die that easily.*

But things were starting to happen, finally. The night before, late, one of the servants had wakened her and Xena with a message from Nossis: Habbish had seen two ships leaving Sparta late at night, plain sails and decks full of men. He'd had the advantage of a short lead, and made the most of it; by morning Menelaus' vessels were well behind him, and he'd seen them putting in along the backside of one of the smaller, unoccupied islands. "They don't want to be seen, then," she told herself.

"Who doesn't?" The soft voice was right against her ear; warm breath lifted the hair along her neck and prickled her skin. Gabrielle snarled a low oath and lashed out with a foot, her staff, and her head. She saw stars as the latter collided with something hard, and the war god cursed in turn. She spun around, rubbing the back of her skull. Ares eyed her in startled surprise. One hand gingerly massaged his nose.

Gabrielle leveled a finger at him. "Don't say I never warned you, Ares! Because I am *so* bored with people sneaking up on me! And that goes double for gods, okay?"

"Got it!" he replied, his quiet voice at odds with the black fury in his eyes. That went, was replaced by a thoughtful look. "You know, if it wasn't so funny, getting bonked by you? I just might call off the whole deal."

"Deal—I got it?"

"You got it."

The bard eyed him narrowly. "And—she's good with this?"

"She's okay with it, shall we say," Ares began; faint, tooth-hurting sound and a flare of pinkish light interrupted him.

Aphrodite shoved him aside, squared her shoulders and formidable bosom. "Don't you even *listen* to my brother," she snarled. "Because, if you want my help it's like, hello? Did I already say I'm not getting on Apollo's bad side, because nettles in the sheets are really not my thing? And like, in case you didn't get it before now, all Apollo's sides are major bad? And besides that, honey, you like owe me in *major* dinars for the—" Her voice rose to a sudden squeak. Ares had a hand twisted in her hair again.

He rolled his eyes, quirked a grin at the bard, who simply sighed.

"Like I said," Ares spoke into the silence that followed. "She's okay with this. She's just putting on the sulk bit for you."

"Am not," Aphrodite replied promptly.

"As if," he retorted sharply. He looked up as Gabrielle cleared her throat ominously.

"Can we *do* this?" she demanded. "Aphrodite, my word I will forget *all* about buying a small bell at some small bazaar or another and taking Joxer on a temple tour, okay? In return, you quit pretending you don't owe Helen something, and you help her out here. All we want is for Menelaus to give up on the woman for good, how hard is that?" Aphrodite flounced out of Ares' reach; watched Gabrielle resentfully. Gabrielle ignored her.

"Explain it to her, Ares. She fixes it for Helen, and in return, I don't pass on any stories about you wimping out in Troy or *her* little party with Joxer."

"You wouldn't dare," Aphrodite sneered.

"Wouldn't I?"

"You know," Ares said finally. "I told Dad, you can't just turn these bards loose with whatever story they think up, and he just doesn't get it. All he can see is, 'Hey, somebody's got a new one about how good I am with the babes!'"

Aphrodite's lips twisted. "Ares, I am like totally bored with this. You're just being snotty because she turned you down—"

"I don't think so," Gabrielle snapped. "Look, will you two cut it out?"

"Fine!" Aphrodite snarled. "Okay. Helen free of Menelaus, for good, that's it?" Gabrielle nodded. "If it gets me rid of *you*, then I'm okay with it—but it'll cost you."

"Whatever," Gabrielle replied shortly. "Let's *do* it." She was suddenly aware of Ares' stillness—a bad omen in itself. Worse. The complacent smile on Aphrodite's face as the two vanished. She clapped a hand over her mouth, much too late to keep her last, unthinking words in. *Sweet singing sirens, what did I just do to myself?*

Four more days dragged by, with little for Gabrielle to do except give Newin staff fighting lessons each morning and make the rounds with Xena. The plan was as ready as it could be. Too much depended on Menelaus—when he arrived, and how he chose to divide his forces, if he didn't simply bull his way up the main road. They made alternative plans for all the possible contingencies Xena and Draco could imagine, but Gabrielle paid little attention. Battle tactics and strategy weren't things she found interesting, and whatever other plans shifted, her part remained the same.

Nossis found a woman among the servants who was close enough to Helen's size and shape to pose as Helen. Her hair needed crimping, but from a distance, they all agreed even Menelaus should be fooled by her. Though if things went as they should, Menelaus would have no glimpse of the fake Helen.

Nossis argued fiercely that a second substitute Helen should be found, but Xena was as firm on this point as Helen herself. "If Menelaus suspects we're trying to trick him, the whole thing falls apart—and he'll destroy the palace, everything, to find her, and take his revenge on you."

Briax spent a good part of his afternoons with the king's soldiers, Joxer, and Newin, all of whom had been assigned to the south side of the island. Gabrielle saw the small company going through various drills at odd times, and now and again some poor captain trying to get his bunch into a proper wall of shields. With Joxer as part of the bunch, she didn't think it was gonna happen anytime soon, but Briax seemed to have nearly as much trouble

253

shifting the awkward, oversized slab of hardened hide and wood.

She seldom saw the village youth—just over evening meals—and he seemed too tired to pay much attention to anything but his plate. *Someone shoulda warned him that fighting's hard work—harder than lugging trays around.* He'd learn, if he came through this mess.

Joxer surprised her by fitting quietly into the scheme of things, taking orders and even seeming to do what was asked of him—but Newin appeared to have influenced him for the better. Great, she thought. Maybe he'd stay here once Helen's problems were taken care of. *Wonder what it would be like, just me and Xena together?* It wouldn't do to let herself think about it, she decided finally. And there had been plenty of times when she'd been glad to have good old Joxer around.

If some of the changes she'd seen the past few days stuck with him once they left, who knew? A mature, sensible Joxer? *Yeah. And an Aphrodite who forgets all about you 'owing' her.*

Another long, dreary evening listening to Draco, Xena, and General Kropin argue over how many men—and under whose command—would guard the main road, and who, if anyone, should keep watch to the east, in case the Greeks decided to try that nearly impossible ascent. Draco finally took charge of that minor problem and talked to a couple of herders who knew the east end of the island well, and who would watch the few possible ways up. Two girls and three boys who were among Crete's fastest runners went with them to bring warning to the palace if need be.

The session was nearly over when King Nossis received a message from the port—from Habbish, whose ship waited at anchor. "Menelaus' ships were off the backside of Melos at dawn today and just before sundown, they pulled back offshore, we saw them. No one seemed to recognize *Wode*; they may think her a merchanter. As dark came on, the two separated, with one going south, the other holding off, just beyond the port. T'is my thought, they mean t'take north and south sides of t'island by surprise."

"Yeah," Draco growled. "With Habbish a sitting duck."

"No," Xena said. "It's an open bay, no way just one ship could block another. Habbish knows that. But he'll have at least one watcher out on the point of the stone mole that blocks the western storms from the docks. By the time the Spartan ship gets past the mole, *Wode* could be long gone." Draco considered this, finally shrugged it aside. At a gesture from the king, the messenger went on.

"T'is in my mind t'help ye with this Spartan bully, and so say my men: *Hammer* cost us time and trade, and *Wode* is a good ship. We can harry either force of Spartans, if ye like."

Nossis stirred; he looked uncomfortable. "He lands at the docks, my people trade with him. Still . . . a known pirate. . . ."

"A man who knows how to fight at sea, and one I'd trust," Draco put in. "Also, if things go wrong, and King Menelaus . . . well, *Wode* could rescue Helen. The king looked even less happy at that suggestion, but eventually he was persuaded, and the messenger went out with word for Habbish to hold his ship close, and await further instructions.

It was very late when Gabrielle followed Xena into their guest apartment. She yawned and stretched, and collapsed onto what she'd come to think of as her side of the bed. "I will be so glad when this is all behind us," she murmured sleepily.

Xena laughed, a low chuckle deep in her throat. "Hey, that makes two of us! But we're doing the right thing, here."

"Oh—" another yawn. "I know. I just—"

"Gabrielle, get some sleep. Things are going down

soon—maybe tomorrow. Remember, you're in charge of a very large part of it all."

"Mmm—yeah. I know." She was vaguely aware of Xena tugging the flimsy little sandals off her feet and draping a lightweight cloth over her, then nothing else.

15

Day broke cool, damp, and windy, three days later. At
dawn, Menelaus' ship stormed the port, apparently taking
the workers and the few soldiers by complete surprise.
The Spartans killed no one, merely herded everyone onto
their ship under the watchful eye of several tough-looking
older fighters, while other men raced to shut down the
messenger tower. The whole was watched over by a man
clad in yellow silk robes, who called out an occasional
order but was mostly content to simply watch.

He and the men under him were unaware that Nossis
had installed young watchers all along the cliff face, and
as the Spartans began the arduous climb from sea level,
they were constantly monitored, with word passed to the
palace, to General Kropin, to Xena, who held a position
near the Maze—and to Draco, who waited on the road
partway down, surrounded by the small force of soldiers
he'd handpicked for the fight to come.

South, the second ship had anchored in the only bay
deep enough for anything larger than a fisherman's cor-

acle. Its sails had been dyed dark, and nothing that might shine or reflect light was uncovered. The men who stole from the ship and began working their slow, cautious way up the steep trail were likewise dark clad, anything metal covered, swords sheathed.

And they, too, were being watched. Gabrielle had one brief glimpse of the men toiling up the steep path before she went over to join the company waiting for her in the arena: the elite fighters Xena had personally picked for her. She wasn't sure she could see what had been behind the warrior's choices: The men ranged from beardless youths to a few graybeards and everything between.

Her stomach hurt. *I hope twenty of us are enough.* She reminded herself of what Xena had said: more would be a liability, where they were going.

She looked past the soldiers, at the dark glory of a woman, the incredible cloud of hair freed to float on the light breeze, except where a band of gold crossed her brow. Helen had exchanged her tutor's dark, plain robes for red and gold silk. *She must be terrified. I would be,* Gabrielle thought. But the woman's eyes were serene. Either she believed Xena's repeated oaths to keep her safe, or she'd given up all hope. Beyond fear, either way.

"He's coming—isn't he?" the woman asked, her voice low and husky.

Gabrielle nodded. "I didn't actually see him, but that's his ship, out south. He wasn't seen on the ship that took the port." She left the rest unspoken, but Helen seemed to need the words said.

"Avicus is there, north; he always fancied himself in yellow. But he and Menelaus would each take a ship, I'm sure of it." Her eyes closed briefly. "But *he* won't be content to wait on a ship for me to be brought to him. He'll come."

"One way or another," the bard agreed.

"Remember," Helen said. "No one is to die—not because of me."

"If we can help it," Gabrielle said. "I feel the way you do about killing people, remember? But I won't hold back if the death of one Spartan means any of these men's lives." Helen merely nodded; her gaze went distant, and Gabrielle turned away to climb into the highest ranks of the arena, so she could keep watch over the palace grounds.

For some time, it was very quiet on the plateau—except for an occasional gust of wind whistling through gaps between stones in the arena walls. Gabrielle descended once to talk to her soldiers, nervous that someone would forget a crucial gesture or command, but no one had. Helen stared at the far wall, or through it, and Gabrielle went back to her high perch without interrupting the woman's thoughts.

South, thirty men stood near the head of that south trail, waiting for the first Spartans to make it all the way up. If Habbish and *Wode* did a good job, if the fighters hidden along the ledges flanking the trail did, Menelaus would have a long trek indeed, and he'd emerge on level ground with fewer men than he'd started with. She couldn't hear anything from down there, but according to the locals, you wouldn't, unless you leaned right over the edge. Joxer had drawn his sword, though most of the men out there still hadn't. Briax looked small and tired, burdened as he was with the massive Cretan shield. Newin was between the two men, a red scarf clutched in his hands. He wore a sword, and a bow and arrows were strapped to his back, but Gabrielle knew he was to have no part in the fighting. She hoped he'd remember that when the time came.

North, she could suddenly see movement, where the road crested onto the plateau. Men were yelling and swords clashed. She shielded her eyes and stared. A dozen or so Cretan soldiers were backing slowly, and she could just make out Draco's distinctive hair in the fore. Spartans were now visible—maybe fifteen of them, distinguishable by those stupid-looking horse-crest helmets. As they gained the pavement, they gave a great yell and leaped forward. Draco lunged at their leader, cutting him down. He felled two more, but the Cretans were on the defensive now, and suddenly, they turned and ran. Someone grabbed Draco's arm and dragged him along. Most of the Spartans cheered and went after them.

Gabrielle grinned. "Yes! It worked!" Five guards remained—reluctantly, she thought—with the man in pale yellow robes who was yelling furiously and waving his arms.

Avicus. The priest dragged at the nearest soldier's arm and pointed toward the palace.

South, the waiting men had crouched down when they heard Draco's skirmish, and she knew that Avicus wouldn't be able to see them from where he presently stood. Gabrielle eased back into shadow and stayed very still, just in case the priest happened to look around; he didn't. His entire attention was fixed on the palace.

The priest gestured for one of the soldiers to precede him, the others to follow, indicated the nearest porch and started for it, striding quickly and with visible assurance. The bard frowned. *Odd. You'd think he knew the place.* Just as he took the first step, though, a terrified scream echoed across the plateau. Avicus leaped back into the open, gazing intently eastward. A woman clad in sheer green threw herself off the family-porch and onto the pavement, long hair flying around her shoulders. She froze as her gaze crossed the six men and fastened on the priest. She fell back, hands out as if to ward him off. "No! I won't—I won't—!" She screamed again, a mindless, horrified shrill, then spun halfway around and ran like a deer, straight for the Maze. With an excited shout, Avicus raced after her.

If he'd been three paces closer, or the woman had been the least bit slower, he might have caught her. Gabrielle held her breath, let it out in a relieved gust as Helen's double vanished into darkness. Avicus would have plunged straight in behind her, but a leather-clad figure came around the near door to block his way. Xena.

A quick glance toward the barracks told Gabrielle that Draco and his men had captured the Spartans who'd followed them—and quietly, since she hadn't heard a thing from her perch. *So far, so good,* she thought—not for the last time. And now the warlord was moving quickly and quietly, slipping up unnoticed behind Avicus's remaining men.

Avicus sprinted toward the open entry to the Maze, yellow silk fluttering after him. Almost—he could nearly—a dark clad, dark-haired figure stepped in front of him, and he fought his way to a halt just before he plowed into her. *Her.* "Xena!" he spat, his eyes narrow slits. She smiled back at him; it wasn't a nice smile.

"Avicus," she purred. "Nice to know you remember me."

"I remember you," he said shortly, and started around her; she moved again to block his way. "I have business in there, Xena, get out of my way, or I'll move you."

"Good luck," she said flatly. "And I wouldn't be so eager to go into the Maze, Avicus. Not unless you want some *real* bad dreams while you're still awake." She moved again as he shifted his weight.

"I know about the Maze," he said; a corner of his mouth twitched up, very briefly. "In fact, I'll tell you a secret, Xena." He leaned toward her, lowered his voice. "Daedalus was a fussy old bastard to work with. And if he's still alive, he probably *still* thinks all the fun twists in there are his." She raised an eyebrow, said nothing. "Guess what? They aren't—they're mine." He waited; no reaction. "The Maze doesn't scare me, Xena. *You* don't scare me. And you're between me and my woman."

"Your woman?"

"Helen," he spat.

"Funny. I thought she was her *own* woman. And I

thought you were helping Menelaus find her."

He laughed shortly. "Menelaus doesn't deserve Helen."

"Or Sparta?" she drawled. "Avicus, you're getting delusions. They'll get you killed." She looked beyond him; the priest smirked.

"Nice try, Xena. I know who's back there: Five of Sparta's best, waiting to take care of you while I retrieve Helen." A startled yell brought him momentarily halfway around, just in time to see Draco take down the third of his men, then leap for the remaining two. Avicus swung back. "Doesn't matter."

Her smile widened, still falling short of her eyes. "You wanna get past me, Avicus? C'mon and *try* it." She went into fighting stance, arms outstretched as the priest raised his hands; he shouted something—more like music than words—and a cloud of purple smoke enveloped her. Avicus darted around her and vanished into darkness.

A moment later, the warrior stumbled forward, flapping her hands in front of her face and coughing. Draco caught hold of her shoulders. "Hey—you all right?" he asked.

"Yeah. I shoulda figured he'd have something like that." She glanced behind her as a distant yell came out of the Maze. "Yeah, Avicus," she said softly, "you started the power trip in there. But it isn't yours anymore." She eased out of Draco's grasp and moved back over to the entry. "King Nossis?"

"Right here," came the steady reply from the inner dark. "I have Esypa with me."

"Good. Stay there. We'll let you know when it's safe to come out." She looked away as Draco touched her arm and indicated direction with his chin. Newin was running across open pavement, waving the red banner. He glanced at them, and Xena firmly pointed toward the nearest porch, but the youth was already on his way, taking a wide path around the fallen Spartans.

Draco waved an arm and several Cretan soldiers came to help him drag the five unconscious men out of sight.

Xena watched them, made certain Newin was inside and the doors closed behind him, then waved a warning toward the arena. Gabrielle eased out of shadow and waved her staff, then scrambled down to ground level. Some moments later, the warrior saw her, the brightly-clad Helen and the small company of guards head toward the path up the mountain. They stopped just short of the first grove, waiting.

She unclipped the chakram, then, and moved out of sight, into deep shadow along the Maze's south wall, watching as Spartan soldiers shot a volley of arrows high in the air and came up, onto the pavement just behind where the bolts fell. Cretans scattered—but not very far. She could see Joxer near the front, trading wild sword swings with a Spartan who looked like his legs were about to give out. More Spartans came on as the first men up cleared a space for them. There weren't as many as she'd have thought; the guards below must have done a good job.

Her eyes narrowed as a tall, lean figure clambered onto the pavement, surrounded by ten men whose horse crests were brightly painted in a checkered pattern: Menelaus and his personal guard. The king let his men storm through the narrowest part of the defense, and now she could hear him bellowing orders: "Find the woman! Find Helen!"

He was twenty tall men's lengths onto the pavement, crossing the red line that had snared Gabrielle's feet, forty lengths—a shrill cry brought him around, staring wildly; he froze in place. Gabrielle's bard-trained voice reached her easily, every word clear: "No! Don't! We'll keep you safe, it's all right, he won't—"

Helen's voice topped hers, shrill with fear. "I won't go with him, I won't!" A struggle. Gabrielle and Helen circled awkwardly, and for one long moment, they froze in place, Helen staring in wide-eyed terror at Menelaus, who stared back. He shook himself then. Helen twisted away from Gabrielle and ran east, into trees. Gabrielle called out orders for the men with her to follow, then turned back, staff at the ready.

Menelaus drew his men around him with an imperious gesture and cried out, "Helen! Come back! I beg of you—" As Gabrielle spun away and sprinted after the woman and her guards, the Spartan king bellowed. "You saw her, she's here, on Crete! There is no way she can escape me now! Get Helen!" But he was at the head of his company, running across the pavement toward the trees.

Just inside the grove, Gabrielle stopped. Helen, her face very pale and her eyes wide, seemed barely able to stay on her feet. The men formed a wall, two across and seven deep, between the two women. "Helen—can you do this?" the bard asked gently.

Helen licked her lips and nodded. "I—it was just . . . seeing him, hearing that voice. The—the worst is over with that. I can do what I have to. Anything."

"It won't come to that," Gabrielle assured her. A look across her shoulder told her the Spartans were well on their way. "Eleven of them. . . . he must be pretty confident."

"He would be," Helen said calmly. "That's his personal guard, specially trained to keep him safe. They're good."

"We'll let them keep him safe, then," Gabrielle said. "But that's all. All right, everyone, let's go. Stick close to me, and Helen—make sure he can see you."

"I know." They moved out into the open again. For several long moments, Gabrielle couldn't see the Spartans, though she could hear them—and the Cretans were making enough noise that Menelaus knew which direction they'd gone. Before long, there'd only be the one trail, heading up—but by then, he'd have a clear view of his once-queen and the pitifully small protective force with her.

By the time they reached the first ledge, Menelaus and

his men were above the trees and moving steadily. One of them had drawn his bow, but the king struck the weapon aside and barked. "No! You might hit Helen!" He drew his sword and held it high. "There's no way back for them, kill anyone who gets within your reach, but remember, your only goal is Helen!"

Helen shook her head; hair flew. "Give up, Menelaus! I won't go back to Sparta with you!"

Gabrielle could see fury and frustration both in his face as she backed up the trail; one of the men kept a hand on her shoulder, guiding her. Somehow, the king managed a smile that almost looked like one.

"Helen. Beloved, you are confused. So many years in Troy, what did they do, to convince you I was your enemy? Helen, you know that I love you, you must know I love you, truly, I would do anything for you. Leave these people, come to me. I will see you are safe, I swear it."

"It's a lie! You don't love me, you want to possess me!"

"Helen, no!" Menelaus started through his men, but was pulled back by two of them. He shook off the restraining hands but didn't attempt to get ahead of his guards again. "I care for you! I want only your happiness—with me!"

No answer. Two of the Spartans darted forward as Gabrielle backed over the lip of the first ledge; one jab to the head and one under the chin flattened one man. She swept the feet from under the second and brought the staff down hard across his throat, leaving him moaning and unwilling to get up. Two of the Cretans moved around her with drawn swords, giving her a chance to sprint across the ledge. One of them wounded a Spartan, and, as the party started up the next steep section of path, someone farther back threw a spear that nearly took out the next of the king's guards. They moved warily, despite Menelaus's furious bellowing. By the time he had them started up the path, Gabrielle was a good forty lengths away.

They moved steadily up, and Menelaus' men continued to feint at them. By the time they reached the broad meadow near the top, he was down to six men, and one of those was bleeding from a cut to the shoulder. Gabrielle looked around and brought her staff down, leaving a dent in the turf. All but one of the men she'd brought with her eyed the Spartans warily as they climbed into the long, narrow bowl, then turned and ran, heading for the side path Gabrielle had found days earlier. She shouted a furious curse after them, grabbed the sleeve of the remaining man and yelled, "You do not leave us, you got that?" He nodded frantically. Gabrielle gave him a shove back, and yelled, "Stay with Helen—go!"

Helen was most of the way across the dell, running, hair and red silk rippling behind her, her sole Cretan guard on her heels. Menelaus gave an exultant, wordless shout, and came on. Gabrielle eyed the Spartans, then turned and sprinted after the two.

Shade enveloped her as she started up the narrow ravine. Ten paces in, she could hear Helen and the guard clambering out, high above. *Time for a little delaying maneuver*, she told herself grimly, and pried a stone loose. It cracked onto the step below her, bounced, flew in a high arc, then dropped. Something below clanged, and she could hear men swearing, scrambling to get out of the way. *Five and counting—I hope*, she thought, and dragged another small rock free. As it clattered downhill, she turned and hauled herself up and out of the narrow pathway, onto level ground.

Helen and the guard stood waiting for her, halfway between the steep drop-off where Menelaus and his men were still climbing and the stone hut. Something new there—it was a brazier, the bard realized. A stone pedestal that now stood just in front of the hut, blue smoke rising lazily and a single tongue of flame licking toward the sky. Gabrielle ran up, then stopped short. The door to the hut was easing shut—and the woman before her was all Helen, except for the eyes, which were extremely blue and highly amused.

"So—how's it look, besides a, like, definite step down for me?" the goddess demanded. Gabrielle rolled her eyes, forced a smile.

"It looks great, except those aren't Helen's brown eyes, and trust me, Menelaus will know the difference."

"Oh—yeah. Sure. Whatever." It was uncanny to watch the sudden change, blue to brown, and suddenly, it might as well have been Helen with her. The changes in body language, grace—style.

The lone guard gave a warning cry and Gabrielle spun back around, her staff at the ready as Spartans spilled into the open. Menelaus shoved his men aside and strode across the wiry grass, sword ready, his eyes boring into Gabrielle's.

"You can die, right here and now," he snarled, "and the man, too. Or you can step aside, and live." He sounded very short of breath, the bard thought. That didn't make him any less deadly. Time to follow the next part of the plan. She flicked a glance at the guard, another toward the red-clad woman slowly backing away. "Either way, woman, you will not stop me from taking her away with me."

"I—" Gabrielle sighed and brought up an apologetic smile. "You know, you're absolutely right about that? Helen, I'm sorry, but—well, he has a point. And you did say you didn't want anyone else dying." A glance to her left assured her the remaining Cretan guard had thrown his sword aside and was racing toward the spire of rock behind the hut. "I'm *really* sorry. We did what we could, but—"

"I won't go with you," 'Helen' said evenly. Gabrielle couldn't tell the difference in the voice, either. She eased her grip on the staff and stepped back and aside, clearing the last obstacle between Menelaus and Helen. He smiled grimly, sheathed the sword, gestured for his men to stay where they were, and started walking slowly toward the red-clad woman, his hands held out, palm up. Gabrielle thought he was trying to smile, but his face really wasn't made for such movement.

"Come," he said quietly. "It's all right. It will be all right. Come to me. . . ." Two more steps. Helen turned and ran toward the hut. Before Menelaus could react, she rounded the brazier and deliberately trailed the fluttering ends of red silk through the flame. The fabric blazed, flames shot for the sky, engulfing the woman who flailed wildly, then ran shrieking across the dell.

"Helen!" Menelaus' horrified cry echoed as he threw himself after her, but too late. He snatched at flames just out of his reach. There was little to be seen but fire as the woman stumbled over black, jagged rocks, and fell out of sight. *"NO!"*

Gabrielle ran over to peer cautiously out and down. She could just make out the fiery, smoking thing hurtling toward the sea—and then, with a high plume of water and a last puff of black smoke, it was gone. She backed hurriedly from the ledge, retreating toward the hut.

Menelaus scrubbed a sleeve across his face, and turned haunted, red-rimmed eyes on her. The hair on the right side of his head and the beard were singed, and she could smell burnt hair. "You," he whispered. "This was your fault. Your doing!"

"No." A deep woman's voice came from the edge of the dell. Xena stood there, Cretan soldiers clambering up behind her. "She didn't do anything, Menelaus. It was your choice, all the way."

"She was mine! Damn you to Tartarus, Xena, she was *mine!*"

"You married her, you didn't *buy* her." Silence.

The tall, gaunt king glared at the warrior. He slumped suddenly and ran a hand across his eyes.

"It's over," Xena said evenly. "Helen's dead."

"Dead," he whispered. "I didn't want that, I never wanted that!"

"Go home, King Menelaus."

He hauled the sword out. His voice was ragged with pain and grief. "I—no, I'll take Crete, I'll burn the palace, destroy everything! I'll—you'll pay, and *she* will, and Nossis, all of you, for daring to hide her from me!"

Xena shook her head. "You've got five men still able to fight up here. I could take them all myself without breaking a sweat, and you know it. Down there—they're all taken, every last one of your soldiers, and your ships are being held by the Minos' men."

"That's a lie! Avicus told me—"

"Avicus is gone."

"But—but he told me—" Menelaus seemed beyond coherent thought. "The Maze, he told me—!"

"Yeah. I know. He helped Daedelus make it what it *was*. The Greek gods don't control Crete, remember? Something older and darker got comfortable in there, after the Minotaur died. Whatever it is, I don't think it liked your priest very much."

"I—" The man's shoulders sagged. Two of his guard came to take hold of him, and he seemed too stunned to throw them off.

"Go home, King Menelaus," Xena said flatly. "The Minos will let you have your ships and your men if you'll leave and vow not to come back. In return, he won't pass the word around Greece about you even coming here, let alone your reason." She stepped aside and gestured for the soldiers who'd come up behind her to get well off the path as the Spartan guard moved. Menelaus suddenly looked like an old, broken man. Tears ran down his cheeks and he made no effort to hide them or wipe them away. Xena watched them until they were out of sight, then beckoned to the Cretan guards who'd followed her. "Stay behind them. Make sure they're all the way down off the mountain—all of them. We'll follow shortly."

She waited, still and silent at the head of the ravine, and when Gabrielle would have spoken, she held up a hand for silence. Finally she sighed faintly and turned away. "C'mon. Let's get this done."

The brazier was nowhere in sight, but Gabrielle hadn't expected it to be. In its place, Aphrodite, now in her filmy and skimpy pale pink, brushed at her arms vexedly. "You know, fire is like, so *unpleasant,*" she began abruptly.

"Yeah, well, it's also effective," Gabrielle replied dryly.

"Oh? So, I totally faked him, is that what you're saying?"

Xena nodded. "You faked him." Aphrodite preened at this; the warrior gave her a grim smile. "About the other thing—Gabrielle owing you? Remember, she's my friend."

Aphrodite cast up her eyes. "Oh, as if I was gonna do anything nasty," she began. Xena cleared her throat ominously and the goddess gave her a slitty-eyed look. "Got it," she said crisply, and vanished.

Gabrielle drew a deep breath and let it out in a gust. "Hey—thanks!"

"You didn't think I was gonna let you get into some situation with her that *I'd* have to get you out of, did you?"

"Hadn't thought of it that way." Gabrielle went over to tap on the hut's only door. "It's okay, they're gone," she said. The door opened a crack. Helen's anxious face peered out. "All gone."

"I can't—you're sure they aren't just—just down there a little ways? Waiting?"

"Xena sent men after them, to make sure they didn't do that. Besides, it's really over."

"He—he believed it?" Helen sagged. Gabrielle caught her, then lowered her to the grass. "I—he thinks I'm dead?" The bard nodded. A high, thin little laugh escaped the other woman's lips, and she clapped a hand over her mouth.

Xena squatted next to her. "It's okay, let it go. You have every right, all these years, waiting for him—" Helen buried her face in her hands and rocked back and forth. Finally she sat up, blotted her eyes, and drew a deep, shuddering breath.

"Thank you," she whispered. "I'll never be able to go anywhere outside Crete openly, but I don't think I would want to anymore. I didn't expect as much freedom as this will give me."

"It worked just like Xena planned it to," Gabrielle urged. "Avicus might have been able to see beneath the trickery, but he wasn't here. So, even if Menelaus hears that someone saw you, he won't believe it, because of what he saw just now. You get close enough to fire to get singed . . ." Helen shuddered, and she fell briefly silent. *Find something else to say.* Something to take the woman's mind off the notion it might really have *been* her, dying by fire and drowning both, to escape Menelaus. "It should be okay to start down, don't you think, Xena?"

"You go first, and keep an eye out," the warrior said. "We'll be right behind you."

Four days later, the two women packed the last items in their bags and went out onto the shaded porch. Draco had already left, sailing with Habbish two days earlier. Xena spoke to him about that, before he left, and he'd taken a polite farewell of Gabrielle. Neither woman had the least clue what the warlord's plans were—Gabrielle doubted Draco himself knew.

King Nossis and Helen waited for the women on the pavement, and just beyond them, one of the rickety-looking carts stood ready to take them down to the port. Joxer was off a ways, talking to a downcast-looking Newin, who stood with Briax and Esypa—the woman who'd drawn Avicus into the Maze.

Xena shook hands with the king, hugged Helen, and stood back so Gabrielle could be hugged by both. The once-queen smiled radiantly, and Gabrielle noticed that her hand had sought and found Nossis'. "Thank you—thank you both for everything you did."

"I'm glad we could help," Xena said. Her eyes went over to the little clutch around Newin. "You're sure Briax will be—"

"He's welcome to stay," Nossis put in warmly. "And Crete can use another good fighting man. My son's tutors and General Kropin all think he'd do well."

"I'm glad for his sake," Gabrielle said. She smiled at them, then crossed the pavement. Briax had one arm around Esypa. The other was in a sling. "You're gonna be okay here?" she asked him.

"Gabrielle—yeah. I'll be fine." He smiled at her—a nice, straightforward, friendly smile, she thought, but the reason for that was at his side. And Esypa seemed to be as taken with him as he was with her. "They like me here, and they think I'm worth something. And—" His gaze slid sideways. "—and, well, *you* know. . . ."

"Yeah, I gather," she said. "Joxer, you coming or not?"

Joxer threw her a sour look. "Gee, Gabrielle—I was just saying good-bye, you know?"

"Yeah, and I know how long you can take, c'mon, there's a ship waiting to get us back to the mainland."

He was quiet as he climbed into the cart behind Xena and Gabrielle and got a good grip on the rails. The driver got the thing turned and the donkeys moving. But that wouldn't last, Gabrielle knew—and it didn't. "Hey, were we great, or what?" he demanded.

"Great, Joxer," Xena said. He eyed her suspiciously. She smiled warmly and nodded. "I mean it. You did a good job up there."

"Well—yeah, as a matter of fact, I did."

Another silence.

"Newin says they found that priest guy—Avicus? Last night."

"Yeah, I heard."

"Well," Joxer added thoughtfully, "what was left of him. . . ."

"Joxer," Gabrielle put in sweetly. "Do you mind? I had a really terrific breakfast, and I would *like* to keep it where it belongs?"

"Hey," Xena growled. "You two gonna start already?"

Gabrielle's mouth twitched. "Was *I* starting?" A look silenced her. Joxer's gaze went distant and his lips moved silently. A faint smile tugged at his mouth. *I know what he's doing,* she thought gloomily. *How many new verses of Joxer the Mighty do I have to listen to before we get back to the mainland? Or before I mangle him?*

She realized Xena's eyes were on her and from the look on her face, the same notion had occurred to *her.* The warrior gave her a smile and ruffled her bangs.

Gabrielle smiled back. "We're going home, aren't we?"

"Wherever that is," Xena began, but Gabrielle shook her head.

"That's wherever we both are, isn't it? Just like—Helen's found a home, up there in Knossos. And so has Briax. I'm glad, and not just because it means he's over *me.*"

"He'll be okay. Remember, being a soldier in Crete is probably the safest job there is."

"Good point," Gabrielle said. She didn't think the youth had enjoyed his first skirmish, and that eventually, he'd find something else to do, back there.

They were quiet the rest of the way down to the port. Gabrielle was glad and surprised that the way down wasn't as steep or scary as she'd feared, and they reached the pier in short order.

The ship was one she hadn't seen before, the crew busy stowing water barrels and crates and bales of things below deck. Joxer immediately left the women to find his own place along the starboard rail. Gabrielle set about picking a spot out of everyone's way to port, and rigged the thin blanket for shade. It was already hot, and the wind was warm and dry.

An hour later, the ship cast off. Gabrielle leaned against the rail, feeling the waves pass under the ship smoothly, watching as the island slowly dwindled. She looked up as Xena settled into place next to her, then went back to her study of the sea and the purple splotch that was all she could see of Crete.

"How's the stomach?" the warrior asked.

Gabrielle considered this, then smiled. "Seems okay so far." She was quiet a while. "Xena—do you really think Helen will be all right now?"

"I don't know, Gabrielle. I hope she will."

"It just doesn't seem fair. With Menelaus still alive, she can't marry Nossis, and anyway, people would find out who his new queen was because royal weddings are such a—a *thing*, and. . . ."

"Gabrielle? I think they'll find a way around little problems like that. And I think they'll be very happy."

"I know they will."

A long, comfortable silence. Gabrielle leaned her head against her close companion's arm. "Xena?"

"Gabrielle?" Both women flinched as behind them, they could hear a rumbling that was Joxer, singing to himself—fortunately, quietly enough that neither could make out the words.

"No more quests, okay?"

Xena laughed quietly. "Gabrielle, you got my *promise* on that one. *No* more quests."

Acknowledgment

My thanks to everyone who has worked so hard for so long to make Xena the success she is: It has been a treasured experience to write books based on a show I so totally enjoy.

To Chris Clogston—a legend among Xena fandom—for her generous bidding that allowed me to cheerfully mangle her good friend Sharon: Ladies, it was good for me . . .

To film editor Rob Field: I had fun, and I hope you enjoyed the walk-on, yellow silk and all. I should say here that the character Avicus is my own creation, aside from the physical description.

My sincere thanks to the legions of Xena fans throughout the world: I'm honored to be one of you, and continually surprised and delighted by how nice you are, individually and as a group.

If you enjoyed the book(s), and would like it/them signed, or would like to receive signed and personalized labels for them, you can E-mail me at XenaBard@aol.com for details.

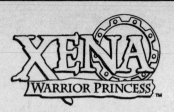